More praise for WILDBLOSSOM

"An English nobleman and a woman from the Wild West—that's a combination you just can't beat. This is a wonderful story filled with adventure, humor, and people who are completely out-of-place in fascinating places. The characters are enchanting and real and will have you cheering for them throughout every delightful page. . . . Don't miss this charming book!"

—CATHERINE COULTER
Author of *Lord of Raven's Peak*

Please turn the page for more rave reviews. . . .

"Curl up with WILDBLOSSOM and lose yourself in its magic! Cynthia Wright is in peak form with this delightful twist on East meets West. You'll fall in love with the irresistible nobleman, Geoff, right along with Shelby, and you'll laugh and cry with them through all the ups and downs of their romance. Colorful settings in Wyoming and England, toe-tingling love scenes, and sparkling dialogue combine with terrific adventures to make this Cynthia Wright's best plot ever. WILDBLOSSOM is a romantic treasure!"

—JANELLE TAYLOR
Author of *Chase the Wind*

"From the moment I read Cynthia Wright's classic *Caroline*, I was hooked! In WILDBLOSSOM, Cynthia uses all of her strengths: humor, unforgettable love scenes, and vibrant characters who linger long after the book is over. Kudos to Cynthia for her best yet!"

—LORI COPELAND
Author of *Promise Me Forever*

"A rootin'-tootin', ripsnorting, rollicking romance between a Wild West beauty and a deliciously dangerous duke. I *loved* it!"

—BERTRICE SMALL
Author of *Love, Remember Me*

"I read WILDBLOSSOM in one sitting, staying up until dawn to see how on earth these totally believable, engaging lovers ultimately find a way to bridge the emotional and societal chasms that separate them. All the delicious qualities I've loved about Cynthia Wright's novels—a marvelous sense of time and place, luscious love scenes, clever plotting—are packed into what may very well be her best book."

—Ciji Ware
Author of *Island of the Swans*

Also by Cynthia Wright
Published by Ballantine Books:

A BATTLE FOR LOVE
BRIGHTER THAN GOLD
CAROLINE
FIREBLOSSOM
NATALYA
SILVER STORM
SPRING FIRES
SURRENDER THE STARS
TOUCH THE SUN
YOU, AND NO OTHER

WILDBLOSSOM

Cynthia Wright

BALLANTINE BOOKS • NEW YORK

 Published in the United States of America by Ballantine Books, a division of Random House, Inc., New York, and simultaneously in Canada by Random House of Canada Limited, Toronto.

Library of Congress Catalog Card Number: 93-90870

ISBN 0-345-38171-8

Manufactured in the United States of America

First Edition: July 1994

10 9 8 7 6 5 4 3 2 1

Dedication

This book is dedicated to my father and soulmate, Eugene Frank Challed, who died on April 12, 1993. No daughter could wish for a better, sweeter Daddy! I miss him deeply, but he remains, vividly, in spirit.

And always, for Jim, whose abiding love enriches every fictional hero and romantic relationship I create.

Prologue

Deadwood, South Dakota
March 1902

Vitality in a woman is a
blind fury of creation.
—George Bernard Shaw

"WHAT IN SAM HILL ARE YOU WEARING?" BENJAMIN Avery exclaimed as he peeked into his niece's spacious bedroom.

Shelby Matthews spun around, her gamine's face radiant with high spirits. She and her uncle would depart within hours for Cody, Wyoming, where they, with family retainer Titus Pym, would run her father's new ranch. "Mama and Daddy are waiting for me at the breakfast table, and I just can't resist the temptation to make an entrance they'll never forget!"

Ben shook his sandy head fondly. "Hard to believe that you went East to a fancy college, Shel."

Reaching for an outrageous pair of white curly angora chaps, she gave him a grin, waving good-bye as he went off to run a bath. "Hurry, Uncle Ben! I'm so eager to be on our way!"

Her bedroom's bird's-eye maple furniture gleamed in the sunlight that streamed through priceless stained-glass windows. Outside, a chickadee warbled *Phee-bee*, causing Shelby to glance down over the rollicking town where her parents had fallen in love a quarter-century before.

The first settlers pitched their tents in Deadwood in 1876, and it had been an eccentric town from the first, twisting its way through a narrow gulch crowned by white rock. Like most gold towns, it grew rapidly, populated by Chinese merchants, gamblers, miners, speculators, prostitutes, and adventurers of every sort. Later that year, when the Lakota people signed away their rights to the Black Hills, Deadwood was there to stay.

In Deadwood's early days, when Shelby's parents, Daniel "Fox" Matthews and Madeleine Avery, had fallen in love and married, they'd lived in a hand-built log house perched atop one of the sheer sides of Deadwood Gulch. Other family members resided next door, and Fox started a sawmill, promising that one day he would build his Philadelphia-bred bride a grand home with a stone tower, a music room, and a wide front porch overlooking the bawdy town they both loved.

Fox wasn't one for idle promises, and he kept his vow. Their Queen Anne–style house was the jewel of Deadwood, proof that the town had some genuine class. The home was big enough for the entire family, including three-year-old Byron, newborn Shelby, and Maddie's father Stephen, her Gramma Susan, and little brother Ben. Even Fox's widowed mother, Annie Sunday, whom fate had brought together in a later-life marriage with Stephen Avery, found a place in the spacious mansion. The two decades since had only enriched the fabric of their family. Even periods of sadness, like Gramma Susan's passing at the age of ninety-six and Stephen's death at the turn of the century, strengthened the bonds of limitless love among them.

A voice called up the servants' staircase near Shelby's bedroom. "Darling, your breakfast is waiting—"

"Just a minute, Mama—I—I—found something else to pack!"

"Can't that wait until you've eaten?"

"I'm probably too excited to each much, but I promise to hurry. You and Daddy go ahead without me!"

Downstairs, Maddie sighed and returned to the dining room, with its splendid mahogany wainscoting, an opalescent Tiffany glass chandelier, and priceless Chinese Chippendale furniture acquired by her great-grandfather, a sea captain and a United States senator. Her chin trembled.

Flawless instincts prompted Fox to glance over the top of his newspaper. "Maddie—?"

"Sometimes I think I tried too hard to raise Shelby more freely than I was raised. I didn't want her to feel constrained by a lot of pretentious rules, especially since we lived in Deadwood rather than Philadelphia . . . but who could have guessed that she'd grow up to behave more like a son than a daughter?"

"You don't really mean that, sweetheart." His eyes caressed the elegant beauty of her face and her upswept marmalade-hued tresses. "You're sad because Shelby's going away and you'll miss her."

"It's more than that," she insisted. "It's her preoccupation with Cody and that ranch. Heaven knows I wanted Shelby to be free, but I did hope that her college years at Smith would bring out a bit more femininity in her . . ."

"Your daughter is a beautiful woman, but you have to allow her, and Byron, the freedom to pursue their own courses in life."

Maddie sighed again. She'd been sublimely content for two decades of marriage . . . until her children grew up. What mother didn't nurture dreams for her offspring, especially two as gifted as Maddie's? Byron was so like his father, and she had fully expected that he would join Fox at the family sawmills and marry Abigail Forrest, who Maddie *knew* would be a perfect wife for him. But after graduating from Yale, Byron announced that he wanted to be an artist and would live in

Paris! For Maddie, the two intervening years had been keen with the pain of his absence and her own dashed hopes.

Shelby, meanwhile, had been strong-willed, strikingly intelligent, and profoundly courageous since birth. Maddie did little to counter her headstrong daughter, and usually was as bowled over by her charm as the rest of Deadwood. Besides, everyone seemed convinced that Shelby would "grow out of it."

"You're brooding," Fox remarked now, interrupting his wife's reverie. "Why not think instead about the fun we'll have alone?"

Annie Sunday came in through the kitchen then, having entered the house through the garden door. "That's right, child. You won't even have me in the way. I'll be in my cottage out in back, putting up preserves and doing needlework. You'll have Daniel all to yourself!" Annie was old now, her chestnut hair gone white. Although her stately form was rather bent and her handsome face lined from years of sun and wind, Annie Sunday Matthews Avery remained a formidable presence in their family. Her gaze missed nothing.

But Maddie seemed not to have heard either of them. "How foolish I have been, believing that either age or college would transform Shelby into a graceful female. Instead, at twenty-one, she seems more stubborn than ever." A tear spilled onto her cheek and she reached for Fox's hand. "How could you have agreed to let our little girl go away to such a place, with only a couple of old bachelors to look after her?"

"Now wait just a minute—" he protested.

"I have doubts myself," murmured Annie Sunday, nodding to the kitchen maid who brought her tea. "This plan of Shelby's does seem to be even more outrageous than usual. What's the name of this godforsaken town she's bound for? Hickokville?"

"Ma, you know it's Cody, Wyoming. Your little jokes about your brain going soft don't work, so behave yourself." Finishing his eggs and muffins, Fox wiped his mouth with a linen napkin and leaned back in his chair. "We've been over this endlessly. You women had dinner with Colonel Cody yourselves, in this very room, while we discussed the plan for us to buy a ranch near this new town of his. Maddie, you were all for it! Deadwood's getting civilized and towns like Cody are the real, *new* West. The land we've bought is spectacularly beautiful—and choice, and Titus and Ben have spent six months out there, supervising the construction of the house and outbuildings. I can't run the place in person, but Shelby is ideally suited to the task, whether you like it or not. She can ride and rope and shoot with the best of them, but more importantly, she has a mind for figures. Both of you know that Shelby will be happier away from Deadwood. She's just not cut out to be the daughter of the richest man in town."

Maddie nodded sadly. "Just like Byron wasn't suited to working with you in the sawmill."

"That's right!" He patted her cheek. "Like it or not, we've raised our children so well that they have minds—and dreams—of their own."

"At least Titus Pym and young Benjamin will be with Shelby," Annie Sunday allowed. "Not that either of them could rein her in if she took it into her head to misbehave."

"No," Maddie agreed, "Titus has always indulged her, and Ben seems more like a youth than a man of thirty-five. He's still content simply to spend the entire day outdoors getting dirty. I've resigned myself to never becoming an aunt, because Benjamin will undoubtedly turn into an old grizzled bachelor cowboy. . . ."

As they continued to chat, Shelby stood poised at the top of the servants' stairs leading into the kitchen. Hearing her family's words of concern over her welfare, she nearly decided against the entrance she had planned, but her wild sense of daring won out as always. Shelby's heart pounded as she clattered down the steep stairs, rushed through the hot, crowded kitchen, and burst into the dining room with a flourish.

"Good morning!" she cried, her cheeks hectic with color. "I'm ready to leave for Cody!"

Fox feared that his wife might faint. Her eyes were huge and her face went white as she stared at Shelby. Across the table, Annie Sunday exclaimed, "Oh my stars!"

Shelby made a little pirouette. "Do you like it?" She was clad in pointed boots, leather gauntlets, the wild-looking curly angora chaps, a holster with a shiny revolver inlaid with mother-of-pearl, a bright yellow kerchief tied around her neck, and a five-gallon Stetson hat. Under its wide brim, Shelby's features appeared especially delicate, and she had wound her hair into two braids that hung down over the curves of her breasts. "Maybe I should take a stroll down Main Street while we wait for Uncle Ben to quit lolling in that fancy bathtub and get me on my way to Cody—"

"Don't you dare leave this house looking like that!" her mother warned. Color returned to her cheeks as she tossed down her napkin and faced Shelby. "I hope you have a logical explanation for this—this *costume*, young lady! Or are you calling yourself a lady these days?"

Guileless as ever, Shelby embraced her mother's stiff form and kissed her cheek. "Mama, where is your sense of humor? I only did this as a lark, to pass the time until Uncle Ben is ready to leave. I don't intend to wear any of these clothes unless I'm working on the ranch. Don't worry, Mama—I won't embarrass you." Shelby stood back, holding her mother's hands, and smiled her magical smile. It was as if a door had opened, letting an ocean of radiant sunshine into the room. "Well, I'll *try* not to embarrass you. Not on purpose, anyway—"

Maddie was caught up, as usual, in the spell her daughter cast so effortlessly. Shelby's outlandish costume seemed fitting, given her rascally nature. And she resembled Maddie in many ways, from her bright hair that was just a shade darker red to her luminous skin. Other features were wholly her own. Shelby's eyes were teal-blue, starry-lashed, and set off by dramatic winged brows. Her nose and cheekbones were finely sculpted, and her mouth was wide and luscious, lighting her entire being when she laughed.

"It's no use making promises you can't keep," Annie Sunday remarked, patting her granddaughter's trim hip. "You've been a naughty girl all your life."

Maddie allowed herself the relief of laughter. She drew her daughter back into her arms and held her closely, rubbing her back. "You are truly certain that this is what you want?"

"I'm very excited, Mama, happy and excited to be embarking on a grand adventure. And if it doesn't work out, I won't be too proud to come home."

"I never envisioned this sort of life for you. In fact, I'll confess that I hoped you'd want to travel East. . . ."

"To look for a husband?" Shelby supplied. "I did that already, when I was at Smith. The East doesn't suit my nature, and neither do the men. They are *unbearably* pretentious! It was all I could do not to burst out laughing whenever one of them launched into a speech about his parents' money and his important friends and his material wealth!" Rolling her eyes, Shelby staggered backward, drew out her pistol, and mimed shooting herself with it.

"For heaven's sake, put that horrid thing away!" cried Maddie.

"Oh, I don't have any bullets for it. Uncle Ben took them all out before he let me borrow it."

As if on cue, a loud *whoosh*ing sound in the upstairs pipes signalled the end of Ben Avery's long soak in his favorite gilt-trimmed marble bathtub.

"I'd better go take off this get-up and change into some proper travelling clothes and lock my trunk!" Shelby was chattering excitedly. "Then, maybe Uncle Ben and I will have time for a few bites of breakfast before we set out on our journey."

She was already accelerating toward the back stairway when Fox caught her hand and she tumbled onto his lap. His weathered brown fingers reached up, pushing back the great brim of the Stetson so that Shelby's wisps of elfin bangs were revealed. In some ways, Fox had felt closer to Shelby than to Byron. He understood her craving for adventure and independence in a way her mother could not, and as much as he secretly resisted the idea of turning her loose in Wyoming without him there to guard her, he loved her enough to cheer her departure.

"Give me a hug, Daddy," she commanded in sunny tones, wrapping her arms around his neck. "Then you have to let *go* of me!"

A moment later, she was scrambling up and dashing through the kitchen door, a comical whirlwind of energy in her Annie Oakley gear. She might be a tomboy, Fox reflected with a fond smile, but she was all woman and more than a match for any man. Would she ever find one brave and crazy enough to take her on?

He turned his attention to Maddie then, rising and going to gather her into his arms. Across the table, Annie Sunday opened the *Lead Daily Call* in front of her face to give them some privacy.

"Perhaps you won't miss Shelby as much as you fear," Fox whispered to his wife. "I have some plans for the two of us."

"You do?"

"Surprises, you might say."

Maddie smiled, pressing her cheek to his. "I realize that I must let Shelby fly off on her own."

There was a little sniff from Annie Sunday then. "Surely you don't imagine that you had any choice? If you hadn't let her go gracefully, the little hellion would have climbed down the trellis in the middle of the night, stolen a horse, and barrelled off to find work as a cowhand!"

Fox and Maddie exchanged bemused glances, and then began to laugh.

PART ONE

What do you seek so pensive and silent?
What do you need camerado?
Dear son do you think it is love?
—Walt Whitman

Chapter One

London, England
April 1902

"DO YOU KNOW, MANYPENNY, QUITE OFTEN OF late I find it difficult to breathe," Geoffrey Weston, Earl of Sandhurst, remarked to his valet, who preferred the title Gentleman's Gentleman.

"Indeed, sir?" Manypenny replied through lips that seemed not to move at all. "Are you ill?"

Geoff, in the act of slipping on his charcoal-gray cutaway coat, looked searchingly at the old man who towered over other people. Manypenny rarely betrayed any humor, no matter how dry, yet Geoff was certain that he must be positively oozing with ironic wit, given his constant deadpan remarks. "Don't worry, old fellow, I'm not ill—only terminally *bored*."

"I believe you have mentioned that previously, my lord."

It's like conversing with one of those hulking great statues in the lobby of Parliament, Geoff thought. Sighing, he regarded himself in the cheval mirror that was tucked into a corner of his dressing room. His clothing fit, as always, to perfection. Tonight he was off to the Haymarket for a comedy featuring Cyril Maude and Winifred Emery, a married couple thought highly entertaining by everyone else. Geoff fought an impulse to yawn just contemplating the hours that lay ahead. Even his various lady friends were tedious in their predictability, and there weren't enough mens' clubs and bottles of champagne in London to elevate Geoffrey Weston's mood.

He met his own gaze in the mirror and decided that even his face was boring. For years relatives had declared that he was the image of Andrew Weston, the third earl of Sandhurst, who had lived during the sixteenth century. Paintings of the fellow bore out the truth of this observation, for Geoff was made in shades of burnished gold, just like his Tudor relative who had been independent enough to purchase this very town house on the Thames for his private use, apart from the mansion where his father, the Duke of Aylesbury, lived. Geoff, too, needed his privacy, for he had two parents who were very much alive and going on at him at every available opportunity.

Manypenny was holding out an engraved silver-spined comb. Sandhurst ran it through his blond hair and searched in vain for some flaw in his reflection. Above the high, winged collar and black tie, his face was tanned, handsome, and shadowed with cynicism. His great eyes were liquid-brown, like chocolate, and his mouth was chiseled. The aristocratic curve of Geoff's cheekbones along with his penchant for athletic pastimes ensured that he would keep his good looks deep into old age.

"What would you think if I grew a beard?" he asked.

"I?" Manypenny drew the vowel out. "I imagine that I would wonder why you would endeavor to cover so fine a face, my lord. If you were cursed with a double chin, or no chin at all . . ."

Bored already with this conversation, Geoff gathered his cane, gloves, and lightweight black coat with a waist-length cape, and took his leave. "Don't wait up for me tonight, Manypenny," he called back from the corridor. "Perhaps I shall run away and become a Gypsy. . . ."

* * *

"What a magnificent evening it's been, don't you agree, Sandhurst?"

Geoff could scarcely hear his friend, Sir Charles Lipton-Lyons, above the din at the Café Royal. The after-theater crowd was lively, fueled by champagne and flirtations. Geoff and Charles were not alone, but their dinner partners had gone off to do God-knew-what in the powder room, and the men would have the table to themselves for nearly a half hour, Geoff reckoned.

For his own part, he wished he were home in bed, but since that was not an option, he drained a glass of champagne and signaled the waiter for yet another bottle.

"Honestly, Charles, I am constantly mystified by your standards for amusement," he called to his friend over the noise. "What, exactly, has happened this evening to inspire an adjective like 'magnificent'?"

Lipton-Lyons, a stocky, pink-cheeked young man with a mustache that curled up at the ends, whacked Sandhurst on the shoulder. "Egad but you are sardonic, old chap! Cheer up! What's happened to sink you this much further into your mire of disaffection?"

"You ought not ask, Charles. I might force you to listen to a recital of my woes until all the other patrons have gone home." A small, grudging smile worked at Geoff's mouth. Charles was one of the few people he actually liked and trusted, for they had known each other since Oxford and had made their grand tour of Europe together, extending it to a three-year revel that nearly ended with the two of them marrying sisters on an island off the coast of Spain. Their temperaments were quite different, but that was part of the reason Geoff valued their friendship and had put forth the energy to maintain it, even though they had recently passed into their thirties and ought to be drifting apart. "Very well, I'll tell you." His eyes hardened as he stared off into the distance. "My dear mother informed me this morning that I've run out of reprieves. She and Father mean to announce tomorrow that their son—that's me, I fear—is betrothed to Lady Clementine Beech. I don't need to remind you that this marriage has been planned for me since the day of Clemmie's birth, when I was nine years old. You'd think that such wheezy traditions as arranged marriages would be extinct by now, wouldn't you? Probably are, except for this one. My esteemed father, the duke, insists that the Westons and the Beeches have been searching for a way to join their massive land holdings in Yorkshire for *eons*, but there was never a suitable match until now. . . ."

Charles Lipton-Lyons had drawn his gilt chair next to Geoff's and turned his ear close enough to make out his friend's speech over the clamor that filled the Café Royal. Everyone seemed to be shouting and laughing at the same time. Charles's brain was quite fuzzy from consuming too much champagne too quickly, but most of what Geoff was saying was hardly news.

They had first spoken of this unofficial betrothal, planned by the two sets of parents, one night when they'd drunk too much ale at The Bear in Oxford. Since Charles's parents were relentlessly modern, he'd found it hard to imagine such a situation could be serious. When the men were in their twenties, Geoff pretended none of it was real, and the only mentioned Clemmie when they were very drunk.

Charles knew Clementine. She was nice enough, if perhaps too no-nonsense, and it seemed likely that she was well aware that her looks were no match for those of the Earl of Sandhurst. Clemmie was a definite English type—raised on horseback and looking rather like a well-bred mare herself: angular, toothy, and cursed with straight hair unsuited to the upswept Gibson Girl style that was all the rage.

"Clemmie's a good sort," Charles offered now, unable to think of any other response. "And . . . you don't seem to have any other woman in mind. I mean, it's not as if you're prone to falling in love in any case. . . ." He was tuning red as he stumbled onward. "You could leave Lady Clem in the country with her horses."

"Someone would have to get Clemmie with child, and logic dictates that it would have to be me, though I really cannot imagine . . ." Geoff's tone was chilly, then bemused as he turned his expressive brown eyes to meet Charles's.

"I could get you a riding crop to pack for your honeymoon. It might be just the thing."

"Hilarious." Each syllable dripped acid. "Don't misunderstand, though. I realize that there's some *sense* buried in that speech you made. Father and I may not be close, but I'm aware that his health is failing, and I am not so wretchedly selfish that I wouldn't like to do something to please him. He'd be glad to see his heir married, particularly to a woman who would bring lands that would double the ducal estate in Yorkshire. And, as you so tactlessly pointed out, I don't care much for *love*, so why not have a marriage of convenience? Clemmie is agreeable, I could go on dallying with actresses and singers, and we'd live separate lives. A fine arrangement, hmm?"

Nodding slowly, Charles waited for the other shoe to drop. "There certainly are positive aspects, no doubt about it. . . .'

"Oh, shut up, coward. You only claim that such a life might be tolerable because you haven't observed me taking great joy in my present existence. What would it matter, eh? When one is already bored to the back teeth, what harm can *more* boredom do? Perhaps there's a bit of truth in that, but I find myself resisting the idea of graceful capitulation. I'd like one last fling, if you will, before I clench my teeth and do the manly thing before God, my parents, the king and queen, and half of London in Westminster Abbey." Geoff idly touched his fingertip to the side of his mouth, thinking. "I find myself longing for a great, thumping *adventure*."

"I take it you aren't referring to a few months spent immersed in debauchery, carrying a bottle and gambling wildly and keeping at least one woman in your bed at all times."

Sandhurst yawned politely. "I can't imagine anything more dull. Didn't we wallow in that trough a decade ago, old boy? No, no, I mean a *creative* adventure. Perhaps I ought to go and live among the bedouins, or sail off to Tahiti like Paul Gauguin."

"Paul who?"

"Never mind. D'you think I might have a talent for art? My ancestor, the one I resemble, was quite an accomplished painter." It began to occur to Geoff that not only had he drunk too much champagne, but also that their female companions for the evening had gotten lost.

"I've a notion that you're drunk, Geoff," Charles decided, "but so am I. What about Wyoming?"

"I beg your pardon?"

Finding this enormously funny, Charles was seized by a fit of laughter. "*Wy-o-ming,*" he enunciated at last in choked tones. "It's a state in the western region of America."

"Whatever possessed you to mention it?"

"You said you wanted an original adventure, and I just happened to speak to my cousin, Trevor. He's friendly with Buffalo Bill Cody." Warming to the subject, Charles picked up the bottle of champagne just delivered by the waiter, got to his feet and cried, "Come on, then. Let's go outside and walk and discuss this subject properly. Those bits of fluff don't care for us!"

Geoff stubbed out his cigar, rose, and linked arms with his friend. "Lead on to Wyoming!"

Swaying slightly, they wove through the crush of tables, emerged onto foggy Glasshouse Street and leaned against a street lamp. "I was losing my voice, shouting in there!" Charles complained. He took a swig of cold champagne and smiled. "Ah—a miracle cure! Now then, about Wyoming. Sandhurst, you surely haven't forgotten the performance of Buffalo Bill's Wild West Show that we attended in our youth—at age sixteen, I'd imagine. Remember? An amazing experience! Even *you* must've been impressed. I had such dreams of seeing the real West for myself one day—if it still exists."

"Well, it's hardly a new concept, Charles. English greenhorns, or whatever they call us, have been stumbling about the West since the Indian wars ended." He pulled his friend upright and started off in the general direction of Lipton-Lyons's lodgings. "What about your cousin? Is he going there?"

"No. Well, perhaps. But he had dinner with Cody himself when he was in New York last autumn. The Wild West Show is still chugging along famously. In fact, Cody's fortunes have improved so much that he now has his own *town*! Trevor, my cousin, was quite caught up in Cody's description of the place, which he's promoting during his travels around the world. You know—he's trying to persuade people to move there, or at least visit. Seems that the town is attracting a colorful assortment of citizens!"

"Where is it located?" Geoff asked quietly. "What do they call it?"

"Call it? Why, Cody, of course!" Charles threw his

head back, laughing, and nearly lost his top hat. "It's rather near that fabulous national park—Yellowstone, hmm? The scenery, according to the old showman himself, is spectacular beyond belief. The town is coming along nicely, Buffalo Bill is constructing a grand hotel this year, and one can have a nearby ranch surrounded by blue skies and woods and babbling brooks or some such poetic stuff, and spend one's days on horseback or fishing and generally enjoy paradise."

Suddenly Geoff stopped on the walkway, gripped Charles's arms and stared at him, his handsome features illumined by the fog-shrouded street lamp. "Let's go there."

Charles could only goggle in response.

"I mean it! What is life for, if not to seize an adventure such as this? I have a confession to make, old chap—I do remember attending the Wild West Show. Vividly. Afterward, there was a party for Cody and the stars of the show, and my family attended. Annie Oakley was there, and that fearsome Chief Red Shirt, and we were invited to visit the Indian village and the stables. . . ." For a moment the Earl of Sandhurst looked almost boyish. "The sort of life they portray in that show is hugely appealing to me, Charles. What a sense of *freedom* one could enjoy! No one would care what you were wearing, or what you owned, or whether you were producing an heir or not!" Filled with the sort of enthusiasm he hadn't felt for years, Geoff talked on until they reached Mount Street and the steps leading to Charles's stylish flat. Again Geoff grasped his friend's arm, demanding, "When shall we leave? There's a ship Monday, I believe."

Looking faintly ill, Charles replied, "See here, oughtn't you give this some serious, *sober* thought? It's not as if you're proposing a jaunt to Brighton for the weekend, after all!"

"I didn't propose it—*you* did!"

"Well, perhaps, but shouldn't you speak to your parents first?"

"Oh, I'll *tell* them, but I damned well don't need anyone's permission to go to Wyoming! I'm nearly thirty-one years old and can come and go as I please. If I agree to marry Lady Clem, that should be enough for 'em. I'll simply explain that I have a few matters of my own to attend to before I'm saddled with a wife and the duties of wedlock." He waved an elegant hand in the mist while the bells of Grosvenor Chapel struck three. "It's all very simple."

"Perhaps," Charles replied doubtfully.

"I'll see you in Rotten Row tomorrow and we'll make firm plans. You aren't looking very well at the moment, Charles. Why don't you go inside to bed before you do something unseemly."

Glad to obey, the young man turned back at his front door. "But Sandhurst, how'll you get home?"

"I'll walk!" His grin flashed in the darkness. "I vow, I haven't felt like this in ages—quite possibly not since we attended the Wild West Show in 1887 and I was granted a hair-raising ride in that fabulous red Deadwood stagecoach. You're a genius, Charles!"

Lipton-Lyons remained on the top step, watching his friend fairly swagger off into the night. It occurred to him that he might have created a monster, but there was nothing to be done about it now except go to bed.

Queen Victoria had died early in 1901, and now her subjects were adjusting to a new king and queen. Change seemed to be creeping in from every direction. Fashions were different now that the moral climate set by Queen Victoria had softened. Great mansions were being sold and turned into clubs or blocks of flats, and new inventions like the motorcar and wireless telegraph were no longer so novel. Yet the British clung to their traditions and resisted change. This morning, as Geoffrey Weston rode his magnificent gelding, Thor, toward Hyde Park, he noticed how few motor cars were yet in evidence on the streets. Carriages and hansom cabs were still favored, with coachmen decked out in top boots and footmen in livery.

Geoff rode through the Albert Gate into the park, which was crowded with light carriages and riders. Women even came for exercise, although they used sidesaddles and were accompanied by mounted grooms. On this mild and fragrant April morning, Rotten Row was thick with the fashionable set, and Geoff had to search for Charles. When he spotted him near Hyde Park Corner, he raised his hand and called out in a most uncustomary way.

Sir Charles Lipton-Lyons, still a bit green around the gills, urged his horse into a lazy trot that brought him to the earl's side. "Hello. Good thing I live so near; might not've made it otherwise. I b'lieve I'll swear off champagne."

Geoff chuckled. "Old story. Do you ever think about the tedious routine we are all caught up in, simply by virtue of social class? Every day, except Sunday, it's the same. We men make our appearance in the Row, then hurry home to change into a frock coat for luncheon at one of our clubs. Then it's on to Wimbledon, or to Hunlingham for polo or pigeon shooting, or to cricket at Burton's Court. Even more ridiculous, we feel obliged to put in yet *another* appearance here in the park before sundown, followed by the ordeal of trussing oneself into evening clothes and tottering off to the opera or a ball or the theater, along with an endless, over-rich dinner. It would be fine if that's what one enjoyed, and I know plenty of fellows who fairly revel in that schedule, but to me it is dull beyond description." His high spirits had gradually faded away as he spoke, now replaced by the shadowed look Charles was used to. "Not that I'm an ungrateful sort. On the contrary, I'm glad to be rich enough not to have to spend my life slaving in a button factory. And, I intend to put my wealth to good use by going to a place where there *is* no Rotten Row or White's Club or West End or any of the pretentious rot that infects my existence here in London."

"I can see that you feel very strongly about this, Sandhurst, and I sympathize."

Brightening, Geoff plucked a twig of apple blossoms from a low-hanging branch. "I'm glad to hear you say that, Charles. I was beginning to worry, as I rode up here this morning, that you might pull out. Not at all sporting after you were the one to raise the subject of Wyoming in the first place!" He laughed at his own seemingly unfounded fears.

"Actually . . ."

"I *knew* it!" Reining in Thor, Geoff fixed his old friend with a stormy scowl. "You have always been the worst sort of coward! This really is beyond the pale, though—to regale me with tales of this far-off place, then be so fickle—"

"See here, Sandhurst, you're not being fair! I thought we were just indulging in a distraction from this business with Lady Clem! You could've knocked me over with a feather when you declared that you really wanted to *do* it!" Passing riders were staring at the pair, who had stopped dead in the middle of the Row. "By jove, there isn't much I wouldn't do for you. However, I have no real desire to traipse across the world to a godforsaken town like Cody, Wyoming, where I would doubtless be the butt of every joke. And . . . I happen to *enjoy* all these pastimes you find so hideously dreary!" Lipton-Lyons's face was flushed with emotion, while Geoff, listening, resembled a statue. Charles couldn't resist one last parting shot. "You may think me mundane . . . but it may simply be that I'm not *jaded* like *some* people!"

A long moment passed, during which Geoff flicked a bit of dust from his sleeve before replying coolly, "I say, old boot, there was no need for histrionics. A simple no would have done just as well."

Charles went even redder, but managed to put out his hand and muster a smile. "I wish you well, Sandhurst."

"Yes—I'd better be off. There are countless arrangements to be made, not the least of which involves informing the faithful Manypenny that he must accompany me to Wyoming in your place. D'you suppose he'll be able to contain his joy?" A familiar sardonic smile played at the corners of his mouth, betraying none of the deep disappointment he felt regarding this setback in his friendship with Charles. He shook his old schoolmate's hand and said lightly, "I'll see you in a year, and you have my permission to squire Lady Clem anyplace you like during my absence!"

Sir Charles Lipton-Lyons found that tears pricked his eyes as he watched the Earl of Sandhurst wheel Thor around and slowly weave his way among the carriages and horses that thronged the Row. When Geoff paused at the corner near Albert Gate, he looked back and tipped his hat, golden hair agleam in the sunlight.

Suddenly overcome with bittersweet regret, Charles put a hand to his mouth and called out, "Godspeed, Geoff! Don't forget to write!"

Chapter Two

Sunshine Ranch, near Cody, Wyoming
April 1902

LYING UNDER PLUSH DOWN-FILLED QUILTS IN HER new brass bed, Shelby wriggled and stretched and considered the day that was spread before her like a wonderful treat. Dawn was edging closer; ice-blue and plum light seeped into the night sky outside her window. In a few more minutes she could jump out of bed, build up the fire against the shivery air, pull on her clothes, and start the fragrant breakfast that would feed six men and herself.

The ripening morning invariably brought more pleasure.

Shelby usually put off her work with the ledgers and statements that were piled on her desk, instead saddling up with Titus, Ben, and their four young ranch hands, Jimmy, Marsh, Cal, and Lucius. In May they'd have their first big roundup and brand all the new cattle and calves, but for now there were other tasks to occupy the days. Fences remained unfinished, stray horses and cattle had to be coaxed out of the hills, and others who had wandered into treacherous mudholes in search of the water they'd craved all winter had to be rescued.

Shelby wasn't strong enough to accomplish much heavy work, but she loved to look for strays, and she found her share. The rest of the time, she made a rousing show of being one of the boys, and they humored her. The simple truth was that Shelby was ecstatic to be outdoors on horseback, deep in the splendor of the Wyoming springtime. The scenery was staggering, even more beautiful than her beloved Black Hills, though she would never say so aloud. The Sunshine Ranch was located in the valley that traced the south fork of the Shoshone River. Snow-crowned mountains rose up behind the ranch, and not many miles beyond lay the magnificent Yellowstone National Park.

Rolling onto her back in bed, Shelby closed her eyes for a moment and remembered the day she and Uncle Ben had arrived at the railroad station. Its location a mile and a half away from Cody forced the newcomers to cross the river to reach the scrappy little town. Nothing was quite as Shelby had imagined.

Faithful old Titus Pym had met them with the buckboard, and they hurried through errands in Cody. Supplies were loaded in back, then Ben made arrangements with a shopkeeper to store all the belongings Shelby had brought from Deadwood that Ben didn't view as necessities. When she protested, the shopkeeper offered to have the wagonload of trunks and crates transported down to the ranch for a reasonable fee. Shelby overrode her uncle and agreed on the spot, knowing that it might take Ben a week or more to retrieve her possessions if he were left to his own devices.

Shelby wanted to have a good look at Cody, but Titus explained that it would be dark all too soon and the horses and buckboard had trouble enough with the road by daylight. Looking around as they lurched out of town, Shelby felt her sense of trepidation grow. How romantic Cody had sounded when Buffalo Bill had described it! This windswept settlement, built on a sagebrush-dotted shelf of land, was not what she had expected. The buildings were generally rough clapboard affairs, the streets were muddy and littered with tumble-weeds, and silent cowboys and blanket-wrapped Crow Indians paused beside hitching posts to stare at her. Shelby was dressed in a practical dark skirt, a white shirtwaist with a high lace-edged collar, and a coat, but she was aware that her looks were singular enough to attract attention. She'd have been happy to hide her luxuriant rusty curls under a wide-brimmed Stetson hat and her annoying curves under baggy shirts, pants, and chaps if it meant that people would stop looking at her. The costume she'd donned at home to horrify her mother might have been a joke, but she did hope to shed some of the restrictions placed on women once she reached the ranch. She could even learn to like this ungainly town, she thought, if it meant that she could have some freedom.

The road they followed southward was barely discernible. It came and went, generally following the Shoshone River, which Uncle Ben informed Shelby had been called the Stinking Water River until recently. "Lotsa sulfur in the water," he added.

Even though the relentless bouncing nearly tossed her out more than once and made her bottom feel sore, Shelby found that the panorama that unfolded before her awestruck gaze more than compensated for her discomfort. Homesteads and ranch houses appeared, tiny dots ringed by toy trees, dwarfed by the distant mountains that seemed to reach toward the edge of heaven.

The Sunshine Ranch, as it happened, was located nearly twenty miles from Cody, and the going was slow. Two hours into the journey it began to occur to Shelby that she wouldn't be dropping into town to visit with townfolk the way she had in Deadwood . . . but Ben laughed and assured her that she'd find plenty of ways to pass the time. During the long ride, she found herself wondering what sort of house Titus and Uncle Ben had produced. Should she brace herself for disappointment? Neither of them was renowned for aesthetic sensibility, and when Shelby glimpsed a wretched-looking sod house in the distance, surrounded by sagebrush, a few half-starved cattle, and one weather-beaten old man on horseback, her fears increased.

"My new neighbors?" she inquired sweetly.

Ben Avery glanced toward the tiny sod house and savored the opportunity to tease her. Deadpan, he waved to the rancher and remarked, "Bart Croll isn't so bad for a fella missing half his teeth. He rolls cigarettes faster than anyone I've ever seen, and he's got a lotta land there." Ben poked Titus in the back. "Titus, didn't Bart mention that he's been corresponding with one of those matrimonial clubs in the East—?"

Titus Pym, a pink-cheeked little gnome who still retained hints of his Cornish accent, took pity on Shelby. He'd been working for Fox Matthews for nearly twenty-six years, before Fox and Maddie even knew they were in love. It was hard for Titus to think of Shelby as anything other than a little girl he was sworn to protect. Now he gave Ben a bewhiskered frown and scolded, "You always were the troublemaker, lad, ever since you was runnin' about Deadwood's badlands in short pants! Don't be foolin' our dear Shelby now. Bart Croll isn't fit to share her company, even if he hadn't already found a wife. I heard that he brought a pretty little thing back from St. Louis a few weeks ago."

"A mail-order bride, huh? Poor thing."

Shelby felt her panic subside, replaced by outrage as she turned on her uncle. "How could you be so horrid to me at a time like this? If I thought it would do any good, I'd tell Mama on you."

"She's used to it, Shel. She's known me all my life!"

Ben laughed and stretched out his long legs, but refused to answer any of her questions except to assure his niece that her new home would not have a mud roof.

At last, in a lushly wooded glade near the blue sweep of the river, Shelby caught her first glimpse of the Sunshine Ranch. At the entrance to the lane that branched off the main road was a sort of archway consisting of two tall poles, one on either side, supporting a long wooden sign. The sign had been carved with the ranch's brand: a circle with eight lines radiating outward like a child's rendering of a shining sun. Shelby was touched in a way she hadn't expected by this symbol of her new home.

Outbuildings had already been erected, and others were in progress, but Shelby's eyes searched through the sheltering stand of old cottonwood trees until she found the ranch house. As they drew nearer, she felt a great surge of relief, then joy.

A spacious veranda stretched across the front of the sturdy log house. She was immediately struck by its resemblance to the first home her father had built in Deadwood, a long structure that still stood and was used by Fox as his office. This ranch house was familiar at first sight. Its proportions were generous and the windows were wide. To Shelby's astonishment, she found that the roof had even been made of real shingles. A stovepipe rose up from one side, and both ends of the house were hugged by mammoth chimneys of river rock.

When the buckboard rolled to a stop, Ben Avery lifted his niece to the ground. In early April the weather was still chilly, although the sunshine and the trilling of birds promised that real spring was at hand. Proud of all that he and Titus had accomplished since summer, with the help of good hired men, Ben pointed out the stable, sheds, other outbuildings, and the bunkhouse that was still going up. There were corrals filled with cattle and wild-looking horses. And, in a sunny area away from the trees, Ben had built a white picket fence around the garden that they would soon be able to till and plant.

"I know you can't cook to save your life, Shel, but you're gonna have to learn, and fast! Did Maddie give you lessons this winter like she promised me she would?" Ben ran a hand through his thick sandy hair and looked boyishly hopeful.

Shelby laughed. "Uncle Ben, you know that Mama can barely cook herself!"

His face fell. "But we were counting on you! I burn everything I touch, and we've got four hired hands to feed—"

"Oh, for heaven's sake, don't whine. What a pitiful sight you are, Uncle Ben! I've spent weeks in the kitchen with Ida, our new cook at home, and Gran Annie, too. Even Mama has a few specialties that she tried to teach me, but I think that they are more suited to dinner parties than ranch suppers. Don't worry, though!" Shelby gave her uncle, who towered above her, a dimpled smile and patted his back. "I can do anything I set my mind to, even cooking!"

And since that day, she had. Through the Sears, Roebuck & Co. catalogue, Ben had ordered a fancy nickel-plated, six-hole sterling steel range. It had arrived by train only the week before, while Ben was in Deadwood, and nearby stood a new oak icebox. They had also sent for every conceivable pot and pan and cooking gadget they could think of, from the latest coffee grinder to a nickel-plated lid lifter. If Shelby had loved to cook as much as she loved to ride her horse, she would have been in a perpetual state of ecstasy. Still, she made the best of it. She was careful to follow her recipes, she listened to the comments of the men and repeated the meals that succeeded the best, she learned from her mistakes, and she did derive satisfaction from being the mistress in the world of her kitchen.

Now, as she threw back the covers and dressed in the violet light, Shelby realized that her first month in Wyoming was passing quickly. Soon it would be May. She was anxious for their first roundup, and she had so many plans for the ranch that she could scarcely contain her excitement. The only obstacles were Uncle Ben and Titus. If she could convince them to follow her lead and take a few risks, the Sunshine Ranch could achieve success beyond anyone's dreams, even those of her father.

Shelby paused before the oval mirror that hung over her washstand. Her clothes had been chosen for utility, but Shelby couldn't help looking beautiful. Today she wore a union suit, shunning a corset, and a split skirt of chocolate broadcloth tucked into soft riding boots. Her flattering blouse was made of ivory cotton with a high neck and sleeves that were full to the elbow, then fitted to the wrist. A thin belt set off her narrow waist, she had fastened a gold bar pin to her collar, and her shining hair was swept up into the wide pompadour that the Gibson Girl had made so fashionable. On Shelby, the style was exquisite, emphasizing her stunning teal-blue eyes, the lines of her cheekbones and jaw, and her generous mouth.

None of these thoughts crossed her mind however. She gave herself a glance to make sure nothing was askew, quickly straightened her bed, then went into the main part of the house. Shelby always smiled when she saw how the big room had been decorated by her uncle Ben. The longest wall was dominated by a giant bear skin. She hated it but didn't want to injure her uncle's pride by taking it down too abruptly. There were some crudely made chairs, plus a striped Indian blanket that decorated the back of the broken-down sofa. No paintings or portraits or fancy clocks graced the walls, but Ben Avery had mounted his prize Winchester repeating rifle and a large tattered poster advertising "Buffalo Bill's Wild West and Congress of Rough Riders." The decade-old relic featured a map of Europe, colored drawings of Indians in Venetian gondolas, and the slogan: "From Prairie to Palace; Camping on Two Continents." Ben had received the poster as a gift from Colonel Cody himself, and the eternal child in him clung to it as an object of priceless value.

Niece and uncle hadn't discussed the objets d'art that were already in place, but each knew that changes would be made. Shelby meant to put her stamp on the ranch, and even Ben Avery had no inkling yet of the force of her determination.

She decided to aid her cause with a huge breakfast that seemed guaranteed to melt any resistance from either Ben or Titus. Her cooking skills were serving her well, and Shelby began to hum, smiling, as she tied on her gingham apron and took eggs, bacon, and butter from the icebox. She'd make pancakes, too, with warm maple syrup. Would hash browns be too excessive?

An hour later the men burst into the house, bringing the bracing clean chill of the dawn with them. The quartet of hired hands looked like brothers, in the way of cowboys. Their legs were slightly bowed from long days in the saddle, their faces were deeply tanned any month of the year, they wore big hats that obscured their faces and bright handkerchiefs knotted around their necks. Shelby liked the music of their jingling spurs and the sharp sound of boot heels on the wooden floor.

Everyone was talking at once, discussing the odds of

another snowstorm so deep into April and how much work needed to be done before next month's roundup. Shelby was glad for the commotion. When all six men were seated at the big drop-leaf table and Ben Avery had said grace, they ate and ate, nodding appreciatively at Shelby with their mouths full. She poured more coffee, passed full platters of pancakes, eggs, and ham, and watched as Titus and her uncle began to smile dreamily and loosen their belts.

"Well," Ben muttered at last with a sigh of pleasure, "I gotta admit that our little Shelby is learning to cook after all."

"Here, here!" Titus cried. Beaming, he lifted his coffee mug in a toast.

"Mighty fine, Miz Shelby," Cal said, eyes fixed on his empty plate. The other three cowboys ducked their heads and made sounds of agreement.

Shelby graced them all with a smile as radiant as the morning sun that now shone into the log house. "I won't pretend to be modest, but I will thank you all for the compliments."

As if on cue, the quartet of ranch hands pushed back their chairs and stood up. "Fences're waitin'," Lucius muttered.

"Wood t'chop," Jimmy chimed in.

"Yup," Marsh said.

"Hope I kin still get up in the saddle." Cal paired this jest with a pat on his flat belly. "Horse'll prob'ly groan!"

The four young men filed out of the house, and when the door shut behind them, Shelby laughed. "Aren't they adorable? Have you two ever heard Marsh say anything besides 'yup'?"

Titus Pym, who was looking particularly elfin that morning, pretended to ponder Shelby's question. "Odd that you should mention it . . . but I don't know as I have!" He gave her a wink, and beamed when she winked right back.

"Shel, you gonna go over the books this morning?" Ben asked. "Seems like you're on a horse a whole lot more than you are at that desk! And speakin' of horses, I oughta go check on that mare that's due to foal soon. Looks to me like she might be further along than we thought." He pushed back his chair.

Shelby took a huge breath; suddenly her palms were moist. "Uncle Ben—wait, please! There's something I'd like to talk to you and Titus about."

"Aw, Shel, can't this keep till—"

She stood up, fingertips spread on the tabletop. "No. We'll talk *now*." When she saw that both men were listening meekly, Shelby began her speech. "I know that you are both aware that Daddy gave me the authority to manage the Sunshine Ranch, but I suspect you thought those were just words and that I wouldn't actually make decisions." She gave her uncle a keen glance and was heartened to find him looking sheepish. "Well, it isn't going to be that way. I have some plans, beyond improving my cooking and keeping the ledgers current and becoming the best horsewoman in the Bighorn Basin. My *real* plans are for the Sunshine Ranch!"

Ben was frowning now. He lifted the blue-enameled coffeepot, filled his mug, and said, "Look here, Shel, I've known you all your life. Why, I was just a kid myself when you were born. I watched you learn to walk and talk and wrap everybody in Deadwood around your pinkie finger. Nobody knows better than I do how smart and stubborn you can be, but that doesn't mean you're qualified to run a ranch like this one! We're not playin' a game out here, y'know! This is—"

"Men's work?" Shelby cut in, leaning forward, eyes ablaze. "You might as well say it because we both

know what you mean! Well, I may be a woman, but I have a mind that's a match for yours any day!"

"You'd better watch yourself, young lady!"

Highly entertained, Titus smiled at the red-faced Ben Avery and remarked, "She has a point there, lad. Let's hear her out."

"Thank you, darling Mr. Pym!" Shelby's own color was high, but she calmed herself with an effort and sat down, realizing that her uncle would feel more defensive if she continued to stand while he sat. "I've been reading, listening to the other ranchers I've met in Cody, and thinking. I am convinced that we need to expand. First of all, we should plant some crops—"

"That's crazy!" Ben cried. "We just started the ranch. We can't be trying to do everything the first year!"

"Uncle dear, please listen! I'm not suggesting that we plant much—just enough to provide extra feed for the cattle and horses in the event of a bad winter next year. It's happened before, and there's no point in taking chances out here where the grass is just scrub as it is. All we need to plant are a few acres of hay and grain, but we'll need equipment. We can buy a horse-drawn threshing machine in Billings—oh, and one of those big hay rakes, and a windmill, and a lot of other supplies. I'll show you a list before you go—"

"I think you've gone crazy!" Ben declared. "You think you can send me off to goldurned *Billings* to buy a bunch of farm equipment just like that? Titus, help me out here! What do you think about this half-baked scheme of Shel's?"

"Well . . ." Pym pursed his lips, considering. "I think I probably ought to go with you to Billings. Shelby's in charge, whether you like it or not; her pa wrote a letter to me stating that plainly. If she botches it, then Fox may hand the reins to you, Ben lad, but for the moment

I'm taking my orders from your niece—and so are you."

Ben Avery's big body sank lower in the chair, and on the back of his head a cowlick rose like a flag. "I give up, boss."

It took the last ounce of control Shelby had to keep from clapping her hands. "I mean to make a success of the Sunshine Ranch, boys! You'll see! I think you'd better head for Billings as soon as possible, so you'll have time to check prices and buy a dozen head of prize horseflesh while you're there. I want to do some breeding, too." Her eyes were sparkling, tilting up just a bit at the corners. "Anyway, we haven't a lot of time before the roundup, and then the ground'll be warming and we can till the soil and plant and—"

"I feel like I'm on a runaway train," Ben muttered.

"Hold on and enjoy the ride," Titus advised. "What's the worst that can happen?"

The younger man gave him a dark look. "Did you have to ask that? Where Shelby's concerned, anything can happen. . . ."

"I know," she agreed. "I mean to make a miracle!"

"You know what I mean," Ben insisted. "By the way, do you have a lot of *money* in your bag of miracles? 'Cause, now that I remember, I think that most of the funds Fox allotted to us are pretty much accounted for. And I seem to remember, too, that he told you that if you could break even the first year with the money he started us with, he'd consider upping the ante. Shel, do you remember something I don't?" The look he gave her was sly and self-congratulatory. "I just can't believe a girl with a college education could've forgotten that she's gotta *pay* for stuff like threshing machines and windmills. . . ."

Shelby was rising to her feet again, sparks catching

in her eyes, and Titus attempted to avert a real clash between niece and uncle. "Don't be assuming so much, lad," he said, extending a hand toward Ben. "You're treading dangerously close to insults, and I can't believe you mean to. No doubt our Shelby intends to take the high road and consult with her father about these plans. There's such a thing as a telegraph, you know, and I'm quite certain that she could persuade him to advance the funds necessary to carry out—"

"No," Shelby said. "I won't ask Daddy. I intend to get the money on my own, without touching the savings we have to use for day-to-day expenses." Suddenly she was up, circling the table and gesturing with both hands as she spoke. "He won't know a thing about our crops or the extra horses, and then when we turn a *profit* at the end of our first year, he'll be simply . . . incredulous! Oh, gosh, we'll all be so proud. You know, one day I hope that my father will allow me to buy this ranch from him. I shall earn that right, and I shall earn every penny of the purchase price by trying a little bit harder than anyone expects and by doing more than Daddy has asked." A ray of sunlight brightened the waves of Shelby's bright, upswept hair as she paused and held up a fist. "If you both lend me your support, we can share in the Sunshine's success!"

Scratching his head, Ben inquired, "You sure you wouldn't rather be a preacher? I feel pretty inspired, but there's still one detail missing, honey. Where are you gonna get all this money?" He glanced over at Titus, whose misgivings were clearly reflected in his expression.

"I have the most wonderful plan—perfect in its simplicity!" Shelby cried. She stopped between their chairs and crouched down to drape an arm around each man's shoulder. "It's so brilliant, you'll both wonder why you didn't think of it yourselves!"

"Somehow I doubt that," Ben muttered. Her glowing face was inches from his, however, and he couldn't help giving her a gruff little smile. She had been irresistible since the day she was born.

"I for one hope you're right, angel," said Titus. "End our suspense now, hmm? How will you get the money?"

"I'll win it playing poker at the Purcell Saloon!" Shelby's incandescent smile widened even more, while her eyes twinkled with mischief. "There, you see, you needn't have worried! I know exactly what I'm doing. With schemes like these, we shall never have to go to Daddy for money!"

Ben and Titus were both too queasy at that moment to reply.

Chapter Three

WHEN THE BUCKBOARD GAINED THE LAST CREST OF the valley road and Cody came into sight, Shelby, Titus, and Ben all sat up a little straighter, grateful that their jouncing trip would soon be concluded. It was a particularly fine late-April afternoon, although still clear and cold. The sky was keenly blue, decorated with puffy clouds, and the trees were thick with leaf buds. Skylarks and robins sang to herald the greening of the land, and prairie roses were opening everywhere. It was a difficult time to be downcast, but Ben Avery managed.

"For Pete's sake, Shel, I think you've lost your mind!" he grumbled, squinting into the distance.

"So you've told me about a hundred times," she said. "You're just upset that I didn't abandon my plan when you announced that no proper female would be seen gambling in one of Cody's saloons. As usual, dear uncle, you underestimated me!" Sitting between Ben and Titus on the splintery seat, she was clad in the cowboy getup she'd worn to shock her parents that last morning in Deadwood. This time, however, she carried the costume one step further, pinning her hair securely out of sight under the Stetson, thickening her eyebrows with a pencil, and gluing a false handlebar mustache to her delicate upper lip. It looked ludicrous, but Titus had made it for her from the mane of her favorite horse, a pinto pony she called Gadabout. They'd tried chin whiskers, too, but the sight of them hanging from Shelby's face was simply too hilarious.

"I don't get it, Titus," Ben complained. "Why are you helping her? If I ever tried to do somethin' this crazy, you'd be all over me like flies on . . . sugar."

The old man averted his eyes. "I don't think I have to explain myself except to say that I feel that Shelby has a great deal of . . . spirit pent up inside, vigor that went unexpressed during her years in Deadwood. People expected her to play the role of wealthy daughter." Titus patted her hand. "I'm inclined to give her her head for a time. Besides, I suspect that Shelby'd go ahead with her schemes with or without us." He gave Ben a bemused smile. "I'd rather be present."

"You are the dearest man, and you both must admit that this is a splendid adventure!" She giggled. "Look at me! What would Mama say?"

"I shudder to think," Titus remarked.

They drew up in front of Purcell's Saloon on Sheridan Avenue. It was one of many such establishments, but probably the best-known and the place where the most money was likely to be wagered.

"Don't forget, Uncle Ben, that I'm your cousin Matt."

Ben Avery scowled at his niece. She wore angora chaps, a holster, boots, fringed vest, orange kerchief, a ridiculous false mustache that they'd coaxed with wax to curl slightly on either side, and her giant white Stetson hat.

"I can't believe you want me to claim you as a cousin. Not one man in my family ever looked like *that.*" He shook his head again. "You little devil, how do you get me into these fixes? Now that I think about it, this is about the hundredth time—"

"Hush!" Shelby raised a gloved hand to Ben's mouth. "Someone will hear you! Just say I'm passing through from some town like Sioux City, on my way to . . . San Francisco. Not that anyone will care. Besides, if they think I'm a little odd, they'll be more apt to bet a lot of money." Her shining smile appeared under the horsehair mustache. "Come on!"

Titus walked into the saloon next to Shelby, while Ben lagged behind several paces. Weatherbeaten cowboys glanced up from their card games, drinks, and smokes; the barest glimmer of disconcertion crossed their faces. When Ben went to the bar to order three beers, and Shelby found a table and began shuffling a deck of cards, the glances from the other patrons became more curious.

"New in town, pilgrim?" asked a dusty, red-faced wrangler at the next table.

"Yeah, I'm passin' through from Sioux City," Shelby declared in the lowest, hoarsest voice she could muster. "Lookin' for a little entertainment."

Muffled laughter rippled through the saloon, and Ben, still standing at the bar, turned crimson. The man who had spoken to Shelby gave her a reptilian smile and leaned over to extend his hand. "My friends 'n' I'll be glad t'oblige you as soon as we're finished with this game. Name's Skinner."

Shelby put her cowhide-gloved hand in his and tried not to wince when he squeezed. "Pleased to meetcha," she growled. "They call me—Coyote Matt."

It took Titus Pym's last ounce of control to remain straight-faced. Amusement began to replace his apprehension and he nodded soberly and clapped Shelby on the back. "Yup, this feller's trapped a passel of coyotes all right!"

"More'n four thousand," Shelby proclaimed recklessly.

His hat pulled low on his brow, Ben sidled up to the table and put down the mugs of beer. One of the other cowboys hailed him, calling, "Hey, Avery, you know this fella?"

Ben stared at the tabletop. "We're . . . distant cousins," he mumbled.

Although she dearly wished to increase his embarrassment, Shelby knew he would never forgive her, so she kept her mouth shut. A few minutes passed. The trio drank some of their beer, Shelby engaged Titus in a few games of blackjack, and they waited to see who would be the first to bet against Coyote Matt. The atmosphere in the saloon was not only rank and smoky, but also uneasy. Men in the West adhered to certain codes of behavior and appearance; there wasn't much space in their ranks for oddity.

Still, the less scrupulous among those present at Purcell's Saloon smelled a pigeon. Soon there were restless noises as bodies shifted in their chairs and heads turned to glance at the buffoon who called himself Coyote Matt.

"Any moment," Shelby whispered gleefully.

Ben sniffed the air, then his gaze settled on his niece's excited face. Beer froth clung to her mustache. Leaning closer, he sniffed again and a smile twitched at the corners of his mouth. "Geez, Shel, you smell like Gadabout when she's been rode wet."

Out on Sheridan Avenue a tumbleweed careened in front of Cody's newest arrivals.

"What's that?" Geoffrey Weston inquired of his gentleman's gentleman.

"A common enough sight in this part of the world,

my lord," Manypenny intoned. "I believe they call it a tumbleweed."

"Ah."

The two men were beginning to attract attention. Immaculately dressed, they stood next to an assortment of expensive traveling trunks and pondered the future. It had been disconcerting enough, arriving at a train station located a good distance from town, and then they had suffered the indignity of paying for a ride into town in the most ramshackle wagon imaginable, driven by an equally broken-down fellow who appeared to shun the concept of bathing. The man had left them here, surrounded by their belongings, and Geoff had decided against soliciting advice from the driver regarding their next move.

"I sense that we are overdressed," Geoff remarked in a stage whisper. His tailored tweed suit was set off by a vest of Prussian-blue cashmere, a round-collared shirt with charcoal pinstripes, a four-in-hand tie, and polished black oxfords. He wore no topcoat or hat, and the afternoon sun picked up the gleam of his plain gold signet ring and his ruffled blond hair. "Did we forget to pack my boots, chaps, and holster?"

"I fear so, my lord," Manypenny replied, deadpan.

Geoff's sculpted features relaxed into an appealing smile as he took in the sight of his manservant set against the backdrop of Cody, Wyoming. Manypenny was closer in height to seven feet than six, and he seemed to own an endless supply of dark suits, gray-striped vests, winged-collared shirts, and black ties. Today, in honor of his appearance outdoors, he had added a black woolen overcoat and a black derby that looked as if it were squeezing the old man's massive head. "My lord," he said now, in a rare volunteered statement, "I hope that you will not forego your personal style of dressing, which is flawless, in deference to your surroundings. To replace your wardrobe with—" He grimaced. "—*chaps* would be nothing less than tragic."

Geoff tried to look serious as he nodded and replied, "I appreciate your advice, Manypenny. At the moment, however, my wardrobe is the least of our concerns. I must seek out some advice about the local hotels before we're held up at gunpoint and stripped of our belongings." He inclined his head toward the group of surly characters gathering across the street and staring at them and their trunks.

"If you don't find lodgings that meet with your approval, my lord, perhaps you would consider turning back. . . ."

"To London?" Geoff laughed at this notion. "Hardly, old fellow. I'm made of sterner stuff than that—and so are you! Now then, I suggest that you have a seat while I go into this saloon and have a word with the bartender." He guided Manypenny to the biggest trunk, watched him perch on the edge, then walked the few yards to Purcell's Saloon.

Now that he and Manypenny had reached Cody, Geoff was more aware than ever of the uncertainty of this undertaking. A vague sense of danger danced over his nerves, and he reveled in each erratic sensation. The farther west they'd come, the more Geoff felt as if he'd been transported to a completely different world than the one he knew. Each minute that lay ahead promised to be unlike any he'd experienced in the previous three decades; it was exactly what he'd longed for. Manypenny would be aghast to learn just how willing his master was to throw off his old ways, including every stitch of his splendid wardrobe.

Stepping into the raucous, smoke-filled saloon, Geoff smiled with irony and thought, It's nothing like

White's—thank God. He felt the keen scrutiny from other patrons and looked back calmly. At the bar, he ordered a whiskey and bided his time. Obviously, he defined the word "dude," but Geoff knew that his prospects for the future could depend on the other qualities these strangers perceived about him. He didn't have to pretend to be unafraid; he had handled every situation in his life thus far, and knew that simple confidence could be the greatest asset of all.

"New in town?" the bartender inquired laconically.

"Very observant of you," Geoff said with a smile. Extending his hand, he added, "My name is Geoffrey Weston. I've been admiring your town."

"Glad to meetcha." They shook hands. "I'm Tom Purcell; this here's my saloon."

From a nearby table someone hissed, "Geez-us! It's one of them sissy limeys!"

Geoff finished his whiskey, then turned and stared evenly at the man who had spoken, immediately recognizing him by his reddening face. No further action seemed necessary, and Geoff's gaze wandered to another pair of eyes that he'd felt burning a hole through his back. To his surprise, he found himself looking at the least-likely cowboy imaginable. He turned back to the bartender.

"Who, may I ask, is that very slight, bizarre-looking fellow seated in the corner?"

Purcell bit back a grin. "Seems to be a relative of Ben Avery's who's passin' through. Ben's the big sandy-haired cowpuncher nexta him; he has a fine ranch south of here. The cousin wants a card game."

No sooner had Geoff digested this information than he felt a sharp tap on his shoulder. Turning his head, he found himself looking down at the very person he and Purcell had been discussing. The fellow was even more peculiar-looking at close range, featuring a small head dwarfed by a five-gallon white Stetson hat, the strangest mustache Geoff had ever seen, an outlandish pair of angora chaps, and oversized cowhide gloves.

"Howdy, stranger!" the odd-looking cowboy boomed in a hoarse voice. "The name's Coyote Matt."

Geoff blinked, but shook the glove extended toward him and felt the daintiness of the hand it concealed. "I beg your pardon." He leaned closer. "Would you mind repeating your name? I'm not certain I heard correctly—"

"Coyote Matt! Yep, I trapped a passel o' them fearsome critters in my day. More'n four thousand, I reckon. Don't s'pose they got coyotes in England."

"I'm not an authority, but no, I don't believe there are any coyotes in England." A wry smile flickered over Geoff's mouth; he was utterly fascinated by this intensely odd and amusing character.

"You got poker over there?"

Geoff's brows lifted slightly. "After a fashion."

"Wanta play? Fancy dude like you could prob'ly win a lotta money from a dumb, scroungy coyote killer like me."

Coyote Matt's voice was so raspy that it was difficult for Geoff to make out exactly what was being said, and he also found that he was constantly distracted by the fellow's physical appearance. "Sir, I suspect that you are trying to draw me into a game of chance because you believe *you* would be the winner, and that might well be the case. In truth, I cannot afford the time, having just arrived in Cody—but I am willing to give you a half hour in the interest of cultivating good will among the townspeople. You see," Geoff explained, glancing back at Tom Purcell and then over the crowded tables of the saloon, "I intend to remain here for some time."

"Yahoo!" shouted Coyote Matt. "Cut the cards, Ben! I got me a game!"

"What extraordinary good fortune," Geoff remarked in apparent amazement as he glanced down at the winnings stacked on the table before him. "Simply extraordinary."

Ben kicked Shelby's shin and she flinched. "Maybe you lost enough, *Coyote Matt*," he said in menacing tones.

"It's my deal," she replied, nearly forgetting to lower her voice. It was beginning to hurt her throat, talking like that, and the clouds of smoke in the saloon didn't help any. "You in, Ben? Titus?"

They both shook their heads, and Shelby stubbornly dealt the cards for five-card stud to herself and the Englishman. It had to be pure luck, his winning nearly all the five hundred dollars she'd brought for this occasion. They didn't have real games like poker in England. Shelby had read her share of Jane Austen novels, and in them the only card games were faro and whist. Certainly not poker! One more hand, she told herself, and the tide would turn in her favor, and then she would win it all back and then some!

Shelby looked at her cards and discovered that she was holding a pair of nines. They had each put in an opening bet of fifty dollars, and now she felt even more hopeful. Watching her pigeon, who had begun to appear more hawklike as the game progressed, Shelby saw that he had discarded only two. She frowned and dealt him replacement cards, pretending to turn her attention back to her own hand but in fact studying his expression under her thick lashes. There could be no mistake to the practiced eye of a girl who had grown up in Deadwood, where gambling was the favorite sport: this fancy Weston character had definitely looked relieved when he saw his cards. At the very least, he must have three of a kind!

Shelby pondered her own pair of nines, discarded three, took three, and found that she had an even worse assortment than before. "It's your bet, sport," she said in her best casual cowboy voice.

Geoff nodded slowly, sipped his whiskey, and added two twenty-dollar bills to the pot.

Clenching her teeth with fear, Shelby capitulated and tossed down her cards. "I fold."

"Do you indeed? What a relief. I only had a pair of threes, but I felt I ought to give you a chance to win back a little of your money. . . ." He shrugged. "Sorry."

Shelby felt as if she were going insane. How could this be happening? Now Ben's big hand disappeared under the table and found her thigh, squeezing right through the chaps until her eyes watered. "Time to go home," he growled.

"One more hand," she said gruffly, and gave the cards to her opponent. "Your deal, Weston."

The fifty dollars that Shelby placed on the table was the last of the money she had . . . and also represented a large chunk of the funds her father had given her to keep in reserve. If she lost it all, not only couldn't they buy farming equipment and more horses, but they wouldn't have enough money to make ends meet past summer. When the new cards lay before her, Shelby held her breath before picking them up. Her heart soared at the sight of two magnificent kings. This was her chance, and she meant to take it!

Shelby discarded three cards, and she nearly whooped with joy when she saw the new trio. One of them was another king!

Across the table, Geoff discarded two cards, but left

the replacement pair lying facedown. Without looking at them, he gazed soberly at Coyote Matt. "Will you bet, sir?"

"Uh-huh. Titus, give me fifty."

"You are nuts!" Ben declared.

"You shut up!" she hissed, then turned burning blue eyes on Titus. "I'll pay you back."

The little gnome of a man appeared crestfallen. "I don't like it . . . but . . ." He pulled some bills from his pocket and handed them over. "All I have is thirty-five."

Shelby put it in the pot. "That's my bet."

"I'll meet you . . . and raise you a hundred," Geoff replied quietly.

Suddenly, she noticed that he had apparently forgotten to look at his new cards. An habitual bluffer! Flooded with elation, Shelby said, "I'm outta cash, but I'll make a deal with you, Weston. I have a ranch I can put up that's worth at least ten times as much as that pile of winnings in fronta you. Whatta you say—how about my ranch against, oh, say, five thousand dollars? That's a *deal*, sport!" She kept her tone husky and offhand, but next to her she heard Ben's stunned intake of breath, while voices began to buzz around the big room. Cowboys who had been gathered around the other card game had by now drifted over to watch.

"Now wait justa minute," Ben shouted. "Titus, you aren't gonna allow this!?"

Titus Pym looked dejected. "I fear we have to, lad. What you don't know is that Fox sent me the deed to the ranch for safekeeping . . . and it's been signed over to—uh, Coyote Matt."

Ben turned on Shelby then. "Did you know?"

Panic began to well inside her. "No, but I had to do

this anyway, and it won't matter about the deed because I am not going to lose."

Speechless with rage, Ben jumped up and stormed out of the saloon, disappearing into the blinding sunlight. Shelby tried not to think about him, or about Titus's words. It had almost been easier to make the bet when it hadn't been real; now the ranch was really hers to lose. She stared into Geoffrey Weston's rich brown eyes and waited for his response, her heart thundering.

"I accept," he murmured, "on one condition. If, as you say, your ranch is worth much more than five thousand dollars, I could not accept more than half ownership of it should I win. I won't cheat you."

"Durned right you won't, cuz *I'm* gonna win! But, okay, them terms sound fair enough." Shelby took a deep breath and lay down her cards. "Three kings, Weston. I doubt you can beat that, seein' as you ain't even studied the new cards you took!"

"So I haven't," he remarked. "Well, let's see what I do have." Geoff displayed the pair of aces and queen of hearts in his hand, then turned over the unseen cards to reveal yet another ace and one more queen. "Egad. What do you call it—a full house?"

Shocked tears stung Shelby's eyes. She nodded blindly, unable to look at Titus or this Englishman who now owned half her father's ranch. Perhaps this was all a nightmare and she would wake up in another moment. . . .

"Well-played," Titus was saying to Weston. "I'll take Coyote Matt and fetch the wagon, and what do you say we meet you in front and take you out to the ranch? That'll give you a minute to gather your winnings." He wanted, above all, to get Shelby out of the saloon before she forgot herself and everyone saw that Coyote Matt was really Shelby Matthews. It was enough that she'd lost all that money and torn the ranch in two, but if the rest of the story got out, she'd never be able to show her face in Cody again. Let them think a crack-brained cousin was responsible.

"It's kind of you to offer, but I'm afraid that I have some trunks . . . and a manservant who is waiting with them outside. Perhaps we ought to hire a separate vehicle."

Titus had taken Shelby's arm and was guiding her toward the doorway, past the dozens of curious cowpunchers. "No, no, we'll make room. . . ." Scared to death she'd faint on him, he called back, "See you outside, then!"

Geoff sat still for a minute, thinking. He felt strangely overwhelmed, a bit guilty, and reckless with anticipation for the adventure ahead. It didn't seem possible that he'd just arrived an hour ago, dipped his toe in the water that was Cody, and now he had a home—no, much better than that, a *ranch*.

Folding the large pile of currency, Geoff put it away, then consulted his watch. Good God, Manypenny had been sitting on that trunk for nearly an hour! He paid for the drinks, added a generous tip, and left the saloon without a second thought for the cowboys and ranch hands who stared after him with a mixture of disbelief and awe.

The sun shone brighter on the mountain of baggage than it had when Geoff bade Manypenny good-bye, promising to return within minutes. To his astonishment, however, the manservant had not changed position or even unbuttoned his overcoat in the warmth of the April afternoon. Like a giant carved sentinel, Manypenny guarded his master's belongings, moving only to lift a folded handkerchief from time to time and blot the rivulets of perspiration that rolled down from under his derby.

"Sorry to keep you waiting, old man," Geoff said when he was beside him, "but I've found a solution to our lodgings problem. I've been playing cards . . . and it seems I've won a *ranch*."

"Have you, my lord?" Manypenny replied mildly. "How very convenient."

"Yes . . ." His tone was absent as he watched the little man who'd been with Coyote Matt drive toward them in a wide, rickety wagon with a seat for passengers raised up in front. "I should advise you that one of the other owners of the ranch, approaching now in that vehicle, is disguised as someone called 'Coyote Matt.' I trust that you will readily observe that he is actually a female, but up to this point, that fact has not been acknowledged." His mouth twitched. "The reasons behind this flimsy charade are a total mystery to me."

Manypenny blinked. "Are you *quite* certain you wouldn't prefer to lodge at a proper inn, my lord?"

As the buckboard rolled to a halt beside them, Geoff's only reply was pure laughter. It dawned on Manypenny then that he hadn't heard his lordship laugh like that in years . . . and that meant they wouldn't be going home to London just yet.

Chapter Four

A LOVELY ROSE AND VIOLET DUSK HAD ENFOLDED the Sunshine Ranch by the time the buckboard turned down the road leading to the log house. A sharp chill had replaced the afternoon's warmth, and Shelby huddled against Titus, trembling with cold and the shock of her own grave mistakes. Next to her, Geoff sat forward for a better view of the house. Smoke spiraled from one of the chimneys, signaling Ben's presence, and the Shoshone River glimmered coral in the distance.

"This is the Sunshine Ranch," Titus said at length. He couldn't help liking Geoffrey Weston, though he could do without the dour servant who sat in back amidst their numerous weighty trunks. Shelby hadn't spoken since he'd led her from the saloon, and Titus felt like a traitor each time he addressed the Englishman who'd won half the ranch . . . yet there was such a thing as common courtesy. Besides, Weston had hardly put a gun to Shelby's head and forced her to bet her last dime, and the ranch as well. Left to her own devices, she'd have gambled away the whole, not half.

"It's splendid," Geoff murmured, then glanced over at Titus and smiled. "I hope my silence hasn't seemed rude, but I've been taking in the scenery. Each view appears more magnificent than the last." They were drawing up in front of the house, and Geoff looked back at

Manypenny. "Aren't you impressed with the fine house these people have built, old man?"

The servant put a hand up to secure his derby as they rolled over a last bump. "It appears a trifle . . . *rustic*, my lord."

"Are you a nobleman, Mr. Weston?" Titus asked, glad to steer the conversation away from Manypenny's cool remark. Even Shelby had stirred at his critical tone, and Titus was anxious to delay the inevitable scenes of conflict as long as possible. "Folks out here won't take to callin' you their lord."

"Please, don't give that another thought," Geoff insisted, throwing Manypenny a dark look. "Manypenny has been with my family for eons. He's old school, so to speak, and enjoys using titles even when they don't apply."

Titus pondered this vague response, but didn't pursue it further. Other matters pushed to the front of his mind. How could the Coyote Matt/Shelby situation best be handled? What would Benjamin's mood be? Preoccupied, Titus climbed down to tie the horses to the hitching post in front of the house. Geoffrey Weston had gone back to give Manypenny a hand down when Shelby jumped to the ground.

"Titus." She paused before him. Her little gamine's face was shadowed under the Stetson's wide brim, but there were tears in her voice. "I am so ashamed . . . but I will not be vanquished. I shall change my clothes and confront that foreigner, and—"

"He's not the villain, lass," Titus reminded her. "It makes me worry from the get-go when you're melodramatic. I'd advise you to accept what's happened and—"

"No. I will *fix* this!" she insisted hotly, then disappeared into the house.

Titus said a silent prayer that Ben wouldn't be waiting for them with a rifle, then he assured Weston that their hired hands would unload the baggage. "I think we all could use a proper cup of tea and something to eat, hmm? Let's go inside and I'll see what we have."

"Lead on." Geoff wanted to pat the poor chap on the back and assure him that this crisis would pass. His heart went out to Titus Pym; clearly he cast himself not only as Miss Coyote's guardian, but also as the buffer between her and that Ben fellow, who Geoff guessed really *was* her relative. A great deal of the picture was muddied, but clarification seemed to be imminent, and Geoff could scarcely wait for the drama to begin in earnest.

When Titus threw open the front door and they stepped inside, Manypenny let out a short gasp. Titus gave him a challenging stare, forcing him to speak. "No offense, my good man. I simply cannot recall the last time I saw a bearskin displayed on a parlor wall. . . ."

"I rather like it," Geoff offered, brimming with high spirits. "The entire room is so . . ." He paused, searching for the right word.

"*Rustic*, my lord?"

Titus bristled like a little porcupine as the indignities mounted. The added fact that he found himself staring at Manypenny's striped waistcoat when he faced him hardly helped. "Now see here, I thought we'd agreed to dispense with all that 'my lord' folderol!"

"I shall henceforth endeavor to refer to his lordship as 'sir.' "

"Much better," Geoff approved. He had wandered over to the great stone fireplace, savoring the warmth.

"Ben must've gone out to check on the fences," Titus decided with a sigh of relief. He went into the kitchen and started the tea. Shelby had baked an apple cake only a day ago, and Titus found himself growing calmer as he set out four plates, cut slices of cake, and began to set the table. Perhaps the world wasn't coming to a crashing end after all.

Still, when the door to Shelby's room opened, Titus jumped. Manypenny was sitting on the very edge of the sofa, holding his derby in his lap, and Geoff was standing, reading the tattered poster advertising the Wild West Show. His expression had been almost dreamy, but the creak of the door returned him instantly to the moment.

"Hello." Shelby stepped into the big room and waited. When she saw Geoff's eyes change, her confidence soared. She didn't care about her looks, yet certainly was aware of them. After discarding her Coyote Matt disguise, Shelby had donned a plum-colored skirt and an ivory, high-necked blouse with a cameo pinned at her throat. Her glorious, dark red hair was swirled into the upswept style that flattered her, emphasizing her striking features. Her small waist and high breasts were set off to advantage by her simple clothing; there was no mistaking her womanhood.

When she sensed that the Englishman had been suitably affected by the sight of her, Shelby walked toward him, one graceful hand outstretched. "I should introduce myself," she began, her tone beguiling.

Returning her smile with an equal measure of charm, Geoff murmured, "Coyote *Mary*, I presume?"

Shelby paled, while across the room the cup and saucer in Titus's hand chattered eloquently. "A lucky guess!" he blurted.

"On the contrary, I am something of a connoisseur of art, and I recognized this particularly fine example of female beauty almost from the moment she tapped me on the shoulder in the saloon," Geoff replied calmly. "The men in Cody do not seem to be particularly observant, or they would have seen through your disguise as well. It was more amusing than effective, Miss . . ."

Feeling as if she'd had the wind knocked out of her repeatedly that day, Shelby managed to whisper, "Matthews. Shelby Matthews."

"That's a lovely name, and I hope you won't be offended if I tell you that you are even more lovely than I guessed you would be." He took her hand at last, his own fingers strong yet well-shaped. "I've been very curious to see the woman behind Coyote Matt's mustache."

Shelby didn't like the current of pleasure that accompanied his touch, or the way her thoughts seemed to scatter just when she needed them most. What was it she had intended to say to him? "Mr. Weston, now that you know I am a woman, I'm sure you will realize that our little drama at the saloon was nothing more than a romp for me . . . an amusement of sorts. How could my appearance in that ridiculous costume be anything else? Did you guess that Titus and I fashioned the mustache from my horse's mane?" She laughed gaily, Titus joined in with enthusiasm, and Geoff was kind enough to smile.

"It doubtless looked better on your horse," he remarked, aware that she was expecting a response, and equally aware of the conversation's destination.

Shelby's amusement seemed to know no bounds. As she laughed she put a hand on his sleeve, as if they were good friends. "My uncle Ben has ever been skeptical of these pranks of mine, but I can see that you are blessed with a sense of humor, Mr. Weston."

"Please, Miss Matthews, call me Geoff," he said on cue.

"Only if you will call me Shelby." She gave him a winsome smile. "May I be frank with you, Geoff?"

"I insist upon it."

She feared that there was a hint of irony mixed with the warmth in his eyes, but charged ahead regardless. "I like you. In fact, I have a notion that this escapade we have been through together will end in a firm friendship between us." Shelby saw that Titus was pouring the tea, and she led Geoff to the table. "Mr. Manypenny, do join us! We don't stand on ceremony here in America."

There was an odd tension in the air as Shelby chatted on through tea. Geoff was hungry; he consumed two large pieces of apple cake with innate good manners. He felt stirrings of sympathy for Shelby, even though he found her vastly entertaining and more attractive than he cared to contemplate. If he were inclined to assume the manners he'd been taught since birth, he might pretend the entire poker game had been only an amusing diversion. But he would not, and the value of his winnings was not the reason.

The cake was gone; the teapot was empty. Shelby fell silent for a moment, then gathered her courage and skirted the point. "Well, that was lovely. And I really can't tell you how pleased I am that you understand."

Geoff appeared to be mildly puzzled. "Understand?"

"Why, yes!" Her heart was thundering again. "You are an Englishman, and gallant enough to understand that that silly game at the saloon was a lark; nothing more! We've laughed about it, we've made friends, and now we can forget about it."

"Oh, no, I don't think so, Shelby. I'm not nearly as gallant as you hoped."

Color stained her cheeks. "But—you can't be serious! You aren't going to *keep* half my ranch!?"

Rubbing a tapered finger against his lower lip, he considered for a moment before countering, "Would you have kept my money if I had been the loser?"

Shelby nearly choked. "That's—different!"

"My dear, you are distraught. Surely you realize that this is a pill you must swallow, no matter how bitter it may seem. However, there is a bright side. I could be worse! I'm hardly an ogre—in fact, there are people who believe that I am replete with attractive qualities—"

"Please!" Shelby cried, giving up any further pretense of good cheer.

"But Shelby, I thought we had agreed to be frank with one another." He chuckled, aware that his continued use of her first name set her teeth on edge. "I can see that you have had a change of heart, but I only meant to reassure you that you could be sharing your ranch with worse people . . . many of whom were sitting near us in the saloon today. Don't worry, we'll deal together quite well, and I shall finance whatever project you were trying to raise the funds for today—if you can convince me that it is worthwhile."

Shelby had a lot of pouting left in her, but Geoff was so casual about it all that she felt stifled. She protested, "You don't understand. This is a catastrophe! I'm not supposed to even know that I own the ranch, let alone lose half of it! My father . . . oh, Daddy will be apoplectic if he hears about this!"

"Where does your father live?"

"In Deadwood, South Dakota." Her misery swelled as she said the words.

"Well, there's no reason he should have to hear about this for the time being, is there? And who is that Ben fellow? I gather he isn't pleased with the day's events."

Shelby poured out the whole story then, beginning with her father's decision to buy land near Cody and ending with her scheme to purchase farming equipment and horses for breeding. "I know I'm right about expanding our operation, but I wanted to prove to Daddy that I could do it on my own, without going to him for more money! Uncle Ben and Titus built this house and the other buildings, and my uncle has been locking horns with me about the proper way to manage the ranch ever since I arrived. When he finds you here, he'll *kill* me!"

"I highly doubt that . . . and while I can understand and sympathize with your sense of despair, I have interests of my own to protect." Geoff stood up, his tone kind but firm. "Perhaps you will learn a lesson from this experience, Shelby—although I would be sorry if it made you shy away from adventure in the future. Coyote Matt was an unforgettable piece of work." He tilted his head, regarding her with something akin to tenderness. "Meanwhile, I trust we'll find a way to get along."

Titus took the two men to the spare bedrooms that opened off the kitchen. It had seemed easier, with Shelby in the house, for Titus and Ben to live in the newly completed bunkhouse with the cowboys, and so there were three extra bedrooms in the house.

Soon it was dark, and Jimmy, Cal, Lucius, and Marsh returned from their day's work rounding up strays and building fences. Titus had them transport the trunks from the buckboard to the rooms of the ranch's new co-owner, who was dozing contentedly in a tub of steaming water.

Ben was the last to appear. Silent, his eyes burning, he listened to Titus's report of the events that had transpired after his exit from Purcell's Saloon. Shelby, he was told, had taken to her bed.

"For Pete's sake, Titus, how could you of let this happen?" Ben groaned when he found his voice.

"Me? So this is *my* fault? I don't really think it makes sense to go blamin' now that the damage is done. Besides, this fellow isn't a bad sort."

Ben shook his big head. "Aw, what in the hell could a dude from England possibly know about runnin' a ranch? This is the kind of gigantic mess only *Shelby* could've made!" With that, he strode through the big room to her door, banged on it, then pushed it open. Her bedroom was pitch-dark. "Shel? Answer me!"

She moaned faintly from the direction of her bed.

"What the hell do you mean to do now, you little so-and-so?"

"Just lie here. . . ." Shelby paused for effect, then murmured in pitiful tones, "My life is over, Uncle Ben. I don't deserve to live! I'll just lie here on my bed until I waste away, and then you'll be rid of me. . . ."

"Aw, geez!" With the firelight spilling through the doorway, he was able to find his way to her bedside. The springs creaked as Ben Avery sat down beside his prostrate niece and gathered her into his arms. "Never mind, Shel. I forgive you. You can't help gettin' us into jams, I guess. It's just the way you are."

A grin spread over her face in the darkness. "Whew! Now that you're on my side again, we can figure out a way to get rid of that awful man! Between us, we ought to be able to make ranch life so horrible for him that he'll *pay* us to take back his winnings!" Shelby clapped her hands, her excitement revived. "I'll bet you I can have him running back to London before the first roundup!"

During the next two days, Geoff saw little of Shelby. He spent most of his time in Cody, getting to know the townspeople, establishing an account at the Amoretti and Parks Bank, investigating the opportunities for investment in the Irma Hotel, which Buffalo Bill was constructing on Sheridan Avenue, and buying new clothing and supplies at the Cody Trading Company.

Geoff's other major purchase was a magnificent buckskin gelding. Pleasure coursed through his veins each time he looked at the horse, and he felt happy beyond words when he was riding him. On a whim, Geoff christened the buckskin Charlie, and each time he said the name, he smiled at the thought of his old friend. All was forgiven now; he was grateful to Charles for guiding him to Wyoming, and immensely pleased with himself for coming.

On the afternoon Ben and Titus were to set out for Billings to make the purchases for the ranch, Geoff arrived back from Cody just in time to see them off. Shelby was standing on the veranda, watching for him, when he rode up on Charlie. It surprised her to observe his horsemanship; somehow she expected him to be inexperienced, but instead he rode with easy grace and assurance.

Ben had slipped through the screen door and come up behind her. "Stop being shocked that he came west with some skills he could use out here," he murmured, reading her mind. "I'd think, considering what happened when you underestimated Weston's talent for poker, that you'd try not to jump to any more conclusions."

"I'll find his Achilles heel yet," she replied stubbornly. "Anyway, I'm glad he's back. I hope he remembered to go to the bank. Are you ready?" Shelby turned to straighten her uncle's coat collar, presenting her back to Geoff as he reached the house and swung down from Charlie's back.

"Yeah, I'm ready, and so's Titus and Jimmy, but we don't like to leave you here alone. You sure you'll be okay?"

"Who'll be alone? Not I! Marsh and Cal and Lucius will be with me . . . not to mention those two *other* people." A spark of mischief gleamed in her eyes as she stood on tiptoe and whispered in his ear, "With a little luck, I'll succeed in driving *him* off before you get back."

"Shel-by," Ben growled, his brow furrowed.

"What's wrong?" Geoff asked in a light tone as he stepped onto the porch. "I hope our dear Shelby isn't plotting my untimely demise. . . ."

Her cheeks burned. She turned to face him, and then embarrassment was pushed aside by an unexpected surge of female appreciation for his appearance. When she allowed herself to consider such matters, Shelby was forced to admit that Geoffrey Weston had looked splendid even when his clothing had been much too fancy for Cody, Wyoming. Now he had made a smooth transformation into the role of gentleman rancher. His choice of horse had been impeccable; the buckskin gelding was simply a prize. Perhaps equally impressive were the clothes that Geoff now wore as if he'd been born to them. This afternoon he was clad in stone-colored trousers tucked into riding boots. Geoff's shirt was faded blue chambray, set off by a chile-red kerchief knotted loosely around his neck, and he wore a butter-soft leather vest that looked as if he'd taken a good year to break in. His physique was both lithe and strong; clearly he had been a sportsman long before aspiring to life in the American West. He was acquiring a golden tan, and his hair shone in the sunlight when he removed his white Stetson and idly reshaped its folds.

"Cat got your tongue, Shel?" Ben taunted her gently.

"I was—" She took a breath, gathering her thoughts. "I was just thinking how quickly our new partner has adapted to our western ways. One would never guess, at first glance, that you are an incurable dude, Mr. Weston."

He shaded his eyes with one hand and gave her his most effective smile. "Have I been insulted?"

"Why do you imagine that I am always up to no good? Actually, I have more important matters than *you* to consider, such as sending Uncle Ben and Titus on their way to Billings with the necessary capital."

"Then you'll be happy to know I have just come from the bank." He took a thickly padded envelope from his vest pocket and handed it to Ben. "I know that you will handle this responsibly. No gambling with the ranch funds, hmm?"

There was a twinkle in his eyes, but Shelby would not acknowledge the humor. "Who's the one passing out insults? I suggest that you save your cruel jokes for a more receptive audience, Mr. Weston!" She retreated into the house, letting the screen door bang for emphasis.

Ben looked at the Englishman and shrugged. "I thought it was a funny thing to say, myself. Don't pay Shel any mind, Geoff. She's madder at herself than anyone, but it's easier for her to take it out on you." He studied the envelope for a moment. "This is a fine gesture on your part; I truly appreciate it, and my niece does, too, even if she's too much of a brat to admit it. Don't let her get under your skin while we're gone. You know . . . she will if you let her."

"She wants her ranch back," Geoff agreed laconically.

"Shel can be downright ornery when she sets her mind to it. I wouldn't blame you, if she misbehaves too much, if you put her over your knee and give her a good whippin'. Might do her good."

He smiled. "An interesting scenario."

"Yeah, ain't it?" Ben happened to glance over toward the door. On the other side of the screen, Shelby was standing in the shadows, glaring at her uncle. Elaborately, she mouthed one word: *Traitor!*

The next morning at sunrise, Shelby made a great show of slaving over breakfast. She juggled pots and pans, stirring oatmeal, frying eggs, and browning french toast, so that when Geoff appeared early and attempted to chat with her, she was able to appear too busy to respond. She reflected that it had been easier to avoid him when Ben and Titus were there, because both men were so embarrassed by her behavior that they went out of their way to keep him occupied at meals and during evenings in front of the fire. They told stories, played gin rummy or checkers, or lured the newcomer outside for a walk and a smoke in the moonlight. Shelby hadn't been much fun these past three days, but there was certainly a fire in her eyes that told Geoff she was far from beaten.

He was tenacious himself, although his personal style was different from Shelby's. Geoff bided his time, drawing on his heretofore untapped reserve of patience. That quality had eluded him in London, where his routine had been so predictable. Dealing with Shelby Matthews required a different sort of forbearance; she challenged his wits at every turn, and he had to remain ever alert because there was no telling what she'd do next. Shelby was vexing, stimulating, fascinating, infuriating, alluring, challenging . . . and often stunningly rude. Now, however, as he poured milk into his strong tea and watched her push a lock of hair off her brow with one hand and flip the french toast with the other, Geoff reminded himself that he had yet to experience boredom in her presence. No one, save Charles Lipton-Lyons, could guess how important that was to him.

Shelby herself imagined that he was put off by her brashness, that he longed for a tranquil, sweet influence from the woman of the house. Englishwomen were elegant and well-mannered, after all.

"Breakfast smells wonderful," Geoff said now, hungrier for conversation than food.

"Good." Brandishing the frying pan, Shelby shook the french toast from side to side. "I can't talk when I'm cooking."

Every so often her looks and gestures and aura struck him with tremendous force, and this was one of those moments. She was clutching a spatula, one hand on her hip, garbed in her usual high-necked blouse and split skirt, and there was an almost whimsical elegance about her just then. Her lush hair was coming unpinned, there was a streak of egg yolk on her blue gingham apron, and her distinctively beautiful face was flushed.

Shelby felt Geoff's reaction to her, for his thoughts had a heat all their own. Spatula in midair, she guilelessly returned his gaze.

"What's burnin'?" Cal called as he came through the front door, followed by Lucius and Marsh.

Shelby crashed back down to earth, yanking the pan from the fire and plucking out the smoking pieces of french toast. Angry and confused, she glared at Geoff. "I have *told* you not to bother me when I'm cooking!"

The only reaction he betrayed was a slight elevation of his eyebrows. Something snapped inside of Geoff, but he was determined not to let her know. Instead, amidst the hired hands' wide-eyed silence, he got up and walked over to the fancy stove where Shelby was dishing up the breakfasts.

"Clearly, you are in need of help," Geoff said, "and fortunately I am here to assist you."

Shelby had to admire his style. "Lucky me," she murmured with a grudging smile.

From the table Marsh whooped, "Yup!"

Shelby also made a show of being an able business-woman. This was a role she could play with real skill if she chose, but she had rarely been inclined to do so since arriving at the Sunshine Ranch. With Geoffrey Weston as her audience, however, she now took a seat at her desk after breakfast.

"Running a ranch is a complicated business," she remarked when he paused behind her chair. Shelby wished she had a pair of gold-rimmed spectacles that she could don for the occasion. Instead she opened the heavy ledger, shuffled a stack of bills and receipts, and took pen in hand.

"I know a bit about such matters, having an estate of my own in England," he replied. "I must confess that I have a manager as well, but I've made a point of learning what goes on. You and I should sit down together soon so that you can acquaint me with the books."

"It will be difficult to find the time, I'm afraid. There's so much to do."

"Has anyone told you that you haven't the manners God gave a cat?" Geoff inquired in a conversational tone.

"No! My friends maintain that I am exceptionally charming and kind." She bent over the sheaf of accounts. "I'm afraid that I have a considerable amount of *work* to do now. If you'll excuse me . . ."

Geoff left her without another word, and Shelby smiled to herself, pleased overall with the morning's progress. He would go off to Cody again, and she was certain that very soon he would realize that it would be infinitely better to stay in town than way out here on a ranch where he was shunned and insulted and made to feel inept at every turn.

The morning was opening like the wildflowers on the hillsides. After scarcely a half hour of daydreaming over the bills, Shelby couldn't bear to stay indoors another moment. With that Englishman out of the way, she was relieved of the pressure to keep up appearances, and happily went off to put on her riding boots and a short Eton jacket.

Shelby fairly skipped out the door, discovering Manypenny sitting in a wicker chair on the veranda. He hadn't taken breakfast with them and she'd nearly forgotten his existence. Today the old man was wearing a straw boater that looked quite comical on his large head. The instant he saw her, he unfolded his giant-sized frame and bowed to her.

"Good morning, Miss Matthews," he intoned.

"Good morning, Mr. Manypenny. What's that you're reading?"

He consulted the spine of the book in his right hand. "It is *The Eustace Diamonds* by Anthony Trollope, miss."

"How delightful! I am a great admirer of Trollope."

"Indeed? In that case you must speak to his lor—that is, Mr. Weston. This volume belongs to him. He brought an entire trunk filled solely with books."

"I see." Shelby backed away. "I'm off then. 'Bye!"

With a nod of farewell, Manypenny slowly lowered himself into the chair and resumed reading.

Shelby hurried to the barn, trying not to think about the trunk of books Geoff was hoarding in his room. How she hungered for new books, especially titles like *The Eustace Diamonds*! If only he were a guest at the ranch—not an interloper! How dare he criticize her manners, when *he* had the effrontery to hold her to the outcome of a silly poker game! Any real gentleman would have laughed and let her and the Sunshine Ranch off the hook.

At the barn door Shelby was surprised to hear voices. Since they were shorthanded until the men returned from Billings, she expected that Marsh, Cal, and Lucius would be at the far reaches of their land by now, tending to the nearly completed fences.

"Howdy, Miz Shelby," Lucius greeted her from the darkened interior of the barn. "I saddled Gadabout an' put her in the corral to wait fer you, ma'am."

"I appreciate that, Lucius, but—" She broke off at the sight of Geoffrey Weston.

He stepped out of the shadows wearing a knowing smile. "Finished with all those ledgers so soon? You *are* a wizard with numbers!"

Shelby's cheeks burned. She looked at the young cowboy. "Why aren't you working on those fences? We can't let the cattle roam free without brands until the fences are finished!"

"I know that, ma'am, but I started talkin' to Mr. Weston about saddles and I guess I lost track of the time. Did you know that he brought an English saddle all this way on the train? Lordy it's a pretty thing! But I convinced him to try a California saddle to go with that fine western horse, Charlie. Now we're saddled up and we was just goin' out to tend to them fences you mentioned, ma'am." The boy sauntered toward her, bowlegged and grinning. "You wanna ride out with us?"

"No." Shelby pivoted and started toward the corral. "And Lucius, remember you have *work* to do!"

A few minutes later Shelby was urging her pinto pony into a gallop. They followed the bends in the river, riding away from the ranch buildings in the direction of the Carter Mountains. Then, turning east, Shelby and Gadabout found themselves in the emerald-green high meadows that were studded with coppices of budding trees and threaded with streams. The air was cooler; a breeze loosened Shelby's hair.

Quite a few of the ranch's cattle were grazing out here; some she actually recognized by their markings. Soon they'd wear the Sunshine brand, that circle with lines radiating out from the center like a drawing of the sun. In spite of everything, the thought of that brand cheered Shelby. No one could take away the love she felt for this ranch.

A little valley appeared, folded into the hillside. Wildflowers spattered color over the grass: yellow, blue, purple, white, and shades of red. Shelby soon longed for a closer look, and wondered if she could transplant some of the flowers into window boxes at the house. Dismounting, she sat down on the damp grass and soaked up the sun-washed view of their land that stretched up the Shoshone River valley. Gadabout seemed to sense Shelby's mood. She meandered around, munching grass and waiting patiently.

Shelby picked lupine, saxifrage, star asters, and blanket flowers. Lulled, she lay back for a moment. The sun was warm on her face, and the next thing she knew the light had shifted and she was chilly. Sitting up, it came to her that she'd been asleep and a considerable amount of time had passed. Her heart began to beat faster as she looked around for Gadabout. The pony wasn't in sight.

She's probably very near . . . or she's gone back to the barn, Shelby told herself, clambering to her feet. *Calm down!*

She called "Gadabout!" and ran around the area in circles until she was dizzy and hoarse. Then, spotting a denser thicket of cottonwoods over the next hillside, instinct told her to look there. When she reached the trees and went beyond them, Shelby glimpsed the mudhole first and then Gadabout. Her heart clenched with sheer panic.

"Oh, girl!" Tears sprang to her eyes. "What have you done?"

The little filly was up to her withers in thick black mud. She gazed back at Shelby for a long minute, then whinnied and struggled to free herself. Now the mud oozed to her mane, touching the bare patch that had provided the makings of Shelby's false mustache.

Shelby was powerless. She had been so distracted at the ranch that she hadn't even brought her usual coiled rope—not that she could've pulled Gadabout out alone even with the rope.

How far away was the ranch? How long would it take her to run there for help? Gadabout was so small and feisty that Shelby feared she'd continue to struggle and drown in the mud before she could be rescued.

"Girl, you're going to have to stay here," she instructed the frightened pony. Openly weeping, Shelby exclaimed, "Stay quiet and wait—I'll bring help, but I don't know how long it'll take. I know you're scared, Gadabout, but I'll save you." She looked heavenward and sobbed, "Dear Lord, please help us get out of this fix! If you save Gadabout, I promise to—"

Before Shelby could finish, the perfect loop of a lasso sailed over her head, seemed to hover above the mudhole, and finally encircled Gadabout's neck. Shelby was lightheaded with shock. Whirling around, she nearly collided with Charlie, the handsome buckskin gelding.

"Surprised?" Geoff looked down from Charlie's back. The rope's other end was knotted securely around the horn of his new California saddle.

The person Shelby hated the most was rescuing her beloved Gadabout.

Chapter Five

"I'VE BEEN WAITING FOR THE OPPORTUNITY TO save you from something," Geoff said as he drew the rope taut. "Will this good deed earn me your favor?"

"I—I—oh, just hurry!"

Geoff talked gently to the pony and to Charlie, too, who seemed to understand his job. The buckskin held his ground, even managing to back up a step or two, while Geoff drew the rope steadily in, hand over hand. Gadabout flailed at first, wild-eyed, but then she must've felt her hooves suck free of the mudhole's bottom. Slowly, she allowed the rope to pull her out of the bog.

Shelby was still crying. Her pristine blouse was smeared with mud, her hair was a riot of curls, and her face mirrored an assortment of emotions Geoff hadn't glimpsed before. A chink in her armor . . . and look what is revealed, he thought. Amazing. He watched as she stumbled while running to meet Gadabout. Heedless of the black goo dripping from the pinto, Shelby embraced her, then removed the lasso from her neck. Leading Gadabout by the reins, she carried the rope in her other hand and approached Geoff and Charlie.

"I suppose you think you're a knight in shining armor now," Shelby murmured as she handed him the rest of his rope.

He considered this for a moment, then swung down

from the saddle and faced her. "Shelby, I probably shouldn't have chosen that particular moment to attempt to be droll."

A shaft of sunlight broke through the clouds overhead and shone directly on Geoff, bathing him in radiance. Shelby's tears had ceased, yet she continued to feel emotional, and wasn't sure why. It was possible that her resentment toward Geoff was mixed with a crazy sort of attraction to him as a man. She'd been considering this possibility for a while, because her body wouldn't stop sending her that message—and the louder it became, the ruder she was to Geoff. That very rudeness had become conspicuous, Shelby now realized.

"I must thank you sincerely for saving my darling Gadabout," she said plainly. "This episode does not erase the other problems between us, but—"

"Will you soften your heart toward me just a little?" His voice was low and rich, his eyes warm. "I'm not going away, you know. I know you wish it, but I will not."

It came to Shelby then that perhaps she did not wish it. How could her feelings be in such utter conflict? "I . . . am ashamed that I could have been so foolish, that I could have lost half of our ranch. It seems like a nightmare—a nightmare that you could banish by telling me you won't hold me to that ridiculous bet!" Her temper was flaring again. "I don't actually dislike *you*—"

"You don't?" Geoff's eyes crinkled at the corners. "Would you be willing to put that in writing in the presence of witnesses?" Recklessly, he reached for her mud-caked hand and held it lightly. "Shelby, I am fully aware of all your hints, subtle and otherwise, that I call off the bet. I don't know why you cannot comprehend the fact that the poker game is over and you lost. There's no going back now. I might see your point about my duty as a gentleman if I had instigated the game instead of you, and if I had suggested that outrageous bet, but it was all your doing. You sought me out, urged me to play with you, and so on. I don't see any evidence that would support your charge that I was the villain of the piece." Geoff paused. Her hands were getting warmer in his, and they trembled a little. "Do you?"

Shelby stared at the toes of her boots, then finally shook her head and mumbled, "No. What's worst of all is that I'm not even one of those women who believes that men should treat us differently, letting us win or giving in to our whims. I know that I'm a match for any man . . . and it was only the spoiled brat in me—the sore loser—who couldn't accept the consequences of that dreadful poker game!" Tears dripped onto their clasped hands.

"Never mind." A sharp urge to draw her into his arms caused Geoff to lean away instead. He felt tantalized by Shelby in a way he didn't recognize, and it worried him. "I've found your tantrums rather entertaining. I've never met a woman like you!"

The warm amusement in his voice made her giggle softly, then step back. "I'm not giving up completely, you know, but I'll try to play straight with you from now on. If I get the ranch back, I'll win it fairly or I'll figure out a way to buy it, but I won't try to drive you away with any more horrid displays. I owe you that much for saving Gadabout."

The pinto nudged her mistress and tossed her mane. Reaching out to gently stroke the pony's neck, Geoff said, "I'll accept that for the moment. Shall we cry peace?" He thought he saw a blush creep into Shelby's lovely face. "This situation can hold more enjoyment than you know."

"That's what I'm afraid of."

One of those crazy waves of captivation hit Geoff then. Shelby's eyes were averted, and he found himself staring at her luscious mouth and wondering what she would do if he bent to taste it. He began to lean toward her when Gadabout pushed between their bodies, clearly more aware of the situation than Shelby or perhaps even Geoff himself.

"Look here," he said to the pinto with mock severity, "I've just saved your life. I suggest you treat me accordingly!"

During the next few days, a real friendship began between Shelby and Geoff. True, there were other stirrings as well, but Geoff's breeding served him well. He was careful with her, aware that she was inexperienced with men and that he might frighten her off permanently if he touched her before she was ready.

In other respects, however, Shelby was strong and daring and self-assured. Geoff had known women rather like her in England, but most of them were outdoorsy girls with lots of brothers . . . and they resembled the horses they adored so.

Not Shelby, Geoff reflected as he watched her stride toward him one sunlit afternoon. How glorious was her cinnamon-hued hair, swirled up into a coil atop her head and fastened with tortoiseshell pins. And her eyes—candidly blue, tilting just a bit to follow the lines of her winged brows. . . . She was the most arresting woman Geoff had ever seen, from her cheekbones and her expressive mouth, to the way her crisp white blouse tucked neatly over her breasts, and even to her style of walking: purposeful, yet with a lovely, innate grace.

"Have you already finished making that stew?" he asked, leaning against the gate to the corral.

"Yes, it's all in the pot, simmering, and not a moment too soon." She shaded her eyes against the sun. "I do wish we were rich enough to have a cook. I've tried, and God knows Uncle Ben has shamed me into some accomplishment, but whenever I'm slaving over that stove on an afternoon like this—"

"I heard that there is an old grub-wagon cook in Cody who has gotten too old for the trail," Geoff said, watching her.

"Oh, we could never afford such a wild extravagance, especially since I'm perfectly capable of doing it myself. . . ." Shelby's attention was wandering as she watched Marsh and Cal come out of the stable with a couple coils of rope, leading a frisky young stallion. "Wait a minute! What are you all doing loitering around here in the middle of the day? There's so much work to do! The roundup is next week!"

The two young cowboys stared at the dirt and scuffed the toes of their boots to and fro, leaving Geoff to explain. Gallantly, he straightened and said, "You've discovered us, I fear. Although I may seem to be adapting to your ways here, I would be glad for instruction in some of the skills particular to ranch life. A day or two ago, when you were . . . elsewhere, the boys and I took a little time off after lunch to practice riding western style, and now—"

"I can't believe my ears! To flagrantly waste daylight hours in such a manner—"

"Ma'am," Cal interjected, "we could use an extra man around here, 'specially with Jimmy, Ben, an' Titus in Billings, but Geoff's not much help unless he feels easy with ropin', shootin', and ridin' western." He finished rolling a cigarette, licked the paper, and added,

"Seems to me that this time spent workin' with Geoff is sorta an *investment*."

"*Geoff?*" Shelby was incredulous. When had this English tenderfoot won the regard of her weatherbeaten, plain-spoken cowpunchers? "You call him *Geoff*?"

"Yup," said Marsh. He threw the extra lariat to Geoff, who caught it and walked over to confer with the two men.

"How long is the rope?" he asked Cal. "Is there a standard length?"

If there was one thing Shelby couldn't abide, it was the sense that she was being excluded because she was a female. So, before Cal could open his mouth, she hurried toward them, declaring loudly, "Forty feet, right Cal? That's twenty-five feet for throwing, and fifteen feet of coil to hold onto." Shelby wedged herself between the corral and Marsh, smiling genially, as if this had all been her idea. "That's what my own father taught me back in Deadwood, and he sure can rope. Sometimes Daddy used a sixty-foot lariat, because he could throw forty feet when the wind was with him." She draped an arm around Marsh's shoulders. "Didn't you rope an elk a few weeks back?"

"That was me," Cal said. He squinted at her suspiciously.

"Who's ready for some practice?" she cried. "You can never practice roping too much, I always say."

"Yup," Marsh agreed, and winked at Geoff.

They decided to let the Englishman start out. The group perched on the side of the corral and watched as Geoff mounted his buckskin and made a few attempts to rope the erratic, elusive stallion who seemed to be dancing away from him, just out of reach.

"It was much easier to find my mark with Gadabout," he called to Shelby in wry tones. "She didn't move—and Charlie wasn't moving, either. I find this business quite . . ." His voice trailed off; he couldn't bring himself to say the word "impossible."

"You hafta swing the rope so the loop'll open in the air," Cal yelled. "Tossin' yer rope before buildin' a loop don't catch the horse!"

Geoff continued to practice, even after an hour had passed and Cal and Marsh decided they'd better tend to the fences while the weather held. There were some questionable clouds stacking up to the north.

When Shelby and he were alone in the corral, Geoff confided, "I feel rather over my head. Just adjusting to the different saddle and the terrain could have been enough to occupy me through the spring." Fingering the lariat, he smiled into her eyes. "I came here with the notion that I was exceptionally skilled because I not only rode and jumped with the best English equestrians, but I also broke horses. Little did I know . . ."

"It's all different?"

"Everything. Even the saddle—my English saddle is as different from this as it would be to ride bareback. These stirrups are much farther back, so everything I do with my legs is different—I'm nearly standing in the stirrups, and gripping with my thighs rather than my knees." Geoff shook his head with a self-deprecating chuckle. "It's rather like relearning all the instinctive movements that go into walking. I've been riding nearly that long. . . ."

"Well, you don't have to change. I mean, you have your own English saddle. You could use it, and simply ride for pleasure, and not bother with all this ranch-hand nonsense."

He liked the way she switched back and forth between western speech patterns and those of a well-brought-up young woman. Very telling. "Then why come—and stay?

If I behave as I did in England, what's the point? Mind you, I don't know if I can bring myself to break horses the way the boys do, by snubbing them up so violently that they often somersault at the end of the rope, but . . . perhaps I'll adjust even to that idea." He tossed the lariat overhead, watching the loop widen perfectly in the air, and grinned. "I want to be useful; to enjoy a full life here at the Sunshine Ranch."

Shelby beamed back at him. "That wasn't bad! If you practice on a few posts first, you'll be roping that stallion by four o'clock!"

Not only was Geoff soon displaying considerable skill with the lariat, but it seemed that he could also shoot. Shelby thought it might be fun to show off a bit, after being so generous of spirit about Geoff's roping and riding, so later that afternoon she suggested that they take turns with her prized Winchester repeating rifle.

"It's just like the one Annie Oakley shoots in the Wild West Show," Shelby announced to him as they lined some bottles, and even a few small stones, on the garden fence.

"Have I told you that I saw them all perform in London in 1887?" He held the rifle and tried to get a sense of its weight and balance. "That afternoon probably led to my journey to Wyoming this spring."

"Really? How amazing! The world's smaller than you'd think." Distracted, she watched him prepare to shoot.

Slowly, Geoff lifted the rifle and looked down the barrel. His finger squeezed the trigger and the first bottle exploded.

Shelby cheered, trying to be a good sport until her own turn.

One by one the bottles shattered and fell, but Geoff left every other one standing. "For you," he told Shelby with the driest of smiles. Then, as her sense of sportsmanship faded quickly, he proceeded to pick off the stones as well, hitting even the smallest with the first shot.

Shelby had begun to pout by the time she accepted her rifle. Even her older brother, Byron, hadn't been able to beat her at shooting. She reloaded, then took aim and fired. The first bottle broke and flew into the air; Geoff applauded.

"I say, I've never known a woman with such an abundance of talent!"

Shelby gave him a sidelong glance before taking aim again. She felt patronized, particularly since he'd lowered the level of difficulty for her by increasing the distance between her targets. When she squeezed off her next shot, the bullet only grazed the side of the bottle, which dutifully fell off the fence and landed in the dirt with a thud. Little hairs bristled at the nape of Shelby's neck, and she struck her remaining targets at dead center.

"Well done! But I don't think the light's as favorable as it was a few minutes ago. Doubtless that was responsible for—"

Shelby interrupted. "You needn't make excuses for me, or apologize for besting me with my own rifle." Turning toward the house, she set her chin and added, "I suppose I must have underestimated you because you're English—again. I keep forgetting that I lost the ranch that way."

"Is that your stew I smell?" Geoff wondered as he fell into step with Shelby. "Gad, I'm ravenous suddenly—and I'd kill for a good cup of tea."

"I'll make a pot." Shelby allowed him to hold the

screen door open for her, adding over her shoulder, "But I'm having whiskey."

By the time the kettle had begun to boil on the stove and Shelby had poured boiling water into the teapot, Geoff had a fire going and the clouds outside had turned ominous.

"I believe we're going to have a storm," he remarked.

Through her kitchen window Shelby saw a white flash of lightning, followed by the boom-*boooom* of serious thunder. "I hope that the boys have sense enough to take cover rather than ride back here in a lightning storm."

"I wonder what Manypenny is doing? I haven't seen him all day," Geoff mused as he stirred milk into his tea. "Perhaps he's reading."

Shelby couldn't resist. "Trollope? *The Eustace Diamonds*?"

He gave her a faintly quizzical look before heading toward Manypenny's little room at the back of the house. A tap at the door brought a muffled "Hmm? What?" which made Geoff's expression even more puzzled. He opened the door.

"What are you up to in here, old man? Did you have your tea whilst I was off roping horses?" His tone was light, but he was brought up short by the sight of Manypenny in bed. The manservant was clad in Oriental-style silk panjamas and a nightcap, and was bundled under several quilts. "What's afoot? Are you ill?"

"I fear so, my lord." The old man's expression caused him to look as if he'd just bitten into a lemon. "I believe it's the . . . ague."

"Good God! This is horrible!" Geoff came over for a

closer look. "I've never known you to be ill before, old reliable!"

"I can only surmise that—" Manypenny covered his mouth with a fine handkerchief, then coughed deeply. "It's this ghastly place, I imagine. There must be an abundance of exotic germs."

"But what can we do for you? Shall we summon the physician? Are you hungry? Let me bring you a cup of hot tea with lemon and whiskey, all right?"

Manypenny looked sleepy. "I'll just have a nap, my lord."

Frowning, Geoff went back into the living area of the house. Thunder continued to rumble outside, raindrops spattered against the glass windows, and the fire he'd built was blazing and popping merrily.

"Your tea is getting cold," Shelby informed him as she stirred the stew. The aroma of gravy-coated beef chunks, carrots, onions, and potatoes filled the house. "As soon as the corn bread is ready, we can eat. Gosh, I wonder if the others will make it back for supper!"

Geoff watched her mix up the cornmeal, eggs, buttermilk, and other ingredients, wondering what in the world corn bread was. When she'd slid the two pans into the oven, he said, "Do you have a moment to spare now? I'm afraid that Manypenny is ill. He believes it's the 'ague.' "

"You mean, a cold?" There was a furrow in her brow. "Why hasn't he said something?" Wiping her hands on her apron, Shelby went into her little pantry.

He followed her. "He's very much the old school, dead against complaints of any nature, particularly outside his class. I suppose Manypenny might let on to another servant, but never to me."

"That's ridiculous!" Shelby was sorting through her shelf of medicines. She threw Geoff a censorious glance, and he shrugged helplessly in reply. "You English are really the limit."

"You won't get an argument from me. Why do you think I came to Wyoming?"

"All right, here's what we'll give him." Shelby held up a box featuring a picture of a mustachioed bandit wearing a large sombrero. "I find that this Mexican Headache Cure works well for fever as well, so we'll start with a dose of it."

"How very . . . unique," Geoff remarked dryly.

She ignored him. "Luckily, I also have the Twenty-Minute Cold Cure on hand. My mother ordered a lot of these things through the catalogue when she knew I was coming out here, and I've never tried it myself, but it certainly does sound promising!"

Geoff consulted the box, reading aloud: " 'A few doses of this grand preparation taken right at the beginning of the first symptoms of a cold will do the work.' Well, I'm admittedly skeptical, but what do we have to lose?"

"I'll take care of him, and he'll be good as new by morning." Returning to the kitchen, Shelby fixed a big cup of tea for Manypenny, adding lemon, honey, whiskey, and doses of the Mexican Headache Cure and the Twenty-Minute Cold Cure.

"Have you tried *any* of these potions yourself?" Geoff wondered as they headed for the sickroom.

"Heavens, no. I'm never sick."

"From the smell of this, I'd guess that it should put him out of his misery one way or another. . . ." he murmured dubiously.

Manypenny, with his red-rimmed eyes and wheezing voice, tried to argue that he was merely a little tired and not in need of assistance, but Shelby waved him off. Instructing Geoff to help the old gentleman sit up, she straightened his nightcap, then held the steaming mug to his lips.

Astonishingly, Manypenny drank the powerful concoction down, then smiled euphorically. "I say, that was frightfully good. Well done, Miss Matthews."

"We're in Wyoming, Mr. Manypenny. Call me Shelby."

He sank back on the pillows and replied woozily, "And I am Percy, my dear . . . only to you." His hand searched for hers, then squeezed. "Like to borrow my book? Do, please . . ."

"That's very kind of you, Percy," she replied, smiling warmly. "I will."

They watched as the elderly manservant drifted off to sleep, then Shelby plucked *The Eustace Diamonds* from the bedside table. Geoff was shaking his head in disbelief as they tiptoed out of the room and closed the door.

"Percy?" he cried when they were back in the hallway. "That is simply outside the bounds of too much. In my entire life I've only heard one or two people dare to use Manypenny's given name of Percival, but the mere idea of anyone saying 'Percy' is beyond comprehension!"

"It was his idea, not mine," she reminded him mildly.

Back in the kitchen, Shelby put plates, cutlery, and napkins into Geoff's arms and told him to set the table. The wind was rushing down their valley now, bringing sheets of rain with it. The fragile windowpanes had begun to rattle with the force of the storm as Shelby dished up the stew and cut the hot corn bread into squares that she served with a little pot of honey. A lantern lent a soft glow to the checkered tablecloth covered with dishes and food, and Shelby dared to smile at Geoff as they sat down together. Alone.

"What's this?" she asked, looking at the little pressed-glass cups filled with amber liquid beside each place.

"You were threatening to drink whiskey earlier, so I thought a bit of sherry might take the chill out of our bones. I brought a few bottles with me from London."

Shelby sipped appreciatively, thinking that it tasted like ambrosia. "I don't suppose you have food like this in England," she said, sounding rather apologetic.

"No," Geoff agreed with an enigmatic smile.

"What would you have for a usual supper?"

"Oh . . . Scotch broth. Turbot with lobster sauce. Mutton cutlets. Cabbage and rice . . . stewed cucumbers . . . stewed pears." He drizzled honey over a wedge of corn bread, sampled a bite, then smiled with honest pleasure. "Nothing nearly this good."

"You're making those up, aren't you?" Shelby couldn't help laughing. "To make me feel better, I mean! Who would eat such things?"

"The English," he replied succinctly. "We stew and pickle foods regularly. It's rather a point of pride."

They laughed together. The lightning and thunder had passed over the ranch, and Shelby relaxed slightly. Nibbling on a piece of red potato, she said, "I suppose the boys are safe and they'll come home when the storm has passed, hmm? I mean, they're used to such weather."

"I'm sure you're right." He had eaten the last bit of stew on his plate, and said, "This is simply delicious. And it's odd that you have Blue Willow dishes; it's what we used for every day at our country house in Yorkshire when I was growing up. I was always much fonder of it than the gilt-edged china my mother favored."

"I chose it myself before I came back from college in Massachusetts," Shelby said. "I never was much of one for a hope chest or anything so nonsensical, but I do have definite tastes of my own, and I knew I'd be unlikely to satisfy them in Deadwood." Shelby watched Geoff refill her glass of sherry and smiled. "So, I forced myself to spend one tiresome day buying some of the things I liked: the Blue Willow, a lot of Belgian lace that I've stored away, bed linens, some Eastern riding gear that I rarely use, and books. I do treasure my books. Unfortunately, Uncle Ben made me leave most of them at home . . . and I agreed, because I was worried that they might be damaged somehow. I wasn't sure what to expect in this wilderness, or what sort of home awaited me."

"I see. And what is all this about *The Eustace Diamonds*?" he asked softly, caught in the spell of the moment. The room was lit from the golden fires within, and by luminous rays of sunset piercing the thunderheads outside. Shelby's radiance was brighter still. "How did you know that Manypenny was reading Trollope? Have the two of you begun a private literary club?"

"Hardly." She found herself warming toward Geoff. His effortlessly dry wit appealed very much to her intellect and her own sense of whimsy, and reminded her of her father. Also, she liked his way of remaining calm under almost any circumstances, unlike Uncle Ben, and certainly unlike her. And finally, there was something more in Geoff's brown eyes that lent substance to his other, cooler traits. He looked at her with an unspoken sense of understanding that made her trust him in spite of all her efforts to the contrary. Emboldened by the sherry, Shelby blurted, "Percy told me about your trunk full of books!"

He looked as if she'd slapped him. "For God's sake,

do not call him *Percy*! I can assure you that he will not appreciate it when his senses are restored!"

Shelby beamed. "I thought, by your expression, that you were angry that I knew your secret."

"Secret? It's nothing of the sort. Would you like to see the books? I'm afraid the trunk's too cumbersome to drag about, so we'll have to visit my bedchamber. Quite innocently, of course!" He spoke lightly, pressed the napkin to his mouth, and pushed back his chair. "I'll help you with the dishes first."

"No—let's just put them in the sink for now—to soak." She could scarcely contain her excitement. "I can't wait! Oh, you have no idea how I've dreamed about your trunk full of books ever since Mr. Manypenny mentioned them days ago. He was sitting on the veranda, reading Trollope, and I was so envious! When he told me that you had dozens more, I confess that I harbored mean thoughts toward you. . ."

Geoff brought the bottle of sherry and both glasses as they walked toward his bedroom. "My dear Shelby, what are you talking about?"

"I thought you were a greedy book hoarder!"

He had a powerful longing to take her in his arms, but instead caressed her with his eyes. "I assure you that, had I been apprised of your passion for literature, I would have invited you into my chamber the night I arrived!"

"And I would probably have been shameless enough to accept."

They stood on the threshold of his bedroom, staring into each other's eyes, and an electric current seemed to pass between their bodies, like the bolts of lightning illuminating the evening sky. It was a feeling unlike anything either of them had ever experienced, and in that instant, they both stepped backward.

"I don't know—" he murmured.

"Maybe it's not . . ." Shelby whispered.

You're a civilized man, Geoff reminded himself. *What are you afraid of?*

Don't be a missish ninny! she thought.

"After you, Miss Matthews." He gestured gallantly for her to precede him.

Heart pounding, Shelby walked into Geoffrey Weston's bedroom and listened as he came up behind her. The room smelled wonderfully of him, and the white iron bed seemed to fill her vision. It was covered with a frayed quilt, hand-stitched in the log cabin pattern, and one of Geoff's soft blue shirts lay casually across one side. There was a dent in the pillow from his head.

Shelby suddenly felt very hot, in spite of the stormy night.

Chapter Six

"THE TRUNK . . ." GEOFF WAS DISMAYED TO FIND that he sounded hoarse. This wasn't at all the self-assured figure he wanted to cut. But then . . . hadn't he fled London society in search of just this sort of shaky, heart-pounding reminder that he was alive?

Perhaps I condemned my tendency toward cool indifference a bit too hastily, he thought as he gestured toward the Louis Vuitton canvas-covered trunk. It really was disconcerting to feel his gut tighten when Shelby looked into his eyes. What was it about her? Why hadn't he reacted this way in the presence of English females?

"Is it unlocked?" she asked, kneeling in front of the trunk at the foot of the bed. Her face shone. "I am so excited!"

Geoff poured himself another glass of sherry and drank it down. "As am I," he murmured ironically.

She watched as he crouched beside her and lifted the lid, gesturing at the contents with one handsome hand. "Have at it."

"Oh. *Oh!* Look at these magnificent books!" They were all leather-bound, stamped in gold, and clearly cared for with love. It came to Shelby that it said a great deal about Geoff that he had needed his books so much that he was willing to risk damaging them by carting them all this way. When she picked up the first one and saw the title, her sense of wonder doubled. "*Ivanhoe*! I love this story! The scene when he returns from the Crusades and jousts, and they don't know who he is until he removes his armor . . . !" She sighed, nearly giddy. "Oh, Geoff, even the paper is fine. You know, my parents have a beautiful library, but I don't think I've ever seen books as rich as these."

"Compliment accepted." He watched as she pulled off her boots and sat down on the floor, cross-legged in her divided skirt and stockinged feet. His fingers itched to reach out and pull the tortoise-shell pins from her hair and let it spill free.

"*Dr. Jekyll and Mr. Hyde*! Oooh!" Shelby pretended to shiver with horror. "Dare I read it? I adored *Treasure Island*, but my teachers thought this wasn't fit literature for a female, and then when I was in college I forgot about it."

Geoff joined her on the rug and leaned against the open trunk so that he faced her. Drawing off his own boots, he wiggled his toes and remarked with a shrug, "It's more disturbing than conventionally scary, in my opinion, and certainly isn't everyone's cup of tea. But you seem a brave sort, and insightful. It's a fable, you see, crammed with insights into human nature and the struggle to balance good and evil."

"I'll read it, then." She set the book aside and took out others, exclaiming in delight either because she'd already read some books or because she'd been longing to. *Moby Dick* was at the top of her must-read list, Sherlock Holmes was a character she'd discovered the summer before, and Dickens had been a favorite of her girlhood. "I always was entranced by the characters' names, and I would cry and cry when tragedy befell them. I read *Great Expectations* at twelve and it made a tremendous impression on me."

Geoff tried to remember the last time *he'd* been entranced—until now—and forgot to speak until she remarked upon his silence. "I was just thinking that you are unlike any woman I've known in the past."

"Is that good?"

"Quite." He smiled at her in a way that made her cheeks color. "And you like my books even though there's nothing by Jane Austen, or the Brontë sisters. . . ."

"I think I'll have more sherry myself," Shelby said, and watched him reach for the bottle and pressed-glass cups. When they each held fresh portions, she offered a toast. "Here's to common interests and uncommon friendships." They were both lighthearted as their glasses clinked. Shelby savored her first deep sip, then reflected, "I will admit that I never would have imagined I could like someone like you. I know we agreed to leave your past in England, but I am curious. You're *something*, aren't you!" She wagged a finger at him in a faintly accusatory manner. "A duke?"

"No, not a duke . . . but, yes, *something*. I'd really prefer that we not—"

"All right, you don't have to say . . . but tell me this: What would you be doing if you were in London right now?"

Caught off guard, Geoff stared out the window for the moment. Rain continued to batter the windows, slanting across the ranch house in blurry sheets of water. Old-fashioned oil lamps provided the light for Geoff's room, reminders of the days before gas lighting, and the air was decidedly chilly. The rag rug on which they sat was scant protection from the hard, roughly sawn boards of the floor. And yet, Geoff felt more content in this rustic environment than he had in his own town house on the Thames, with its priceless rugs from the Orient, crystal gas-lit chandeliers, modern marble bathrooms, plush feather beds, servants to attend to every need, and motorcars in a newly constructed garage.

Shelby touched his arm. "Are you going to answer?"

"If I were in London tonight . . ." he replied slowly, "I'd be at the theater in the West End, or the symphony or opera. Or I might be dining in the very exclusive home of leaders of society, followed by a grand ball. . . ."

Her eyes were wide, sparkling like sapphires. "Truly? But if that's so, why did you come here? We don't even have a phonograph, let alone the sort of entertainment you're used to."

"I'd really rather not discuss this—"

"Are you in *disgrace*?" Bracing her hand on the trunk, Shelby leaned forward and whispered in his ear. "Were you forced to flee to America to lie low until a shocking scandal dies down?"

A lazy smile tugged at the corner of his mouth. "I'm sorry to disappoint you, but—no, I came to Wyoming by choice. I don't expect you to understand, but I found those pastimes in London to be excrutiatingly boring."

She studied him as he spoke, taking in his profile, etched in the glow of the lamplight, and the keen intelligence in his brown eyes. He was every inch a person of breeding, of quality: it was apparent without hearing his cultured accent and speech. Yet, Geoffrey Weston was acquiring a harder edge. Golden stubble glinted on his jaw, and his hair was tousled, curling over the collar of his green checked shirt. But though he might be toughening into a cowboy, he clung to certain civilized habits, like the washing up he'd done before supper tonight.

Shelby found herself powerfully drawn to this man

who was determined to follow his own star and saw no reason why he couldn't straddle two worlds, thus carving out his own niche.

"Why shouldn't I believe you?" she said at last. "I may like culture, and I miss the books and art and music and drama sometimes out here—but I *don't* like pretension, and that's what your life in London sounds like. I'd be bored stiff with all that posturing, too!"

Geoff could scarcely believe his ears. He almost reached for her then, but Shelby was skittish in her artlessness. She drank down her little cup of sherry and began rifling through the trunk again. Discoveries were exclaimed upon and sorted through. They traded opinions about literature until the shadows multiplied around them in the little room and Shelby shivered, reaching for the bottle of sherry and helping herself.

"I know that we should check on Mr. Manypenny again, and you're probably bored with my chatter—"

"On the contrary," Geoff interjected, tipping up her chin. The sight of a slow blush creeping into her cheeks sent a shock of desire through him.

"Before we pack up," she said shyly, "I have an idea—for sort of a game—I used to pass evenings with a college friend this way."

"A *game*?"

"Will you choose a favorite poem and read a bit of it to me? It's very revealing."

Geoff didn't hesitate. He plucked a slim volume from those Shelby had heaped on the rug and leafed through it. "It's not a definitive choice, merely one that reflects my mood."

"Better yet," she decided, scrambling over to sit beside him so that their arms touched. Happiness welled up from the depths of her soul. Could it really be that she had spent these last hours with a man who enjoyed the same mismatched pleasures as she? Of course, it was all too good to be true, but for now Shelby meant to enjoy the moment.

"What poet?" Her voice throbbed with anticipation.

"Tennyson."

"Spectacular! Let me guess . . . 'Locksley Hall'? 'The Lotus Eaters'?"

"Keep quiet, scamp." His long fingers found the page, then and he read slowly, clearly, portions of the long poem called "Ulysses."

> "How dull it is to pause, to make an end,
> To rust unburnish'd, not to shine in use!
> As tho' to breathe were life. Life piled on life,
> Were all too little, and of one to me
> Little remains: but every hour is saved . . .
> And this gray spirit yearning in desire
> To follow knowledge like a sinking star,
> Beyond the utmost bound of human thought."

Shelby closed her eyes and mouthed the words when Geoff reached the passages that she most adored: "Come, my friends, 'tis not too late to seek a newer world . . . To strive, to seek, to find, and not to yield."

Silence, rich and full, reigned until Shelby opened her eyes and found him gazing at her in a way that made her feel hot then cold. Her breasts tingled and so did her heart. "That was beautifully done."

"The sherry's made you effusive," he mocked gently.

"Yes."

"Go on. It's your turn."

Beaming, Shelby opened the tiny volume that lay waiting on her lap. "I choose Fitzgerald's 'The Rubáiyát of Omar Khayyám,' " she announced.

"Smashing. I must confess, I'm enjoying this game. It's an excellent change of pace."

"I'll only read a little." She began then, her voice warm with regard for the words:

"Then to the Lip of this poor earthen Urn
I lean'd, the secret Well of Life to learn:
And Lip to Lip it murmur'd—'While you live,
Drink!—for once dead, you never shall return.'

"I think the Vessel, that with fugitive
Articulation answer'd, once did live,
And drink; and that impassive Lip I kiss'd
How many Kisses might it take—and give!"

When her voice trailed off, Geoff mused, "Do you think it's about drinking? There's a lot of talk of wine in the Rubáiyát."

Shelby leaned close, until she could smell his hair and skin, a mixture of fine-milled soap and, faintly, the scent of dust and horses. It was a heady, arousing blend. "I thought that, too, when I was very young and naive. Now I believe that he's speaking of life. 'Drink' means *live*."

"And 'kiss'?" Geoff was appalled at himself. Was it something in the air here?

"I think he means . . . this." Shelby slipped her arms around his neck and crawled onto his lap. "I've never done anything so bold before," she confessed, even as his arms took her prisoner. "Please don't misunderstand."

"Certainly not," he assured her in muffled tones, then his mouth was slanting across her lips, so hungry to taste her sweetness, aching to be satisfied. It seemed that he'd wanted Shelby since that first moment in

Purcell's Saloon. Somehow, despite her ludicrous disguise, he'd been captivated.

And now, Shelby thought, she had surrendered utterly to the man who ought to be her nemesis. Clearly she had no pride anymore, only this powerful urge to get closer and closer to the person who'd tricked her out of the Sunshine Ranch.

Kissing was one thing; being relentlessly curious, she'd kissed her share of boys in Deadwood, but none of them had been in a league with Geoff. His mouth was hot, firm, deft, demanding. His body was lithe and masculine, his hair curled when she ran her fingers through it, and he was caressing her with those fingers that looked like they'd been sculpted by Michelangelo.

Shelby was so intoxicated with sensation that she was almost overcome. A voice from her gut commanded, *You will* not *faint like some wilted pansy! Kiss him back!* The feeling of his hands on her back, through her shirtwaist and chemise, was exciting not only for the caresses, but even more for the promise of other pleasures that Shelby had only imagined.

Geoff, meanwhile, was mystified by the power of the passion that held him in its grip. For years he'd simply gone through the motions, and sensations that had once been acute seemed to deaden over time. Now, kissing Shelby's extravagant mouth, breathing in her fragrance and holding her in his arms, he realized that he'd forgotten what true passion was. And this was hotter still.

What was happening to him? Dimly, Geoff realized that he was enchanted by much more than Shelby's physical beauty. It was as if a light shone from within her, kindling an answering spark in him. . . . For God's sake, don't go all mawkish! he chided himself. He had dismissed true love years ago and had built up too many layers of cynicism to go starry-eyed just yet. Still, kissing Shelby was enough to make him wonder if the poets hadn't written with one foot in reality after all. . . .

He was burning to open her shirt and find her breasts, to unfasten her skirt, to carry her to his bed, but that wasn't possible. Passion was one thing, but Shelby was gently bred, inexperienced, and Geoff knew that the sherry had helped push her into his lap.

Eventually he managed to draw back and find his voice. "Perhaps . . . we ought to rest for a moment."

"Why?" Shelby was flushed, damp with perspiration, and her hair grew curlier by the minute. "Why do we have to talk?"

Realizing that she'd lost her head, he forced himself to behave like a gentleman. "Look—we can't just go on and on like this without . . . going forward, you understand, and of course, that's simply out of the question—"

"I'm of age," she gasped. "Over twenty-one—"

"Most impressive." He kissed her brow. "We don't want to be too hasty, though. You'd certainly regret it later—never mind your uncle, who'd doubtless shoot me upon his return." With a grim smile, Geoff lifted her away from him, then helped her to her feet. "Perhaps I've already taken advantage of you."

She watched him run a hand through his golden hair and longed to touch it again herself, to lay her cheek against the roughness of his, to taste his mouth and feel the pressure of his hard chest on her soft breasts. Deprived, Shelby pouted. "You're being very stuffy, I think."

His face darkened. "My dear girl, if you believe that I am going to allow you to control the situation between us the way you are clearly accustomed to controlling the other aspects of your life, you are quite mistaken. I have a mind—and a will—of my own, and I'm confident that they are a match for yours." The distant sound of Manypenny coughing made Geoff cock his head. "I'll see to him while you choose the books you'd like to borrow. I trust that you'll neatly replace the others in the trunk and close the lid when you're finished."

Watching him leave the room, Shelby looked down at the priceless books that were strewn, helter-skelter, across the rag rug and the splintery, planked floor. Her eyes stung. Had she been scorned? It was hard to know for certain, but her heart was in conflict: on one hand she felt frustrated and confused, and even outraged by his high-handed dismissal, but on the other hand, she was just plain euphoric. Every nerve in her body sang with awakened passion and the heady joy of budding love.

Marsh, Cal, and Lucius turned up about midnight, after the rain died away. Seeing the light burning in the kitchen of the ranch house, Cal knocked at the back door, soaking wet, clutching his sodden Stetson in both hands.

Shelby wore a long dressing gown over a muslin nightdress with a ruffled collar, and her hair hung down her back in one thick braid. Opening the door, she beamed at the dripping cowhand. "Don't be scandalized by my appearance, Cal, but I had to wait up for you and I wanted to be comfortable. Where are the others? You all must put on some dry clothes, then come in for stew and tell me everything!"

"They've gone to the bunkhouse, ma'am." He nodded to Geoff, who had appeared behind Shelby. The Englishman also wore pajamas and a dressing gown. "We found a cave up in the mountains, one we'd seen before, and waited the storm out there. There was too much lightning to do anything else. I'm no fool!"

"Of course not! And we felt quite sure that was where you were. Now then, go and fetch the other boys and I'll dish up the stew. I've kept it warm all evening."

Cal's bloodshot eyes became even more pained. "Much obliged, ma'm, but everybody's awful tired, an'—"

"Shelby," Geoff spoke up, to her surprise, "why don't you dish up the stew and Cal can take it over to the bunkhouse to eat while they get to bed."

Licking his lips in anticipation, the cowboy agreed, "That'd be a real godsend! That is—if you wouldn't mind, ma'am. . . ."

"Of course not." She bade him wait, then gave Geoff a narrow glance en route to the stove. After assembling a basket of dishes and forks, Shelby brought it along with the Dutch oven that had a swinging handle on it for easy transport.

"It sure does smell good," Cal said as he accepted the food. "Good night, Miz Shelby, Geoff . . ."

When she was alone again with Geoff, Shelby marched past him to clean up the drips of gravy on the stove. "I still can't believe that he calls you *Geoff*! What would your subjects say?"

He laughed. "I don't have subjects and you know it. I think you're just annoyed because you imagine that I'm taking over here. You're used to doing things your own way, and you resent interference from me, no matter how inconsequential."

Scrubbing harder at the nickel-plated stove, Shelby snapped, "Well, can you blame me? After all, it is my house!" And then the truth returned with a sting, reminding her of how little she *did* control these days. Geoff had even taken command of the expression of her romantic yearnings, and it felt as if he'd treated her like a willful child. "I'm very tired. Will you let me have my way in *this* and leave me now?"

He swept his arm before his chest and bowed. "Your obedient servant," he replied, unable to keep a slight taunting undercurrent from his voice.

Geoff stopped to see that Manypenny was sleeping peacefully, then went into his own room and closed the door. She's far too volatile, he thought. Mercurial. He pulled off his dressing gown. *Pigheaded! I must have been possessed earlier tonight, but now I've come to my senses!*

"Thank God," Geoff muttered aloud, for emphasis. He got into bed, put out the light, and lay wide-awake for the next hour, staring at the ceiling.

In the morning, Shelby was stirring Irish oatmeal into a pot of boiling water when she noticed lacy flakes of snow gliding past the window. Eyes widening, she put a lid on the oatmeal and removed it from the flame, then went to the front door for a better look.

When Geoff came out of his room, his first glimpse was of Shelby, fresh and lovely, standing in a doorway aswirl with snowflakes. She wore her oldest boots and a divided skirt made of worn leather, which signaled her intention to ride with the men that day. From the waist up, however, she was classically feminine, in her crisp white shirtwaist with its high embroidered collar, and her newly washed upswept hair, fastened with pearl-studded pins. Hearing his footstep, Shelby turned, her expressive face alight with pleasure.

"Look, Geoff! It's snowing—in May! Can you believe it?"

When he drew near, she reached out and took his arm, all affection. Geoff wondered if she'd really forgotten their episodes—both passion and discord—of the night before . . . or had the snow simply wiped the slate clean again?

"Quite lovely," he agreed, looking at Shelby.

"I wish there were enough to build snowmen and go sledding." She leaned her cheek against his shoulder for a moment, then the back door flew open and Cal, Lucius, and Marsh stamped into the kitchen. Shelby caught Geoff's sleeve before he moved to join them. "Did Mr. Manypenny have a good rest? I thought I'd let you have the first visit, to protect his pride and modesty."

"Tolerable," he replied, leading the way back to the stove, where strong coffee simmered in an enamel pot. "He seems to sleep most of the time, so he's spared the conscious knowledge of how sick he is."

Over a gigantic breakfast of oatmeal with fresh cream, raisin muffins, eggs, and ham, the group discussed the need to make up for lost time and get the fences finished. When Ben and Titus returned in a few days, it would be time for the first roundup, and Ben certainly expected the fences to be in place. Until every animal they owned was branded, or fences were finished, their claims of ownership were fairly empty.

No one expected the snow to continue. Even Lucius, who'd lived in Wyoming all his life and had seen some serious spring blizzards, scoffed at the idea that this would amount to much.

It seemed a lark at first, bundling up and going off to work outdoors in the snow. Shelby put on longjohns and two pair of socks, then donned the leather skirt and boots she'd worn earlier. Adding a thick sweater over her blouse, she put on an oilskin duster she found in Titus's things, and since he was a small man, it fit her.

To her surprise, when Shelby came into the house's big room, she discovered that Geoff had done more shopping in Cody than she'd realized. He owned longjohns himself now, and wore red ones that were visible under his plaid flannel shirt. Chaps covered his dungarees, and last but not least, he unfolded a new duster and displayed it for Shelby's inspection.

"Magnificient!" she assured him. "Much nicer than this one of Titus's!"

Geoff laughed and put on the duster while she watched. It seemed that the long garment had been designed with him in mind, for the heavy white ducking complemented his blond hair and tanned skin, and its loose, double-breasted cut, split up the back to facilitate horseback riding, was rakishly flattering. He added his white Stetson and drew on cowhide gloves, while Shelby followed suit.

"Did Mr. Manypenny eat his oatmeal?"

"A bit." Geoff held the front door for her and they went out into the storm.

"I must say, this would be a lot more fun if I felt more . . . myself." She glanced up at him, adding, "I think I may have drunk a bit more sherry last night than was . . . prudent."

So she means to dismiss it all, Geoff thought, and gave Shelby his oldest world-weary look. It held an element of disenchantment, but one had to know to search for that. "Say no more. I drank so much sherry myself that I don't even remember seeing you."

Her burden lightened, she scampered ahead of him into the thickening curtain of snowflakes. Arriving at the corral, Shelby found that Gadabout had already been saddled and was prancing to and fro in anticipation of the day's adventure.

For several hours the adventure held, and all five of them had fun. They'd eaten so much at breakfast, and they were so busy all day, that no one wanted to return to the house for lunch. Instead the men toiled over fences at the far reaches of the property while Shelby did what she could to help, like unrolling coils of barbed wire or holding a post still while a man pounded it into the mushy ground.

The previous day's rain made working conditions less than ideal, for though it was cold enough to snow, it wasn't so cold that the mud had hardened. Sometimes they got tired of slogging around in sloppy boots, but then Shelby would hit someone with a playfully tossed snowball, or they'd realize how close they were to finishing the fence once and for all, and decide to work on. "Just a few dozen more yards!" became an oft-heard yell.

Everybody pretended not to notice that the snow had begun to stick to the ground and was falling harder by the hour. When Lucius snapped at Cal at about three o'clock, Shelby diplomatically suggested that everyone was hungry and tired. She would go back to the house and get some food.

She was in the kitchen—packing rolls and ham into saddlebags, and heating lots of coffee—when Cal burst into the back door, accompanied by frigid gusts of snow, and more snow.

"It's a whole lot worse, Miz Shelby!" he exclaimed. Red-faced and gasping for breath, Cal added, "Geoff says I should tell you to stay put right here, where you'll be safe 'n' dry. We're doin' our best to round up the cattle and bring 'em back—"

"What about the fence? Did you finish?"

"Yes'm." Snow dripped off his hat, reminding Shelby of the storm he and the others had endured the night before. Exhaustion creased his gaunt face. "I b'lieve so. The only part that wasn't done was way out to the south, beyond the grazin' land your cattle favor. We'll do our best to round 'em all up and get 'em in anyways, so they don't freeze t'death."

She made him drink down a cup of hot coffee with cream and let him go back to join the others, though she hated to stay behind. In the meantime, Shelby warmed some stew, cut the meat and vegetables into tiny pieces, and took the dish, plus a cup of tea, into Mr. Manypenny. He was snoring mightily, his domed brow pink with fever, but Shelby managed to rouse the manservant and encourage him to eat. Then she saw to the chickens and cows they kept to provide eggs, milk, butter, and cheese for the household. After feeding and watering the animals, she brought in the snowy bales of hay that stood in the yard, and latched the barn doors against the blizzard.

Manypenny was dozing, still holding the fork in his long, pale hand, when Shelby returned. He'd eaten most of the stew, and drunk the tea laced with the Twenty-Minute Cold Cure. "Mr. Manypenny," she whispered, "will you be all right if I leave you for a bit? I think I should check on the men."

His hooded lids flickered and a smile touched his mouth. "Call me Percy, my dear. And, yes, indeed, do look for his lordship. He has no business mucking about in a snowstorm." Slowly, he looked toward the window, adding, "It is snowing, is it not? I was momentarily fearful, given the season, that I might be in Heaven."

Shelby wanted to hug him, but instead patted his hand. "No, you are very much alive . . . Percy." She had to smile, imagining Geoff's expression if he could hear her. "I'll be back soon, with . . . his lordship."

"Fine, fine. Enjoy yourself." In the next instant, he was once more asleep.

Even though she was well aware that Geoff would be furious with her, Shelby couldn't stand to wait any longer. Waiting behind was the kind of female role that drove her absolutely insane, even as a child when there had been a fire or some other emergency in Deadwood and her father or Byron would stop her from coming along with those galling words: "You're a girl, Shel. You have to stay home where it's safe."

Buttoning the oilskin duster, wrapping knitted scarves around her neck and mouth, and tying another over her hat to hold it in place, Shelby tugged on her gloves and left the house.

The wind had worsened, blowing so hard that it was difficult to see at all. Gadabout whinnied when her mistress came into view. The pinto pony still wore her saddle, since Shelby hadn't planned to stay inside very long, and now it was covered with snow, and the drifts reached her knees. Shelby talked to her gently as she brought her out of the corral and mounted her, which turned out to be a challenge, given all the clothing she wore.

Heading back in the direction from which she'd ridden not long ago, she imagined that she'd reach the men shortly. They might be almost back to the corral themselves by now! It was that sense of certainty that kept Shelby in a feisty mood, in spite of the swelling winds and thickening snowflakes. At first she admired the beauty of the lacy bits of snow, then was amazed that the flakes could grow so large and sting so when they struck her face. Snow filled her vision, swirling madly in the distance.

Gadabout paused and Shelby patted her and called over the howl of the storm, "It's all right, girl! Don't be afraid!"

A tingly, hard knot of panic began in the pit of her stomach. How much time had passed? Her sense of cold was crossing the line from distress to searing pain.

What if her nose froze and had to be amputated? Shelby was on the verge of tears, and full of regret for the ordeal Gadabout was forced to endure, and then, miraculously, she glimpsed a gray shape through the dense curtain of snow. She'd found someone!

"Hello!" she screamed. "It's me! Shelby!" But when she urged Gadabout on, struggling against the force of the wind, the form melted into a mere shadow. Terror seeped into Shelby's heart. Her father had told stories of being caught in a blizzard so horrendous that he'd seen mirages, just like those that played tricks on people lost in the desert. . . .

Her heart pumped harder, driven by fear and her own resistance to weaker emotions. Should they turn back? But which way were the ranch buildings? All her markers were gone and the world had become a roiling sea of frigid white.

And then, over the wind, Shelby heard a voice that seemed to shout her name. Gadabout turned on her own and sought aid, and together they made their way toward another shadow, which mercifully grew clearer as they neared.

The human figure on horseback turned out to be Lucius.

"You was lost, huh?" he barked, an oversized, frost-crusted neckerchief wrapped around the lower half of his face. "Shouldn't be out here, Miz Shelby. Follow us home." With that, he turned his attention toward getting the cattle back to the ranch buildings.

The suffering cattle were straggling along the fence line, two and three abreast as they followed Lucius and then Marsh. Instinctively, Shelby caught herself counting them. There had been 183 head of cattle accounted for this week, and before the roundup, they hoped to discover the other seventeen mavericks in the hills. It would make life so much easier when all the animals were branded, but at least now the fence was completed, and even if they missed a steer or two today, the animals would be confined to the Sunshine Ranch until the storm died down.

The blizzard limited Shelby's sight to only a few yards. Now she recognized Cal's red roan, its rider also disguised by layers of clothing. He was helping to herd the cattle onward, but paused to shout at Shelby, "What're you doin' out here, ma'am? Beg yer pardon, but Geoff'll tan yer hide if he finds you." He pointed back into the swirling currents of snow. "Better git outta here before—"

Shelby thought that the wind had carried his last words away. Edging Gadabout closer to the cowboy, she yelled, "*What?* I can't hear you!"

But Cal was mute now, waving her off, wheeling his roan around to continue on his way. And when Shelby decided to follow, she brought Gadabout nearer the fence line, which was the only landmark in the sea of white.

An instant later an ear-splitting crash rent the air just inches from Shelby. Her heart leaped and so did Gadabout, rearing up on her hind legs just in time to miss being crushed by an enormous dead cottonwood tree that had splintered and toppled under the weight of the snow, ice, and driving winds.

Not only had Shelby escaped by inches, but so had a pair of passing steers. Numb with shock and cold, her heart pumping as she gasped for breath and blinked back tears, Shelby saw that the fallen tree had landed squarely on their new fence, crushing one of the posts and flattening several yards of ice-tipped barbed wire.

The approaching Herefords seemed to eye the opening in the fence with curiosity. It seemed only logical to the half-delirious Shelby to dismount and get a closer look at the damage. The snow was drifting toward her thighs and she clutched the pony's reins with one gloved hand and tried to move cottonwood branches with the other. What a nightmare! she thought. How could so many catastrophes be occurring—and in May, for God's sake! They should be frolicking in flower-strewn meadows! She tried not to think about the burning, pins-and-needles sensation in her extremities, or how long the ride back to the house would take. . . .

Mentally, she added up the amount of barbed wire they'd need. The wind shifted slightly, roaring into her face, and for a moment Shelby feared she'd lose her hat. She was holding it in place with one hand when something caught her by the collar of her oilskin duster, lifting her clear out of the snow, and her general mood of fear and despair wildly escalated once more into terror.

"Oh, God! What . . . ? *Help!*" she shrieked, hysterical. Was it a bear? The storm picking her up the way it had the tree?

"Help?" repeated a familiar voice, still deadly calm even when shouting above the wind. "I can't imagine why I should lift a finger to help you, when you've clearly created this predicament for yourself—against my orders."

Dimly, Shelby was startled by his strength, for he had bent over and swept her up onto Charlie's back as if she were a sack of feathers. Now, pinned there by arms that felt like steel, she was forced to look into his eyes—and it wasn't a comforting sight. "Really, Geoff—there's no reason for this display of temper. I'm an adult, after all, and not to be locked away simply because of my sex—"

"Shut up," he ground out harshly. He pulled down the snowy woolen scarf that had covered his mouth and glared at Shelby with hard eyes, his face windburned, his brows coated with ice. "There are no words to express my *rage*! First you lose your ranch, and now you're about to lose your life! You're spoiled, willful—"

Shelby's eyes flashed even as her voice wavered on a sob. "Look, this is still my ranch, too, and I have a right to protect my land and my livestock! You have no right—to tell me what to do and call me names!"

"I will not argue with you now, when we're both perilously close to freezing to death. Your face is turning blue!" His fury was driven by emotions that frightened both of them. Using Gadabout's reins, he drew the pinto pony alongside Charlie and fairly tossed Shelby onto her saddle. "Get home!"

"But the tree," she argued stubbornly, "the fence—"

Geoff wasn't listening. He slapped Gadabout on the rump and sent the pony trudging northward toward the line of cattle heading for shelter.

Chapter Seven

THE MAY MORNING WAS SPARKLING. A ROBIN'S-egg-blue sky stretched overhead, the meadows and mountains were quilted in white, and the sun blazed down, scattering diamonds on the snow even as it dissolved it.

It could have been a magical day but for the tension between Geoff and Shelby. Declaring that they all should enjoy a holiday until the snow had melted, the Englishman spent the day taking care of the napping Manypenny and reading *Jude the Obscure* by Thomas Hardy in front of the fireplace. Every time his eyes happened to meet Shelby's, sparks seemed to fly, brighter with each hour that they nursed their separate tempers.

"Why are you in such high dudgeon?" Manypenny inquired of his master while eating a buttered muffin and a coddled egg for lunch.

Feeling a bit silly, Geoff told him a little of it, dwelling on Shelby's refusal to do as she was told. "She could have lost her way and frozen to death out there!" Then, to drive home his point that she was rather mad, Geoff added, "And, although I've never been one to tell tales out of school, I think you ought to know that she has taken to referring to you as—" He paused, as if so appalled that he could scarcely repeat the word himself. "—as *Percy*! I don't mind telling you, my dear Manypenny, that it shocked me deeply when I first heard her say it! I begin to think, in light of her generally rash behavior—"

"I want Miss Matthews to use my given name," the manservant interrupted. "I enjoy her tremendously, and am not inclined to stand on ceremony when we are together. And, although I hesitate to interfere, this fever has loosened my tongue enough to let me say that I believe you are more angry with Miss Matthews for defying you than for endangering her own life. Has anyone defied you before, my lord?"

Geoff's face darkened in consternation. "I say, old man . . . you never let *me* call you Percy!"

"That's true," Manypenny replied mildly, "and I do not intend to alter that tradition at this time, any more than you should suggest that I address you as—" He cleared his throat and muttered in tones of distaste, "—*Geoff*. Now then, my lord, I find that I am fatigued. Will you leave me to my nap?"

Carrying his servant's dishes, he did as he was bade, stunned by their conversation. Perhaps life in London hadn't been so bad after all. At least there Geoff knew who he was and what to expect from the people in his life. If an old boot like Manypenny could fly off this way, what other wretched surprises waited for him in Wyoming?

By the time he'd made a proper pot of tea—a skill Americans seemed incapable of mastering—Geoff had decided that Shelby was directly responsible for the world going askew. She was much too impulsive, stubborn, and self-confident for a female. It threw the entire scheme of things into disarray.

And where was she?

A while ago, after they'd all eaten lunch together, Shelby had mumbled that she was going to milk the cows. She should have been back long ago. So, after drinking a cup of tea, Geoff put a towel over the pot, donned his boots, and went outside.

It was warm enough for him to go coatless, and although the sun felt splendid, the mud and slush were another matter. Until most of the snow had been absorbed into the ground, there didn't seem to be much point in mucking about outdoors. Still, a couple of the boys had gone off to repair the fence, while Marsh was putting out hay for the cattle.

"Have you seen Miss Matthews?" Geoff asked as he approached the big corral.

"Yup." Marsh's hat was pulled low over his eyes and his cheek bulged with tobacco as he pointed to the south.

"I understand that we are missing eight head of cattle?"

"Yup." Marsh spat tobacco juice, then turned loquacious, adding, "Through the fence, I reckon."

"Do you suppose that Miss Matthews has gone to look for them?"

Apparently worn-out by his speech, the cowboy merely nodded this time, then returned to his chores. Geoff went into the barn and had a chat with Charlie, whose demeanor told him that he had no desire to go out for a gallop in knee-deep mud and sloppy snow, having far too much regard for his buckskin coat. Since they were in agreement on that score, the Englishman returned to the house and decided to spend the rest of the afternoon acquainting himself with the ranch accounts. Shelby would probably shoot him outright if she knew, but then she was off sticking her nose where it didn't belong—and he did own half of the ranch, didn't he? He was tired of waiting for her to show him what was what.

To his chagrin, Geoff discovered that there were bills overdue in town: they owned the Cody Trading Company, the livery stable, the implement store, and the Maverick Market. Folding these neatly, he put them in his pocket and returned Shelby's desk to its original condition.

When she came in, windblown and mud-spattered, Geoff was caught off guard by the force of his response. On one hand, he felt angry with her for going off on her own without even telling him, while on the other hand, he reacted as a male to her vigorous, glowing beauty. She stripped off her gloves and pulled the ribbon from her hair unselfconsciously, and yet it seemed to Geoff that somewhere in her soul she knew how irresistible she was when she shook her curls and straightened her shoulders before confronting him.

"I want to talk to you about our missing cattle," Shelby announced, striding gracefully into the big room and pulling up a chair next to Geoff.

"I appreciate that." His tone was astringent.

"Well, you are a . . . partner." She folded her hands and narrowed her teal eyes for an instant, adding suddenly, "You're not in charge, though! I won't be bossed, sir, especially by someone who swaggers around here claiming to be a nobleman!"

"I beg your pardon!" His jaw hardened. "I have made a point of *not* talking about my past, and I have made every effort to be fair, and to work as hard as the other men."

Shelby waved a hand dismissively. "It's an attitude you have, then; it's probably inbred, like those receding chins so many Englishmen are cursed with." It pleased her to see sparks kindle in his eyes. "Anyway, my point is this: I came to Wyoming because I needed to be given my head. That's why Daddy let me manage this ranch. I would have wilted away if I'd stayed in Deadwood, where I was a rich man's daughter, and I wouldn't have been happy staying in New England after college, either. I like to be *free*." Shelby paused. Both of them were sitting forward in their chairs now, eyes locked in a battle of wills. "I won't take orders from you."

"Even when it's a matter of life and death?"

"I don't foresee those circumstances arising." She tossed her hair, sat back and tried to appear relaxed and competent. "Now then, about the cattle. I have reason to believe that Bart Croll, the owner of the next ranch south, has appropriated our steers. The broken fence adjoins his land, and from what I've heard, he's just the type to keep someone else's property."

Geoff blinked. "For God's sake, why do you always imagine that some tremendous drama is under way!"

"Don't scold me."

"All right, all right. I apologize." He held up his hands, but his attitude was marred by condescending undertones. "I'll tell you what—tomorrow morning I'll go over to Mr. Croll's ranch and have a little chat with him."

"At dawn? It's important that we don't let any more time slip by!"

"Now who's giving orders?" Geoff arched a sun-bleached brow. "If it will please you, Miss Matthews, I shall ride to the Croll ranch as soon as I'm awake and dressed. All right?"

"Great. I'll be ready."

"No. You're *not* going." He stood up with a note of cold finality. "This is a matter that must be handled with finesse—a quality that *you* were born without."

* * *

Geoff soon discovered that the Bar B Ranch, owned by Bart Croll, made the Sunshine Ranch seem like a grand estate. Riding over there the next morning when the sky was still streaked with carnation and peach, his eyes took in the underfed cattle chewing at sparse patches of grass, the haphazardly built fences, and finally, a sod house that was decaying at one end.

The barn, such as it was, was made of sod, too, and the horses in the corral needed a good meal. A post with a rack of elk antlers on top appeared to serve as the hitching post, so Geoff looped Charlie's reins around one of the horns and went up to the sod house's door. There was one glass window, and through it Geoff saw the dim glow of a lantern.

What am I supposed to say? he wondered. Ask the man if he stole our cattle? But he was here, and he had to carry through with his mission. Shelby wouldn't have had any qualms about demanding the return of her animals, and she certainly wouldn't want to hear that he had been too polite to do the same.

So he knocked. A moment later a rangy old man with white stubble covering his hollow cheeks opened the door. He wore faded gray longjohns, overalls, mud-caked boots, and carried a rifle. "Who are you?" he asked.

Geoff extended his hand. "My name is Geoffrey Weston, sir. I believe that we're neighbors—I'm half owner of the Sunshine Ranch, to your north."

The old man grunted. "You a limey? Thought so. M'name's Bart Croll an' I been out here long before that fancy fella Cody decided to make a town fer hisself." He rubbed his whiskers, then demanded, "Whatta you want?"

"Well, I'd like to talk for a bit, get acquainted—"

Bart grunted again, opened the door, and gestured

with the rifle barrel for Geoff to enter. "Come on in while I finish my coffee and get m'coat, then you kin ride with me while I check the livestock."

Geoff did as he was bade, closing the door, and then immediately wished he'd left it open. There was a damp, smoky, rancid, musty, sour smell inside the tiny dwelling that made him want to cover his mouth and nose. The walls were crumbling, the floor was a mixture of dust and mud, and the furnishings were pitiful. Next to the hay-burning stove stood a pale, thin woman with huge blue eyes and flaxen hair braided neatly into a crown atop her head. She was stirring something in a pot. When Geoff nodded to her, she dropped her eyes, but managed a smile.

"How do you do, madame," he said, hoping she hadn't seen his disgusted expression, and introduced himself once more.

"This here's m'wife, Vivian," Bart put in as he pulled on his dirty coat. "I guess you could call her a mail-order bride."

"Indeed!" Geoff affected cheerful interest at this news, when in truth he was horrified. Why would a passably pretty young girl marry a cranky old geezer who offered her a home that was no better than a squalid hut? "And where do you come from, Mrs. Croll?"

"St. Louis," she replied softly. "My parents were killed at Christmas in a fire, and I had no one . . . until Mr. Croll offered me marriage."

Against his will, Geoff's eyes wandered to the narrow bed against one dank, sod wall. Neatly covered with a hand-stitched quilt, the bed was barely wide enough for one person, yet there were two meager pillows. It was almost enough to make him sick.

"Let's go," Bart said, draining his tin cup of coffee

and heading out the door without a word of good-bye to his young wife.

"It was a pleasure meeting you, Mrs. Croll," said Geoff.

"Likewise, Mr. Weston. I do hope you'll come back, and bring your wife if you have one!" There was a note of urgency in her voice, and her eyes were bright with pain.

Outside, when the two men were on horseback, Croll came alongside Geoff's buckskin and barked, "Stay away from m'wife, you smooth-talkin', sissified limey! She don't need yer sympathy!"

"I can assure you that my intention was only to be polite," Geoff replied coolly.

They followed the fence lines together for a bit, while Geoff chatted as amiably as he could about his new life. They traded horror stories about the recent blizzard, then Geoff asked Croll's advice regarding the Sunshine Ranch's first roundup, which was approaching next week. How many extra men might he need? He tried to think of other meaningless questions that would make the old man think that he was too much a novice to suspect him of keeping their cattle, which might have wandered onto his property during the storm.

Bart Croll waxed nostalgic about the old days on the range, before barbed wire, when cowboys knew no boundaries and slept under the stars with only a blanket.

Finally, sensing that he was sufficiently softened up, Geoff said, "Well . . . I won't take any more of your time, sir, but—I don't suppose that, by chance, you might have seen a half-dozen or so Hereford cattle on your land—unbranded?"

Rolling a cigarette, Bart narrowed his eyes at Geoff. "What're you gettin' at, mister?"

"Nothing at all! I only thought to let you know that,

since the storm, we are missing eight head of cattle. The ranch is new, they haven't been branded yet, and it occurred to me that they might have wandered over here—and that you might not have noticed they weren't carrying your brand." He grinned. "Perhaps you'll let us know if you happen to come across them."

"Why wouldn't I?" Bart growled.

"Why not indeed?" Geoff was just about to bid the old grouch good day and ride away when he noticed Croll squinting toward some cattle herded together farther north along the fence. Shading his eyes, Geoff saw that there was a *horse* in the midst of the cattle—a pinto pony that he recognized all too readily. Its petite rider had dismounted and appeared to be hiding among the animals, but clearly there was one pair of legs that were human.

"What the hell's goin' on over there?" Bart Croll snarled, dragging on his cigarette. "I don't take kindly to rustlers, 'specially ones who come on my land in broad daylight!" He began loading his rifle.

Geoff didn't see that he had a choice. Sighing, he confessed, "Mr. Croll, I know that this will seem suspicious to you, but I think that horse belongs to the little Matthews girl, Shelby. She's a scamp, always into mischief, and I would venture a guess that she was bored this morning and decided to follow me over here. I'm certain she's only having a bit of fun. No harm intended!"

As the two men approached the cattle, Shelby climbed back onto Gadabout's back and waved, smiling brightly. "Good morning! Are you wondering what I'm doing in the middle of a lot of cows?" She guided the pinto out into the open and gave Geoff a naughty smile. "Don't be angry with me, Mr. Weston! It was just a game, to see if you wouldn't notice me!"

"I don't take kindly to folks playin' games on my property!" Bart Croll put in. "If it'd been upta me, I'd've shot first and asked questions later! Remember that next time, missy!" He glared at Geoff. "Take her home. I gotta get to work; ain't got no more time for you crazies."

Watching them leave, his dark eyes burned like coals.

Too angry to speak to Shelby until their own house was in sight, Geoff finally slowed Charlie and allowed her smaller pony to catch up.

"Good grief!" she cried breathlessly, when they were nearly even. "I've been chasing you for miles!"

Having eased Charlie into a brisk canter, he glanced down at her with an expression of dark fury. "I could wring your neck! You are the most foolhardy, contrary—"

"For a titled gentleman, you sure are free and easy with the double-barreled insults!" Shelby protested. "Didn't you ever learn manners from all your governesses and private schools?"

"*My* manners are not the issue!" His jaw clenched and his eyes narrowed. "Your madcap, hell-raising behavior is. Don't you realize that you could have been killed back there? I didn't even know you were on that ranch, sneaking around, until Bart Croll saw you himself! He would have *shot* you, for God's sake, if I hadn't interfered!"

"Could, would, might!" Waving a hand dismissingly, Shelby declared, "I'd rather talk about what *is*!" She reached over and caught his coat sleeve. "Slow down and listen to me—this is important! Don't you see, I had to go over there this morning. I knew he'd never tell you the truth, and I was hoping that you two would stay in the house, or nearby, and talk, so that I would be free to check his cattle—"

"Well then, why didn't you tell me? I could have concocted an excuse to stall him from riding the fences!"

Shelby widened her eyes with exaggeration. "Gosh, why didn't I think of that? *Maybe* because I didn't think you'd let me! Maybe because I was afraid you'd chain me to our hitching post before you agreed to such a scheme!"

Fuming, Geoff looked away. For a person who was accustomed to feeling nothing, these forceful responses to Shelby were almost more than he could endure. Sometimes he wondered if steam were coming out of his ears. "If you'd just behave yourself in the first place, you'd save us all a lot of trouble. . . ."

"But then we wouldn't know that . . . Bart Croll *has* our cattle!" Shelby stood up in the stirrups, wearing her broadest, incandescent grin. "Oh, Geoff, I saw them with my own eyes—all eight! I'd just about given up hope, when I came to that last batch—and there they were!"

"And how can you be certain? Our animals hadn't been branded yet."

"Why, I recognized them!"

"Shel-by," he cried in exasperation.

"It's true! He doesn't have many Herefords, especially any as fine as ours. Didn't you see how thin his cattle were? But beyond that, I was able to definitely identify nearly every one of the eight, and the others were right by their sides."

The Sunshine Ranch buildings were in sight now, and Charlie eagerly picked up his pace. "Devil take it, how could you possibly make a positive identification of a steer?" Geoff challenged over one shoulder.

"They have faces, too, you know. Markings that set them apart! And our cattle know me." Stubbornly, she came alongside again, long enough to add, "They miss us and their home—and they made cow eyes at me!"

In spite of himself, Geoff burst out laughing.

After considering the situation overnight, Geoff decided to speak to the town marshal in Cody, a fellow by the name of Burns, about Bart Croll and their cattle.

He would have liked to ride into town alone, but by now he knew better than to attempt to exclude Shelby. If he did, she'd only pop up at the worst possible moment. So, over breakfast the next morning, Geoff casually mentioned that he would visit Marshal Burns that afternoon. Would she like to come along and do some shopping at the Cody Trading Company?

Shelby felt that it was a waste of time to bring the marshal into their affairs, but refrained from arguing. After all, Geoffrey was from England, where one assumed that the justice system worked properly. Law and order in the West was another matter. But she humored him, and that strategy earned Shelby a place beside him on the buckboard at midday.

They shared a festive mood as they set out, for the weather remained splendid, the snow was nearly gone, the sunshine had helped to dry up the mud, and birds were singing as if intoxicated. Spring had bounced back, its magic more potent than ever.

Even from a distance the little town of Cody seemed to be infused with all the vigor of its namesake, the celebrated Buffalo Bill. There appeared to be a lot of activity under way, as if fueled by the vitality of spring.

"As I understand it," Shelby explained, "Colonel Cody has had two primary projects in mind to get his town on its feet. First, he has been determined to build a road connecting Cody to Yellowstone National Park's eastern entrance, about fifty miles away. He sees the town as a jumping-off place for visitors to the park—"

"Quite farsighted of him," Geoff remarked as they came to the edge of Cody.

"Indeed, and I believe they expect to finish the Cody Road this summer! His second project is his grand hotel—over there. . . ." She pointed to the corner of Fourth and Sheridan streets, where a huge building was nearly constructed out of sandstone, and a spacious veranda extended nearly all the way around. The hotel already dwarfed every other structure in sight. "Colonel Cody means to name it for his daughter, Irma. I heard every room will be heated by steam and lit by gas—and Uncle Ben says it will cost nearly eighty thousand dollars when it's finished!"

Drawing gently on the reins, Geoff slowed the buckboard and stared at the magnificent two-story hotel. "I'm impressed by Cody's vision . . . but who will stay in all those rooms? There are only a few hundred people in this entire town. What need have they for such a huge hotel?"

Shelby laughed. "Colonel Cody doesn't think that way! I believe that, for him, the hotel is a symbol of his hopes for Cody. It's almost as if by building this he has willed prosperity for his town."

There was plenty of other news that May afternoon. Two telephone companies had been granted franchises by the town council, and now poles and wires were going up everywhere. The *Cody Enterprise* had just opened its offices across from Dr. Chamberlain's residence. When Geoff went in to buy a newspaper, he discovered that the telephone exchange was being set up in a little back room of the Amoretti and Parks Bank, and everyone was anxious to ring up "Central."

"I perceive that even the West isn't safe from progress," he remarked dryly as they leaned against the buckboard and scanned the newpaper together, both hungry for information. "Soon enough everyone will want a motorcar, and horses will be obsolete. . . ."

Shelby sensed that his thoughts were elsewhere and she was about to be put off. "Will you take me with you to your meeting with Marshal Burns?"

"If it were a simply matter of principle and fairness to you, I would, certainly, but I don't think your presence would aid our cause." When Geoff pushed back his gray Stetson, a lock of gold hair fell across his brow. "Frankly, I think that if we're together, he'll wonder what's afoot at Sunshine Ranch—and I don't think he'll speak as freely. I promise to tell you everything that's said, however—and I further promise to pay for anything you want to buy at the Trading Company!"

Her eyes flashed. "I hate it when men patronize women that way—believing that any conflict can be defused by sending a female *shopping*!"

Vastly amused, he turned his palms up in a gesture of mock despair. "I'll meet you at the Cody Trading Company no later than one hour from now—much sooner, I hope."

Conscious of the curious stares of passersby, Shelby could do no more than put her hands on her hips and glare at him. Geoff tipped his hat to her, then sauntered off down Sheridan Avenue toward the marshal's office. Against her better judgment, Shelby found herself staring at him from a purely objective, female point of view. It was hard not to, for Geoffrey Weston was an exceptionally fine-looking man, and there was another quality about him that she couldn't describe but that multiplied his attraction.

It had something to do with the way he was gradually

adapting to their western ways. Shelby found that endearing—the sight of him from behind, walking more like a ranch hand than a nobleman. And his attraction had something to do with the gleam in his soft brown eyes, and the curve of his cheekbones, and the way he was laughing more, and getting tanned and hard in the western sunshine.

His shoulders were straight and wide, heart-meltingly appealing in the flannel shirt he wore. His hips were lean, and the muscles in his thighs were long, shaped by a different sort of horseback riding than they did in the West, Shelby suspected. Sometimes, when she gazed at his legs, she imagined Geoff in proper riding attire, sailing over a hedge or a stream during a fox hunt.

But for now, he was here with her in Cody, Wyoming. Shelby scolded her heart to be still as Geoff disappeared into the new jail, where Marshal Burns had his office.

Did he really expect her to go *shopping* at a time like this?

Biting her lip, Shelby contemplated the Cody Trading Company, then shook her head and set off in the opposite direction. There was more than one way to skin a cat, wasn't there? Surely the marshal's office had windows, and surely they'd be open on a beautiful day like this!

Why should Geoff care if she just *listened*—as long as no one knew she was there?

Chapter Eight

"I REMEMBER YOU," SAID THE OLD MAN SITTING AT the rolltop desk inside Marshal Burns's office. His bald pate was sunburned, and his large stomach and bulbous nose betrayed his affection for strong spirits. "I was at Purcell's Saloon the day you come to town and won the Sunshine Ranch."

"I see." Geoff wasn't sure whether this fellow was Burns or not. He didn't wear a badge. "Well, everything has worked out quite agreeably between the Avery-Matthews family and myself. We've developed a good partnership." He extended his hand. "My name, incidentally, is Geoffrey Weston. It's a pleasure to meet you. . . ."

"I'm jest the deputy." He pretended not to notice Geoff's hand as he shuffled papers on the desk and aimed a stream of tobacco juice into a battered spittoon. "You kin call me Ted."

"Ah, rather like your President Roosevelt!" Geoff rejoined, hoping to coax a smile from the fellow.

"Uh-huh." He found a match on the cluttered desktop and began to pick his teeth. " 'Spose you're lookin' for Marshal Burns . . ."

"Yes."

"He's out collectin' fines, and buryin' a dog, I think. He gets an extra dollar for every dog he buries."

"I see . . ." This didn't seem to be a subject worth pursuing, so Geoff glanced at the oversized clock ticking on the wall. "Given the distance I have to travel to town, I'd rather not make two trips. Perhaps I could explain my problem to you, uh, Deputy Ted, and you could then tell Marshal Burns."

"Mebbe."

At times like these, his restrained British upbringing served him well. *Patience, patience,* Geoff's inner voice cautioned as he drew up a chair next to Ted's and said, "You see, during last week's blizzard, we lost eight cattle that had not yet been branded. Our ranch hasn't had its first roundup, and although we had finished the fences, a tree fell on one section, and it seems that these cattle must have slipped out during the storm."

"That was mighty careless of you folks." Deputy Ted wiped the end of the match onto his overalls, leaving a smear of soft food particles.

"Actually, we did everything possible to make certain that the cattle got back to the corral—short of losing our lives. But when a count was made the next day, we were eight short."

"You makin' an accusation, mister?"

"Shelby Matthews and I have reason to believe that our cattle are now on the Bar B Ranch, which adjoins our property to the south. I asked Bart Croll about it, and he assured me that he hadn't seen our animals, but Shelby identified them among his steers."

Deputy Ted fixed Geoff with a watery eye. "Oh, yeah? How'd she do that when they ain't been branded yet?"

"She . . . recognized them. Unique markings." He shrugged. "You know how women are. They remember the most amazing details."

A loud crashing sound interrupted their conversation.

Determining that it had come from the alleyway next to the jail, Ted heaved himself out of the chair. "Geez-us! Sounds like our bank robber from Sheridan's tryin' to escape!"

Pure instinct made the fine hairs on the back of Geoff's neck stand up. "Let me check for you, Ted. I think it sounded like a cat in someone's garbage." Before the fat old man could move, Geoff was out the front door. He caught up to Shelby with just a few long strides, grabbed the collar of her flannel-lined jacket and pinned her against the jail's brick wall. "I *knew* it! This time I really *am* going to whip you!" he hissed in menacing tones. "I suggest that you run for your life!"

"But you mustn't tell him anything else, Geoff!" she whispered excitedly, not frightened a bit by his threats. "Ted is Bart Croll's cousin! I've seen them together more times than I can count! I completely forgot that Marshal Burns had hired him."

Geoff's eyes changed as he took this in. "All right, I'll take care of it, then, and you scurry like the devil to the Cody Trading Company. I'll see you there momentarily."

She went tearing down the muddy alley, her coppery braid flying behind her, and Geoff had a funny sensation of warmth in his chest as he watched her. It went away, though, when he thought about Deputy Ted. Grimly, he went back inside and found the old geezer sneaking a swig of whiskey from a bottle in the desk drawer.

"Was it a cat?" he asked as he licked his lips.

"Hmm? Oh, yes, I believe so. It knocked a crate over."

"Oh." He yawned. "Well, nothin' left for you and me to talk about, Weston. I kin tell you that Bart Croll is as honest as the day is long. Prob'ly the finest, most upstanding citizen in the Bighorn Basin, an' you're mighty lucky to have him for a neighbor. Helluva man."

"I see." Geoff nodded slowly. "And the cattle . . . ?"

"Like you said yourself—we know how women are. And everybody knows Shelby Matthews is crazy as a bedbug." Ted tapped the side of his head with a stubby finger. "I wouldn't waste my time worryin' about this if I were you, Weston. Folks lose cattle from time to time out here. Plenty of bad luck to go around fer everyone."

"I appreciate your advice, Deputy Ted. . . ." Smiling, Geoff stood up to go, then gave the other man a perplexed glance. "What did you say your last name was, sir?"

"I dint." He winked at him, then spat out more tobacco juice. "Ted's plenty."

"I tried to tell you that visiting the town marshal wasn't a good idea," Shelby whispered as she and Geoff examined the harnesses on display in the Cody Trading Company. "The law's a very iffy thing in the West."

His only reply was a decidedly ironic glance, accompanied by an arched eyebrow.

"Talking to Ted Croll has probably made our problem worse. Now Bart'll know we're on to him."

"I begin to think that Ted's advice that we forget this entire matter was sound. It's not worth the trouble we're making for ourselves." Geoff moved toward the row of rocking chairs, adding softly, "In any case, I assured the good deputy that we would simply write the lost cattle off to bad luck, and I pretended to believe his assertion that Bart Croll is a man of sterling character."

"Bart joined a matrimonial club, I heard, and found himself a mail-order bride." Shelby shuddered at the thought. "Poor woman!"

"I met Vivian Croll." Seeing the store owner coming

toward them, he added, "I've been meaning to tell you about her. Remind me during the ride home."

Jacob Schwoob, just twenty-six, was one of Cody's earliest and most prominent citizens. He and his wife Louisa also claimed the distinction of producing the first baby born after Cody's incorporation in 1901. The Cody Trading Company occupied a big new building and was filled with an ever-growing array of merchandise, from groceries to hardware to furniture to clothing to ranch and farm equipment.

"Mr. Schwoob," Shelby greeted him brightly, "how are you? I was just telling Geoff here that every time I come in, you have a larger selection of goods! I hardly know where to look first!"

"Have you seen our new dishes? Louisa chose the patterns herself, and some came all the way from Paris." He turned to Geoff then, exclaiming, "I've missed seeing you, my friend! Did you survive our spring blizzard? I hope you all waited out the storm, tucked in before the fire."

"Well, we survived, Jakie—though it was difficult to persuade everyone to come indoors, where it was safe." Geoff cast a sidelong glance at Shelby and was pleased to see her looking perplexed as she tried to figure out his friendship with Jakie Schwoob. Clearly she'd forgotten all the trips he'd made to Cody on his own in those first days after coming to the ranch. "How's the town band coming? Have the uniforms arrived from Colonel Cody?"

"What band?" Shelby demanded.

"Oh, some of the boys started a brass band this past winter," Jakie explained, "and when Colonel Cody heard about it, he offered to donate the uniforms. They got here a while back, and they're quite handsome—embroidered, cowboy style, with matching hats!" He was smiling broadly. "My brother Loren has joined, and he's been urging me to do the same . . . but I don't play an instrument. I'll confess that those uniforms are mighty tempting, though! Do you suppose the crowds would heckle me if I just dressed up as a band member and marched in the parades?"

They all laughed, including a group of eavesdropping women from the next aisle. The ladies seemed especially anxious to hear Geoff speak, and they were rewarded by his revelation that he had played an instrument in his youth: the French horn!

Jakie threatened to give Geoff's name to Frank Williams, the president of the band, and then rambled on awhile longer. Eventually it came out that Jakie was thinking about buying an automobile. "It would be the first machine of its kind in Cody."

"How exciting!" Shelby exclaimed as she picked out canned goods for her pantry shelves.

Schwoob trailed along after the pair as they shopped, regaling them with a tale about a recent trip that Colonel Cody and George Beck, one of the other town founders, had made to Washington, D.C., to raise funds for the road to Yellowstone Park.

"Speaking of automobiles," Jakie revealed, "George and the colonel got hold of one and went for a ride down Pennsylvania Avenue. George was at the controls, and apparently not making fast enough time to suit Colonel Cody." All shopping in the big store had come to a halt while everyone within earshot openly listened to Jakie Schwoob's story. He spoke with relish, gesturing for added entertainment value. "George Beck made the automobile rush down the avenue at a great speed, and soon it became apparent that *pedestrians* might be at risk! The colonel suggested that George let up a little, but when he tried to shut off the power, nothing happened. Colonel Cody shouted 'Whoa!'—to no avail! Policemen chased them on foot, shaking their clubs, but the vehicle continued at its breakneck speed. Members of Congress, crossing Pennsylvania Avenue, were knocked down by Beck and Cody's auto!"

"That's terrible!" Shelby covered her broad smile with both hands, delighting in the drama. "How did it all end?"

"Alas, the mobile perambulator finally struck a granite fence, forcefully enough to throw George Beck and Colonel Cody out on the grass! They were immediately grabbed by policemen, who charged them with racing through the streets. Fortunately, a friend who had political influence happened to be passing, and he persuaded the policemen to let our founding fathers go free."

Geoff was laughing with pure pleasure, leaning against a display case. "It sounds like a scene from Buffalo Bill's own show!"

"He says that this just proves to him that it's better to stick to horses, especially in the Wild West Show!" Jakie affirmed as he laughed along with his customers. "And when George Beck returned to Cody from Washington, he refused to speak about his misadventure!"

"Rather a lowering experience for the president of the Cody Club," Geoff agreed with a chuckle. "I suppose that we should be going, if my partner is ready . . . ?" He looked at Shelby with raised brows.

"Now that I've filled my basket with items chosen on impulse, I'm trying to decide among them." A pretty flush crept into her cheeks. "While I was being entertained by those stories, I picked up everything that struck my fancy!"

Geoff looked into the basket filled to the brim with ribbons, cooking utensils, a new lace tablecloth, writing paper, a pepper mill, and a box of rifle shells. "Don't deprive yourself, Shelby. We'll get all of it." He took the basket from her before she could protest, and he and Jakie walked together up the aisle. "Did you have my other purchase loaded in the buckboard?"

"What other purchase?" Shelby asked as she hurried to keep up with the two long-legged men.

"Can't you ever allow yourself to be surprised?" Geoff retorted. He heard the fond note in his own voice and wondered at it.

Shelby looked confused.

"My stock clerk took it out," Schwoob assured Geoff. As he added up the bill, along with the past amount due that the Englishman wanted to pay, he made idle conversation. "So . . . are you two partners in more ways than one these days?"

Turning pink to the roots of her hair, Shelby said, "Why, Mr. Schwoob—I—"

"I *see*!" He winked broadly at both of them.

"No, it's not like that! I mean, Mr. Weston and I are friends—nothing more—except for business associates."

Jakie looked disappointed as he wrapped up her purchases. "Too bad. This town could use a lively romance." Another thought occurred to him then; he studied Geoff over the tops of his wire-rimmed spectacles. "Since you're unattached, maybe you'll be interested to know that Cody will soon have three new, unmarried female citizens! Our new doctor, the esteemed Louis Howe, tells me that his family is on their way—including a trio of lovely daughters!"

Frowning, Shelby reached for one of her parcels, but Geoff had to linger to count money into Jakie Schwoob's hand. "It's a little stuffy in here. I think I'll wait for you outside. Nice to see you, Mr. Schwoob!"

Striding up and down on the boardwalk that protected

pedestrians from Sheridan Avenue's mud, Shelby found that she was very upset by the notion that Geoff might become interested in another woman. What if he decided to court one of Dr. Howe's pretty daughters? They were probably bright and entrancing, yet ladylike and graceful, with carefully coiffed hair and stylish gowns. She glanced down at her divided skirt and dirty boots, and at the long braid that fell over her shoulder, and frowned so that her lower lip stuck out.

"What's amiss, scamp?" Geoff asked lightly as he came up behind her, his arms full of packages.

"I don't think you should call me that," she fretted. "It makes me sound like some sort of . . . ragamuffin tomboy."

"I disagree." He set off toward the buckboard, and Shelby was forced to hurry to keep up. "I think the word scamp could also refer to an enchanting gamine . . . which is what you are, when you're not making me furious."

"What's my surprise?" She caught his sleeve as they approached the buckboard.

"I'll show you when we get home. Waiting will develop your character." Geoff led her away from the back of the wagon, adding, "Your habit of acting on impulse could lead to serious trouble for both of us!"

Geoff insisted on stopping to pay bills at the other businesses where the Sunshine Ranch was in arrears, explaining to Shelby that he'd looked at the ranch ledgers for her own good. She pouted for a bit, but softened by the time they began the long ride home. The late afternoon light was luminous as the sun slid down behind the mountaintops to the west of Cody, and the Shoshone River sparkled in a wind that sent tumbleweeds rolling across the road.

"You promised to tell me about Bart Croll's wife," Shelby reminded Geoff. "Is she awfully horrible?"

"Gad, no," he replied, laughing in spite of himself. "How can you live like that—saying the first thing that jumps into your mind?"

"If you knew my family, which included assorted grandparents, you might understand. Everyone is very strong-minded and enthusiastic, so as the baby daughter, I had to learn to fend for myself at the dinner table—or never be heard at all!" She propped her feet on the front of the buckboard and smiled at him. "Your family meals must have been very proper in comparison."

Geoff smiled derisively. "Most of my meals were taken at private school, where conversation was generally forbidden."

"That's awful!" Stricken, she felt her eyes fill with tears. "How sad to be a child and have to grow up away from home and the love of your family! How old were you when you went to live at school?"

"Eight, perhaps—or six? I don't recall. And it wasn't terribly tragic, since my family isn't warm and demonstrative by any means. Most evenings, when I *was* at home, I dined with my nanny."

"Stop! I'll start crying, my nose will run, and I don't have a handkerchief!"

Geoff laughed, warmed by her spirit. "Don't waste your tears on the past. I certainly don't; I locked my memories away years ago. They aren't so much sad as boring." He reached over and touched her cheek with a newly callused forefinger. "You'd be better off weeping for Vivian Croll. There's a tragic character if ever I've seen one."

"I can see why you'd feel sorry for anyone who had to live with that man, but why did she marry him in the first place?"

"I certainly didn't have a long, heart-to-heart talk with Mrs. Croll, particularly with her evil husband glaring at me, but it's true she was a mail-order bride. Apparently, she was living in St. Louis, and lost her family in a fire this past Christmas. She was all alone in the world, so this proposal from Bart Croll was her salvation." Geoff flicked the reins to urge the horses home before darkness settled in. "It must feel like she made a deal with the devil, though, because her eyes are positively haunted."

Shelby shivered. "I can only imagine how I would feel were I in her place."

"That sod house may be the worst of the bargain for her. One had the feeling that Bart Croll built and furnished it on a Sunday afternoon. . . ."

Studying his pensive features in the twilight, Shelby felt an odd pang, and again she spoke before the words were formed in her mind. "Is Vivian pretty?"

"Pretty?" *Oh Shelby, I adore you,* he thought, then answered calmly, "Yes, I'd say so, given her circumstances. She has light hair, and very large blue eyes, and she looks quite fragile. My heart went out to her; it would be wonderful if we could find a way to help her."

Minutes later they were home, and Shelby went off to the barn to feed carrots to Gadabout and Charlie. All the while, she was pondering ways to retrieve their stolen cattle. Back in the house she saw that a fire had been lit, but no one was about. Assuming that Geoff was looking after Mr. Manypenny, Shelby went on to her own room to freshen up.

On a whim, she decided to relax by changing into something decidedly more comfortable. It felt glorious to take a sponge bath with the French-milled soap she kept for special occasions, then brush her cinnamon-tinted hair loose, tie it back with a big ribbon, and get into her favorite fleece-lined, drop-seat, red union suit. The fuzzy fabric felt almost indecent against her bare skin, and Shelby was smiling as she added a long white dressing gown, secured with a satin sash around her waist. Warm socks and slippers completed her ensemble, which seemed ideal for the plotting session for the cattle restealing she had in mind.

Only Geoff was available to judge her outrageous getup, for the boys were out repairing the crushed fence and there was no telling when they'd be back. Why not be comfortable? she wondered as she emerged from her bedroom.

There was a definite mood shift in the house; Shelby felt it instantly. The glow from the fire and several freshly lit oil lamps flickered over the framed Wild West Show poster and giant bearskin that decorated the room's walls. Her eyes found Geoff then, casually attractive in fresh tan denim trousers and a starched white shirt with a plain neck band. He'd left one button open, and his hair shone like old gold in the soft light.

Geoff stood beside the broken-down sofa and its table, which now held a magnificent new gramophone. It was even finer than the machine owned by Shelby's parents, with an oak sound box, a brass amplifying horn, and a nickel-plated carrying arm. Awestruck, she came closer. This gramophone was made to play flat records rather than the cylinders that had been popular until recently, and a stack of black records waited beside the machine.

"This is fantastic!" she murmured, already dreaming of the magic music could bring to the ranch house. "I've missed listening to songs at home—and playing the piano. When Daddy built Mama her dream house, he made a music room, tucked into a tower."

"I had a feeling you might love music." He smiled

into her eyes. "I was ready for a diversion myself. I daresay there's a limit to how many games of checkers I can play, and I may be closing in on that number."

Shelby's face was shining. She literally caressed the gramophone, then began looking at the records. " 'Bring Back My Bonnie to Me,' 'Listen to the Mockingbird' . . ."

"I had to take what Jakie had in stock," Geoff explained with a light shrug. Meanwhile his eyes roved over her. "What the devil have you got on?"

Her laughter was playful. "I wanted to be cozy—and I thought we were going to sit down at the table with a pot of tea and decide how to get our cattle back."

"Let's dance first."

"Geoff! I look ridiculous! I can't dance like this—and besides, I'd feel like a clumsy ostrich dancing with you. You probably are used to dancing with princesses."

"Nonsense. Besides, princesses are the most boring partners imaginable." A tender expression passed over his face as he took in the sight of Shelby, delightful in her red union suit and dressing gown with the sash tied around her small waist. How could he ever explain to her that he'd stopped dancing long before he came to Wyoming, unless he was cornered, because there'd been no pleasure in it anymore. It occurred to Geoff then that he'd had more fun with Shelby than he'd known in years. Extending a hand, he gazed into her sparkling eyes and said, "Lady Shelby, would you do me the honor of sharing this first dance with me?"

She made a mock curtsy, her red-clad legs showing. "I accept . . . my lord."

After winding up the gramophone, Geoff put on a record of a waltz called "Love Comes," and as the uneven tune filled the room, he gathered Shelby into his arms. It did not surprise him to discover that she danced well, for she had attended an excellent college in the East and her education colored everything she said and did, in spite of her efforts to the contrary. What did surprise him was the utterly beguiling outline of her soft, diminutive body, for even though she was covered from head to toe, these were clothes that allowed him to feel her true shape. There was something about Shelby that intoxicated him to a shocking degree.

And yet, it was inexpressibly sweet to feel alive again.

Shelby, too, was caught in the spell. The ranch house's main room was big enough for them to waltz properly, and Geoff's touch was deft, a combination of grace and strength, which made Shelby feel as if he were lifting her off her feet when they turned with the music. Happiness welled up in her. None of it made sense, but it was real.

When the record wound down, Geoff put on another: "In Love With the Man in the Moon." They danced on and on, beaming at one another, caught up together in the magic so potent that it needed no words or explanation.

By the time the second song slowed, Shelby's face was flushed, her heart racing. They stopped together, resting, and Geoff lightly held her against him, his hands framing her hips. She was so soft, and she smelled fresh and lovely. The pressure of her breasts on his chest aroused him beyond reason. It was like a fierce hunger that he could scarcely understand, since all his life he'd had more of everything than he needed. Geoff's desires had been fulfilled before they could ripen . . . until now.

When Shelby slowly looked up at him, and her little hands crept up to twine about his neck, he was lost. It was impossible to hold her closely enough, so fierce was his embrace, and the ribbon fell from her hair as he sank his fingers into the shining mass of curls. For her part, Shelby nearly whimpered when his mouth finally closed over hers. She was ravenous for the taste of him, the torturous pleasure of his kiss, and the need that built inside her in a way she was beginning to recognize.

The sash securing her dressing gown came undone. The red union suit beneath should have been a decidedly unfeminine garment, but on Shelby it became purely alluring, drawing Geoff's hands to slide over the visible curves of her back, hips, rib cage, and finally, daringly, her breasts.

She gasped, astonished to feel the hot moisture between her legs, the pulsing ache that surpassed any yearning she'd ever imagined.

Bang! The back door flew open, followed by the sound of stamping feet and Cal's voice yelling, "Anybody home?"

Shelby's first impulse was to dash into her bedroom, but there wasn't time. Cal was already coming through the kitchen. Her discomfiture was such that all she could do was press her hands to her hot cheeks. It took Geoff to firmly close her dressing gown and knot the sash.

"Tidy your hair," he whispered, then went to meet the ranch hand. "How did it go out there, Cal?"

"Fine." Grimy and sunburned, the young man's eyes were startled under the brim of his hat as he focused on the gramophone. "Chrissakes, where'd that contraption come from?"

"The Cody Trading Company—Jakie Schwoob's store."

Regaining a little composure, Shelby came forward to join them. "Excuse my appearance, Cal, but when I heard the music, I couldn't resist hurrying out here for a closer look."

"Well, I'm glad you're here, Miz Shelby. I got some news for the two of you. Serious news, I'd call it."

Unconsciously, Geoff reached out and fit his hand around the bend in her arm. "Go on."

"It's the fence. When we fixed it today, we saw that it wasn't broke by that tree." Cal squinted at them in the firelight. "Somebody's already cut the barbed wire—or they cut it after the tree came down."

"What are you saying, Cal?" Shelby pressed.

He shrugged. "Looks to me like your cattle didn't wander over to the Bar B by accident. I'd say that somebody cut that fence to make it easier to get through, and then those eight head of cattle was outright *stole*."

Eyes flashing, Shelby waved a fist in the air. "I *knew* it! I knew that there was more to this!" She looked at Geoff, who wore a grim, thoughtful expression. "Now we have to go over there and get our cattle back, and there's only one way to do it! This isn't London, it's the West, and if we try to go through the town marshal, we'll have a worse mess on our hands. No, we're going to have to *steal* them back—and don't try to tell me otherwise! I won't listen to your arguments!"

"Arguments?" Slowly, Geoff raised his eyebrows and looked down at her animated face. "For once, scamp, we are in complete agreement."

Chapter Nine

GEOFF SPENT THE ENTIRE NEXT DAY IN CODY, CHATting with townspeople on the pretext of hiring extra hands for the Sunshine Ranch's first roundup. He even dropped by to meet Marshal Burns, who was in the office at lunchtime, and had a drink with him and Deputy Ted. By using patient and circuitous conversational gambits, Geoff managed to extract a couple pieces of information about Bart Croll.

The first was that the Bar B wouldn't begin its roundup until the next week, so Geoff didn't have to worry that the Sunshine's cattle were now wearing Croll's brand.

Secondly, the men suggested that Geoff might like to join them for a regular weekly poker game, held every Thursday in Purcell's back room. Geoff wondered if he lived too far out, but Ted assured him that even Bart Croll made the trip to Cody to socialize with the men. "Sometimes he even stays over," the marshal added with a wink.

When Geoff arrived back home with this information, he found Shelby pacing back and forth out in the yard. The sight of him riding Charlie down the ranch road prompted her to run to meet him, then nearly pull him off the buckskin's back.

"We just have to wait one more night," he told her,

raising a cautioning hand. "Croll won't be around tomorrow; Thursday nights he has a poker game in Cody."

Shelby thought she'd die before another thirty-six hours passed. And, on a practical note—what if Uncle Ben and Titus returned? They were due any moment, after all. If not for the blizzard, they would have already gotten home, she reckoned.

"I'm adamant about this," Geoff said firmly as he walked Charlie to the trough for water. "There's no point in doing something as mad as this if the risks are too great. Do you want to be tried and hanged in Cody for this prank?"

"Prank! *Prank?!*" Indignant, she ran after him as he started toward the house in search of food. "I demand that you take that back! This is an honorable mission, a quest for justice—"

"And you love the notion of sneaking around rustling cattle in the middle of the night!" Geoff ducked behind a cottonwood tree, pulled down his hat as if disguising himself, and lowered his voice to tones of mock drama. "It's the adventure that has you so worked up, and it's no use trying to convince me otherwise. I'm afraid I know you too well."

Shelby knew she ought to be outraged, but instead she giggled, and had to restrain herself from touching him. "If you're trying to incite me, it won't work. I'm in no mood for an argument. Come inside for supper and we'll work out the plans for tomorrow night. . . ."

"Psst! Geoff!"

The Englishman drew back slightly on his reins and waited for Gadabout and her rider to come alongside. "You must not speak!" he whispered harshly. It was a wonderfully atmospheric night for such an adventure, with a glimmering new moon on the rise, bracketed by diamond-bright stars. The brisk air was scented with sagebrush and, it seemed, danger.

"I'm too excited!" Even though Shelby wore a big gray Stetson, pulled low on her face and concealing her hair, as well as a coat with a turned-up collar and a big kerchief tied around her neck and chin, there was no mistaking her radiant visage. She couldn't help reaching out to Geoff, and was rewarded by the clasp of his black-gloved hand. "It's a thrilling night, but I feel that this is a noble mission. This might sound silly, but I've missed those cattle. I worry that they're not being cared for properly."

Geoff's own face was darkened and disguised as thoroughly as possible, but nothing could hide the ironic glance he directed toward the silvery heavens. "I won't dispute your affection for livestock, my dear, but I think we should get on with this." He nudged Charlie to walk over to Cal, Lucius, and Marsh, who were on the ground next to the barbed-wire fence. They'd cut it again, at exactly the same places the thieves had, just in case anyone checked later. In a low, clear voice, Geoff reminded the quartet of their plans. He would keep toward the Croll homestead, watching for any sign of Bart, guarding Shelby and the others against discovery. Shelby, meanwhile, was the only person who claimed she could identify the eight head of Sunshine Ranch cattle. It was up to her to move among the Bar B livestock, bring out their own, one by one, and Cal would lead the cows back to the fence. There, Marsh would guide them through, and finally, Lucius was responsible for moving them back into the nearby herd.

It was very lucky that Bart Croll didn't have a larger herd of his own. If there'd been hundreds, rather than a few dozen, and fewer stars to provide a bit of light, Shelby's task would have been much more daunting.

As it was, Geoff found himself worrying. He decided to carry her into the other herd by scooping her onto Charlie's back and slipping one arm around her to hold her secure. There wasn't any point in Shelby having Gadabout out there with her; the pony was just one more thing to stand out if someone came. And when he slowed Charlie to a walk beside the Croll cattle, Geoff looked at them and wondered how the devil she could ever figure out which eight belonged to them. It seemed impossible enough in daylight!

"I feel like Robin Hood," she whispered, defusing the tension.

Against his better judgment, Geoff kissed her. Both their bodies radiated heady anticipation for the adventure ahead, and that aura was intensified as they clung together, tasting, hungering, while the night breeze nipped at their faces.

Finally Geoff drew back, his eyes stern. "For God's sake, be careful, Shelby."

"Why, I'm always careful!" She gave him a jaunty grin and slipped from the saddle to the rugged ground.

"When you've found the last steer, hop on with Cal and ride back to the fence line. I'll check on you from time to time, but don't wait for me before you get yourself to safety." He leaned over and caught the collar of her denim coat. "Agreed?"

"Sure!" Waving, she scampered off toward the herd of cattle, disappearing into the shadows.

Geoff worked his way toward the Croll house, marked in the distance by a thin ribbon of smoke that curled from the roof. It was a pretty night, and his solitude gave him a chance to contemplate the differences between England and Wyoming. At his estate in Gloucestershire, spring was dazzlingly lush, brilliantly green, and gloriously perfumed. Here, spring was a simpler matter: pure, pungent, and thrillingly real. The thawing ground and greening plants lent a quality to the air that made his nostrils flair when he inhaled deeply, and it was still crisp enough that his breath steamed as he let it out.

There were sounds in the darkness: quavering owls, rascally coyotes, and whippoorwills whose song was shortened in the West to simply "poor-will."

Circling the acre or so closest to the sod house, Geoff saw a light move in one of the windows. The breeze shifted, rustling the new leaves of the cottonwoods and peach-leaf willows that flanked the house. Time passed.

Geoff went back to check on Shelby, and found that Cal was with her. "Everything's fine, boss," the ranch hand assured him. "This is number five, an' she's pickin' 'em out like they're wearin' signs!"

Arms akimbo, Shelby stood in a shaft of moonlight and beamed at Geoff. "What can I say? It's a gift."

He rode past her and reached down to touch her cheek, wryly murmuring, "Scamp," then returned to his lookout post. However, even as Geoff approached the sod house, something in the air disturbed his high spirits. Straightening in the saddle, he glanced around. Nothing moved; even Croll's ramshackle barn and corral were quiet.

The door to the house opened then, and Geoff's heart lodged in his throat. *Damn!* The distance was great enough that he couldn't see who it was immediately, but he knew that he was close enough to be noticed. Charlie seemed to stiffen beneath him.

"You there! I see you!" called a woman's tremulous voice. "Come over here, stranger, and don't try anything! I have a gun, and the trigger's ready to be pulled!"

Splendid, Geoff thought grimly, and did as he was bade. Approaching the sod house, he made out Vivian's figure more clearly: she wore a man's coat over her long dark skirt; her hair, pinned up on her head, shone pale in the moonlight; and she was aiming a large shotgun straight at him.

"What're you trying to steal?" Vivian cried when he was a few yards away. "Are you a rustler? My husband tells me to shoot first and ask questions later, and maybe that's good advice!" Her voice shook as she added, "We don't have much, you can see that. Why don't you leave us alone?"

He drew off his hat. "It's Geoffrey Weston, Mrs. Croll. Do you remember me?"

His cultured accent had a jarring effect on her. Her eyes got big as saucers and she lowered the rifle. "But—what—what're you doing over here, Mr. Weston?"

It came to him that she was blushing, which made him sad for her, but probably was a good sign that he'd get out of this mess. "I don't suppose you'd believe me if I said I needed to borrow a cup of flour?"

"You can tell me the truth," she said softly.

"You won't shoot me if I come down? You can trust me not to harm you, Mrs. Croll."

"I know that." Vivian set the shotgun against the hitching post and waited while Geoff dismounted and led Charlie over to stand before her.

"Would you believe me if I told you that your husband stole eight head of our cattle?" he asked gently. "I have proof."

"Yes. I believe you." She looked down. "I'm sorry."

Her defeated tone stirred up deep feelings of sympathy in Geoff. "We came tonight to take them back. That's all; we aren't looking for revenge, and we know that the law is on Bart's side, so that's not a choice, either. We just want our cattle back."

"Of course." She nodded sadly. "I don't blame you." Her blue eyes studied his romantically shadowed face for long moments before she whispered, "I wish there were someone to come for me, as you have come for your cattle—to take *me* away from him. . . ."

Geoff felt as if he'd been punched in the stomach. "I thought as much. You're not happy here, are you?"

"No. How could I be?" Tears thickened her voice, and in the next instant she caught herself. "I have to stop thinking of other people's lives and count my blessings. I owe him everything. I had no place to spend the winter, until Bart took me in. I am—his wife. . . ."

"Look . . ." He lay a hand on her coat sleeve, feeling the thinness of her arm through the bulky material. "I'll send Shelby to meet you, and then at least you'll have a friend. Shelby Matthews is the young lady who manages the Sunshine Ranch. I won part of it in a poker game, and live there as well."

"That sounds romantic. Are the two of you . . . promised?"

Smiling dryly, he replied, "No. We're partners—and friends. And we'll think of a way to help you, Mrs. Croll. You certainly deserve more from life than—"

They were interrupted by the sound of hoofbeats approaching on the ranch road, and both of them paled.

"Get inside!" Geoff ordered. Then, in one movement, he pulled his hat on to hide his blond hair, swung onto Charlie's back, wheeled around and galloped away.

Like a nightmare, he heard the hoofbeats coming on, after him—enough noise for at least two horses. His lungs burned and his heart thundered as he urged Charlie forward, grateful for the horse's great speed. *Please God, let Shelby and the others be back at the house by now!* Geoff thought wildly as he approached the spot where he'd left Shelby in the midst of the herd. Surely she was finished—and he'd made his instructions crystal-clear that she should look after her own safety above all else.

"Hey!"

She stepped out from among the cattle, waving her arms, wearing a panicky expression. Without looking back to see how far back his pursuers were, Geoff slowed Charlie just enough to hold out a hand to Shelby and haul her up as they passed. Resuming the hard gallop, he kept one arm gripped around her midsection and looked for the fence. It wouldn't be far.

"I—I can't—breathe," Shelby gasped.

"Good!" he barked, but relaxed his hold on her a bit. Countless decidedly unfriendly words and epithets waited on his tongue, but he couldn't spare the effort speaking would require. When they came to the fence, he would need every ounce of concentration he possessed.

Hanging on half sideways, secure only in the iron grasp of Geoff's arm, Shelby saw the glint of barbed wire in the distance. Shots rang out from their pursuers, occasionally missing her by inches. Her thrilled state gave way to raw terror.

"I'm scared!" She assumed they'd turn and follow the fence line until they could lose the pair of riders chasing them through the darkness. Instead, the wire came closer to closer, and she had to bite her lip to smother the scream that rose in her throat. When Geoff leaned forward in the saddle, taking her with him, Shelby closed her eyes, utterly terrified.

Charlie sailed up, up, and out, seeming to fly—like

the paintings of fox-hunting English horses Shelby had seen. No western horse was trained to perform a feat of such magical grace, but Charlie landed softly and safely, in spite of the considerable burden on his back.

"Where are the boys—and the cattle?" Geoff demanded roughly once they'd landed on their own side of the fence.

"Back—I told them—to go back to the house." She was shocked to discover that she was nearly faint from fear and relief. And it wasn't over—the hoofbeats were coming closer across the scrubby range.

Before she could recover, Shelby found herself being virtually pushed off the horse, while Geoff jumped with her. Holding the reins in one hand and her arm in his other, he scrambled forward in the darkness, heading straight toward a shallow gully that was apparently a remnant of an earlier path carved by the Stinking Water River. Using that meager protection, and aided by the cover of night, Geoff coaxed Charlie down into the hollow.

Shelby recovered her senses enough to see what needed to be done. Slipping her arms around the buckskin's neck, she drew him down, and together she and Geoff persuaded Charlie to lie down. Then, with each of them flattened against the ground on either side of the horse, they stroked him and waited. The chilly spring air seemed to vibrate with tension and danger.

Only a minute or so passed before the pursuing horses stopped short at the barbed-wire fence.

"I think you was seein' things, Ted! I shoulda stayed at that game tonight, where I coulda won some money! I knew this'd be a waste of time!"

"Whatta you mean, Bart? You saw that horse same as me!"

"Then where'd it go? Didn't just disappear into thin

air, and in case you didn't notice, this here's a fence. You think the horse crawled under the barbed wire?" He laughed. "I bet it was a deer. You're just too suspicious fer your own good. That sissy limey comes sniffin' around and you think he's up to somethin', when he prob'ly ain't got the brains to wipe his own butt!" Croll laughed at this display of wit, and his laughter shifted into a coughing spell.

"I got instincts about these things," Ted insisted as they turned away from the fence. "If that dude wasn't upta somethin', why wasn't he at the game tonight?"

"Cuz he's wettin' his wick in that nutty Matthews broad! Gotta get all he can before her uncle comes back from Billings!" More laughter, more coughing, and then, as Bart got farther away and more difficult to hear clearly, he added, "Tell you what. We'll settle this by askin' Viv if she saw or heard anythin' tonight. I got her trained to keep an eye on the ranch when I'm not home. . . ."

There was no rational explanation for the wildly heightened mutual attraction that both Shelby and Geoff felt that night. He pretended to be angry with her as they returned to the house, but in truth, as she sat in front of him on the saddle and leaned back into his chest, he was captivated. To his own chagrin, his body betrayed him, and he was powerless to stop himself from growing hard and hot inside his denim pants. Given the fact that Shelby's backside was flush with his crotch, Geoff could only hope that she was too naive to notice.

A self-deprecating smile twitched at the corners of his mouth as he thought, *Maybe she thinks it's my holster. . . .*

Contentment flowed through Shelby's body like an

intoxicating nectar, all the more pleasurable in the aftermath of danger. The bond between Geoff and her was strengthening every day, as even their quarrels brought them closer together. Snuggling back in the circle of his arms, Shelby thought, He may yell and threaten, but underneath, he likes me this way.

When they got home and stabled Charlie, Shelby checked on Gadabout, then went into the corral with a lantern and found the lost cattle. All eight of them stood at the trough, eating and drinking, and the sight of them brought stinging tears to her eyes.

"Look how happy they are to be home, where they needn't go hungry like Bart Croll's cattle! Some people might think it's silly for me to care about these poor creatures," she said to Geoff in an emotional voice, "but I don't care. They may be dumb, but that's all the more reason for us to look out for them and protect them." She stroked the brown and white head of the nearest steer, and he looked over at her and lapped her hand.

From the other side of the corral fence, Geoff reached out and drew off her oversized gray hat, watching as her hair spilled free. "Your eight lost children are home again, safe. Let's go in now."

Cal, Marsh, and Lucius were just filing out of the kitchen, bound for their bunkhouse. "Hope you don't mind that we heated up some stew," Cal said. "Nothin' like danger to give a man an appetite!"

"Yup!" Marsh agreed, then burped and blushed, hanging his head.

"Glad to see that the boss found you okay, Miz Shelby," Cal added. "I hated to leave you there like that."

"Next time, do not," Geoff advised him in astringent tones. "I was nearly overtaken by Croll and his cousin, and Miss Matthews and I made an escape that was precarious at best. Shots were fired. In the future, I would advise you to follow your own instincts rather than allowing my . . . associate to persuade you to behave otherwise." He smiled then. "However, I must congratulate you fellows for rescuing our cattle and bringing them, as well as Gadabout, home safely."

Cal opened his mouth as if he would speak, but then thought better of it and simply said good night, and the trio shambled off. When Shelby went inside the ranch house, she began to shiver, hugging herself in her coat.

"What's wrong with me?" she wondered, teeth chattering so much that she nearly giggled.

Geoff, having looked in on Manypenny to assure himself that the nearly recuperated old gentleman was fast asleep, returned to wrap his arms around her. "You've had too much excitement, I imagine." The fragrance of her hair aroused him.

"It *was* exciting, wasn't it?" Shelby was still shaking, but there was a subtle shift in the mood as her body fit itself to Geoff's and his embrace hardened. Her face found its way beyond his open coat, seeking his flannel-clad chest. "This was the sort of night I've always longed for, but because my family are the pillars of Deadwood, I was forced into another style of living. I thrive on *this* life, though! I adore the ranch and the animals and the mountains and the river—and Cody! Just breathing on a night like this makes me happy. . . ." And you—I adore *you*! Shelby thought so loudly, she felt certain he could hear her emotions.

"Might I be so bold as to add one more element to your list?" Geoff murmured with a touch of irony, still holding her close.

Her heart began to pound. "All right . . ." She felt her face getting hot and was glad he couldn't see.

"What about *danger*? Wouldn't you agree that you seem to relish being in peril?"

"Maybe," she agreed. "I have never been any good at prudence."

"No." Geoff's voice thickened as longing broke over him like a cloudburst. He'd known it was coming, but hadn't been able to predict the exact moment of impact. "Shelby . . . I . . ."

Her arms, encumbered by her thick coat, searched upward to fasten around Geoff's neck, and she turned her face up to his as if searching out the sun. "Yes." The word was an affirmation rather than a question. A voice from a distant corner of her mind reminded her that this was absolutely outrageous behavior, but her true self triumphed as always. "Yes."

He pressed her back against the oak icebox and feasted on her extravagant mouth. No other female had tasted, felt, or responded to him like Shelby, and this was a matter quite beyond common carnality. Geoff had long ago grown bored with the quest for intensified lust. His opinion was that heightened sexual excitement, for its own sake, marked an immature individual.

Yet, by opening her mouth to his hungry kisses, Shelby opened a new vista of complex sensations inside of Geoff. How perfectly she combined pure desire with innocence and curiosity—and a chemical reaction that only the two of them, together, seemed capable of creating.

The edges of the real world began to blur, muted by the rapture of their kisses and incendiary caresses. Staring into Geoff's brown eyes, Shelby managed to get out of her coat, and to pull his off as well. Now she was no longer shivering with cold, but hot, her cheeks flushed.

He returned her gaze solemnly, his face inexpressibly beautiful, in Shelby's opinion. She was accustomed to good-looking men, having a father and brother who constantly turned heads, but Geoff stood alone in her eyes. Sculpted and golden, lean and graceful as a lion, he lifted her into his arms now and carried her out of the kitchen.

"Music?" he whispered, his breath warm on her ear, and Shelby nodded, nearly faint with pleasure. Geoff gently laid her on the sofa, lit one lamp, then put on the first record he could find. The gramophone magically produced the tinny strains of "Bring Back My Bonnie to Me," and Shelby dreamily sang along.

"My Bonnie lies over the ocean, my Bonnie lies over the sea . . ." Shelby warbled while Geoff laughed aloud and pulled off her boots, then his own. He joined her in singing the chorus: "Brinnng back! Brinnng back! Ohh, bring back my Bonnie to me, to me!"

Soon the music died away and they rose together, holding hands, and went into Shelby's big bedroom. "Manypenny?" she said worriedly as Geoff lit the lamp by her bed.

"Snoring with gusto," he assured her.

Shelby's heart thudded again, but when Geoff opened his arms, smiling, all her nerves dissolved. She went to him in her stocking feet and hopped up, wrapping her arms around his neck and her legs around his waist, laughing joyously. Again their mouths came together, kissing, kissing, gasping for breath, tasting, nibbling, while Geoff's hands cupped her buttocks through the trousers she'd worn for the night's adventure.

"Yes . . ." Shelby heard herself murmur again. It was as if the word was pulled from the depths of her soul. All of her trembled with a fierce need to blend with all of Geoff.

He sat down on the edge of the bed so that Shelby was on his lap and they were bathed in the soft glow of the lamp. Slowly, his long fingers ran through the mass of her cinnamon curls, feeling their glossy texture, then he caressed Shelby's winsome face, whispering, "Enchanting" in husky tones.

She had always been self-conscious about her wide mouth, but when Geoff outlined it with his fingertip and worshiped it with his eyes, Shelby felt sensual, touching his forefinger with her tongue. The aching core inside her grew hotter, more insistent. She found the buttons on his shirt and opened them with surprising ease, drawing a grin from Geoff. When his shirt was open, her hands reached inside to explore the mysterious territory of his male chest. His body felt thrillingly alien to her: hard tapering contours comprised of only muscle and warm, smooth flesh—no fat. Shelby had never touched a man in this way. She was on fire with not just desire for him, but curiosity as well.

Geoff indulged her, wondering when she'd wander below his waist and discover the real evidence of his maleness. At the same time, he was wary of that touch, for tonight he was reminded that several weeks had elapsed since he'd been with a woman. When he combined that overdue need with the extraordinary passion Shelby inspired in him, Geoff realized that he must make every effort to rein himself in. *This must be Shelby's night. . . .*

His fingers were tender yet sure as they swept back her hair and drew her closer so that he could softly kiss from her cheekbones down the satiny column of her neck. He slipped loose the buttons of her shirt, then kissed her bared shoulders with feathery softness.

Shelby closed her eyes, drifting, caught in a powerful current of new sensations. She didn't see Geoff's sudden smile as he took in her undergarment. Instead of a boned corset, worn by every woman of fashion he'd undressed in recent memory, Shelby was charmingly clad in a fine-ribbed cotton vest that resembled a child's undershirt, with lacy straps at her shoulders. However, the thin material clung to her beautiful breasts in a manner that was anything but childlike. A soft groan escaped Geoff's lips, and he knew he was in deep trouble.

Shelby sank her fingers into his hair as Geoff eased her back onto the pillows of her bed. Through her lashes she saw him above her as if through a mist: the incarnation of her fantasies, smiling at her with tenderness, lifting her hand to kiss her palm, her wrist, the sensitive inner side of her arm.

"My God, Shelby, you're exquisite."

When Geoff said it, she believed him. He kissed her throat, then cupped her breasts over the soft, ribbed vest. The shivery heat between her legs became a congested ache; when he slid her pants off, and his own, then embraced her, Shelby wore only cotton drawers and they didn't seem to hinder her first discovery of the anatomy of a fully erect man. And she wanted more. She opened her bare thighs, instinctively pushing so that the hot ridge of his maleness could separate her puffy nether lips, even through the drawers.

Passion began to overtake Geoff, not just from his own body, but from Shelby's. She was so eager, meeting him kiss for kiss, her hands wandering over him in constant exploration, her arms and legs joining in the shared embrace. Geoff found that he couldn't get enough of her full, delicious mouth, or the curve of her neck where he could inhale the fragrance of her hair. Her breasts were so warm, pressing against his chest, and finally his lips trailed fire down Shelby's throat. Her nipples were puckered under the ribbed Egyptian cotton, their dark rose hue showing through, and Geoff suckled them through the fabric, the sensation of his warm, wet mouth and cool breath stunningly exciting to Shelby.

"Oh. Oh!" She threw her head back on the pillows, arching against him, throbbing with needs she had never imagined.

That was all Geoff needed to hear, for he had been hovering dangerously near the precipice for many long minutes. Gently, he drew off the rest of her underclothes, then held her close so that they could each savor the feeling of that full-length naked embrace. He kissed her again, smoothing back the hair from her damp brow, and waited for her incandescent smile. Shelby further responded by parting her legs to the slight pressure of his hard-muscled thigh. She found Geoff's long, lithe body to be as amazing as any sculpture she had ever seen in museums or books; she couldn't stop touching him, even in places she'd expected to be shy about. His buttocks were perfectly curved, and unyielding as marble.

And he let her eventually find him, although the pleasure of her touch was nearly excruciating, and Shelby guided him into her body, jerking at the first shock of pain, but bravely urging him to continue.

So sweet! Geoff thought, closing his eyes against the painful ecstasy of Shelby's snug warmth all around him. Her fingernails dug into his back, her mouth uttered low cries against his throat, her firm, rounded breasts seemed to scorch the surface of his chest. And each thrust was more exquisite than anything he'd ever felt in his life. There was so much he wanted to give to Shelby tonight, but his traitorous male body galloped toward fulfillment—and when it came, in a burning, shattering explosion, Geoff wondered if he could survive.

Strangled, primitive sounds seemed to be wrenched

from the depths of his soul, and Shelby would never forget them. She clasped his shuddering body to her own, their sweat mingling, their hearts thundering in unison, and understood what it was that had bound her own parents together over the years. It was a bond of fire, the ultimate act of sharing—of intimacy, and of exposure.

Geoff buried his face in her neck and she stroked his hair, murmuring, warm from head to toe with satisfaction.

"Shelby . . ." he whispered in reverent tones.

"I know." Her eyes stung. She blinked and tasted her own salty tears. "I know."

Chapter Ten

"JUST WHAT IN THE *HELL* IS GOIN' ON, I'D LIKE TO know!"

Dimly, Shelby registered the familiar voice, then felt how sore her muscles were. She was exhausted. Without opening her eyes, she turned toward the wall, seeking to shut out the rude voice, the morning—but instead she was blasted with a windowful of bright sunshine.

A hand whacked her backside. "For Pete's sake, wake up, Shel!"

Geoff . . . where is Geoff? The last time she'd checked, he had been right here in this bed, spooning with her.

"I'm not gonna ask you again, you little hellion!"

When a hand caught the edge of the sheet she had tucked under her chin, Shelby hurtled awake. *Ohmigod!* It was Uncle Ben—he was real, here in her room—and she was naked! Her eyes opened in terror and she gripped the sheet and quilts with both hands, holding fast to her modesty and her secrets, while hot blood flooded her cheeks. "For heaven's sake—leave me alone! How dare you barge in here like this!"

Benjamin Avery looked chagrined. "Geez, Shel—it's almost ten o'clock in the morning an' the whole house is asleep! After I been gone this long, you can't blame me for wonderin' what in Sam Hill is goin' on in my own house!"

Her guilty blush deepened as Ben held up two coats in one hand, then mismatched boots with the other. "I—Well . . ."

"I come in the house and I find these coats on the kitchen floor, then these boots in front of the sofa, and a kerchief lyin' in between! When there's clothes all over the house and nobody around or answerin' my call, I began to think maybe you'd all been murdered!"

Shelby wanted to crawl under the covers and hide. "Where is Geoff?" she inquired in a tiny voice.

"Sawin' logs, when I looked. And I'm not talkin' about the kind that we burn in the fireplace." Ben shook his head disapprovingly. "Mr. Manypenny's sittin' up in bed reading *Collier's* and waiting for somebody to bring him breakfast. Told me he's been *sick*! Geez, Shel, that wonderful gentleman coulda died by the time you hauled your spoiled little rear out of bed and—"

"That's about enough from you!" she cried, rallying. "I didn't mean to sleep so late, and I'm certain neither did Geoff, but the fact is that we're both tired after a night of successfully rustling our own cattle back from Bart Croll's ranch!" It pleased her to watch Ben's eyes grow big as he took in this news. "As for Mr. Manypenny, he's doing quite well now, and if he truly wanted or needed something, I'm confident he could get it unaided." She drew herself up with dignity. "Now then, if you'll allow me some privacy, I shall dress and join you. I'm very anxious to see Titus—and Jimmy—and hear all about your trip! Was it wonderful?"

He shrugged, chastened. "Yeah, I guess. Not the word I woulda picked, but sure, it fits. Sorta like the word 'duchess' seems to fit *you* these days. . . ." Backing out the door with a victorious grin, Ben felt generous. "I s'pose I could make some coffee while you get dressed, Your Grace."

"I'd really appreciate that, *dear* Uncle Ben." Shelby willed herself to ignore his gibes, favoring him instead with her most winning smile, which she held in place until the door had closed behind him. Then she went limp, nearly overcome with the new realities of her life. Even Ben Avery, who thought her quite capable of almost any wild act, would not suspect that she was naked under the covers and had spent most of the night making fiery love with Geoffrey Weston.

She colored anew at the thought.

I'm not a virgin anymore. But what am I?

What are we?

Shelby longed for a hot bath, but instead she slipped into a navy-blue skirt and fresh white shirtwaist with a high collar. Standing in front of her mirror and brushing her hair, she gazed at her reflection and alternated memories of Geoff's touch with a search for visible signs of the changes she had undergone overnight. *Surely, now that I am privy to the secrets of womanhood, I must look different. . . .*

It was so difficult to come back down to earth, and Shelby scarcely knew how to react when she emerged from her bedroom to find Manypenny shuffling into the main room of the house. The elderly manservant was impeccably clad in dark, faintly striped trousers, a white shirt, gray silk vest, and a striped tie. He even wore shoes, although they weren't tied very well, and his efforts at barbering himself had been less than successful.

Shelby rushed to his side, touched by his dignity. "Mr. Manypenny, how handsome you look!" She slipped a hand through his arm and felt him lean against her as they walked toward the kitchen. "Are you sure you're well enough to be up and around? You know, your strength won't return all at once. What does Geoff say? I hope you let him help you get dressed."

"If I may be so bold, Miss Matthews, I would offer the opinion that his lor—ahem! Rather I should say *Mr. Weston*—is currently behaving with a deplorable lack of discipline." He shook his big head to indicate just how deeply in disgrace Geoff was. "I believe he has only *just* decided that the morning is sufficiently well-aired to merit his conscious attention."

Shelby laughed at Manypenny's starched wit. "I've been very lazy myself, sir. Last night we had to rescue our cattle from the neighboring ranch, and I think we're both very tired this morning."

"I daresay." Each syllable was so weighted with irony that Shelby reddened, wondering if he knew more than she and Geoff had imagined. She was spared a reply, however, by the sight of Titus Pym, who was pouring himself a cup of coffee and watching her with a twinkle in his eyes. When Manypenny spied the Cornishman, he reached for a chair back and said, "There's your friend, Miss Matthews. Go and greet him; you must not give me a thought."

Shelby helped him into a chair, then rushed to embrace Titus, surprised by the tide of affection that broke inside her. "Oh, Mr. Pym, I've missed you. It seems that you three have been gone an eternity!"

Surprised by the tenacity of her hug, the little man drew back and scanned her face. "Are you all right, my dear? I don't mind telling you that I had second thoughts while we were away, for your parents entrusted you to my care, and, well . . ." He tossed a meaningful glance at Mr. Manypenny, who was reading the newspaper the men had brought from town. Titus finished in a conspiratorial whisper, "We don't really know these folk very well, now do we? Have they been kind to you?"

"Yes—of course! And you know that I'm much too bossy to allow anyone to run roughshod over me, Mr. Pym." Shelby released him then and began pulling out pans. "I know it's after ten o'clock, but I imagine everyone could use a nice late breakfast, like the kind Mama and Gran Annie used to fix on Sundays after church. Pancakes and eggs and bacon—wouldn't that taste delicious?" She realized that she must appear overanimated, but couldn't seem to stop herself. While cracking eggs, sifting flour, and slicing bacon, Shelby explained to Titus how ill Manypenny had been for many days, then went on to effectively dramatize the spring blizzard, the discovery of the lost cattle, the journey she and Geoff had made to Cody to report to the marshal, and the purchase of the gramophone. She was flipping pancakes, and the bacon and eggs were sizzling, when the back door opened and men filed into the house.

It made Shelby happy that her uncle was back home where he belonged, and she grinned at the sight of Jimmy back among his fellow ranch hands, but when Geoff brought up the rear and their eyes met, Shelby's heart began to skip. Her palms and the soles of her feet broke out in a sweat. She was giddy and shaky, but she loved each palpitation.

Geoff's spell on her seemed to be more potent than ever. A shaft of morning sunlight followed him through the door, bathing his burnished hair and tanned face in a golden haze. His smile of greeting to Titus was magically friendly, and the body Shelby had learned so well during the past night now wore khaki pants and a crisp white shirt with purely masculine élan. Perhaps, she reflected dreamily, the perfect man was actually a cross between a nobleman and a cowboy.

"How did you get outside?" Shelby asked, knowing that she looked starstruck, yet helpless to stop it. "I mean—Uncle Ben said you were still getting dressed. . . ."

His smile at her seemed to light up the room. "I slipped out the front door while you were doing a one-woman pantomime of the blizzard for Mr. Pym. I felt guilty for not having a look at the animals this morning."

"How are they?"

Before Geoff could reply, Ben pushed between them and grabbed for the spatula. "For Pete's sake, Shel, the pancakes are burning! What's eatin' you, anyway?"

"My fault." Geoff rushed to the burly fellow's aid, adding, "I distracted her."

Shelby removed herself from the fray by setting the table, and soon they all were seated together, eating with gusto and all talking at once. The journey to Billings had apparently been a success. Some of the new horses had come south with Titus, Ben, and Jimmy; the others would arrive with friends who were coming this way. Some of the new farming equipment they'd purchased was already in Cody, waiting to be picked up; the rest would be delivered on the next train.

Titus urged Shelby to finish the story about the stolen cattle, so she and Geoff took turns filling them in on Bart Croll and the previous night's great adventure. The men were shocked to hear of Shelby's direct involvement in such a dangerous undertaking, but she was quick to defend Geoff's decision to let her participate.

"You both know me too well to think I'd have stayed behind, and Geoff knows that I would have sneaked after them if I'd had to! It was easier to agree from the beginning—"

Gruffly, Ben interjected, "Sounds to me like I need to give our friend here some lessons on teachin' you to behave, Shel."

"Oh, don't be a pompous ass, Benjamin," Titus scoffed, stirring sugar into his coffee. "You can't control her any better than the rest of us."

"In my own defense," Geoff said sheepishly, "I will say that I might have tried chaining her to the fireplace if not for the fact that only Shelby could identify our eight steers with certainty. Since they weren't branded yet, we couldn't afford to make a mistake, especially given the handicap of darkness." He exchanged a look with Shelby and decided to gloss over the very real danger they'd encountered. "It was a risky venture, no doubt about that, but Shelby was determined—and I suppose one could conclude, 'All's well that ends well.' "

"I hope I don't see my niece's face on Wanted posters the next time I go into Cody," Ben grumbled. Then, perhaps a bit too casually, he exclaimed, "Geez, whatsa matter with me? Almost forgot, Weston—you had a letter waitin' for you at the post office! Looks pretty *important*." He waggled his brows while reaching inside his denim jacket. Holding the envelope out so that Shelby could see it clearly, he slowly turned it over as he passed the letter across the table to Geoff.

She recognized immediately that the impeccable handwriting was a woman's. It was addressed:

Geoffrey Weston, Earl of Sandhurst
Cody Township. The State of Wyoming.
The United States of America.

* * *

Shelby didn't want to look at the back, where another name was engraved on the flap, above the broken wax seal, but she couldn't help herself. *Lady Clementine Beech*, it proclaimed. Shelby thought, It's probably his old maiden aunt, or better yet, his nanny! She might have been able to convince herself of this if it hadn't been for Geoff's face. He colored guiltity at the sight of the letter, and next to him, Manypenny lifted one meaningful brow. It all lasted perhaps five seconds, then Geoff got the creamy envelope out of sight and regained his composure. No one else would guess a thing—except Shelby, who now was privy to the cadence of his heart, the green sparkles in the depths of his eyes, and the taste of his sweat.

Lady Clementine Beech played a key role in Geoff's life in England! Her feminine instincts proclaimed this assumption as fact.

Shelby's happiness must be too good to be true.

She was possessed with curiosity about the letter—and despised herself for it. Deep inside, Shelby could already envision herself sneaking into Geoff's room, rifling through his things, and reading the *letter*, and she was revolted by the scenario. Her faults might be numerous, but dishonesty, skulking, and violating the privacy of another person were not among them.

Yet she knew she would sink to that level, because she had to know. It occurred to her to simply ask Geoff, but she sensed that some defense mechanism in him would compel him to blur the truth. Clearly, if he were truly in love with Lady Clementine Beech, he would be in London rather than Cody—or he'd at least be talking about her. Geoff wasn't sneaky, any more than she was, Shelby reflected, but he was a nobleman—the *Earl of Sandhurst*, her subconscious kept trumpeting—and everyone knew that titled people had to live their lives according to other people's expectations.

She just had to know the truth—not Geoff's truth, but Clementine's. She'd given herself to him willingly (had she thrown herself at him?), and had no regrets, but something had happened to her. She had feelings for Geoff that were powerful and tender, and they wouldn't leave her alone.

So, later that afternoon, when everyone was out working with the new horses, Shelby slipped away. Just in case anyone asked, she mentioned to Lucius that she needed to wash the breakfast dishes and would be right back.

Approaching the house, she suddenly remembered Mr. Manypenny. He was sitting in his favorite wicker chair on the veranda, reading another volume of Trollope: *Phineas Redux*. In the sunlight, it was all the more apparent that he was thinner and, if possible, paler, but the smile he bestowed upon her was quite cheerful.

"Mr. Manypenny, may I ask you something?" Shelby inquired playfully as she stepped onto the porch.

"Of course."

"Do you remember any of the things you said to me during your illness?"

"A *lady* would not remind a gentleman of such lapses," he remonstrated with mock solemnity, eyes twinkling. "However, if you are referring to my insistence that you address me as 'Percy,' my reply is affirmative."

Shelby wanted to throw her arms around his neck and kiss the top of his bald head, but refrained, beaming instead. She giggled. "Geoff went absolutely wild every time I said 'Percy' to him."

"No doubt. I should enjoy that spectacle myself. I suggest that you say it to my face when he is present."

Laughing, Shelby agreed, then remarked that she was going to tidy up inside. A bad liar, she could feel the heat in her face the very instant she spoke the words, but hoped that the brevity of her deceit prevented Manypenny from noticing.

I am a terrible person, she thought miserably. Her heart was pounding as she crept down the hallway to Geoffrey's room, clutching a silly-looking feather duster in one hand. The door was ajar. Shelby stepped in, nearly sick with anxiety, and inhaled Geoff's appealing scent. It clung lightly to everything he touched; it was still on her other pillow. *Geoff's pillow,* she thought, welcoming the giddy tide of infatuation. Anything to distract her from the self-loathing that kept rising in her throat.

It was the first time in her life she'd done such a thing. Shelby had always been honest to a fault.

She looked around the room with loverlike fascination. The quilts on Geoff's bed were smoothed and folded back to reveal two snowy pillows. Tasteful ivory-handled grooming implements were arranged in a row on the bureau: a brush and a comb, a small mirror, and a razor. Nearby were a tin of after-shave alum and a blue and white mug containing a worn piece of shaving soap. Shelby lifted the cup and smelled it, analyzing Geoff's own scent—part fresh "gentleman of quality" soap from Trumper's, part Wyoming sunshine and mountain breezes, and part horses and sweat and a bit of smoke. It was a highly potent combination.

Steeling herself then, Shelby began to search. She opened his drawers, where fine underclothes and handkerchiefs were arranged, There was a book in the drawer. Thumbing through it, she discovered that Geoff kept a journal, writing sporadically rather than daily.

The letter wasn't in the journal, so she replaced it and went on.

Other drawers held clothing purchased in Cody: trousers of khaki and denim, union suits in soft gray and faded red, cotton shirts, heavy socks, bandannas. No letter.

A noise set Shelby's heart thundering again. She tiptoed to the hallway and listened, but the house was quiet. Hurrying back, she lifted the lid of the canvas-covered trunk at the foot of the bed and rifled through the books she and Geoff had shared. Just the sight of the leather-bound, gold-stamped volumes of Tennyson and the *Rubáiyát* made her eyes sting.

Memories, but no letter.

Short of looking under his mattress, Shelby could only turn to the one other trunk that Geoff still kept in his bedroom, for the others were stored now in the barn loft. This was a huge, magnificent wardrobe trunk, standing on end in the corner by the bureau, and it was open a few inches . . . beckoning her to explore. Tentatively, she pushed the two sides farther apart, awed by the Louis Vuitton trunk's expensive interior.

One side featured a brass bar on which were hung various tweed suits, apparently designed for shooting and other sports, jodhpurs for riding, smoking jackets, and handsome gabardine trousers and wool jackets. The rest of the wardrobe trunk was made up of compartments for such necessities as different styles of hats—boater, fedora, and even one of beaver lined with sheepskin—pajamas and silk dressing gowns, handmade shoes, and accessories, including braces, collars and cuffs, ties, gloves, and driving goggles with glass lenses, made of buff leather.

Shelby's palms were damp with anxiety. She was ready to give up when she pulled open a last built-in drawer and discovered stacks of personal items. There was jewelry: a gold watch and cuff links, and a signet ring engraved with the Earl of Sandhurst's crest. A slate-gray ribbon bound photographs of people whom Shelby assumed were family members, and letters. One had come to him a few days ago in Cody, and the paper was engraved with the crest of the Duke of Aylesbury. The terse missive was signed only "Your Father."

Shelby was just about to run out of the room to safety when she glimpsed, stuck in the side of the compartment, the ivory envelope from that morning. *It's going to change everything,* she thought, but freed the heavy pieces of paper and unfolded them with shaking fingers.

> My dear Sandhurst,
>
> I find it impossibly dreary that you've gone to that place at the end of the world, but I suppose I shall have to adjust. What do you *do* there all day? The one comfort is that there are doubtless plenty of horses. If you find one to bring me as a wedding present, I imagine it would be a tremendous conversation piece. Perhaps we could have it properly trained and race it at Ascot . . .

The rest of the letter blurred before Shelby's eyes as one word rang in her mind: *wedding*. But no—Clementine Beech hadn't *named* her future bridegroom, had she? Clinging to a thin reed of hope, Shelby read on:

> I'm wretched at letter-writing, darling, but I saw your mother yesterday and she urged me to dash off a note to you. It wouldn't do for you to forget me, would it? At least I am consoled by the fact that there are more

horses than females in Wyoming, hmm? I've no doubt that you'll come home to me, and sooner than you think. You're an Englishman, Geoffrey dear, and a nobleman, and you belong here. Mummy longs to begin planning a Christmas wedding. I must run now. We're trying a new course for field trials this afternoon and I've a new gelding to ride. Gloucestershire is lovelier than ever . . .

Your own Clementine

"Damn!" Shelby whispered as she digested the harsh facts dished out by Lady Clementine Beech. A heavy weight of despair pressed her heart. And yet, in spite of the bitter disappointment, she was grateful for the truth. If she kept trying not to think about the real life that was waiting for Geoff back in England, she'd only be more devastated in the end.

After all, it couldn't really be possible that her recent bliss could be pure and unfettered, could it? she asked herself. She had been a practical person since babyhood. Perhaps it was better to know how matters really stood, and then she could guard herself a bit more carefully, against the day when Geoff would go away.

Still, it hurt. Tears burned Shelby's throat and her thoughts tangled in confusion. *Could real love be turned off like a faucet?*

"Ah-hemmm!" The sound of Manypenny loudly clearing his throat rumbled from the hallway, jolting Shelby back to reality. It almost seemed that he was warning her of his approach, and she barely had time to stuff the pages back into the envelope and push it into the wardrobe compartment. Flushed with panic, she looked around for the feather duster and grabbed it just as the elderly manservant appeared in the doorway. He merely regarded her, tilting his big head slightly to one side—knowingly, Shelby thought.

"I—I was just—dusting!" she exclaimed, and flicked the feather duster to and fro over Geoff's trunk with exaggerated vigor. But the room was already spotless.

"Miss Matthews," he intoned, each weighted word bone-dry, "if you felt that it was necessary to make a special effort to put my master's bedchamber . . . in order, then I can only hope that you accomplished your objective."

She scurried past him, cheeks burning, and paused to dust the door frame. "Every now and then I feel the urge to do something domestic. . . ."

"Of course you do. And that is your right." After a moment's effective silence, Manypenny added, "I came to tell you that we appear to have a visitor. He won't come down from his conveyance, but he is making a great deal of noise, and I thought you should be informed." The Englishman watched the blood drain from Shelby's cheeks before he added, "Although I have not been formally introduced, my powers of deduction suggest that our caller is the knavish Mr. Croll."

"I'd like to know where you was last night, limey!" Bart Croll was shouting at Geoff as Shelby came running out of the house. When he gestured with a fist, he nearly struck his wife, who cowered beside him on the buckboard seat.

"Are you accusing Mr. Weston of a crime?" countered Titus, who had just come from the corral to join Geoff and Ben on the ground. "If so, why not come to the point? Make your charges and state your proof."

The weatherbeaten old man narrowed his eyes. "I don't got proof, I got suspicions." He looked at Geoff again. "Why didn't you come t'the poker game in Cody?"

"Me an' Titus got home from Billings last night," Ben put in. "Geoff was ready to go, but he gave it up when we came."

"You should be glad, Mr. Croll!" Shelby said, laughing. "After all, the last time Geoff played poker in Cody, he won half our ranch! He's dangerously good." As she spoke she glanced over at Vivian Croll, who couldn't take her eyes off her. "I don't believe we've met, Mrs. Croll." Warmly, Shelby reached up to clasp the older woman's hand. "My name is Shelby Matthews and it's a pleasure to meet you. Would you like to come in for a cup of tea?"

"No!" her husband barked, and Vivian flinched. "She don't need any of your goldurned fancy *tea*!"

Geoff spoke at last. "Mr. Croll, I'm curious to know what exactly it is you suspect me of *doing* last night . . . ?"

"I—well—" he muttered, eyes darting furtively, "I'm missin' some cattle."

"Really! Then we *share* that problem! Perhaps there's a rustler at work in the area. Will you inform Marshal Burns?"

"Nah. Can't prove nothin'. I, uh, hadn't branded 'em yet."

"Were they calves, then?"

"I gotta get home now. Viv's got chores t'do." Bart Croll slapped the reins on the horses' backs and they lurched forward, circling the yard and starting back down the drive toward the road.

"Good-bye!" Shelby, Geoff, Ben, and Titus called in unison.

Only Vivian Croll turned back, daring to raise a hand to wave farewell. Even from a distance her expression was tragic, and Shelby understood why Geoff had been so moved by her plight. She looked up at him now, Clementine Beech forgotten in the midst this present drama, and saw that his brown eyes were agleam with emotion.

"She didn't tell him," Geoff said softly to no one in particular. "Last night, Vivian came out—virtually caught me on their land—and I told her the truth. She even had a gun, but when she heard my story, she agreed that we were right. She hates him." He sighed. "I was afraid that he would break her with his threats, or worse, but she must be stronger than she looks."

"It's more than just hatred that Vivian feels," Shelby cried, seizing on this distraction from her own heartache. "She's afraid! We'll have to find a way to help her."

"Yeah, right, and probably get ourselves killed for tryin'!" Ben said with a derisive snort. "Bart Croll and his cousin Ted don't give a damn about killin' folks who step on their toes. I should of known that you'd find a way to get on his bad side while my back was turned! If there's trouble, you find it, and now you're takin' Geoff with you." He shook his head of sandy hair. "I'm tellin' you, Shel, you can't mess with that man's *wife*. He lives by the laws of the *West*, an' he'll shoot you as soon as look at you."

PART TWO

What of soul was left, I wonder,
when the kissing had to stop?
—Robert Browning

Chapter Eleven

THE RETURN OF BEN, TITUS, AND JIMMY BROUGHT work back to the forefront of ranch life. The first roundup, which should have started a week ago, commenced immediately.

Spring would no longer be denied, and when Geoff rode his buckskin gelding over the ranch at dawn, he was enchanted by his surroundings. Birds had returned for the summer, and the thickets were crowded with them. Meanwhile, the skylark and white-shouldered lark bunting sang while soaring overhead against the rosy sky. Shelby could identify these and other calls Geoff had never heard before, and sometimes he rode with her so that she could teach him to separate the songs of the bluebird, the mountain chickadee, the sage thrasher, the robin, and the raucous pinyon jay.

More often, though, there was too much work to indulge in such pleasures. Geoff could only try to soak up the beauty of the sunrise, the staggering silhouette of the mountains behind the river, the prairie roses carpeting the ranchland, and the heady mixture of fragrances carried on the breeze. Always, in the back of his mind, was the realization that it couldn't last. When next year's spring unfolded in Wyoming, the Earl of Sandhurst would be back in England, doing his duty.

The roundup would last perhaps a month. If they had

more cattle, it would take six weeks, but then again, they were new at this business, and every steer they owned had to be searched out of the hillocks and coulees and thickets and bogs, then branded against its will. Jimmy, Cal, Marsh, and Lucius knew more about this procedure than their employers, and Geoff was the first to acknowledge it. With Cal's advice, he signed on a few more hands to get them through the roundup. Then, on a whim, he brought a cook—inventively called Cookie—out to the ranch to help with meals so that Shelby could do what she loved best: chase cattle all over the ranch and beyond. These were generous indulgences that further softened Ben Avery's heart toward the Englishman.

All this activity helped to keep Geoff and Shelby from dealing with each other—and the consequences of their night of passion. They all rode and roped until they cared only about a hot meal and a bed, with little or no energy remaining for emotions. However, even if the roundup hadn't intervened, Geoff had been permanently unsettled by the arrival of Lady Clem's letter. It was like a thorn, sticking his mind and his heart. The letter—and the memory of Shelby's expression as she watched him accept it just hours after their lovemaking—made him realize that it was no use pretending that his other life didn't exist.

On the contrary, it seemed to be shadowing him. Geoff spent a lot of time pondering this bristly situation while hunting down strays at the base of the mountains. He felt certain that Clemmie hadn't meant any harm, sending that letter to him here. However, his mother might have guessed that he was communing with more than horses in Wyoming. The Duchess of Aylesbury never did anything by chance, and her suggestion to her son's fiancée that she write had not been made on a whim.

That sort of long-distance interference was particularly annoying. The discreet machinations practiced by people like his parents was one of the reasons Geoff had begun to chafe against the constraints of his life in London. Couldn't he escape even in Wyoming's Bighorn Basin?

Or was Lady Clem's letter gnawing at him for a different reason? As he chased down a rebellious steer and prepared to throw the noose of his lasso over the animal's horns, Geoff reflected that the basis for his ill humor might well be guilt. Was it fair to blame Clementine or his mother, when he was the one who had made love to Shelby? He was a cad to have drawn so close to her without being courageous enough to tell her the truth.

This is a different world, he protested on his own behalf, and I'm not the Earl of Sandhurst here! His conscience, however, was quick to retort, This isn't the real world for you—but it is for Shelby! You made her a part of your fantasy, and she'll end with her heart dashed!

And indeed, when he headed back to the barn at midday with the two steers he'd turned up, Geoff saw Shelby straddling the corral fence, staring at him as he approached. He had to shade his eyes against her radiance, but there wasn't a way to shade his heart.

Throwing herself into the exciting, strenuous work of the roundup, Shelby had cast off her split skirts and high-necked blouses and now charged out of the house each dawn clad in denim pants, boots, and a shirt made of either a plain cotton or flannel, tucked in. These garments fit her in a way that made Geoff badly want to hold her; to run his hands over the curves of her hips and bottom and breasts and the length of her back. Some days, when she was working a lot in the corral,

Shelby even wore leather bat-wing chaps, and they looked terrific buckled around her pretty hips. The blue bandanna around her neck set off her teal eyes and sun-pinkened cheeks. Her fair skin would have been burned if not for the protective brim of her dusty white Stetson, and she'd taken to braiding her hair into one thick plait that emerged from the back of her hat, hung down her back, and flicked to and fro when she moved.

In short, Shelby was more beguiling than ever. And she had changed, though Geoff would have preferred to deny it. Depending upon the moment, when she looked at him, Geoff was liable to see either new vulnerability . . . or defiance in her eyes. The rest of the time, Shelby's guard was up, and she joked with him as easily as she did the other men. Her attitude said, I'm fine—I'm looking ahead—no regrets—don't worry about me—let's just forget it ever happened.

As Geoff rode closer to the corral, he realized that he not only couldn't forget, he didn't want to. He was hungry for her still, and those yearnings brought more guilt.

"Hey!" Shelby called, flashing her broadest smile. "You're back just in time to help plant the first rows of crops! Ben wants to start the hay and grain after we eat. Now that summer's coming, we decided that we can't afford to wait until roundup's over."

Geoff pushed back his hat, swabbed his brow with a black kerchief, and replied wryly, "God forbid we should have any leisure time, hmm?"

"What would we do with it, anyway?" Shelby willed herself not to blush. "A person can play records like 'My Bonnie' and 'Listen to the Mockingbird' just so many times."

"I imagine you're bored with dancing, since all the men want to practice with you. Evenings, I half expect to find Manypenny in line behind Titus and Ben and all the boys." He wished he could shut up. Did she think he was shameless? "I suppose that the novelty of dancing must be wearing off."

"No." Shelby shrugged, her chin raised in the manner of a child fighting back tears. "I thought you were the one who had grown bored with dancing. You watch the rest of us as if we're quite bourgeois."

Charlie nickered to her and stepped forward to nuzzle her hand. Geoff wanted to reach out himself, now that his horse had brought him within touching distance, but there was a warning gleam in Shelby's eyes. Cookie came out on the veranda then and rang a big bell to summon everyone into the house for noon dinner.

"Good!" Shelby cried with visible relief. She jumped to the ground, enjoying the agility afforded her by pants. "I'm starving!" After a pause to stroke Charlie's face and kiss his big horsey mouth, she ran toward the house without another word to Geoff.

He wished he could call to her and say, laughing, that she became more of a scamp with each passing day. Those times were over, though. Geoff blamed himself for spoiling their friendship.

June rolled in on a wave of sunshine, and the men began building a second barn. Not only did they need it for their added horses and cattle, but also to house the new farm equipment, and eventually to store the supplemental feed crops when they were harvested.

It was an exciting time. Their first spring roundup was finished off with the branding of the calves born in the past few weeks. The Sunshine Ranch was growing; thriving in spite of the fact that Shelby had lost half of it to an Englishman.

She had decided that God had brought them all this activity for a reason. The physical work and the excitement of making something new brought Shelby happiness at a time when she would have otherwise been very blue. Putting on pants and rolling up her sleeves every morning, then sweating during the day, gave her a lot of pleasure and kept her from thinking too much about Geoff and her heartache. There was nothing she could do to change what was real: his title, his life in England, and his wedding, which was being planned by Lady Clementine Beech at that very moment.

Shelby also turned her thoughts to Vivian Croll, particularly when Ben brought home some stray mongrel puppies he'd found on the road to Cody. Who better to adopt one of the orphans than a lonely mail-order bride?

One Thursday afternoon, she tucked the curly gray pup into a carpet bag, attached it to her saddle, and waited on the road until she saw Bart ride off to his poker game in town. Reaching the pitiful sod house, Shelby found Vivian planting flower seeds in newly turned earth by the door. When she heard her visitor ride up, the girl got to her feet and wiped her hands on a threadbare apron.

"Miss Matthews! What a surprise!"

Shelby dismounted, untied the carpet bag, and dared to give Vivian a momentary hug. "I've been wanting to come for days. I get terribly lonely with all those men at the ranch, and I hope that you and I can be great friends."

"I don't think Bart wants me to entertain." She looked down.

"We'll find ways around that," Shelby assured her. "Even today, I knew he was going out and I just waited. I'm pretty crafty when the need arises!" Trying to think of something cheerful to say about the dusty, depressing house, she pointed to the new garden. "What kinds of flowers are you planting?"

"Just some wildflower seeds Mr. Schwoob gave me. Bart wouldn't like me wasting my time on something so silly, when there are more chores to do than I can finish in a lifetime."

The more Shelby heard about the awful Mr. Croll, the more upset she felt, but what could be done? For the moment, all Shelby could offer was her friendship. They went inside, where Vivian poured weak tea for her guest and showed her the tablecloth she embroidered whenever Bart was away. Nearby, a basket overflowed with mending that must have been saved for all of Croll's bachelorhood.

"I allow myself a few minutes' work on the tablecloth for every sock or handkerchief I patch," Viv explained.

"I know I don't have any right to comment on your life or marriage, but . . . don't you think he's being a bit hard on you?"

Her eyes pooled with tears and she looked away again. "There's nothing I can do."

Nor, it seemed, could Shelby; at least, not yet. "Well, you have a friend now—me!" A warm smile lit her face as she reached into the carpet bag. "And I've brought you a present."

Vivian began to weep with joy when Shelby put the puppy into her arms. He wriggled and licked her hands, then her face, while Shelby explained his origins.

"We have no way of knowing what sort of dog he is, but Uncle Ben guesses he won't grow terribly large." She laughed, adding, "This seems to be a case of love at first sight!"

"Oh, Shelby, no one has ever brought me such a wonderful gift! He is the sweetest thing ever! I shall call him Willy, after my little brother who died." Cuddling the puppy closer, she crooned, "Willy-boy, do you love me? I think so! And I love you!"

Tears stung Shelby's own eyes. "I'd better get back now. At least, I don't have to worry that you'll be lonely anymore."

In the doorway, Willy in her arms, Vivian bit her lip and turned pale again. "I just hope that Bart lets me keep him. . . ."

"He'd better! If he is that cruel, I want you to bring Willy to me, and stay yourself!" Her eyes met those of her friend. "We women have to stick together out here," Shelby said, smiling. "I know we don't know each other well, but I think some people are meant to be friends. If you need me you must let me know."

"That's kind of you, but my first loyalty is to Bart."

"But, if he isn't kind to you—" There was so much about this situation that Shelby simply couldn't fathom, and she had to struggle not to be impatient.

Viv glanced away. "I'm his wife."

At least, as she rode home, Shelby could console herself with the knowledge that Willy would bring some affection and pleasure into Viv's barren life. Besides, who was she to judge anyone for settling for crumbs, or living with heartache? She was hardly a paragon herself.

As always, her thoughts returned to Geoff and the feelings that continued to percolate inside her. She tried not to give them a name, and thankfully was so bone-tired again that night that she didn't lie awake pondering the mystery of the human heart.

It helped to realize that Geoff probably didn't understand any more than she did. Just because he had a lot more experience, that didn't mean he knew about . . . *love.*

Maybe he hurt, too.

* * *

As the weeks passed, Shelby's thoughts continued to circle on the prickly topic of love, and she searched for distractions. Ben seemed to sniff out a bit of what was in the air, and helped by bringing Shelby a gift. It was a beautiful .32 caliber Remington rifle with a walnut fore end and stock. Prodded by her uncle, she began trying some tricks—chiefly aiming at rocks that Ben would throw into the air. Someday, he said, he'd get some glass balls, like the kind Annie Oakley blasted to smithereens.

By late June, Shelby had worked her way up to hitting every third rock. Ben was coaching her, tossing rocks and whooping with excitement one sunny afternoon, when Geoff passed on his way to the barn.

"I see you're making progress," the Englishman remarked, pausing to chat.

"Shel's got talent, no doubt about that," Ben bragged. "I'm gonna get us a mirror and start her practicing that trick Annie Oakley's famous for—the one where she's looking into a mirror and shootin' over her shoulder at a far-off target!"

When Geoff looked to Shelby for a reaction to her uncle's plans, she shrugged and smiled. "It's something to do to pass the time. We can't work unceasingly, after all. And . . . this is fun." Her eyes said that it could be a lot more fun if Geoff were involved rather than Uncle Ben. How they'd laughed the day they'd practiced rope tricks and shooting together!

"That's a beautiful rifle." Geoff's tone was affable.

"Well, I had to do something to prod Shel into showin' some enthusiasm around here," Ben said. "She was starting to act like my sister, all domestic and dreamy-eyed. I even caught her lookin' at all those fancy dresses in *Harper's Bazaar* one afternoon! I'm just relieved she hasn't gone completely soft yet." He gave her a teasing poke in the ribs, but Shelby was blushing.

"Mama sent that fashion book to me. How could I not look at it?"

"For Pete's sake, I was just havin' some fun with you! Since when are you so sensitive? Don't worry, Shel, I don't really think you're going to put on airs anytime soon, 'cause you've been a flat-out hellion since the day you were born. Remember what Gran Annie used to call you? *Incorrigible.*" He reared back and laughed at that, but Shelby seemed to be fuming and embarrassed under the brim of her Stetson.

"I really appreciate the compliments and praise, Uncle Ben."

Geoff watched them with a faint crease in his brow, waiting for a chance to speak. "If I leave you two, will you promise to make up and be nice to one another? Good enough. I'm off to Cody for the remainder of the afternoon."

"You gonna pick up the disk harrow Jakie's got in?" Ben asked. "I think there's room for it in the new barn now. It's got that seeder attachment, and we sure could use it."

Geoff nodded. "I thought I might, yes. And Cookie's given me a list of supplies." He paused a moment before adding, "Since the last newborn calf was branded this morning, Cookie was wondering how much longer we'll need him and the other extra hands. I said that I thought the other boys would go when the barn is finished this week, but I didn't know if Shelby would want to return to the kitchen or not. . . ."

When Ben started to answer for her, Shelby threw him a warning glance. "I would like to think it over. I admit that I do love being outdoors, unrestricted, all day long. If I took over Cookie's duties again, Uncle Ben, I shouldn't have so much time for shooting practice."

"Yeah. You got a point there—but can we afford t'keep Cookie?"

Geoff gazed into Shelby's eyes for a moment and gave her a tender smile. "We can afford anything that makes your niece happy." He drew on his gloves then and went off to hitch up the wagon.

Ben Avery looked puzzled. "What's he talkin' about, Shel? I keep having the feelin' that there's something I don't know. Are you two sweet on each other? Titus mentioned it to me, but I told him he was crazy, 'cause you wanted to run Geoff off the ranch!"

Her heart ached so much that she couldn't answer. Instead she just shook her head and set about reloading the rifle, all the while avoiding her uncle's eyes.

The new little town of Cody wore summer well. The trains were running nearly on schedule, the telephone lines were working, the new Methodist-Episcopal church was finished, and the Irma Hotel was scheduled to open in the fall.

Dr. Louis Howe's recently arrived trio of lovely daughters were the most popular subject for discussion in Purcell's Saloon. The married men, however, were more inclined to wonder if the road to Yellowstone Park would be open in July, as planned. Geoff kept his ears open as he slowly drank a beer at the bar, and heard many a conversation turn to rustling. Cattle had been stolen from the Allison ranch, but the identity of the thief hadn't been determined. Meanwhile, James Doyle, another supposed rustler, had been arrested and skipped the country after forfeiting his bond.

"People won't put up with it anymore," muttered one North Fork rancher. "I'm thinkin' of runnin' an ad in the *Enterprise*, with a promise to kill any man I catch on my land. Maybe if we keep the heat on Marshal Burns, and he keeps on arrestin' the criminals, they'll quit completely."

"What's happened to Deputy Ted?" Geoff asked casually.

The man snorted and paused in the midst of licking a cigarette paper. "People started sayin' things about him, and he left town. I heard he went to Sheridan. Good riddance, I say. Now if his sour-faced cousin'd leave, too, we'd all be better off."

Ironically, Geoff saw Bart Croll when he emerged from the saloon. He and Vivian were loading boxes onto the back of their rickety buckboard, and Bart abruptly shouted something at his wife in a voice so shrill that it carried down the block to Geoff. The Cody Trading Company had been his destination anyway, so he quickened his pace, arriving just in time to see Croll grab Vivian by the arm and twist her around to face him.

"You silly *idiot*! What were you thinkin', setting that box down on my finger? Do you think you can get away with it just because we're in public?" His eyes blazed like hot coals.

"Croll, unhand the lady." Geoff had come up behind him, quietly, and spoke in a cold, vaguely menacing voice. "You're hurting her—and frightening her—and I won't have it."

"Oh, you *won't*, won't you?" Oozing sarcasm, the older man dropped Vivian's arm only because he'd shifted his attention to Geoff. "And how come you got this sudden interest in my wife, limey?"

"I'm interested in helping anyone who is being mistreated." He noticed then that the gray puppy adopted by Vivian was sitting on the buckboard seat, staring worriedly at Bart. Geoff reached out to pet him even as he continued the confrontation with Croll. "Your wife is a fine lady, and I won't stand by and watch you browbeat her."

"A *lady*? Geez-us, have you got that wrong!" The old man sneered. "Nothin' you kin do about it, anyway. She's my wife."

Viv took that opportunity to clamber into the buckboard and take Willy onto her lap, her hands trembling all the while.

"People don't own one another," Geoff said coolly. "Furthermore, I think, in view of your cousin's departure from the marshal's office, there are numerous actions I could take against you. If you're wise, you won't force me to make that decision." With those ominous parting words, Geoff took in Viv's grateful look, turned away and went into the Cody Trading Company. Not until he was well inside and shielded by a display case did he venture to peer around a corner at his nemesis. Geoff's mouth curved slightly as he watched Bart Croll climb up beside his wife. Whatever words he spoke were rewarded by a tentative smile from the beleaguered woman.

"Somebody ought to put that vermin out of his misery," a voice said at Geoff's shoulder.

He glanced around to find Jakie Schwoob watching the couple in the buckboard and shaking his head. "If it were just Croll, I might be able to tolerate him, but my heart goes out to his wife," Geoff replied. "She's a lovely woman."

"I know." Jakie sighed heavily, then turned away to watch another customer. "It's a sad business. Oh, by the way, I have something to show you."

Geoff gathered the supplies on Cookie's list, had them boxed to load beside the disk harrow, then sought out Schwoob. “All right, you’ve piqued my curiosity. What’s the surprise?”

Schwoob left the other customer to choose among several packages of buttons, and led Geoff to the back of the big store. “First, I have a new record for you. I hear it’s all the rage in the East—called ‘In the Good Old Summertime’! Shelby’ll love it.”

Smiling in spite of the pang he felt, remembering, Geoff accepted the record, then inclined his head. “And secondly?”

Jakie threw open the door to his storeroom, illuminating five new bicycles lined along one wall. He gestured with a flourish. “Aren’t they handsome? The finest models in production today; they’re called the Napoleon and Josephine bicycles!” He was beaming from ear to ear.

Geoff listened to the sales speech about the bicycles’ three-crown flush nickel-jointed construction, the Morgan and Wright double-tube pneumatic tires with piano wire spokes, and the latest 1902 design frame, forks, and sprocket. The Napoleon model was painted black, and the Josephine had a maroon finish. Finally, when he couldn’t bear another excessive word, Geoff interrupted. “Save your breath, Jakie. I’ll take them both.”

“You will? Shelby’ll love them! They’re only sixteen dollars a piece, which is a bargain for the highest quality—”

“I know!” They started back into the store, and Geoff began to list some other items he wanted Schwoob to order for the ranch. Cookie was longing for a fancy butter churn, and Geoff had decided to purchase a hay loader, a windmill, a horse-powered grain thresher . . . and a piano. “I noticed Shelby looking at the pianos in the Sears Wishbook,” he explained. “I wrote down the one I’d like, based on those.”

"Seems like you're pretty smitten with that girl. Takes a good man to look past her rambunctious ways and see the lady underneath. . . ."

"Do you think so? I liked her immediately, precisely because she is *not* like all the other ladies."

Standing at the counter and adding up Geoff's purchases, Schwoob glanced up. "Really! Do you think your kin in England would feel the same way?"

"We'll never know, my friend. Shelby is adamant about her freedom, and staying on the Sunshine Ranch. I, on the other hand, was born to a more restrictive life. Beyond one brief escape like this year in Wyoming, I'm not able to choose my fate the way Shelby can." He arched an eyebrow and smiled. "Life is not always fair, hmm?"

This was a situation Jakie Schwoob didn't understand, so he fell silent, totaling the day's purchases and writing up an order for the upright parlor grand piano. Meanwhile, a pretty young female customer sidled up next to Geoff and gave him a smile that could only be categorized as suggestive.

"How do you do, sir?" she murmured, allowing her breast to brush his arm. "Will you think me terribly bold if I confess that I overheard a few of your remarks about your ill-fated romance?"

Amusement played over Geoff's mouth. "Have we met, miss?"

"My name is Etta Feeley." Her smile widened knowingly, and she almost seemed to wink while looking him over with highly appreciative eyes. "My friends and I have been *dying* to ask you to visit us, your lordship."

"I'm Geoffrey Weston," he supplied, and accepted her outstretched, perfumed hand for only a moment. "I must tell you in all candor that I cannot accept your invitation, but I do thank you—and your friends—for asking."

Jakie Schwoob gave his friend a wild look to remind

him that Etta Feeley was the town's principal madame. Then he said to her, "Miss Feeley, I can't have you making those invitations in my store. When you come in here, you have to be . . . discreet."

Abashed, Etta colored and replied, "Why, I thought I *was* being discreet!"

Geoff couldn't help laughing at that, and Jakie soon joined in, in spite of himself. Etta Feeley was a good sport and didn't take offense.

At six-thirty the sun was still hot overhead, and the ranch hands went back outside to work when supper was finished. Now that the roundup was officially over, everyone was concentrating on the new barn and their fledgling crops.

Shelby went to her bedroom for a bath, glad for Cookie's help in the kitchen and her own freedom from domesticity. Even Manypenny seemed to be enjoying his new life on the ranch now that he was fully recovered from his illness. He had made no attempt whatever to take up his old servile routine again, and Geoff never complained. Manypenny now spent most of his waking hours rocking on the veranda, reading, dozing, and admiring the dramatic landscape.

Shelby pumped water for her bath at the kitchen sink and was carrying in the last bucketful when she encountered Manypenny in the hallway. He was coming out of his bedroom with a copy of *The Red Badge of Courage*, tieless and very nearly relaxed. "It's a perfect summer evening, don't you think?" she murmured with a smile.

"Indeed it is. I never expected to become so fond of Wyoming . . . or this ranch," he confessed.

In her big bedroom, Shelby put her new folding bathtub to good use. It featured a built-in heater for the water, and she had spent many a contented hour soaking away the dust and exhaustion of the day's work.

A clock in another part of the house struck seven, rousing Shelby, and she emerged from the tub, wrapping herself in a robe and her wet hair in a towel. She had just patted on powder and slipped into a fresh blouse when she heard a knock at her window. At first Shelby thought she was hearing things—or perhaps it was a jay, breaking open a seed. But when the sound came again, she hurriedly pulled on a pair of denim pants and drew back the curtain.

There was Geoff, balancing on a shiny new bicycle, waving to her. "Come out for a ride," he called.

How irresistible he was, eyes twinkling, the sleeves of his pin-striped shirt rolled up, his Stetson replaced by a straw boater set at a jaunty angle. And Shelby couldn't resist. She didn't allow herself to even think, but finished dressing and quickly pinned her damp hair atop her head before dashing through the house to meet him. Manypenny watched with a dubious smile as Shelby emerged onto the veranda and saw the gramophone perched on the top step. Round and round went the new record while a tenor voice sang, "*In the good old summertime, in the good old summertime . . . Strolling through the shady lanes with your baby mine . . .*"

It was like a dream. Geoff steadied the bicycle with one foot on the ground and extended his arms to welcome her. Shelby had no qualms about sitting between his legs, sidesaddle on the bar, and if Manypenny hadn't been watching from the veranda, she might have turned her face up to his for more than a smile.

When they set off, the bicycle wobbled precariously, and Shelby's excited laughter was music to Geoff's ears. Gradually, as they gained speed and the threat of toppling over at any moment passed, Geoff let go of the handlebars with one hand and wrapped it around Shelby's little waist.

It came to him then how much existed between them. Shelby was a tremendous friend, great fun, wonderful to talk to, and he'd missed her. Just the sensation of her body against his, as she had been the night they'd ridden Charlie home from the rustling adventure, was profoundly satisfying. Her damp hair was scented from her bath, and her ear and neck were alluringly moist when his face touched her there.

The last strains of the song came to them from the veranda: "*You hold her hand and she holds yours, and that's a very good sign . . . That she'll be your tootsey wootsey in the good old summer-time!*" They rolled down the lane to the valley road, passed under the crude wooden arch that bore a carving of the Sunshine Ranch brand, and turned south, following a row of quaking aspen.

"I surmise that 'tootsie wootsie' is an American endearment," Geoff remarked at length.

"Well, perhaps it comes from New York," she allowed with a straight face. Then, unable to restrain herself, Shelby added, "This bicycle is just splendid. How do you hatch these ideas?" All the unspoken difficulties that had stood between them in recent weeks were swept away on the warm evening breeze.

"Jakie Schwoob suggested it. . . ." His cheek rested against her hair. "Would you be angry if I told you that I actually bought you your own ladies' bicycle . . . but I gave it away on a whim?"

"To Vivian Croll?"

"You and I think alike." Geoff steered the front tire around a rock, then related the story of his confrontation with Bart Croll that day. "I think I must have been having some sort of heat stroke during the trip back here, because it suddenly came to me that Vivian should have a bicycle—that perhaps it might bring her some pleasure. The idea that we might somehow help her to smile is hard to resist."

"I certainly don't mind riding a man's bicycle—and I hope you're right about Vivian. Maybe I'll send a note to ask if she wants to practice with me." She fell silent for a bit then, and they both soaked up their own pleasure. There was something mysteriously thrilling about the way he balanced her on the bicycle bar, his long-muscled equestrian's legs pumping smoothly so that she no longer feared they might tip over. "Do you know, I've never ridden a bicycle before! I've always wanted to, but Deadwood is built on the walls of a canyon, and my family's house is on a street that goes nearly straight up and down."

"I'm glad, then, that this bicycle turned up for us. You and I both needed a bit of fun. And we needed to laugh . . . together." When they were a mile or more down the road, well out of sight of the ranch house and corral, Geoff let the bicycle coast for a bit, gradually dropping his feet down for balance.

They came to a standstill, and Shelby leaned back into the familiar contours of his chest, her eyes closed against a wave of bittersweet happiness. He wrapped his arms around her. It was good to feel the thin cotton of her blouse and the warm, firm flesh of her upper arms.

"I've been missing you, scamp."

His tender tone made her eyes sting. Turning, Shelby let her upper body meld with Geoff's, wrapping her arms around his neck, burying her face in the hard strength of his shoulder, breathing in his mixture of Trumper's and Wyoming scents. Words failed her.

Geoff's hands traveled over her back as if committing her to memory. Through the fabric of Shelby's blouse, he discerned a delicately ribbed undergarment identical to the one she'd worn to bed with him. He wanted to cup her breasts again, to kiss them, to feel her nipples pucker against his tongue. Instead Geoff settled for tipping her face up and searching her eyes.

Shelby reached to touch his hair, gilded in the gathering twilight, and the side of his jaw. "I've been missing you, too."

His body urged him to put the bicycle down and lead her into a grove of trees. Was it passion or something more that gripped him so intensely he could taste it? Whatever it was, he had to rein himself in, or Shelby would never trust herself alone with him again. He forced himself to be gentle, to cradle her in his arms and kiss her with measured restraint.

But she felt the chemistry, too, and opened her mouth with a muffled groan. Her breasts tingled; a slow flush spread over her body. However, Shelby wasn't so enthralled that she couldn't sense that Geoff was holding back. Her women's instincts intervened to protect her.

When their mouths parted, Shelby made herself look into Geoff's hooded eyes. She saw the arousal, and the conflict, and knew that they must face reality together. "Oh, Geoff . . . there's someone waiting for you in England, isn't there?"

His head snapped back almost imperceptibly. *The letter—that's why it was half out of the compartment in my wardrobe trunk! Shelby knows.* He didn't fault her for searching. She'd done what she had to do to protect herself.

He sighed, and it burned his throat. "I'm afraid it's true." His fingers tangled in her hair. "I've had obligations since birth. But that doesn't mean it's what I want . . . or that I haven't begun to question the future others have planned for me."

Chapter Twelve

IN JULY THE ROAD FROM CODY TO YELLOWSTONE was finished and Geoff decided to spend a few weeks in the magnificent wilderness. A family friend had traveled there twenty-five years ago, and Geoff had never forgotten the stories he'd heard over London dinners as a child. (Only because the friend was spinning those tales, and the little boy had begged to hear them, had he been allowed to sit at the table with the adults.)

And, he had decided it might be a good idea to put some distance between himself and Shelby. Since the evening he'd taken her bicycle riding, Geoff felt more torn than ever about their relationship. If they just kept getting closer, wouldn't there be more pain in the end?

Yet, riding home one hot, windy afternoon at the end of July, following his days in the wilderness, Geoff dared to wonder if there might not be another answer. His time alone in Yellowstone had left him aching for Shelby. He wouldn't have to return to England for good until next spring . . . and now he considered the possibility that Shelby might love him enough to come back with him.

Perhaps he was just dreaming, he thought, instead of facing reality, for he had yet to figure out what to do about Lady Clem or his parents. He'd given his word that, after one year of travel, he would return and fulfill his obligations without complaint.

He just hadn't counted on Shelby—on emotions he'd believed weren't possible. Passing the entrance to William F. Cody's TE Ranch, he straightened in the saddle and urged Charlie to pick up his pace. The Sunshine Ranch wasn't far now.

It felt like coming home.

Furtively, Shelby leaned against the fireplace and studied the advertisement in her fashion book for the "Princess Bust Developer." Nearby, on the same page, was a drawing of a huge jar bearing a label that shouted, BUST CREAM OF FOOD—*Unrivaled for Enlargement of the Bust.* What sort of bosom did Lady Clementine Beech have? she wondered.

"What're you frowning at?" Ben Avery looked over her shoulder as he spoke, before she could slap the *Harper's Bazaar* closed. "Aw, geez, Shel—what would Maddie say if she could see you lookin' at stuff like that?"

Cheeks burning, Shelby tried to retain a semblance of composure. "Mama knows what it means to be a woman. She would probably be glad to know I'm thinking about something besides guns and horses."

He looked her over. "That's for sure. I can't figure out for the life of me what in the Sam Hill has got into you. One day you're out branding calves and struttin' around in pants, and the next day you start wearin' dresses and buying lace doilies to put on every table in the house!"

"I'm a girl, that's all. And these clothes are cooler than heavy denim trousers." Still blushing furiously, Shelby smoothed the creamy voile layers of her skirt and glanced at herself in the nearby mirror. She looked almost as good as the models in *Harper's Bazaar.* Her luxuriant dark red curls were perfect for the Gibson Girl style, unlike poor Vivian Croll's hair, which was too thin to hold together. Helping Vivian had been a good excuse for Shelby's own experiments with her appearance, and until now Ben hadn't grown suspicious.

"I never could figure out females," he muttered.

She gave him a wide smile. It was funny how keenly she'd felt Geoff's absence, for she'd never been particularly sentimental in the past. Shelby had tried to stay occupied by visiting Vivian, and Viv's cooking and sewing gradually piqued her interest in more feminine pursuits—those that had to do with making herself look more attractive and feathering the ranch house nest.

Then, almost immediately, Shelby began to fantasize about Geoff's homecoming. She imagined that he'd come through the door, stare at her, spellbound by her beauty, and then look around at the pretty touches she'd added to the house. There were bright bouquets of flowers on every table, lace doilies and tablecloths, new gingham curtains, and ruffled pillows. It might have been mistaken for a love nest . . . if not for all the other men around, and the fact that the absent Geoffrey Weston was betrothed to another woman.

But that last circumstance was cast aside in Shelby's fantasy, crushed by the force of true love. Each hot July night, she lay in bed under a sheet and spun her dreams. They all shared the same essence: Geoff would renounce his birthright, his title, his engagement, his country, his *obligations*—and stay with Shelby on *their* ranch, where he was happy. It was the only outcome that made sense, after all.

And after weeks of fantasy, reality seemed vague and uncertain.

"I gotta say this for you, Shel, you sure look pretty."

Ben touched the scalloped lace yoke and high collar on her dress and smiled. "In some ways, you're prettier than Maddie was at your age, because you're . . . lively. You've got a way about you she didn't have until she was older. Fox had to bring it out in her, I guess."

"Daddy is still the one person who understands what Mama is capable of," she agreed. "I wish we weren't so far away. I'd love to visit them right now."

"Yeah. You're just going through a phase, though, right?" His rugged face had a worried, little-boy look. "Titus says he thinks you're just checking to make sure you know how to be a girl, and that's fine, as long as you aren't givin' up on shooting and—"

"Don't worry, Uncle Ben, I won't give up my rifle. . . ." Her voice trailed off at the sound of an approaching horse. Shelby's heart skipped. Was it crazy to believe she could recognize Charlie's hoofbeats?

Ben stepped onto the veranda, leaving the screen door open, and she found that she couldn't move. Through the door frame, she saw the horse and rider, their coloring strikingly similar. The buckskin gelding looked a bit tired, but Geoff was more devastatingly handsome than ever, his good looks roughened by nearly a month spent in the sun and wind.

He handed Charlie's reins to Jimmy, who came with the others to welcome him back, then Geoff took off his hat and walked up the steps to shake hands with Ben Avery. Through the screen door, he saw Shelby watching, wide-eyed, and he smiled at her.

"What's happened to our sharpshooting, cowpunching Shelby?" he asked Ben. "Am I seeing things, or is she wearing a dress?"

Hope surged within her. She didn't hear her uncle's mocking reply, for all her senses were filled with Geoff. A ray of sunlight created an aura around him, burnishing his hair, which was curly with perspiration, picking up the twinkle in his eyes, the flash of his smile, the contrast between the brown of his arms and the blond hair that covered them; noticing every nuance of the way he inhabited his travel-worn clothing. No longer was Geoff a dude, for even the denim of his pants was faded and soft, skimming the hard contours of his body.

When the screen door opened and he came inside, Shelby knew that her heart was in her eyes. "Hello, Geoff."

"How did you know I was coming?" His voice was gently laced with amusement.

"Know?"

"I assume that you are decked out in this finery in honor of my homecoming . . .?"

Ben seemed to find this especially hilarious, throwing back his head to howl over the notion that his niece would dress up in honor of any man. Shelby blushed at first, but then irritation with Ben overtook all else and she gave him an elbow in the ribs. "You are impossible!"

"I forgot how funny Geoff can be," he gasped at length, red-faced. "Must be that English sense of humor."

Geoff regarded them both with a tentative smile, brows raised. "Clearly you've been lacking entertainment, old chap. I never meant to make a joke at Shelby's expense."

"I'll pour some lemonade," she said, and started toward the kitchen. "Perhaps we can sit down for a few minutes and you can tell us about your trip. How I envy you, traveling around Yellowstone Park!"

What the devil is this all about? Geoff wondered as he watched her go. Shelby was a vision in her simple dress of cream voile and lace, her dark cinnamon hair a luxuriant swirl atop her head. She was even wearing a corset that accentuated her breasts and the tiny span of her waist. He looked around and took in the doilies, pillows, and flowers.

Was this Shelby's way of telling him that she loved him enough to give up her freewheeling tomboy existence on the ranch, after all? That she could conform to the role of Countess of Sandhurst as long as they could be together? The mere thought flooded him with utter joy. It wouldn't be easy to get rid of Lady Clem, and his parents would surely balk, but perhaps there might be a way to get happiness for himself—if Shelby was truly willing to make the tremendous sacrifices that would be necessary. It would take time to convince her properly, but Geoff felt hope begin to bud.

He couldn't take his eyes off her as they sat down with glasses of lemonade and she cast her own eyes down in the manner of a shy, well-bred young lady.

"I should take a bath before I soil the house," Geoff said. "I must look a wreck."

"Not at all," she replied.

Ben cast a suspicious eye on both of them, but then Titus and Manypenny came in to hear about Yellowstone, and he was distracted. There was a lot of talk of water: spouting geysers; colorful, iridescent hot pools; the magnificent Yellowstone Lake, which Geoff described as being ultramarine in color; and the Tower Falls, which were said to descend 350 feet.

"I had heard about these sights and have even seen paintings," he said, "but being used to the gentler beauty of England, I truly could not imagine the . . . *grandeur* in advance." Geoff shook his head, still awestruck. "There are tourists coming in even by motor car now, so it's hardly a wilderness, yet one can get away.

The forests are dense, and the variety of animals is amazing. . . ."

Manypenny spoke up in nonchalant tones: "Isn't it sad that people have spoiled the place? I'll never forget my own visit there in 1863. Of course, there weren't roads then of any kind! We hoped to make a new trail in from the east, but were prevented from doing so by some Indian troubles. Instead, we approached from Bozeman Pass, descending into Yellowstone Valley. I must say that my first sight of the Yellowstone River struck me quite mute."

Everyone stared, agog, while Manypenny gazed off into space, smiling slightly at his memories. When Geoff found his voice, he cried, "Are you having us on, old fellow?"

He looked hurt. "Of course not."

"Why didn't you tell me you'd been here before?"

"It never came up, sir."

"But 1863 was nearly forty years ago. How old *are* you, Manypenny?"

In sonorous tones he replied, "Eighty-*two* on Sunday last, my lord."

"No wonder you're so fond of the rocking chair now!" Titus laughed. "Once you let yourself sit down, it must've been hard to get up again!"

"Quite," he agreed with a sniff.

While questions continued to pour out for Manypenny about his view of the West at the time of America's Civil War, Geoff happened to glance out the window in time to see a young man ride up to the house. He would have gone himself to see what the boy wanted, but as soon as the knock came at the door, Titus and Manypenny challenged each other to get there first.

"Don't move, sir," Titus said to Geoff, putting a hand on his shoulder. "I'll get it."

"I believe I should go," Manypenny countered with a frown. "It seems to be one of *my* duties."

When the two older men were out of earshot, Shelby said, "Those two have been rivals ever since Titus came back from Billings. Mr. Manypenny was so happy, rocking on the porch, until Titus began making remarks that seemed to imply that the old gentleman was lazy." She laughed fondly.

A moment later Titus came back around the corner of the kitchen area. "This fellow has a telegram for Mr. Weston!"

When Geoff emerged onto the veranda, escorted by Titus Pym, he found that Manypenny was guarding their visitor. The sunburned, gangly teenager said, "I'm supposed to deliver this to the Earl of Sandhurst. That you?"

"It is," Geoff replied with authority.

"Well, then—here." He turned over the telegram, and looked shocked when Geoff gave him a few coins in return. "Gee, thanks, Earl!"

Titus had wandered off to the new barn, and Manypenny returned to his rocking chair in the shade. Cold with dread, Geoff went to the other end of the veranda, near the kitchen window, and tore open the yellow-tinted paper.

It took him a full minute to make sense of what it said. His father, the duke, was seriously ill. He might die. Geoffrey was needed at home, and must return to England immediately.

He leaned against the log house and attempted to absorb the shock. *Home.* But . . . this was home! If he'd known, he would never have gone off this month; he'd have stayed right here, cherishing each hour, courting

Shelby properly so that she would want to spend the rest of her life with him.

His heart hurt at the thought of her. What could he do now? Was it possible that her dressing up of the house and herself *did* mean that she could give up the style of life she adored, and her home in Wyoming, out of love for him? Everything Shelby had ever said about needing freedom echoed in his memory. How many times had she insisted that she could never tolerate the posturing and pretensions of London society?

Ben Avery's agitated whisper carried out the window to him. "Shel, I gotta tell you that I can't believe what I'm seein' with you and Geoff!"

"Shh—he'll hear you!"

"He's gone outside, and I might not get another chance to let you know that you're makin' a fool of yourself! I didn't want you to be rude to the man, but that doesn't mean you should turn into a slobbering idiot, primping and sending for bust food and makin' calf eyes at him!"

"Uncle Ben!" she gasped.

"Hey, I bet I know what you're up to!" Abruptly, he sounded relieved. "I bet you're tryin' to get Geoff to marry you so you can get the ranch back!"

Shelby didn't answer at first, then spoke in an odd, hurried tone. "Well, I can think of worse reasons to marry, can't you? Now, hush up, before he hears you."

Rather than walk past the window and be seen, Geoff turned the other way and left the veranda. It wasn't until he was well away from the house, leaning against a cottonwood tree near the vegetable garden, that he allowed the tide of emotion to swell up from his heart. Tears like acid stung his eyes until he couldn't bear the pain any longer.

Geoff's old armor was still available; stored away,

but quite serviceable. He called it up, along with the mask he'd worn daily in his past life, and started back to the house.

Shelby was tidying the kitchen, avoiding Ben's accusatory eyes, when Geoff reentered the house. Worried about the contents of his telegram, she certainly hadn't had the energy to deal with her uncle's outburst.

She'd never been any good at acting, and unfortunately, Ben had known her since birth, so he was even harder to fool. His gender was a help, though. Even less perceptive and sensitive than most men, Ben seemed willing to be talked out of the notion that his niece was in love with Geoffrey Weston. With an effort, then, she managed to keep her manner offhand as she looked toward Geoff.

"Was your telegram important?"

"Rather."

A cold chill ran through her. This was a man she had never met before. It was as if he was only the shell of her Geoff, and Shelby realized immediately that it was not a momentary change. "Are you all right?"

"Not really." He was wearing his signet ring again, and twisted it back and forth. His jaw was hard; a muscle flicked there before he spoke again, in a more pronounced accent. "It seems that my father is quite ill. I'm afraid that I'll have to leave immediately . . . so, I am forced to bid you both good-bye."

Shelby gave a strangled gasp. Her teal-blue eyes were huge, horrified. "But—you can't just *go*! I mean—this ranch belongs to you, too!"

Even Ben looked stunned. "Shel's right, Geoff. We sure don't think of you as a visitor. . . ."

His gaze wandered here and there, anyplace but Shelby. Shrugging, he murmured, "Oh well, it can't be helped. I hadn't thought to leave so soon, but perhaps it's better this way—to go before any real attachments are formed, hmm?" At length, Geoff looked at Ben, adding, "You mustn't worry that I'll continue to claim half the ranch. It was an amusing diversion, but I'll sign my half back to Shelby before I go. It's only fair. I never would have kept it this long if I hadn't wanted to stay here with you all."

"I can't believe this!" Ben cried, beset by unaccustomed emotion. "I mean—it feels like you're family or somethin'! Are you just gonna go back to England and become a duke and forget all about us?"

Shelby blinked madly to keep back the tears, while Geoff went ashen. "No, I won't forget. . . ." he said, too calmly. "But I was born to another life, and I have no choice but to accept it and go on." He swallowed, then managed a wan smile. "Besides, I'm sure it's better to shove off now than to wear out my welcome, hmm? I'd better go tell Manypenny the news. He won't be happy, I'll wager. This means he'll have to start working again, beginning with the packing of my trunks."

Unable to speak, Shelby watched him turn away. She stood in front of the nickel-plated range, one tiny fist pressed to her mouth, trying to hold in an ocean of tears.

When Geoff and Manypenny left the Sunshine Ranch, Shelby stayed in bed, pleading a sick headache. She still couldn't bear to speak to Geoff for fear she'd sob hysterically and beg him not to leave her.

He was secretly relieved to be spared good-byes. What could they say to one another?

Geoff had let down his guard only once before leaving, and that was with Charlie, who would never tell anyone about the bitter tears that were shed during their last dawn ride over the ranch.

Finally, Ben and Titus took the two Englishmen and their mountain of luggage to Cody in the wagon, and it was a scene reminiscent of their arrival, except that the season had changed—and Shelby was missing. Lying in bed, she had waited for the sounds of the departing wagon to die away, and then rose and walked barefoot through the house.

Geoff's room looked like a monk's cell. Clothes, books, toiletries, and the wardrobe trunk with Lady Clementine's letter in it—everything he owned was gone. The only proof that Geoff had ever lived in this room was the faint scent of him, still in the air. Yearning and grief clenched at Shelby's insides. She crawled onto his bed, hugging his pillow, and let the tears come.

How could this have happened? How could she ever go back to life without him?

Shelby wept until she was spent, then went out into the hallway. Manypenny's room was bare, too, reminding her of the hours she'd spent there during his illness. It had been the beginning of the most unlikely friendship of her life. Was he hurt that she hadn't said goodbye?

Perhaps they'd come back. Some days the train just never arrived! Perhaps it might have been attacked and robbed by Butch Cassidy and the Sundance Kid and their Wild Bunch, in which case the train wouldn't be able to take Geoff and Manypenny away!

But when Shelby came into the eating area and saw the sheaf of papers lying on her new lace tablecloth, her heart knew the truth. Geoff didn't mean to return, even if the train was late. There were papers deeding his half of the ranch back to her, and a short letter that avoided sentiment until the very end. Geoff reminded her of their obligation to look out for Vivian Croll—"I trust you'll find a way to improve her situation, even without my help. Just be careful!"—asked her to take care of Charlie for him, and closed,

> Shelby, I have regrets about the way things turned out for us, but I'm too selfish to undo the past. We had some adventures and memorable experiences together, and I'd like to think our lives are better for them. I'll remember you with a smile, scamp . . . especially when I hear songs like "In the Good Old Summertime."

She looked around and saw that the gramophone was still on the little side table, left behind by its owner as a token of the past. Someone had put a certain record on the turntable, and Shelby knew what it would be.

There was no room for doubt: Geoff would not be coming back.

Chapter Thirteen

BUFFALO BILL WAS COMING TO CODY FOR THE grand opening of the Irma Hotel, which would take place on November 18, 1902, just four short days away. On the Saturday morning of Colonel Cody's arrival by train, it seemed that everyone in town was en route to the depot to greet him. Businesses and houses alike were decorated with bunting, flags, and portraits of the great man, and the neighboring town of Meeteetse had sent its cornet band and orchestra to add a special flourish to the gala occasion.

Shelby Matthews and Vivian Croll were riding side by side on their bicycles, trailing at the end of the procession of a couple hundred carriages, marching musicians, and mounted dignitaries who were all heading down Sheridan Avenue toward the train station.

"Sometimes I wish he'd never come to Wyoming at all," Shelby remarked with a heavy sigh.

Vivian looked puzzled. "Colonel Cody?"

"What? Oh . . . no, I mean Geoff!" The sky above them was white, and the wind pushing tumbleweeds through Cody warned sharply of winter's approach. Shelby wrapped her muffler tighter and added, "If I had never met him, I wouldn't know I was missing anything now."

Vivian gave her friend a wan smile. Although she understood that Shelby had been devastated by Geoff's departure and continued to pine for him more than three months later, it was difficult for Viv to feel much sympathy for someone who enjoyed the sort of life she could only dream of. Shelby was safe, loved by her family, and, most importantly, in control of her own destiny.

"Do I sound like a terrible brat?" Shelby steered her Napoleon bicycle close enough to touch her friend's gloved hand. "I promise to say no more about it for the rest of our day together. This is too fine an occasion to be spoiled by my lamentations . . . and besides, I suspect that you have problems I don't understand. Isn't that so, Vivian? And you never complain; never speak a word."

The other woman glanced away, her eyes smudged with fatigue. Courage had begun stirring in her months ago, when Shelby and Geoff had first come into her woeful existence. She still felt powerless against Bart's inhumane treatment, but her thoughts were increasingly rebellious. He could beat her down further and further, mentally and physically, but she did not have to break. Shelby's radiant presence in her life, and that of darling Willy, not only lifted her spirits, but gave her hope that better days lay ahead. Still, it was too dangerous for her to confide in her friend. Bart was capable of anything. And so she looked back at Shelby and murmured, "You have no idea, actually. It was a great victory for me to get permission to come out today."

"*Permission!* How can you talk that way? You are supposed to be his wife, not his slave!"

Viv could only sigh. Life was much more complicated than Shelby realized, and rarely fair or just.

Sensing her momentary weakness, Shelby pounced. "Please—tell me the truth. I can help you!"

"I—" Stricken, Vivian broke off. No more, she thought. She mustn't say another word, or she wouldn't be able to stop—and somehow he'd find out! If she involved Shelby, it would only mean that two of them were at risk. And so, instead, Viv tried to change the subject, pointing to the Irma Hotel, which was decorated with even more bunting than the rest of the buildings in town. "Goodness, doesn't it look handsome?"

Shelby choked back her pleas and speeches, knowing by now that once Viv grew skittish, she could not be reached. Instead, Shelby gave her a warm smile and nodded. "Wait until you see the magnificent bar that Queen Victoria sent Colonel Cody a couple of years ago, in appreciation of his command performance in London. The mirrored back bar all made of beautifully carved cherrywood, and Uncle Ben said that it was terribly difficult to get here. It was made in France, then shipped to New York by steamer, then to Red Lodge, Montana, by train, then they had to take it apart and bring it here by horse and wagon. Isn't that amazing?" She smiled brightly. "Of course, we'll see the bar at the opening celebration for the hotel on Wednesday evening."

"I can't wait to hear all your stories," Vivian said. "Will you promise to visit me the next day? I do hope that Bart has other work on the ranch so we can talk freely. Now that winter is coming again—so quickly!—there is less and less for him to do outdoors, and that little house seems so . . . crowded."

"But Viv, I want you to come with me to the party!" Shelby cried. She stopped her bicycle and fished in the pocket of her coat for an invitation stamped at the top with a gold buffalo. "Look, Colonel Cody sent out a thousand of these, and they aren't addressed to us by name. You'll come as our guest! It won't be any fun for me if you aren't there!"

Vivian refused to hold the engraved invitation, but she did glance at it sadly, catching the phrase *Colonel W. F. Cody earnestly desires your presence.* "I can't, Shelby. Thursday is Thanksgiving. It's impossible. I know Bart simply wouldn't allow it." She paused. "I'm afraid to leave Willy with Bart. In fact, I shouldn't stay out long today."

"That's ridiculous! What's he going to do, physically harm you if you disobey?" Instantly, she wished she could take back the hastily spoken words, for Vivian went dead-white and her haunted eyes filled with tears. "Oh, Viv, I'm sorry! But I don't understand! I know he's a bully, but surely he wouldn't *hit* you! I mean, that's just too terrible to imagine!"

Her little chin was trembling as she boosted herself back onto the bicycle seat. "You just don't know how perfect your life is. You have so much to be grateful for."

Shelby watched Vivian pedal away toward the rest of Colonel Cody's welcoming procession. Shock, horror, and guilt clashed within her as she wondered how she could have been so blind . . . and, now that the truth was out, what she could do about it.

Oh, Geoff, I need you! Shelby thought. She tried to swallow the lump in her throat, though, and put the invitation back in her pocket before cycling furiously to catch up with Vivian. Somehow she would cope without Geoff, and find a way to rescue her dear friend from a husband who was a much worse villain than Shelby had ever imagined.

"For Pete's sake, Shel, I wish you'd quit talking all the time about Vivian Croll!" Ben complained while his niece helped him with his tie. They stood in the kitchen, amidst the ruins of a Thanksgiving dinner that had been devoured by all the men of the Sunshine Ranch. "This is supposed to be such a great night—and it won't do any of us any good to spoil it worrying about her! I mean, I feel bad for her, too, but it's not my marriage—" Feeling the heat of her threatening stare, he broke off.

Her heart hurt all the time, especially when she sighed, but Shelby knew Ben was right about one thing. Tonight was special, and nothing would be gained by ruining it with more of her fretting about Vivian, or brooding about Geoff's absence.

"God's foot!" Titus cried, appearing at the edge of the room. "Don't you two look magnificent! Ah, darling Shelby, if only your parents could see you tonight! How proud they'd be. You're just as beautiful as your mother, and I must tell you I always believed she was the most stunning female in all the world!"

"You are terribly dear, Mr. Pym." She gave the little Cornishman a kiss on his ruddy cheek. "Every woman at the Irma Hotel will envy me for being with you two handsome men."

It was a night to remember, largely because Ben, Titus, and Shelby had not looked so splendid since arriving in Wyoming. By reminding the men that they should have proper suits for church and other occasions, Shelby had been able to persuade them to purchase clothing for tonight's gala party. They both wore single-breasted dark suits with bow ties, striped vests, and pocket watches. Shelby had also talked them into buying warm Ulster coats, which looked handsome enough to serve the occasion, but would also keep them warm through the long winter. Freshly barbered and smelling of bay rum, they were ready for a night of celebration.

Shelby did a little pirouette to show off her own

gown. Fashioned of pale yellow silk that accentuated the striking dark cinnamon of her hair, it featured a deep neckline inlaid with lace, and more lace decorating the sleeves. A sash of emerald-green silk encircled Shelby's tiny waist, in contrast to the pouf of her bodice and the full hem. Her hair was upswept in a style that showed off her arresting eyes. Her cheeks were rosy with excitement, and the four-stranded pearl dog collar that gleamed round her neck was her only jewelry.

"You sure we could afford all this finery?" Ben mumbled as he held up his niece's new fur-lined cape.

Shelby fastened the closure at her neck, reached for her matching fox-fur muff, and gave him a patient smile. "You know full well that we have a tidy sum in the bank, thanks to Geoff. I don't intend to squander it, but by the same token, we do have the good name of our family to uphold. I'm sure that Daddy and Mama would insist that all three of us have a set of good clothes for special occasions."

"You had plenty at home, as I recall, but were too stubborn to bring 'em," he grumbled. "You were determined to go around in angora chaps and a Stetson all the time."

"Well . . . perhaps I've grown up a bit since then."

Titus gave Ben a nudge in the ribs. "Be glad for that, and stop acting like a parsimonious old *bachelor*!"

"Hey! I'm not that old yet! I'll get married some day!"

Titus and Shelby rolled their eyes at each other, then burst out laughing. With that, they all went outside, got into the leather-topped buggy, and set out for Cody.

"Too bad we don't have snow," Ben observed as the chill crept around them. "The sleigh would be a lot faster on a cold night like this."

Still, excitement helped to keep the trio warm, and

the journey up the South Fork Road went quickly. The sky was deep blue, rose-tinted where it met the great mountains to the west, but by the time they reached Cody, darkness had fallen and snowflakes fluttered down as if Buffalo Bill had ordered them for decoration.

Dozens of buggies and even automobiles were lined around the Irma Hotel's location on the corner of Sheridan Avenue. The sprawling sandstone building truly was the town's crowning jewel—more magnificent than the population could support, yet in keeping with Buffalo Bill's image of himself and the town he had founded. There were no other structures in sight when one stood in front of the hotel, with the moonlit mountains providing a backdrop.

"He'll never see a profit," Ben remarked as they drew closer. Lights blazed in every window, people crowded the veranda that nearly wrapped around the hotel, and more guests stood on the second-floor porch that opened off the corner suite upstairs.

"I heard there's a telephone in every room," Titus marveled.

"Well, I think Colonel Cody was simply wonderful to do this for the town," Shelby said, "and I for one think that eventually the Irma *will* turn a profit! More and more tourists are traveling to Yellowstone Park, and I predict that this hotel will be a much-needed jumping-off point."

"Cody's building a lodge at the eastern entrance to the park, too," Ben revealed. "Calling it Pahaska Inn." He broke off at the sight of a fetching young lady, smiling at him from the hotel steps. "Hey, why're we wasting time? Let's go to the party!"

Shelby went into the Irma Hotel on Titus's arm, happy, smiling, and beautiful . . . yet constantly aware of the space in her heart that had ached since the day Geoff had returned to England. Occasions like this one should have helped her to forget, but instead Shelby found herself missing him more. They had discussed Buffalo Bill and the progress of his hotel many times, and everything that she saw tonight she wanted to share with Geoff.

"Our friend Geoff would have enjoyed this occasion," Titus murmured, knowing it was better to bring it out in the open. Perhaps that would help her to have fun without him.

Shelby blinked. There was a lump in her throat, preventing words, and all she could do was nod over and over again.

"I understand more than you know, darling girl." He patted her, kissed her cheek, and took her cape. "Go on in there and watch all the men drop at your feet."

She glanced down at herself, coloring, then back at Titus. "Daddy would thank you for taking care of me this way, Mr. Pym. Uncle Ben means well, but—"

"Don't I know all about him! I've been tryin' to tame that lad since he was no higher than my elbow." He saw that she was shy about moving among the guests alone, perhaps because so many people were staring at her already, so Titus led the way. "Let's find ourselves a glass of champagne, all right?"

The Irma Hotel was more impressive than Shelby had dreamed. The lobby was spacious and well-appointed, with a paneled desk that spanned one wall, and stylish wallpaper decorated with framed paintings of Buffalo Bill and some of his colorful friends. Staring at Shelby from high on the far wall were the stuffed heads of animals that appeared to be elk. The lobby was crowded with people, but in the middle of the room, she saw a large circular ottoman upholstered in tufted leather occupied by five elderly guests. Some of the furniture wasn't quite Shelby's own taste, but it was undoubtedly grand.

Some people greeted her, but clearly few recognized her in this guise. They were used to seeing her in her trousers and boots and braids.

The band was playing "A Bird in a Gilded Cage." Shelby peeked into the huge dining room to see the musicians and the guests who had begun to dance. Ben was there, dancing with the fetching girl from the porch steps. In the barroom, gaslights shone in the mirrors backing the bar given to Cody by Queen Victoria, and Shelby stared at it for a moment, then took in the heavy billiard tables, the bentwood chairs, and the paneled booths on the far side of the room.

"Here's your champagne, dear," Titus said, touching her elbow. "I hear that Cody himself is about to speak to the guests from the bottom of the stairs. Shall we go and listen?"

She was excited by this news. The day he'd arrived at the depot, the crowd had been so huge that Shelby hadn't been able to get near, even though Cody was a friend of her family and had stayed at their home when Fox Matthews decided to buy the Sunshine Ranch. Besides, Vivian had needed to start home early . . . and Shelby had felt awkward about mentioning her acquaintance with the incredibly famous Colonel William F. Cody. The differences between her luck and Vivian's were beginning to become apparent to her, and there was no use rubbing salt in the wounds.

Still, approaching the staircase, Shelby wished Viv could be there—and be able to enjoy this sort of party like the truly fine woman she was. Why couldn't Vivian have the sort of life she herself took for granted? Shelby thought. It ought to be her due!

Cody stopped partway down the stairs, flanked by his daughters: Irma, for whom the hotel was named, and Arta. Both were quite pretty and fashionably dressed. Colonel Cody appeared to be in good spirits, but perhaps a bit tired, a reminder that he was nearing sixty and kept a grueling schedule. His long hair was white now, as were his goatee and mustache, but he retained an air of dignity and magnetism. Shelby had read in the newspaper about the late-October death of Arta's husband, Horton Boal. Boal had committed suicide in a Sheridan hotel owned by his father-in-law, and Shelby decided that the family was bearing up well under their tragedy.

The band struck up "Hail to the Chief," but Buffalo Bill soon begged for quiet. After introducing his daughters and the hotel manager and staff, he orated, "To those who ask how I would like to be remembered, I now reply that I should like to be known as a pioneer and a developer of civilization, rather than simply as a scout and a showman. I have worked with more diligence on the former endeavors than on the latter. I love the Bighorn Basin with all my being, and this hotel means more to me than anyone here can imagine. Homecomings like this one are the great red-letter days of my life, and I will now swear to you, my dear friends and neighbors, that I intend to make the Irma Hotel the talk of the West!" Cody paused, then added, "Tonight, I also am honored to announce the engagement of my lovely daughter, Irma, to Lieutenant Clarence Stott, who is stationed at Fort Mackenzie, Sheridan, Wyoming. This truly is a red-letter day for the Cody family!"

The crowd roared in response, their cheers filling the building, and the band struck up "Hail to the Chief" again. Since Mayor Edwards was confined to bed with a broken leg, a fellow named Ridgely went up to Cody on behalf of the townspeople and extolled the aging showman's virtues. Then, when the ceremonial portion of the evening was ended, Buffalo Bill encouraged all his guests to eat, drink, and be merry. Shelby and Titus were about to turn back toward the lobby when Irma Cody came to the bottom step and called softly, "Does anyone know if a Miss Shelby Matthews is present tonight?"

Startled, Shelby raised her hand amidst the crush. "I am she!"

Irma gave her a sweet smile. "My father has wondered how you and your uncle have fared on your ranch. Won't the two of you come up to his suite and speak to him?"

Titus promised to send Ben along, and moments later Shelby found herself with a Cody daughter on either side. Buffalo Bill had already climbed the stairs, deep in conversation with his friend, Dr. Powell. Shelby couldn't help wondering about the whereabouts of Cody's wife, Louisa, and why no one mentioned her in speeches about the virtues of their family. Were the rumors of divorce true?

What was the use of fame and genius and wealth if one couldn't enjoy it with a loving mate? How sad that Colonel Cody didn't have a wife by his side, laughing with him, holding his arm, and worrying over his well-being. Again Shelby felt that familiar stab of yearning for Geoff.

Where is he tonight? She scarcely dared consider the possibility that he might have married Lady Clementine Beech by now . . . but it was hard not to remember the words she had written to her fiancé: *Mummy longs to begin planning a Christmas wedding . . .*

"How long have you been living out here?" Irma asked.

"Oh, a long time! At least, it seems like a very long time. I came here from Deadwood in April." She gave both women a smile that was rich with complex emotions. "So much has happened to me since then." It occurred to Shelby that she must guard her tongue, for the Cody sisters' hearts were in very different places. Irma was in love and about to marry, while Arta's husband had just killed himself with chloroform, leaving her with two children to raise alone.

Fortunately, Shelby didn't have to make conversation with both women when they reached Colonel Cody's suite. Arta wandered off into another room, and Irma happily soliloquized about her impending nuptials.

The corner rooms Cody had reserved for his own use were handsome. There was a private parlor, two bedrooms, and a bath and closet, all crowded with stylish oak furnishings. As downstairs, there were many portraits of Buffalo Bill on the walls. Since her father seemed to be otherwise occupied at the moment, Irma suggested that Shelby look around. "Everyone wants to speak to him, and he is happy to oblige," she explained.

Shelby decided to go into the bedroom an explore the porch that was constructed upon the veranda roof. There was a great corner window opening onto the wide makeshift balcony, the edge of which was marked only by a low-railed fence. It was a perfect spot to escape the stifling crowds that filled the hotel, and Shelby stepped out into the frigid air and inhaled deeply. The struggling town of Cody was spread below, silvered by moonlight and dusted with snowflakes. Most of the homes were dark, since nearly everyone had come to the party.

"Too bad Geoffrey Weston had to go back to England," a kindly voice said from behind her. "I miss him, too."

"Oh!" Shelby pressed a hand to her heart, whirling.

"I didn't know anyone else was out here!" In the shadowy light she recognized Jacob Schwoob, and felt a throb remembering the happy afternoon she and Geoff had spent at the Cody Trading Company.

"I didn't mean to frighten you, Shelby, but you looked so lonely, and I thought I could guess the reason."

"You could? Were my feelings for Geoff that obvious?"

Jakie Schwoob gave her an indulgent smile, then took off his wire-rimmed spectacles and polished them as he spoke. "I know that the two of you denied any romance the day you came into my store, but as time passed, I saw more and more of Geoff, and he stopped trying to hide his feelings for you."

Shelby's heart was pounding hard and her legs felt weak. "I—I'm getting cold. Could we go inside?"

He took her elbow to help her through the tall window, and in the glow of the gaslights, Schwoob looked more benevolent than ever. "I just think you ought to know that Geoff loves you. Everything he bought, from the gramophone to the bicycles to the piano, was a way for him to express that love."

She was so numb it seemed the voice was coming to her through gauze. "Piano?"

"It's finally arriving this week," Jakie said, beaming. "Geoff ordered it the same day he took the bicycles home."

She wanted so badly to believe him, but was afraid to let herself. "I know that Geoff was fond of me, but if it were more than that, wouldn't he have stayed?"

"Who knows? Maybe he had doubts about *you*." He shrugged, then glanced across the room to the spot where Ben Avery and his evening's companion were chatting with Colonel Cody. "See that girl? Do you know who she is?"

"No . . ."

"It's Etta Feeley. When she first arrived from Red Lodge, people assumed she was a lady, and her visit was written up in the Society column. Since then, some folks are still confused about her . . . but the fact is that she owns the biggest—" Jakie pondered the best turn of phrase. "—fancy house in Cody. And Etta's a friendly girl; shops in my store regularly. She's spent a lot of money on her . . . establishment, and that's good for the whole town—"

"Does my uncle know this about Miss Feeley?"

"Probably. But I mentioned her to *you* because she approached Geoff one day in my presence. Etta made her intentions quite clear." He smiled at the memory. "My point is this: if Geoff hadn't been in love with you, I think he would've gotten to know her a little better. What did he have to lose? She invited him, and he declined, flat-out. The only men in this town who do that are crazy in love or securely married."

"Mr. Schwoob . . . what good does it do for me to know all this?" Tears glittered in Shelby's eyes and she sighed as if a heavy burden was pressing against her breast. "To think that Geoff truly loved me only increases my pain! I miss him constantly. I do believe that he was—is—the mate God intended for me, but now that cannot be. He has gone back to another life in England, and he is promised in marriage to another woman!"

He looked stricken. "My dear girl, I only thought—I mean, is there no hope, no way this gulf between you can be bridged?"

Accepting his handkerchief, Shelby delicately blew her nose and shook her head. "I think that I am doomed to spend the rest of my life ranching and caring for the men. I'll be an eccentric spinster, looking after my old bachelor uncle. . . ."

"I cannot imagine that is your fate!" Jakie felt terrible for bringing on this case of the doldrums. "Dear Shelby, I see that Colonel Cody is waving to us, and pointing at you. Are you well enough to speak to him?"

Shelby looked like a fragile little dove in her lovely gown and upswept hairstyle as she tottered off bravely to join Ben, Buffalo Bill, and the notorious Etta Feeley.

Etta was the first to greet her, reaching out with both hands. "I've heard a lot about you, Miss Matthews!" She wore too much perfume and rouge, and her hair was probably dyed, but her smile was genuine. "We've been helping Colonel Cody hatch a plan for you, and I hope you will give him your attention!"

Shelby greeted her in return, glanced at Ben—who was looking warm and uncomfortable—and put her gloved hand in Cody's. He bent low, kissing it, his goatee wiggling slightly. Then, as if on cue, Ben cleared his throat and announced that he and Miss Feeley would be going downstairs for refreshments.

Cody gave Shelby an intense look. "Miss Matthews, there is a matter I would like to discuss with you. Will you grant me a few minutes of your time?"

"Of course, sir! I would be honored!"

He liked that. Clasping her arm, Cody led her to a long, tassled sofa in the corner of the parlor. Something in his expression convinced the other guests nearby to leave them alone.

"May I be frank, Miss Matthews?" When she nodded emphatically, he smiled. "You are charming, and I understand that you are very talented as well. Is it true that you are an extremely proficient horsewoman . . . and a sharpshooter, too?"

"I don't mean to sound conceited, but yes, sir! I love to practice riding and roping, and especially shooting, for hours on end. Uncle Ben has helped me learn some marvelous tricks." Shelby was brightening again in the wake of her scene with Jakie Schwoob. "I must confess that I idolize Annie Oakley."

He looked extremely pleased, then his expression turned somber. "I don't know if you are aware or not that I, and my Wild West Show, have had a very difficult year. Have you read about my poor son-in-law? Ah, yes, of course it would be all over the newspapers here. . . . Well, aside from that tragedy, there have been other trials. My old friend and partner, Nate Salsbury, has been ailing, unable to travel with the show much of the time. . . ." He heaved a sigh. "Perhaps the biggest blow was the train wreck involving the Wild West Show a year ago. We lost more than one hundred of our show horses, including my own mount, Old Pop."

Shelby gasped. Cody's eyes glazed over for a moment, then he patted her hand. "Yes, young lady, I'm afraid it's true. We were lucky not to lose any human lives—but Annie Oakley was so badly injured that she was hospitalized for many months."

"Oh, dear! I didn't know that!"

"Well . . . we've tried to keep it out of the newspapers, hoping that she would make a full recovery. However, that seems doubtful now." At last his compelling gaze fastened on Shelby. "I'll confess to you that we've also had a few money problems of late, and I am worried about the success of our upcoming tour abroad without Annie to draw the crowds."

"But Colonel Cody, your show is jam-packed with stars and spectacles, like the Indian attack of the wagon train! People will come with or without Annie Oakley!"

"I'm not prepared to take that chance, Miss Matthews."

Shelby was puzzled. The air was dense with cigar smoke, perfume, and the heat of bodies and steam from the nearby radiator. Why was Buffalo Bill telling her all of this?

"I can see that you are too modest to guess my intentions, and I won't keep you in suspense any longer," Cody said genially. "Miss Matthews, I would like you to take Annie Oakley's place—performing as a female sharpshooter with the Wild West Show. We sail for England on December fifteenth!"

It was too much for Shelby to take in. She stared, made a little sound of disbelief, then fell to the floor in a faint.

Chapter Fourteen

"I CAN'T BELIEVE I *FAINTED*!" SHELBY CRIED, HER voice all the louder in Vivian's tiny sod house. She shook her head in disgust. "I can't *bear* women who faint! There I was, at the great turning point of my life—and I made a complete fool of myself!"

"That's silly!" Vivian laughed and petted Willy, who still weighed no more than ten pounds. He was her constant companion, shadowing her as she did chores and cuddling beside her the rest of the time. "I think that you fainted because of the corset. You aren't used to being cinched in like that. Besides, it sounds as if Colonel Cody didn't think any less of you for it, so I suggest that you stop fretting."

They were seated together at the splintered table, which was covered by the cloth Vivian had embroidered with such painstaking care. Already, like everything else in Bart Croll's house, it was stained and spoiled where he had touched it. If Shelby didn't care so deeply for Viv, she couldn't bear to set foot in this hovel. It had repulsed her the first time she'd visited, in dust-choked summer, but now it was even worse because there was no air from outside. Shelby's eyes burned from the smoke.

Vivian read her mind. "If there were love in this house, I could be happy in spite of the hardships. . . ." She tried to smile. "At least it's too cold to rain! The last time it rained for two days in a row, I had to hold an umbrella over my head when I tried to stand at the stove and cook."

"Our roof leaks sometimes, too," Shelby lied.

"I wouldn't mind if it was rain that dripped through—but our roof is covered with sod." She glanced away. "It leaks big globs of mud, and they fall in the soup, on my sewing, sometimes on my face when I'm sleeping."

Shelby didn't know what to do except cover her friend's hand with her own. "Oh, Vivian, won't you please reconsider and come with me to England?" It seemed to her that Viv might change her mind, just as she herself had, if enough pressure was applied. "I thought it was a crazy idea at first, too, but everyone convinced me that it will be the best thing for me even if Geoff won't have anything to do with me."

Already Vivian was fond of imagining the reunion between Shelby and Geoff. Ever since the starry night when he'd been so kind to her, rustling back Shelby's cattle, she had felt her own heart flutter each time they'd met. It was a harmless secret, her girlish infatuation with Geoffrey Weston, and seemed to have no connection with her best friend's very real love for him. Perhaps it made her cheer Shelby on all the more. She never expected her own dreams to come true, but Shelby was different. She was charmed, somehow.

"You must write to me immediately after he sees you in England," Vivian said softly. "I want to know every single detail, every word the two of you exchange—please?"

"No. I won't tell you anything."

Vivian looked crushed. "But why not? I promise not to tell anyone else; you know you can trust me, Shelby!"

"That's not the point. I want you to be there yourself! I'll need someone to help me. Even Colonel Cody suggested that I have a maid to see to my costumes and look after my things when we travel. The only person I want to be with me is you, Viv!"

They stared at one another, the crux of the matter left unsaid. Shelby meant for Vivian to leave Bart, to divorce and start life anew in England. The naked fear in Viv's eyes was more eloquent than words.

"Are you just going to stay here for the rest of your life?" Shelby asked urgently, her voice breaking. Her friend looked away. "Why can't you ever meet my eyes when I try to discuss these matters? What has he done to make you so terrified that you would subject yourself to this torture forever?"

Vivian pressed her lips together, then murmured, "At least I have my darling Willy. And, Bart may not live to be very old. Already he has an awful cough from those cigarettes."

"But Viv, can't you see how crazy that sounds? You need love from *people*, not just from a dog. Why should you waste your own future waiting for Bart to die?"

"Sometimes I think that animals are better at loving than people, because they don't make demands, or find fault, or indulge in cruelty or betrayal." Her thin hand stroked Willy's wiry gray fur. "As for Bart . . . in a perverse way, I owe him my life. After my family died in that horrible fire, and I found myself homeless in St. Louis in the dead of winter, I actually thought I might either freeze or starve to death. Bart brought me here and gave me a home. . . ."

Shelby wanted to shake her. "At what *cost*?" She felt like crying at the sight of her friend's gaunt, ghostly face, her deep-set blue eyes and her dull hair. "Your life has *meaning*! I don't have a sister, and sometimes I pretend that you and I are sisters. I certainly love you that much. How can I go away to England and leave you here with that monster?"

"I'll be all right. You have to go. I want you to."

Shelby shook her head. "I have to go home and finish packing, but that doesn't mean I'm giving up. I just wish I had more time to change your mind before I leave for England."

"I thought you said the Wild West Show isn't sailing from New York until the middle of December?"

"Yes, but I want to visit my parents, and there are only two trains a week right now—so I have to take the one tomorrow." They stood, and Shelby stepped forward and dared to hug Vivian. Her friend was clearly afraid to be touched, even by a loved one, and stood with her arms pressed to the sides of her painfully thin body. "I hate good-byes. I'm a terrific coward when it comes to saying good-bye. Did you know that I stayed in bed rather than face Geoff when he left?" She sighed. "If you don't come to the ranch with your bags packed tonight, I'll do everything in my power to come over here on the way to the train and try one more time to change your mind."

"Don't—I mean, if Bart is here, it will only make my lot harder after you're gone."

Deep affection swelled Shelby's heart and brought hot tears to her eyes. "Oh, Viv—why are you punishing yourself this way?"

The other woman looked away again, shaking her head, then squeezing her eyes closed so Shelby wouldn't see the raw depths of her misery. Little Willy whimpered and licked her hand.

When Bart Croll saw Shelby Matthews riding away from his house, he was so mad he took a bite out of his cigarette by accident, then chewed it up and swallowed it. That bitch made him crazy. She'd stolen the cattle back, he knew it for a fact. He'd seen 'em back on her land, branded now with that stupid sun symbol.

She went riding around like a hellion, roping and shooting and dressing as if she thought she was a cowboy. Today she was wearing a duster that flapped down around the toes of her boots, and a scarf around her ears and an old Stetson on top of that. That long red braid of hers flipped in the wind, just as sassy as Shelby herself.

Bart dreamed of killing her. Just shooting her outright—*boom!*—right through the heart with a big gun. He also dreamed of fucking her so hard she'd beg him for mercy, crying. Maybe he'd tie her hands behind her back and push her head down on the table and screw her like a dog. Croll didn't know which he wanted more—the killing or the fucking.

He was hungry as hell, too. Dismounting, he went into the house and discovered that nothing at all was cooking on the stove. Worse, Vivian was sitting at the table, staring off in the distance dreamy as a half-wit, petting that stupid dog.

Bart tried not to lose his temper. Instead he batted her on the side of the head and shouted, "Lazy bitch! What the hell you doin'? Where's my dinner? You think this is some kind of society hotel I'm runnin' here—and you're a guest?"

"No, Bart. I'm sorry." She started to her feet, eyes downcast, and pushed the cowering Willy under the table. Usually, when she heard him coming, she locked the dog in the outside shed, where he'd be safe and out of Bart's way. "Shelby stopped by to say good-bye. She's taking Annie Oakley's place in the Wild West Show." Bart only gave her his meanest bored stare. "Anyway, I guess I lost track of time. I'll get your dinner just as quick as I can—"

"I don't want dinner yet."

Nausea swept over her at the tone of his voice. Pretending not to understand, Vivian hurried toward the stove and reached for a cast-iron skillet. Her hand shook so much that it rattled against the burner, and Willy peeked out from under the tablecloth.

"Go lie down, woman."

Bile rose in her throat. "Please, Bart—not now . . . please!" She heard herself whimpering and despised the terror he evoked in her. When Bart came toward her and twisted her arm behind her back, Willy scurried out from under the table, growling ferociously. Fearlessly, he latched onto the rancher's pant leg.

"Get away, mutt!" Croll gave the little animal a savage kick that sent him hurtling across the cramped room. Undaunted, Willy returned to defend his mistress.

Viv made the mistake of beginning to weep. "Please, Bart, please, don't hurt him. I'll do anything you want, just don't hurt Willy. I love him so. . . ."

He stuck the dog in a bureau drawer, pushed it shut, and grabbed her by the back of her skirt. "Git on that bed an' spread your legs!"

Please God, Vivian prayed soundlessly as she fell across the meager bed, *make me numb*. Bart was there in the next instant, raking up her skirts. When he lay heavily on top of her, his sour, rank smell filled her nostrils and made her want to retch. Turning her face to one side, she squeezed her eyes shut and held her breath, willing herself not to feel, not to be sick, not to sob out loud. His hands were permanently stained and cracked, like sandpaper on her soft belly. He tore away her underclothes, always liking it when she had to mend them later, and thrust a finger inside her, then two, grunting like a pig. Dry and frightened, Vivian cried out in pain.

It never took very long for him to rape her, but Viv felt as if she were spiraling down a black hole into the bowels of Hell. To not be allowed to consent to such a violation of her most intimate being was worse than one of his beatings, which sometimes left her black and blue. This was an assault of her soul.

Bart pushed inside her, but his erection shrank away after a few moments. He was getting old, and she prayed each night that the time would come soon when his pride would keep him from trying again. Today, though, the failure of his manhood enraged him. He kept thrusting at her, cursing.

"This is your fault, you stupid bitch! I might as well be fucking a block of ice for all the good you are!"

As always, Viv kept her face turned away, eyes closed, willing herself to detach from the degrading ordeal. He struck her, hard across the face, but she didn't respond.

"Why do I put up with you? What good are you?" Veins stood out in his red face. He pulled out of her, clambered up and fastened his pants. Vivian curled up in a ball, facing the wall. "Yer no good, that's what! I was better off alone!"

"I'll leave, then," she whispered.

"The hell you will! Think I'll let you go? You owe me, bitch!"

Willy had been crying in the drawer all the time, but now he began to yip in Viv's defense. Infuriated by his own impotence and his wife's indifference, Bart narrowed his eyes at the bureau.

"I *hate* that mutt. All he does is yap and eat my food and get in the way! Never shoulda let you keep him in the first place." Reaching for his gun, he opened the drawer and held Willy aloft by the scruff of his neck. The pup made plaintive crying sounds. "Time for you to go, mongrel."

Stricken and stunned, Viv sat in bed, her eyes like saucers in a dead-white face. "W-What? You don't mean—"

Pleased to have found a way to strike her very core, Bart Croll grinned, showing his broken, yellowed teeth.

"Time you remembered who's in charge here, you ugly whore." With that, he went out the door, the whimpering Willy clutched in one hand, his pistol in the other.

Viv began to shriek, and the sounds were bloodcurdling, reverberating with all the raw pain buried deep within her. Her legs felt numb, but she stumbled forward, screaming, *"Noooooo—"*

A gunshot cracked outside the window.

Bart's satanic laughter drew Viv to the doorway. *It's only one of his sick jokes! It* must *be!* When she stepped through the door into the dirt yard, she saw Willy, a curly gray mop lying by the hitching post. Blood oozed from his broken little head.

Shelby tried not to think too much as she washed clothes and packed for her new life. If she thought about leaving the ranch and how much she'd miss everyone, she'd be grief-stricken, so she just told herself that she was getting away for the winter. Ranch winters were terribly long anyway. Colonel Cody had insisted that there would be no contract, and that had been what finally convinced her to agree. If she didn't like performing with the show by spring, she could come back to Wyoming.

Shelby tried not to think much about the Wild West Show, either. She was proud of her skills as a sharpshooter, but she'd read so much about Annie Oakley that she felt like a complete amateur in comparison. But Cody had promised that she wouldn't have to perform when they first got to England. A trainer would work closely with her until all concerned felt secure about her performance.

She was glad to have visited England before, so she didn't have to wonder what life would be like there, but of course that was the least of her worries anyway. Shelby spent most of her time trying not to think about

Geoff. Still, lying in bed alone in the dark the night before her departure, she swung back and forth between potent memories and jarring uncertainty. It was impossible not to imagine various scenes in London. What if he were already married when she arrived? *Never mind, I'll just pull up my socks and get on with life—and my job! There's no reason for him to think I came to England to win him back, is there?*

There were shadows under her eyes when she got dressed the next morning and let Cookie fix breakfast for her. She felt years older than the carefree gamine who had popped into her parents' dining room in full cowgirl regalia, but that had been just last March. It was odd to consider how life experiences and heartache and friendship could combine, just so, to carry a girl over the brink into womanhood. . . .

Titus, Cal, Lucius, Marsh, and Jimmy all joined Shelby for breakfast, and they reminisced about the good times they'd shared on the Sunshine Ranch. Already they treated her a little differently, though, for she was clad in a rather sophisticated traveling suit of green wool trimmed in black velvet—a gift from Buffalo Bill. Titus and Ben were going to take her to the depot, so when the buggy was loaded with her luggage, Shelby sadly kissed each of the ranch hands on the cheek.

"I'm awfully fond of you boys, do you know that?"

Before the others could speak, Marsh exclaimed, "Yup!" and everyone started laughing.

It was Cal who dared to turn serious. "We're glad that you're goin', Miss Shelby, cuz we expect that you'll bring Geoff back with you. Right?"

"I don't know. Unfortunately, Geoff was born to the sort of position that makes it hard for him to do as he pleases . . . but I have decided that I am worthy of the Earl of Sandhurst, after all." She gave them one of her wide, shining smiles. "However it all turns out, at least we'll know we tried!"

"Atta girl," the quartet of cowpunchers all said at once, and began to clap. Lucius added, "All them dukes and earls would be lucky to have you!"

Shelby stood in front of the mirror to put on her new hat, a confection with a brim that turned up on each side, its crown decorated with feathers and ribbons. It made her look mature and startlingly like her mother. Outside, she consulted Ben's pocket watch. "I want to allow enough time to stop and say good-bye to Vivian. We won't linger; I don't want to cause trouble for her." She looked perplexed. "I really had high hopes that she'd come last night. I tried every bit of persuasion I could think of to get Viv to be my ladies' maid in England. Colonel Cody said he'd pay for one, and it seemed the perfect way to get Viv to leave Bart—"

"Look!" Ben shielded his eyes against the winter sun and squinted at the horse coming toward them from the Croll fence line. "It's Bart's horse, but the rider looks like . . ."

"Vivian!" Shelby cried, overjoyed. Heedless of her expensive clothing, she lifted her skirts and ran to meet her friend. Viv reined in the horse, jumped down, and hugged Shelby without any prompting. She was shaking all over.

"I'm coming," she gasped. "I'm coming with you! I didn't have time to pack anything except this one little carpetbag—"

"It doesn't matter, we'll get you everything you need later." For a moment Shelby was almost overcome by emotion, but then she managed to whisper, "Oh, Viv, I'm so happy—more for you than for me. We'll have a wonderful time, but what's important is that you're going to have a new life. Starting this moment!"

"Y-Yes." She nodded like a doll.

"Where is Willy?"

Glassy-eyed, Viv looked away. "Oh . . . he got killed. Last night. An accident." Sobs overtook her. "I—can't talk about it, Shelby!"

"Of course not!" Shocked, she wrapped an arm around her broken friend. "I'll take care of you. Lean on me, sweetheart."

Ben and Titus appeared startled by this new development, but they, too, were fond of Vivian and happy that she'd found the courage to leave her husband. The longer they knew Bart Croll, the more they despised him and were repelled by his presence. Titus maintained that he was more reptile than human.

On the way to Cody, Shelby took a few minutes to remind the men of Buffalo Bill's assurance that Gadabout and Charlie could also come to England with the Wild West Show. It would be up to the Sunshine Ranch to deliver the horses to Cody's nearby TE Ranch before December sixth. "The colonel and his friends will return from their hunting expedition then, and soon after that he'll organize the train to New York."

When they arrived at the depot, Shelby sent Ben inside to purchase their tickets, and her friend decided to go on board the train to rest. Shelby stayed on the platform and watched her uncle load not just her own things onto the train, but also a trunk she didn't recognize. She was in the midst of bidding Titus a tearful good-bye when she saw Ben pass by with the luggage on his shoulder.

"Mr. Pym, how can I ever thank you for all you've done for me? I have to admit, there were times I felt a bit lost among all you men, and you always came to my rescue with an extra helping of kindness and understanding."

"It's no more than I've been doin' since the day you were born, darling girl . . . and no more than your parents expect of me." He hugged her tight, then stood away, smiling and pink-cheeked in the November wind. "I'm glad you're going on this adventure. I have a feeling that it holds a lot of surprises, and you'll come home to us an even better person than you are now."

"I hope so, Mr. Pym."

"I shouldn't be tellin' you this—but I will." He winked. "Mr. Manypenny and I may not've seen eye to eye on a lot of things, but by the time he went back to England, we agreed wholeheartedly that you and Geoff were a splendid match."

Shelby kissed his cheek again, holding onto her hat as one of Cody's famous zephyrs threatened to pull it from her head, hatpins and all. "Take care of yourself and—" She broke off as Ben came up behind Titus. "Uncle Ben, I don't think you care at all that I'm leaving! It's time for me to board the train and you haven't given me so much as a pat on the back! And what was that ugly old trunk you took on board?"

He gave Titus a conspiratorial grin. "That was *my* trunk, Shel. I'm on the payroll of the Wild West Show—and I'm going with you to England! Titus an' the boys can run things here during the winter." Ben gave her cheek a tweak before adding, "You need me! Who else did you think could train you to do all those tricks?"

Titus chuckled. "Sometimes I think it's the other way around, lad. Shelby's had you jumping through hoops since she was a baby!"

A conductor leaned out of the train and drawled, *"Allll aboarrrdd!"*

Her heart began to pound with exhilaration. "Come on, Uncle Ben! We can't be late!" And then, heedless of her fine clothing, Shelby clutched her hat with one hand and ran into her future.

* * *

Tucked in a narrow, twisting gulch, the town of Deadwood was receiving a fanciful coating of snow. Pine trees, rocky cliffs, and steeply pitched roofs were all frosted like decorations on a cake.

Madeleine Avery Matthews stood in her tower music room and looked down over the town through a tall window of curved glass. "I hope it stays this way for Christmas," she murmured wistfully. "Perhaps the snow will bring us good luck."

"And what do you need luck for?" Maddie's half sister asked from her seat on the piano bench. Sun Smile, who was a member of the Teton Sioux Indian tribe, had met Maddie for the first time when they were nearly twenty years old. Maddie had been a proper, Philadelphia-bred lady, new to the Black Hills, and Sun Smile had been the grieving widow of a Sioux warrior killed at Little Bighorn. Their father, finally revealing an old secret, had brought Sun Smile into the fold of his Irish-English family.

"Luck?" Maddie repeated, smiling at her sister. "I need luck to bring my children home for Christmas . . . and to keep you with us, too. I always wish you would not go back to the agency."

"Fireblossom, I only came at all because Fox wrote me of the loneliness *you* were not telling me about." The mild remonstrance was softened by her use of the name Maddie had been given by the Sioux, in honor of her glorious hair. "But I cannot stay here until Christmas—I have a husband and three children waiting for me at home! Besides, I have another plan I am working on for my life."

Maddie joined her on the piano bench and lightly fingered the keys. "You've been visiting a week and you haven't told me yet? What is it?"

"I am going to college. We are moving to Yankton, where Running Elk is going to work among the Yankton Sioux, and I am going to start college there." She was radiant.

"That's wonderful! I'm jealous." Maddie felt a rush of memories as she looked at her sister, who had traveled a long road since the summer of 1876, when they met at Bear Butte. Sun Smile had been wracked by grief then, mute, dirty, and hostile. Now, remarried and in her early forties, she was a handsome mixture of Sioux and Anglo-Saxon: tan-skinned, black-haired, gray-eyed, and both humorous and dignified. Her turbulent, often tragic past had shaped her into a woman of pure character.

"What are you jealous of?" She appeared to be puzzled.

"Your . . . sense of direction. Fox says I need to have a project of my own, beyond my work in the gardens, our marriage, and caring for the home and Gran Annie. . . ." Maddie sighed. "So many of the people who helped make my life full and rich are gone now."

"I have always thought Fox was a very wise man," Sun Smile replied warmly. "What new colors would you like to add to the fabric of your life?"

Maddie glanced around the music room with its rose moiré wallpaper, an imported marble fireplace made more splendid by a crackling fire, and the eighteenth century piano and harp. "I mean to write a book for children . . . about two sisters, one of whom is from the East and very fancy, and the other of whom is a beautiful Sioux girl." Shyly, she met Sun Smile's wide eyes, eyes that were exactly like their father's. "I think I have talent. I've been making a plan for the story, and I'm going to start writing when I'm alone again."

"I know that your book will be wonderful, my sister, and that you will discover that there are many more stories waiting in your heart to be told."

The moment was broken by the sudden appearance of Annie Sunday Matthews. She burst from the paneled serving area that connected the front of the house with the dining room, and their newly adopted black kitten came scrambling in her wake. "Madeleine! I was peeling potatoes in the kitchen when I saw Fox driving straight up our icy, perpendicular hill in that ridiculous automobile of his. It's a wonder he didn't slide straight back down and kill everyone! They were waving and honking the horn, and—"

Before Annie could finish, there was a clamor on the front porch, followed by the sound of the front door being thrown open. Sensing that longed-for excitement was here, Maddie hurried into the entry hall just in time to be swept by a flurry of snowflakes. Fox came next, clad in warm tweeds and driving goggles. The moment he saw his wife, he exclaimed, "Maddie—look what the storm has blown in!"

Shelby popped through the door next, laughing, all bundled up and looking quite grown-up. Over her daughter's head Maddie could see Ben, who would always be her little brother even though he was at least as tall as Fox. The sight of her family, flushed and laughing and framed by lacy snowflakes, brought tears to Maddie's eyes.

"Oh, Mama, I swear that you are more beautiful every time I come home!" Shelby plunged into her arms just as she had since she was big enough to crawl. "I didn't realize how homesick I've been until just now."

Maddie closed her eyes, soaking up all that was familiar and dear about her daughter. "It's so good to have you home, sweetheart." Still hugging Shelby, she heard the front door close and opened her eyes to discover a complete stranger standing next to Benjamin. The pale, wide-eyed girl wore an old coat buttoned to her chin and hugged herself with both arms. Was it possible that her brother had . . . married?

"Benjamin, aren't you going to introduce your young lady?"

He rolled his eyes and the girl looked even more discomfited. "Maddie, this is Vivian Croll, and she's Shel's friend, not mine. Oh—wait, I didn't mean that the way it sounded." Ben screwed up his face, pained. " 'Course we're *friends*, but not what you thought."

Holding her mother's hand and reaching for her grandmother's, too, Shelby drew them over to the spot where her Vivian was cowering against the door. "Gran Annie and Mama, Vivian has been my one female comrade where we live—and that's a long way from Cody. She's a very dear person and I know you'll make her welcome."

"Naturally!" Annie Sunday wore a smile that was comfortingly no-nonsense. "It appears that a hot, nourishing meal is in order. If you'll excuse me, I'll go and see what we have on hand."

Maddie was greeting Vivian and gently insisting that the girls take off their coats when Sun Smile quietly came out of the music room. Shelby's mouth dropped open.

"Auntie, I didn't know you were visiting! It's wonderful to see you!"

Sun Smile's eyes were warm with affection as they embraced. "I have missed you, little Wildblossom," she said, using the pet name she had bestowed on her niece when she was learning to walk. From the beginning, Maddie's sister had recognized Shelby's nature.

"And my cousins? Are they here?"

"No, they are at the agency school. Your mother needed someone to hold her hand now that all her children have flown the nest," Sun Smile said as she smiled wryly and patted her niece's cheek. "She doesn't seem to understand that you were much farther away when you were at college in Massachusetts."

"That was different," Fox rejoined, slipping his arms

around Maddie's waist. "Ben was here then, and he's always given Maddie plenty of mothering to do!"

"Hey!" Ben cried. "No insults!"

It was a joyous scene: the family reunited in the beautiful mansion, where fires danced in every fireplace while snowflakes fluttered past the windows. Maddie felt nearly overcome as she took it all in.

"I can't describe how happy I am!" She reached for her daughter's hand. "And how pretty you look, Shelby. I'm glad you've passed through that outrageous cowgirl phase." She paused then to bestow an extra smile on the starry-eyed Vivian. "To have you all here with weeks to spare before the holiday . . . this will be the best Christmas we've had in years! Only Byron's absence will keep it from being perfect. Shelby, you'll never know what it means to me that you came so far to be with your family for Christmas."

Shelby's own smile faded. She looked at her father, than at Ben, but neither of them offered any assistance. "Uh, Mama . . . I guess there's only one way to break this to you. We can't stay for Christmas. We have to be in New York by December fifteenth. . . ."

"But—*New York*? What on earth could be taking you to New York?" Then she looked faintly hopeful. "Are you engaged?"

Fox tightened his arms around his wife and gave Shelby a pointed look. "You'd better get it all on the table, honey. The details can be sorted out later."

As if sensing the building drama, Gran Annie's face appeared around the corner of the dining room. Sun Smile was calmly attentive, Maddie looked distraught, and Shelby now wore a sickly smile as she surveyed her audience. "Well . . . you see, I haven't *quite* passed through the cowgirl phase, Mama. Colonel Cody has asked me to take Annie Oakley's place as the female sharpshooter with the Wild West Show, and I've accepted. From New York, we sail to England!"

Never in her life had Vivian enjoyed such a luxurious bath. The Matthews mansion featured four incredible bathrooms upstairs, and the one adjoining Shelby's girlhood room was especially pretty. There was a mosaic floor, a marble sink, a modern water closet with an oak tank, and, best of all, the huge tub that now held an awestruck Vivian. Shelby had even added something to the water that made drifts of froth, and had given her friend some scented French shampoo paste to wash her hair, which had never felt silkier or smelled sweeter.

Scrubbed and relaxed, Vivian lay back in the bathtub and closed her eyes. Through the door, which was slightly ajar, she could hear Shelby talking with her mother. They had been sitting together on Shelby's brass bed when Viv had gone off to her bath, and she thought it would be nice to let them finish their conversation before she reentered the room.

"I must admit," Maddie murmured, "your Geoffrey Weston does sound like a wonderful man. Never in my wildest dreams would I have expected you to fall in love with a gentleman, much less a *nobleman*—but perhaps it's a case of opposites attracting. That's rather what happened with your father and me, and no two people could have shared a happier marriage than ours."

"But Mama, you do understand that Geoff is betrothed to someone else. Just because I'm going to England, and will probably meet him again when I am there, doesn't mean he'll change his mind." Shelby sighed. "He's duty-bound, you might say."

"Well, of course—if he is a *duke*, he was born to a life of both great privilege and great obligation. Oh, darling, it makes me giddy just to think that there is even a tiny char.ce that you could one day be a *duchess*!"

"Geoff is an earl," Shelby corrected. "His father is the Duke of Aylesbury, so I suppose he will one day inherit, but I don't think he cares about his title—beyond feeling that he must, in the end, do the honorable thing."

"And you two discussed this? Whether or not there was a way you could be together?"

"Not exactly . . ." Shelby went back over the events that had led up to Geoff's departure for England, as she understood them. "I truly was beginning to believe that, in spite of everything, he might change his mind and stay in Wyoming with me. I could see his feelings for me, and his pain, in his eyes. I think that, perhaps if he'd been able to stay the whole year, he might never have gone back. Even before the telegram came saying that his father was ill, I was trying to show him that I could be a lady as well as a cowgirl. I wore a dress, and I fixed up the house—"

"Perhaps he was hoping you would offer to live in *his* world?" Maddie suggested softly.

Her daughter sat wide-eyed, considering this. "I said many times that I couldn't bear to live as he had to, in English society. . . ."

"Oh, *Shelby*."

"But surely he'd have known, by August, that I loved him enough to do anything if it meant that we could be together! After all, I wasn't the one who was betrothed! His fiancée was writing letters to him at our ranch!"

"I still cannot believe that you could have been so foolish as to bet your father's ranch in a poker game," Maddie scolded. "Will you never learn to think before you act?"

"Great-Gramma Susan used to say that I was just like her mother! Meagan Hampshire was practically legendary, Mama, so I can't be all bad." Shelby paused.

"Geoff deeded the ranch back, so it's all fixed. You won't tell Daddy—at least not yet?"

"No, of course not." Maddie leaned closer and slipped an arm around her daughter, who was wearing the lace-trimmed flannel nightgown she'd received for her sixteenth birthday. "You're wonderful and delightful . . . but now you are venturing into a very crucial chapter in your life, and you must try to take care. Your Geoffrey moves in *royal* circles, and he has more to consider than the desires of his heart." She thought for a moment then, finally lamenting, "Oh, Shelby, *must* you make your entrance in London as a sharpshooter in the Wild West Show?"

"Yes, Mama. I would never have gotten up the courage to go at all if Colonel Cody hadn't convinced me, and I won't go back on my word. With Annie Oakley hurt, he genuinely needs me." A winsome smile lit her face. "Besides, it's no use pretending to be someone else. I am what I am, and since I can't compete with Lady Clementine Beech on her own terms, I may as well come in with a bang of my own!" Shelby giggled. "No pun intended."

Vivian came out of the bathroom then, wearing another of Shelby's old nightgowns and toweling her fine blond hair. "I hope I'm not intruding, but if I'd stayed in there any longer, I was afraid I'd be terribly wrinkled!"

"I was just leaving. I know you girls are tired, so I'll let you get to bed." Maddie kissed Shelby, then rose to embrace Vivian. "We're awfully glad you're going with our daughter to England, my dear. I know you'll look after her."

When her mother had gone, Shelby went into the bathroom to clean her teeth. Vivian, meanwhile, got into bed and stared at the elegant snow-white monogrammed bed linens. Her pillow was the deepest and softest she'd ever seen, and there were enough quilts on the bed so that there was no chance of feeling chilled in the middle of the night.

She called to Shelby: "I hope I didn't look too shocked when I saw your aunt Sun Smile! You never told me that you have an Indian aunt!"

"I've known her all my life, so she's not unusual to me," Shelby replied as she padded back into the room. "I don't give her Sioux blood any thought."

"I like her very much! It's just that . . . I had always heard that Indians were . . . heathens."

"Well, now you know better!" Shelby parried cheerfully. Putting out the light, she got in on the other side of the bed. "Viv, I hope you don't mind sleeping in here with me. I never even asked if you'd prefer a room of your own."

Unbidden, tears filled Vivian's eyes and throat. "Oh, after what I've had for the past year, this house is a palace, and this bed is big enough for ten of us."

Moonlight streamed into the bedroom through the long windows on the far wall, lending just enough light for Shelby to make out her friend's features. She turned toward her and whispered, "I hope I'm not prying, but I haven't been alone with you since we boarded the train in Cody. You haven't told me how you were able to get away from Bart. . . ."

The silence seemed bigger than the house. Vivian made sounds that weren't quite words, and then at last she managed to say in a curiously unemotional voice, "Well . . . I had to poison him."

"Poison him?" Shelby echoed, aghast.

"Yes. I put rat poison in his potatoes."

"Viv—do you mean that you *killed* him?"

"I had to." She turned the other way, snuggled down into the down pillow and savored the exquisite softness of the sheets. How could Shelby ever understand what had gone on in the Croll home? *"I had to."*

Chapter Fifteen

"I COULDN'T BE MORE RELIEVED TO HAVE CHRISTmas behind us," remarked the Earl of Sandhurst as he went into his dressing room to slip into the impeccably tailored charcoal-gray jacket that Manypenny was holding up. "Don't you agree, old fellow? All that *family* congeniality, coupled with the endless repetition of holiday customs, becomes tedious beyond endurance." He waited while the manservant whisked microscopic bits of lint from his back with a small silver brush. "I'll confess to you that my future in-laws are even more trying than my own parents. Of course, it's only because of the impending wedding that I was subjected to so *much* Christmas celebration—" The sight of Manypenny's barely perceptible flick of an eyebrow brought Geoff up short. "What was that about?"

"I have no idea to what you are referring, my lord."

"You arched your eyebrow; it's no use denying it, I am attuned to every nuance of your being."

"I am flattered to hear it, my lord."

His jaw hardened. "Manypenny, answer me!"

"I *may* have been thinking that you could be out of temper with Christmas because of the company you keep. I might believe that there is at least one person in this world who could persuade you to sing carols and drink wassail and eat plum pudding and decorate the entire house with pine boughs . . . and you wouldn't find any of it *trying* in the least."

Geoff closed his eyes against the pain. Sometimes he wondered if his heart was truly damaged, for memories of Shelby could pierce him like a dagger. But he was learning how to recover more quickly from such episodes. He clenched his teeth, took a deep breath, then opened his eyes . . . and saw the newspaper lying on his dressing table. It was open to an article with an unmistakable headline: WILD WEST SHOW OPENS TODAY AT EARL'S COURT.

"My lord, are you ill?"

Picking up the paper, he threw it into the waste bin. "Manypenny, I do not appreciate these decidedly unsubtle hints that I break all my promises here and dash back to Wyoming. You may as well face reality; I have."

"Allow me to beg your pardon, sir, if I have offended you. I only thought that you might wish to visit Earl's Court for a slight taste of that other world. . . ."

"If you assume that I have not been aware for weeks that Cody and the Wild West troupe were returning to London, you gravely underestimate my powers of observation. The city has been covered with advertising posters." His tone was cold. "I am going out. Where is my umbrella?"

"Here, my lord." Manypenny watched his master stride out of the dressing room: wide-shouldered, lean-muscled, and defiantly civilized in his superbly tailored and tasteful clothing. It gave the old manservant a lump in his throat just to watch him.

"Oh, incidentally . . ." Halfway across the spacious bedchamber, Geoff turned and looked back through the doorway. "I am off to Gloucestershire this afternoon, and I believe I shall ask Charles and Lady Clem to come along. London is a dead bore. You'll have to pack us up, Manypenny."

"Thank goodness Mama doesn't know how we're living," Shelby said to Vivian with a beleaguered smile. "Of course, I didn't know myself. If Colonel Cody had told me we'd be occupying a tent throughout the winter, I'm not certain I would have agreed to come."

"At least it has wood floors, and a stove to keep us warm."

"At least there's plenty of room for both of us," Shelby agreed. She was sitting on the edge of her cot, wrapped in sweaters and a coat, and sipping the hottest tea she could stand. "We were lucky to get Annie Oakley's own tent. Most of the others are smaller." She sighed. "I'm relieved, too, that I needn't perform yet."

"Very true."

"Can you think of anything else we should be thankful for?"

"Yes." Vivian's teeth chattered for a moment. It wasn't so much the cold that plagued them as the bone-chilling dampness of the London winter. "I'm thankful we aren't at sea any longer. I've never been sicker in my life. And—" She stole a sideways glance at her friend. "—I'm most grateful of all that I don't have to live with Bart Croll anymore. This is heaven in comparison."

"Shh!" Shelby cautioned. "You mustn't even say his name, Viv. If anyone should find out . . . I mean, I may understand completely, but I don't think the police would."

Vivian glanced down at her pale hands. She hadn't worn her wedding band since that day. As soon as he'd stepped over Willy's body and headed to the outhouse, Vivian had torn the ring from her hand so hard her finger had bled. And then she'd begun searching for the rat poison.

Shelby knew everything now. During the long sea voyage, Viv had been sick most of the time and Shelby had stayed beside her in their tiny stateroom. There, half delirious and plagued by horrendous nightmares, Viv had resurrected long-buried memories. She'd shown Shelby scars: a permanent welt on her back from Bart's belt, and the burn from the cigarette he'd put out on her thigh. Before long, however, it became clear to Shelby that Viv's innocent soul had been injured much more seriously than her body. "If only you'd told Geoff and me how bad it was," she had whispered, blinking back tears as she pressed a cool towel to her friend's brow. "We would have found a way to save you!"

Shelby might not have been able to rescue her in Wyoming, but she was determined to protect her now.

"Did you see that the flags in the arena are flying at half-mast?" Viv asked.

"Yes! Poor Colonel Cody is so broken-hearted over Nate Salsbury's death," Shelby replied. "First his son-in-law and now his partner—dying on Christmas Eve. I knew he wouldn't cancel the show, but I heard from Uncle Ben that the cavalry banner will be wrapped in crepe."

"Do you want to watch the show this afternoon?"

"No, I don't think so. I'd rather wait for better weather. Do you mind?" Her thoughts began to pick up speed then. "And, since I obviously can't practice while the show is in progress, why don't you and I go off to see London? Uncle Ben's been an absolute slave driver ever since we arrived at Earl's Court. Don't we deserve an afternoon off?"

Vivian had brightened. "Where shall we go?"

"To tell you the truth, I'm dying to visit the British

Museum, but perhaps we'd have more fun in Mayfair. I know my way around a bit from my journey here during college, so I can take you to Fortnum and Mason's to buy biscuits, jam, and tea for our lowly tent, and to Hatchard's Bookshop next door. After that . . . perhaps we'll go over to Harrods. It's a magnificent store, and there's a restaurant adjoining the Floral Hall, so we can have a nice hot luncheon." Shelby was brightening as she spoke. "What do you say, Viv? Let's get out of this dreary place before the mud oozes in and carries us away!"

Earl's Court was located on a big railroad junction in the West End. The grounds were comprised of twenty-three acres of gardens, courts, and exhibition halls. The Wild West Show had been performing there for fifteen years, and it felt like home now to the regulars. They had stables, a corral, and a grandstand that could seat twenty thousand spectators. The camp village, where Shelby and Vivian and Ben now lived, was erected among a grove of trees, and ran with surprising efficiency.

Vivian couldn't quite get used to the Indians, who strolled past her in full regalia, complete with feathers in their long black hair, and sometimes even wearing war paint. And there were countless other exotic performers from all corners of the world. Shelby constantly reminded Vivian that she needn't be afraid of strangers just because they happened not to be white.

Today, in spite of the drizzle, the mood in the camp was festive. As the girls headed toward West Cromwell Road, everyone they passed was in costume and excitedly anticipating the troupe's first show back on English soil. "Good luck!" Shelby called over and over, and Vivian managed to smile as well.

No sooner had they climbed into a hansom cab than Vivian forgot her intention to caution Shelby against being so friendly to a particularly fearsome-looking Brulé Sioux. Instead, as they rolled through the crowded, misty streets, she found herself pointing at every building and park they passed. "What's that?" became her refrain, and their driver, Nigel, was happy to act as tour guide.

They passed Kensington Palace, then the palace gardens adjoining the famous Hyde Park. Presently, Nigel yelled, "This 'ere's the entrance to Rotten Row," as he pointed to the archway on their left. "That's where all the dandies ride their fancy 'orses ev'ry mornin' an' afternoon! The lot of 'em need a honest day's work, *I* say!"

Shelby glanced over to find Vivian's staring, saucer-eyed, her thoughts as loud as if she'd spoken: *That's where* Geoff *comes to ride! If the sun were shining, would we see him right now?* Shelby's own preoccupation with Geoff's possible presence in London was so overwhelming that she wanted to keep it to herself. She wished now she'd never confided so much about her feelings to Vivian. Now that they were near him, Shelby wished her unrequited love were a secret.

"Shelby!" whispered Vivian. "Do you suppose—"

"No. He'd never be in London in the winter. The Season doesn't begin until spring." She looked away, erecting a barrier of privacy. "Please, don't even think about finding him."

"Oh." Viv bit her lip. "All right."

She fell silent for a time, pouting a little until Nigel made a slight detour to show them Buckingham Palace. "That's where King Edward and Queen Alexandra live! Not bad, eh? 'Course, we all miss dear Queen Victoria, God bless 'er, but me wife says it'll do England good to have young blood." He went on to explain that Queen Victoria hadn't even lived in London, preferring the quiet country atmosphere at Windsor Castle.

Vivian forgot to be cool toward Shelby. "Oh, mercy, just look at that! Do you suppose the king is looking out at us right now? I vow, never in my wildest dreams did I imagine that I could ever see such a place, and it's all thanks to you, Shelby!"

They passed some of London's finest homes along Green Park, and then the cab turned onto Piccadilly. There was the Royal Academy on the left, and St. James church on the right, and the most splendid carriages and richly garbed people that Vivian Croll had ever seen. She was speechless by the time the cab pulled over in front of Fortnum and Mason's.

" 'Ave a wonderful day, ladies!" Nigel cried, beaming over the tip Shelby had given him. "I'll keep an eye open for you later, a'right?"

As they walked toward the entrance to Fortnum and Mason's, Shelby held the umbrella aloft in one hand and guided her friend with her other hand. Vivian had never been anywhere except St. Louis and Wyoming until these past weeks, so Shelby could forgive her for staring openly at each new sight.

"Oh, God—Shelby!" she gasped suddenly, pointing toward Hatchard's Bookshop, which was located next door. "Look, look!" Realizing that Shelby seemed determined *not* to look, Viv gathered her wits and cried, "For pity's sake, it's *Geoff*! Hurry, before he's gone!"

Nearly swooning, Shelby stood on tiptoe and tried to find him. There seemed to be a sea of black umbrellas, plus lots of dark-suited men wearing bowlers. And then there he was . . . the recalcitrant aristocrat. Hatless, Geoff stood out in the crowd because of his golden hair and tanned skin. Even in December, he wore the lingering mark of the Wyoming sun, and his burnished looks were perfectly accentuated by a tasteful camel hair topcoat and a deep blue wool scarf. Under his arm he carried an unopened umbrella. It made Shelby feel giddy just to look at him.

In chiseled profile he spoke to the driver of an enclosed Mercedes motor car that was idling at the curb. The other man leaned out and replied, smiling, in the familiar way of a friend. Geoff turned back, looking toward Hatchard's again, and for an instant Shelby feared he might see her. Just then a woman came hurrying out of the bookshop, nearly dropping her parcels.

"For God's sake, Clemmie, come along before we begin to rust out here!" Geoff scolded genially.

The sound of Lady Clementine Beech's laughter sent a sharp pain through Shelby's heart, and yet she had to look. Her rival's face, half hidden by a Gainsborough hat, was plain at best. Yes, but her blood is blue! Shelby brooded. Geoff returned then to Clementine, gallantly carrying her packages and handing her the umbrella, while Shelby wept, unseen. Moments later the door of the cream-colored Mercedes closed behind them and it eased into the Piccadilly traffic, taking care not to frighten the horses.

"Are you all right?" Viv dared to whisper.

Shelby couldn't help straining for one more glimpse of his blond hair inside the Mercedes, but then it turned a corner and was gone. A powerful sense of hopelessness swept over her. She stood outside Fortnum and Mason's and pressed her hot, wet cheek against the cool gray stone while Vivian looked on in concern and passersby moved to and fro without even noticing her plight.

"It's too late," Shelby managed to say at last. "It's over."

"How can you say that? How do you know?"

She took out a lace-edge handkerchief and wiped her eyes. "He's not the same, Viv. And he was with her. It's too late."

"What are you going to do?"

"Why, just what I came to England to do. I'll fulfill my promise to Colonel Cody, and you and I will enjoy ourselves." Her voice was hollow, even as she forced herself to straighten up and smile. "It's not the end of the world! Let's go and have a cup of tea and buy ourselves some presents. I think that I should have lots of presents, don't you?"

As they went through the doors of one of England's oldest stores, Vivian offered, "My mother used to say, 'There are plenty of other fish in the sea where that one came from!' "

Shelby kept on smiling, but her heart said, *There is only one Geoff. . . .*

Deep in the Cotswolds of Gloucestershire, a picturesque village called Sandhurst nestled in a fold of rounded hills. The town's buildings were fashioned of golden limestone, the meadows were thick with sheep, and Geoffrey's ancestral home was located just a few miles south.

"It's as if time has stopped out here, don't you agree?" Charles remarked as he steered the mud-spattered Mercedes up the last hill leading to Sandhurst Manor.

"You always say that," Geoff murmured, stretched across the back seat, half asleep. Long ago, when they'd stopped for petrol, Lady Clem had climbed up in front with Charles for a better view, not to mention better company.

"I may as well tell you that my mother is terribly put

out with you for luring me to this remote spot without chaperones, or even my maid in attendance!" Clementine feigned shock herself, wagging a finger at Geoff although she wasn't certain whether he saw her under his hooded lids. "Do you have something *beastly* in mind, Geoffrey?"

At length, he replied sardonically, "No, actually. I thought I might save the beastliness for our wedding night."

Charles seemed to find this hugely amusing, laughing so loudly that Clementine gave him a sharp look and snapped, "Are you quite *finished*?"

A quarrel was averted when they gained the crest of the hill and Sandhurst Manor came into view. A fanciful salmon-brick concoction of turrets, half gables, and odd-sized chimneys, the house had been built in sections dating back to the fifteenth century. It was tucked all by itself into a deep valley, surrounded by extensive stables, ancient groves of beechwood, and lush gardens.

"Isn't it *odd* that I've never been here before?" Clementine remarked.

"Is it? Not to me." Geoff sounded bored. "You've spent lots of time at my parents' estates. This one is my own. There wasn't a reason to show it to you until now."

"Hmm." She looked unconvinced.

"I've always preferred the other name for the manor," Charles chirped, starting down the other side of the hill. "Have you heard, Clemmie? They call it Sandhurst-in-the-Hole."

"It is rather odd-looking." She squinted at the sprawling house. "Perhaps it's time to pull it down and put up something modern . . .?"

That roused Geoff. Sitting up with a start, he thundered, "Absolutely *not*! Not one brick of Sandhurst Manor will be altered unless I say so, is that clear?"

Shrugging, she glanced away. "There's no call for hysteria, my dear. I'll simply spend my time in the stables when we're here. Will that meet with your approval?"

The servants were lined up in anticipation, as if an entire house party of guests was arriving instead of this rather peculiar trio. Geoff always felt uncomfortable about these sorts of traditions, but felt equally powerless to change them. If he told Parmenter, the butler, and Meg, the housekeeper, that he didn't want them and their staff to go to so much trouble on his account, they would be crushed. So he gave them the kind yet slightly imperious greeting that they expected, and presented his friends.

"My lord, isn't Lady Clementine also your *betrothed*?" Meg ventured. As tall and spare as Parmenter was portly, Meg Floss was not much older than the Earl of Sandhurst, and had inherited her exalted position a year ago when her mother had died of influenza.

"Yes, you're right about that," Geoff replied. "She, uh, is." Why was it that the words invariably stuck in his throat? It killed him to introduce Clemmie as his future wife, although he had nothing against her. As chums, they dealt together quite well. "I'd like a bath, Meg, and I've left Manypenny behind in London. Can you show my guests to their rooms, then send someone to see to my bath?"

"Haven't you more luggage?" The housekeeper had a hopeful thought then. "Perhaps it's coming separately—with the others?"

He knew she was referring to the added guests and servants who usually would complete this sort of grand affair. "There are no others, and no more luggage. We've just popped in for a couple of days, Meg. Sorry."

Just as Geoff began to walk away, Parmenter called, "Beg your pardon, my lord, but I have wondered about His Grace's health. We've not heard very much since summer, when he had that spell. . . ."

Realizing how little thought he gave his father, Geoff felt another twinge. "He is much better, thank you. His heart appears to have strengthened, and he's been taking exercise. I spent a good deal of time with him over Christmas, and felt quite encouraged by his progress."

"His color is very good," Lady Clem put in, "but he refuses to give up his pipe."

"Ah, good for him," Parmenter agreed. "A man's got to protect his pleasures, after all, hmm?"

"Here here," Charles chimed in.

Geoff caught his sleeve and dragged him away, muttering good-naturedly, "Bloody idiot. I can't stand it when you wax philosophical. Come and have a drink in my room after a bit, all right?"

"What about Lady Clem?"

"She can have a drink in her own room."

The wings of Sandhurst Manor were grouped around a square courtyard of sculpted gardens, trellises, and stone benches. Inside, the house was a warren of rooms that included twenty bedchambers, a two-story great hall with an arched ceiling, a long gallery lined with Flemish tapestries on one side and courtyard windows on the other, and a magnificent library. One of the most splendid aspects of the manor was the generous application of intricately carved linen-fold paneling that dated back to the sixteenth century.

Bored with his grand suite upstairs, Geoff had decided last year to move to the ground floor. He liked being away from the other guests, if there were any, and favored French doors that opened onto a stone terrace. Also, he had had the sixteenth century buttery converted into a Moorish-style bathroom that featured a tiled pool-bath sunk in the floor. Blue and ocher baked-clay tile covered the walls in a colorful design, and there were stained-glass windows to let in jeweled sunbeams.

Few things gave Geoff as much pleasure as a long soak in his pool, though he'd only been in it a few times before setting off for America. Now he emerged from the steamy bathroom wrapped in a toweling robe, his tawny hair damp and curling slightly.

Charles Lipton-Lyons was standing by the fireplace, where a cheerful blaze was roaring. "I've brought the brandy," he said, and made a little toast with his glass.

Joining him, Geoff perched on the end of the mammoth testered bed and sipped the liquor. "Now that we're here, what do you suggest that we do?"

Charles laughed. "I thought you were the host! The weather doesn't seem to favor croquet, and we'd need a fourth for bridge." He paused, then added, "I thought that this outing was rather last-minute . . . almost as if you were anxious to get out of London. Wouldn't have anything to do with the Wild West Show, would it?"

"Have you been talking to Manypenny?"

"No, but I have enough wit to surmise that Cody's visit to London might remind you of Wyoming . . . and that, uh—ranch girl. What's her name again?"

"Shelby." It burned his throat to say it. "Stop calling her a ranch girl."

"Sorry, old fellow. No offense intended, but you really must get on with it, don't you agree? It's not fair to Clemmie that you're dreaming about this—Shelby person, when you're supposed to be thinking about marriage." It was difficult for Charles to put his heart into this speech since it was quite clear that Lady Clem was no more in love with Geoff than he was with her. What Charles did want was to find a way to bestir his old friend. "See here, you were supposed to come back from America revived, but instead you're even more . . ."

"Bored."

"Yes, more bored than you were before!"

"Perhaps that's because I know now what I'm missing." He finished his drink and gazed at Charles with expressive brown eyes. "I miss Shelby."

"I thought you told me, when you first returned to London, that it could never work. Do you remember that night? You may have had a bit too much whiskey, but you were impassioned all the same. You certainly convinced *me* that it was a brief affair that must be relegated to the past. You said that she could never live in your world, and you were unable to stay in hers, so it was better to face reality and—"

"I was probably trying to convince *myself*," Geoff murmured. "And I have tried. Why else would I subject myself to all that Christmas torture?"

"We can't run away from our responsibilities forever," he observed, starting on his second drink. "It may not be pleasant, but we have to marry, soldier on, produce heirs, and—"

"Egad, you make it sound as if we're in our dotage! Ready for a reserved table every noon at the club, followed by a pipe and a nap!" Geoff got up and paced across the room, then began getting dressed. "I would appreciate it if you'd leave me alone about my shortcomings, at least for the remainder of the weekend. I feel rotten enough as it is that I'm not more eager to please my father by sacrificing myself on the altar of our title. Then, there's my lack of enthusiasm for my betrothed—"

"You called?" Clementine poked her nose in, caught a glimpse of Geoff's bare calf, and withdrew.

The two men exchanged uneasy glances. "You weren't eavesdropping, were you, Lady Clem?" Charles called in jovial tones.

"I only heard Geoffrey utter the word 'betrothed.' It seems I'm more on his mind that I had guessed!"

"Come in for a drink," Charles urged. He drew her into the room.

"There isn't a lot to do in this hulking great castle," she remarked. With practiced ease Clementine poured three fingers of brandy into the glass and drank happily. Out of the corner of her eye she observed her fiancé buttoning a fresh pin-striped shirt from the tails up. The glimpse of his brown chest made her tilt her head to one side and smile.

"I believe I ought to make a telephone call to my parents," Charles exclaimed, and then he was gone.

Geoff wished he could leave the room, too, but clearly that wasn't the point. Instead he smiled at the woman who would be his wife. "Did you enjoy Christmas? I hope my family didn't drive you to distraction."

"No, not at all. I get on quite famously with Her Grace; she's so very certain about everything, rather like I imagine I shall be at her age." Lady Clem smiled, showing lots of teeth. "As for His Grace . . . as long as I let him beat me at chess, we did very well. Did *you* enjoy the holiday season?"

He blanched. "I? Why—I suppose so, as much as one might expect." Fastening another button, Geoff looked at Clementine and wondered why he had to be engaged to the one young woman who stirred not a single spark of desire within him. Of course, he didn't recall feeling aroused in the company of any female since he'd returned from America, but Lady Clem was singularly uninspiring. Her face was just a bit too angular, her jaw too pronounced, and her form too streamlined for his taste. There was nothing soft about Clementine that might invite his touch, nor any fragrance wafting out that made him instinctively long to smell the back of her neck. Her eyes were fine, but too no-nonsense; Geoff missed the warm luster and playfulness of Shelby's gaze. He also missed something even more important—the spiritual sympathy he and Shelby had enjoyed. With Clementine, he envisioned a lifetime of conversations involving the weather, deadly dull gossip about titled friends, problems with the servants, and perhaps on a good day, politics.

Or, the *children*. What sort of children might they produce?

Of course, the English aristocracy routinely married for convenience, then carried on separate lives. If he were lucky, he might not have to spend more than a few days a year in her company.

Geoff walked to the mantel and poured himself another glass of brandy, all too conscious of Clementine watching him.

"We'll manage somehow, you know," she said at length.

"I suppose so." He bit the inside of his lip in a way that made him, unknowingly, look even more appealing; then he sent her a flickering smile.

Emboldened by the liquor, she took a silver-backed comb from the bureau and walked up to Geoff. Summoning all her womanly arts, Clementine pressed lightly against him, reaching up to comb his damp hair into place. "I've loved your hair since we were children. It's like the sun."

You may as well give it a try, Geoff thought, and slid his hands around her waist. When he drew her into his embrace, yearning for Shelby nearly overcame him, all the more acute because Clementine felt nothing like Shelby, smelled nothing like Shelby, and, when he kissed her, tasted nothing like Shelby. Her arms were around his shoulders. Her breathing changed; she was returning his kiss, parting her lips, but for Geoff it was a moment completely without inspiration. He felt sick inside, more at himself than anything.

Clementine slipped a hand inside his shirt, eagerly caressing the contours of his chest and the light gilding of hair that curled above his collarbone. She kissed him there and it was clearly a signal.

Deliverance took the form of a knock at the door. His heart jumped with relief as he went to answer it. There stood Charles, looking as if he'd seen a ghost. "Come out into the hallway for a moment, all right?"

"What is it?" A strong sense of unreality permeated the entire scene.

"I'm sorry to tell you, old chap." Charles put a hand on his shoulder, where Clementine has just been clinging with such unlikely fervor. "I've spoken to my mother—"

"Yes?" Geoff prodded.

"Your father—His Grace died peacefully early this afternoon." Charles's voice seemed to come from a distance. "Your mother didn't know where to find you at first. I think they have sent someone from London to tell you. Dear old friend, you are now the Duke of Aylesbury. . . ."

Chapter Sixteen

"USED TO BE THAT IT WAS ENOUGH TO BE ABLE TO shoot a cork from a bottle, especially if you happened to be female," Buffalo Bill remarked to his newest protégée. They were standing in the middle of the showgrounds at Earl's Court, where Shelby and Ben practiced for hours each day. "But now there are so many fancy shooters that the audience demands a moving target. Missie had to outdo herself every year. . . ."

Shelby knew that "Missie" was his nickname for Annie Oakley, who seemed to be hovering over her shoulder, at least in spirit. As the winter wore on and her own March debut with the Wild West Show neared, it was hard not to compare her own skills with those of her predecessor, an international star.

"Annie Oakley sent me some of her favorite Schultze gunpowder," Shelby told Colonel Cody now as she paused to reload. "And she wrote me a very nice note, wishing me luck. I am so sorry for her injury."

The Wild West Show wasn't doing as well this London season as it had in the past, and sometimes Cody looked as if he had a heavy weight on his shoulders. "We seem to be plagued with bad luck, ever since beginning of the new century, and Missie's train crash was a big blow. I still think maybe it's time for me to retire and concentrate on my projects in Wyoming. I'm too old for this punishing life, and I don't want to die a showman."

Ben patted him on the shoulder and smiled. "You'll know when it's time to pack it in, Colonel. I still see that sparkle in your eyes when the show starts and you ride into the ring!"

"I imagine you're right . . . although even that's changed now that I've lost Old Pop, my faithful horse. This replacement just isn't the same." He sighed, drew off his hat, and ran a hand through his long, snowy locks. "You know, I'd like to cut my hair, but I'm not sure if it would hurt business. Do you suppose the public would stand for it?"

Shelby sensed what he really wanted to hear. "I believe, sir, that it's reassuring to people to see you looking the same, year in and year out. You're a living legend." She looked to her uncle. "Don't you think, Ben?"

"Yeah, I do. Listen, I'm ready for some lunch. What do you say we take an hour's break, then meet back here to keep working on the mirror trick?"

"Missie was shooting while looking into a mirror years ago," Cody informed them.

"I can only hope that the audience will allow for the fact that I'm new, and younger, and not expect as much of me," Shelby said honestly.

"You're prettier, too, little girl. And you're saucy. Missie liked to play to the audience and make them laugh. If you can do that, it won't matter if you miss a shot or two, or leave out some of the harder tricks." He gave her a smile so charming that it nearly restored her spirits, then tipped his hat to them and went off to confer with a group of blanket-clad Indians waiting at the edge of the field.

The weather was frigid and dank, causing Shelby to

turn up the collar on her coat. "Perhaps I'll take Gadabout for a ride around the ring while it's quiet here. I feel badly that we brought the horses over and haven't more time with them."

"I still say you oughta give Charlie back to Geoff," Ben said. "You want me to do it?"

"No!" Her cheeks flamed. "No. If he had wanted Charlie, he would have said so when he left Wyoming."

"Did you see the newspaper I put in your tent this morning? Viv said she'd give it to you."

"I didn't have time to loll around reading the *Times*. I was out here before you were! And what on earth does the newspaper have to do with Geoff's horse?"

"Not the horse—*Geoff*." Sensing that this wasn't a subject to make light of, he softened his tone. "Did you ever see anything printed about his father's death?" When Shelby didn't reply, but continued to wait with a wary expression, Ben continued, "Well, today's article said that he died the day after Christmas. Geoff's the Duke of something-or-other now, and him and some Lady Whoosit are gettin' married in a few weeks. They had a small reception last night just to announce the wedding date, and the new king and queen showed up to congratulate them."

"Oh." Shelby heard herself speak; felt her head nod. "I see."

Ben's heart went out to her, but he could tell she didn't want to be hugged, which was just as well because he wasn't any good at that. "Who can figure out men? I'm one myself, and even I get confused. We all know how Geoff felt about you, Shel, but I guess that over here *duty* is more important than just about anything else. It seems like it doesn't count that he was happy on the Sunshine Ranch, with you and Charlie and the rest of us."

"I'm hungry," Shelby said abruptly. "I'll see you after lunch." She gathered up the shotgun, revolver, and converted rifle she'd been practicing with, and trudged back to the camp village.

Vivian was emerging from their tent just as Shelby arrived. She wore her best clothes: a dove-gray skirt with a white, lace-trimmed blouse that Shelby had purchased for her in New York City as a surprise. Viv's protection from the elements was a three-quarter-length blue wool coat that had belonged to Madeleine Matthews, and she wore a matching feather-trimmed hat that made her hold herself a little straighter.

"Oh, Shelby—I'm surprised to see you!"

"Why, Viv, you look as if you're rushing off to an assignation!"

"No! I'm . . . just going out for a bit. I've just grown tired of the same surroundings."

"Good for you. I wish I could go along!" Shelby saw the flicker of panic in her friend's eyes, but was too preoccupied to wonder what it meant. "I'm just going to get a bite of lunch, then go back to practice some more. And by the way, Uncle Ben said that he gave you the *London Times* this morning. Is it inside?"

Her cheeks turned even pinker. "Let me check." Viv rushed back into the tent and rifled through the wire wastebasket, plucking out the newspaper just as Shelby came in herself. "There's really not much worth reading—"

"I've already heard about Geoff, if that's what you're intent on keeping from me."

"I can see that you'd rather I let you alone." She handed over the *Times* and gave her friend a long look. "I'll see you later."

Alone in the tent, which was quite cozy now, with a Persian rug on the floor, books and china and pieces of furniture, and the stove going constantly to keep the girls warm, Shelby took the newspaper and sat down with it on the edge of her cot. Dry-eyed, she read the article through about Geoffrey Weston, Duke of Aylesbury, who was such a great support to his mother, the dowager duchess, in the wake of the old duke's sudden death. "Friends of the family have remarked on the impeccable behavior exhibited by not only the new duke, but also his betrothed, Lady Clementine Beech. She has been a tremendous support to one and all." The writer, having long since abandoned any pretense of impartiality, went on to predict that "the wedding, on April the fourth, of the Duke of Aylesbury and Lady Clementine Beech, will be the crowning event of the spring of 1903. These young nobles are shining examples of the newly begun Edwardian Age, already marked by the welcome return of royalty to London."

Shelby hurt terribly. Why had she ever come to London at all? Looking back, she felt foolish to have imagined for one moment that there was a possibility that Geoff would have second thoughts and choose her over the life to which he had been born. There had not been even the smallest hint of indecision when the time came for him to leave the Sunshine Ranch. Shelby had been told all her life that she must learn to take no for an answer, and now, for the first time, she was prepared to accept that advice. She wished she were back home in her own bed, tucked in, with her mother smoothing the hair back from her brow with cool fingers.

Tears splashed onto the newspaper. Shelby wiped her eyes with the back of her hand, then reached around under the front of her cot and drew out a violet-papered hatbox. Inside were little reminders of Geoff: the horsetail mustache she'd worn as Coyote Matt, a box from the Mexican Headache Cure he'd mocked so charmingly, the slim volume of Tennyson that he'd left behind, a blue bandanna that she'd borrowed from him, the recording of "In the Good Old Summertime," the soft-ribbed vest she'd worn that night in bed, the goodbye letter he'd written her, and the pillowcase from his bed.

So many things, like the bicycle and the gramophone and Geoff's smile and his touch and the sound of his voice, wouldn't fit in the box, but it comforted her to have even a few mementoes of the most truly happy time of her life.

Everything that happened to her from now on would be measured against those few achingly sweet months.

As tears slipped down her cheeks, Shelby opened the volume of Tennyson and looked at the poem Geoff had read aloud to her that night of their first kiss. *"How dull it is to pause, to make an end/ To rust unburnish'd, not to shine in use . . . 'tis not too late to seek a newer world . . . To strive, to seek, to find, and not to yield . . ."*

Deep in Shelby's soul, she felt a faint quiver of hope. If she wanted it, life would go on.

The last time Vivian had gone for a walk alone, she'd run back to Earl's Court after ten minutes because she'd caught a glimpse of a man looking out at her from a closed carriage—a man with burning eyes who seemed to look exactly like Bart Croll. Vivian told herself it was impossible; no one could have survived the amount of rat poison she'd put in his potatoes. He'd writhed so much that she couldn't watch, couldn't bear the cursing and accusations that marked his death throes, so she'd said she was going for the doctor and had never come back.

Everyone might agree that he was a horrible person

and deserved to die, but what did God say? Even Shelby had been shocked that she had really *killed* another human being, no matter what he might have done to her first. Had Bart's ghost come to haunt her, to get her to confess her terrible crime to the police, to accept the punishment?

Today, when Vivian was tempted to glance back to see if Bart was watching her, she tried instead to concentrate on the importance of her errand. It was nearly noon when she reached the Strand, emerged from a hansom cab, and hurried down a cobbled alleyway that led to a great house built of white stone. One side faced the River Thames, affording its occupants a magnificent view of all manner of activity on the water.

Were those footsteps she heard coming from behind? Vivian was rounding the corner of a black iron fence as she allowed herself a backward glance, and then collided with a strange man. Nerves overcame her and she let out a scream as she tumbled backward toward the pavement.

"I say! I'm dreadfully sorry, miss!"

The fellow who had frightened her now looked perfectly gallant, reaching out to help her up, smiling with the kindest eyes she'd ever seen. "Thank you, sir." She smiled in return. "It was my fault. I wasn't looking where I was going."

"Permit me to introduce myself. I am Charles Lipton-Lyons, a childhood friend of the new Duke of Aylesbury. Do you know His Grace?" Intrigued by her American accent, Charles set her on her feet and found that she was much smaller than he. There was something fragile and vulnerable about this mysterious young woman.

"Actually, I do, sir, but you mustn't tell him you've met me!" Her eyes were big as she lay a finger over her lips. "It's a secret! I've come to see Mr. Manypenny, not Mr. Weston."

"Then, let me take you to Manypenny. Geoff's right in the morning room in front of the house, trapped with his mother, so I'll sneak you in the back, all right?" He took her tiny hand and noted the flush that crept into her pale cheeks. "Aren't you going to tell me your name?"

"Promise not to tell?"

"If you'll call me Charles."

"All right, Charles." She leaned forward, feeling coquettish for the first time in her life. "My name is Vivian."

Powerfully relieved to find that this wasn't Shelby the ranch girl, Charles beamed at her. "Good enough. You can tell me the rest of your name the next time we meet." They started toward the servants' entrance to Sandhurst House. "Are you going to be in London very long? I would be delighted to show you the sights!"

"That would be very nice." They lingered outside the door for a moment, shivering in the wintry wind that blew up from the Thames. "But Charles, I'll have to send word to you . . . and first you must promise again that you won't breathe a word to your friend about me."

"I do promise, and I'm becoming quite fed up with saying so! In any case, Geoff has so much on his mind right now that he doubtless wouldn't register—"

This time Viv lay a finger over Charles's mouth, then drew back as she realized how daring she'd been. With his neat dark hair, mustache, and ruddy complexion, he seemed kind and sweetly earnest, and best of all, he made her feel safe. "Just promise."

"I bloody do." His heart was thudding with excitement as he reached into his breast pocket and took a calling card from a silver case. "You can reach me anytime. Would you like to have dinner, and then perhaps go with me to the Hippodrome?"

"I have to go now. Mr. Manypenny is waiting for me." With that, Vivian slipped through the door and left Charles Lipton-Lyons wondering if he'd been conversing with a fairy. Vivian was the most ethereal woman he'd ever met.

"If not for your approaching nuptials, my dear Geoffrey, I would have returned to Yorkshire within the week of your father's passing." Edith Weston, Dowager Duchess of Aylesbury, sat stiffly on a gold gilt chair in the pristine morning room. Still beautiful at sixty, she wore her widow's black as if it were a fashion statement; a stunning contrast with her upswept mass of snow-white hair. "I would much prefer to spend the winter at Aylesbury Castle, where I might grieve in private. Now I understand why Queen Victoria stayed at Windsor Castle, removed from London, after she lost Prince Albert."

Geoff squeezed lemon into his tea. "For God's sake, Mother, I hope you don't hold the queen up as your model for widowhood. She was in mourning for *forty* years!"

"I will not allow you to make clever remarks on this subject."

He took a breath before replying, "You might save yourself aggravation if you could accept the fact that you are not able to control the words I speak."

"If only fate had not decreed that you would be the only child born to us, I might place less importance on your behavior. As it is, all the world is focused on you, Geoffrey. Everyone is watching, waiting to discover if the new Duke of Aylesbury is half the man his father was." She paused, pursed her lips slightly, then added, "Don't gulp your tea, dear boy. One must *sip*."

Rising, Geoff walked to the windows facing the Strand and suppressed an urge to claw the glass. *How can this be happening? How can she say such asinine things? Why was I born into this world?* "Mother, I realize that you are having a difficult time of it, and I do sympathize. After all, I have lost my father, so I'm grieving as well."

"*Are* you?" Edith parried in acid tones. She knew just the way to prod his guilt. She might not have spent much time with Geoff, but she was his mother, after all, and instinctively she understood him . . . when she chose to.

"I am not going to apologize to you for refusing to be molded like a lump of clay," Geoff said coldly. "I won't pretend that I'm enjoying my life here, but I am trying to cultivate the sense of obligation that Father believed to be so crucial to a worthwhile existence. I am aware that I have certain duties simply because I am the sole heir."

"This privileged life is a blessing, not a curse, dear boy."

He walked back to stand before her, impeccably turned out in riding clothes, a white four-in-hand tie, and gleaming black boots. "I wish I believed that; it would make everything so much easier."

"Well, at least you *look* like a duke! I couldn't wish for a handsomer son. And we've found you a bride who understands the noble life, so one can only hope that it will all work out in the end, hmm?"

"I wish I could stay and continue this thought-provoking conversation, but I must exercise Thor. May I see you out, Mother?"

The dowager duchess gave him a bored smile that

was eerily like his own. "I'm not going just yet. Our wonderful Clementine is arriving momentarily, and we are going to sort through your china, crystal, and linens to see how much will have to be discarded. Your bachelor things simply won't do for your married household, Geoffrey."

It felt to Geoff as if a vise were tightening around his chest. From the doorway, he turned to deliver a subtle counterattack. "Oh, by the way—did I tell you that I'm dismissing the estate manager at Sandhurst Manor?"

Her Grace gasped. "Is this your notion of a jest?"

"Not at all. I'm going to begin looking after the estates myself, not only because the work will do me good, but also because we can do with a bit of economy. Have you any idea how large a death duty we must pay?" His brows arched slightly. "Times are changing, Mother, and I intend to face reality."

"Why . . . this is simply shocking, Geoffrey!" She sank back in the chair, her hand to her heart. "Managing one's own estate would be so . . . undignified!"

"I mean to do it anyway. Good-bye, Mother." He strode out of the morning room and left the house by the front door, nodding to the servants.

Outside, Geoff noticed a tall, bald-headed man resembling Manypenny. The fellow was on the other side of the fence, handing a thin young woman with pale hair and a blue hat into a hansom cab. Geoff was about to dismiss the two strangers and turn toward the stables when the cab set off briskly and the bald man started back toward Sandhurst House.

"Gad! Is *is* you!" Geoff couldn't help laughing as he walked up the drive to meet Manypenny. "I thought my eyes were playing tricks on me."

The old gentleman was decidedly uncomfortable. "No, Your Grace, they were not . . . playing tricks."

"How many times have I asked you not to call me that?"

"More than I can count . . . sir."

"Then unless you've gone soft in the head, I see no reason for you to persist in using that ridiculously exalted form of address!" Geoff scowled, then a twinkle returned to his eyes as he remembered the spectacle of his manservant skulking about with a fair-haired girl young enough to be his granddaughter. "Now then, you must tell me what you were up to with that pretty young lady I glimpsed. You aren't carrying on some sort of love affair in secret . . . ?"

"Certainly not, sir!" Manypenny spluttered. He then had a thought that caused him to recover his composure. "Am I not entitled to a bit of privacy? Yes? I thought so. If you'll pardon me, sir, I must return to my duties."

He left Geoff staring after him in consternation. Walking back to the house, Manypenny dipped his head, not only to avoid the wind, but also to hide the smile he could no longer suppress. How smashing it had been to see Vivian Croll, and to know that Shelby and Benjamin and even the horses, Gadabout and Charlie, were right here in London! It would be hard to refrain from seeking Shelby out, for Manypenny truly adored her, but Mrs. Croll had convinced him that they must work together to bring off a grander scheme. Since neither His Grace nor Shelby seemed to know what they must do, it was left to others to intervene. . . .

Shelby had been practicing relaxation exercises for two weeks preceding her debut with the Wild West Show, and now, on March 14, 1903, she lay on her cot with her eyes closed just an hour before the performance was scheduled to begin.

"I can't believe you're this composed," Vivian exclaimed as she burst into the tent. "Ben is *shaking*, and his part is nearly all behind the scenes!"

"Well, you know me." Slowly, Shelby sat up and smiled at her friend. "If I'd been left to my own devices, I would have been a bundle of nerves by today, and then I'd've shot someone's head off! It was Chief Iron Tail who explained that I could train myself to be calm. He's a wonderful, wise man."

"Are you going to get dressed now?" Vivian opened the beautiful trunk that Buffalo Bill had given Shelby when she joined the Wild West Show. A near duplicate of the one Annie Oakley traveled with, it unfolded to reveal drawers that held her costumes, and a dresser top with a mirror built in.

"I've never seen you so excited, Viv!" Laughing, Shelby put her arm around her as she was swept by a wave of affection. "Have I told you that I couldn't manage without you? Even Colonel Cody is grateful for your presence, especially since you persuaded him to invite King Edward and Queen Alexandra to attend today. He had been uncertain, thinking that it was too soon since their August coronation for such frivolity, but now that they're coming, he's convinced that this is the event that will turn things around for the tour."

"I was afraid that you'd be angry when you learned I'd suggested that they sit in the royal box the same day as your debut," she replied nervously.

"Well, I've decided it's just as well. I'll admit just to you, Viv, that I do think about Geoff. At least so far, no one knows I'm here and my name hasn't been in the advertisements. If the king and queen had attended after I'd begun performing, Geoff might've accompanied them, and I couldn't bear that."

"Don't you think he might be here today?"

Shelby shook her head emphatically. "No! It's too near his wedding, and I think that if he were nostalgic for reminders of Wyoming, he would have visited already. I've decided that he's avoiding memories of me as much as I'm avoiding him." Her eyes shone as she added, "It's just as well, Viv. It would break my heart to see him again, and I've had enough heartache. I just want to get this tour over with so that we can go home."

Vivian wasn't so sure she would go home, given her hasty departure just before the inevitable discovery of Bart's body. She also wasn't sure she wanted to leave London. Charles Lipton-Lyons had taken her out for two long, exciting, chaste evenings of suppers, theater, and opera, and it was all she could do not to tell Shelby about him. Shelby thought Viv was visiting an ancient aunt who lived in Bayswater.

"This costume is ridiculous," Shelby pronounced as she turned around to be fastened up the back. "Maybe Annie Oakley could get away with it, but—"

"You look just perfect!" Vivian handed her a wide-brimmed straw hat. From a distance they could hear the opening notes of the "Star Spangled Banner" wafting into the camp village. "We'd better hurry! You're the third act on the program!"

Taking deep breaths to keep herself calm, Shelby looked around to make certain Ben had all her firearms and accessories at the showgrounds. She took a last peek in the mirror, laughed at her reflection, and let Viv pull her out of the tent.

"It was splendid of you to accompany us today, Geoff," King Edward VII said as his party settled itself in the royal box. "Having just come from the American West, in the vicinity of Buffalo Bill's own town, you doubtless will bring an authentic perspective to our outing."

"It really is so exciting," Queen Alexandra chimed in. "The last time we attended, the performance was spectacular. Have you been to the Wild West Show, Lady Clementine?"

"No. I haven't."

The queen took a moment to see that her grandsons, Prince Edward and Prince Albert, were settled, leaving the bride-to-be an opportunity to fume.

The last thing Clementine had wanted to do was remind Geoff of his months in Wyoming, for it was quite apparent to her that the experience had changed him. Even before he went away, he certainly hadn't been happy, but at least he'd been witty and bold and fond, so she'd heard, of sex. Since his return to England, and especially since he'd become Duke of Aylesbury, Geoff's characteristic air of boredom seemed to have a harder edge. That didn't bode well for their marriage . . . but when Lady Clem discussed the matter with Charles Lipton-Lyons, he had assured her that Geoff would forget about Wyoming in time.

The American ambassador and Mrs. Choate were seated behind the betrothed couple, and now they leaned forward to engage Clementine in conversation about her wedding plans. Geoff was grateful, for he found it impossible to behave as an attentive fiancé ought. Listening to the cowboy band play a sort of overture, he felt a painful yearning for everything he'd loved about Wyoming. It hurt even to think of the town of Cody, of the tumbleweeds and Jakie Schwoob and Purcell's Saloon and the splendid views that marked the South Fork Road . . . but he still tried to block Shelby from his mind. When she did appear, unbidden and burningly real, Geoff felt angry—with fate, he supposed.

I shouldn't have come. I shouldn't have let Manypenny convince me that it would do me good.

When the band struck up the "Star Spangled Banner," Geoff clenched and unclenched his hands, then pressed them to his tense thighs. He had dressed with special care that morning and wore a suit of soft gray wool, a crisp white shirt, and a waistcoat of blue-gray corded silk. There was a hint of spring in the air, heightened by sunshine, and Geoff hadn't needed an overcoat.

As the band played on, Buffalo Bill suddenly burst into the arena, riding a black charger. The audience roared and the two young princes jumped to their feet. Cody rode toward the royal box and announced in his distinctive, resonant voice, "Your Majesties, ladies and gentlemen, allow me to introduce to you the greatest Congress of Rough Riders in the world!"

The king raised his hat to acknowledge the old showman, and the American ambassador explained, "Perhaps Your Majesties do not know that Colonel Cody coined the term 'Rough Riders' five years before our great President Roosevelt used it for his cavalry during the Cuban war!"

Geoff sat forward, intent on the spectacle that was unfolding below them. There was a grand review that led off the show, featuring colorfully dressed Indians, cowboys, gauchos, Cossacks, Mexicans, Arabs, as well as mounted soldiers from armies around the world. They paraded around while the band played, and the princes could scarcely contain their excitement.

Seeing the cowboys, in their Stetson hats and sheepskin chaps and bright kerchiefs tied around their necks, Geoff ached again for that way of life he'd left behind.

He felt Clementine staring at him, and knew he ought to reach for her hand to reassure her, but he could not. It was as if his heart, opened by Shelby, had closed tighter than ever when he left her. He couldn't manage even to pretend.

"And now, folks, it's my pleasure to introduce the newest member of our troupe!" Cody was shouting, still on horseback. "She's every bit as lovely and spirited as our beloved Annie Oakley. Give a warm welcome to our Little Trick Shooter: Shelby Matthews!"

Geoff opened his mouth, but no sound came out, not even a gasp. No sound could equal his feelings at that moment. It wasn't possible . . . yet with his own eyes he stared as Shelby came capering into the arena, holding her Winchester repeating rifle at a jaunty angle. She was smiling her wide, winsome smile, as if she'd been performing for years.

Chapter Seventeen

THE APPROVAL OF THE CROWD WAS LIKE A TIDAL wave of goodwill rolling over Shelby, and she responded immediately. In her navy-blue dress with white trim, which showed off a tiny waist circled by a silk sash, and with blue-stockinged calves and matching slippers, she was an intriguing blend of schoolgirl and beautiful woman. Her hair rippled down her back, gleaming like cognac in the sunlight, and under the brim of her boater-style hat, Shelby's piquant features had never been more irresistible.

Ben Avery, in full cowboy attire, followed his niece into the arena at a discreet distance. It did him good to see her light up this way; it was the first time she'd looked truly happy since Geoffrey Weston had left the Sunshine Ranch half a year ago. Waiting by a table draped with silk and laden with rifles, shotguns, and various props, Ben looked for the royal box, which was decorated with both American and British flags. It was easy to spot the king, with his Vandyke beard and portly physique . . . and sure enough, there was Geoff—just as Vivian had predicted. He reminded Ben of a watchful lion, leaning partially into a shadow, but there was no mistaking the curve of his shoulder or the amber gleam of his hair.

Shelby was almost laughing as she scampered back

to join her uncle. "It's going to be fine!" she whispered happily. "I can feel it!"

They had decided to keep the act easy today, then add tricks as their level of confidence grew. Shelby started off with an exhibition of elementary rifle shooting, then caught the audience off guard when she threw up a glass ball high in the air, quickly aimed her rifle and hit the target. The cheering was so sustained that Ben wondered if they shouldn't stop right there.

They tried a number of stunts. Ben pulled the trap and Shelby shot clay pigeons; first one, then two, and finally three at a time. She stood with her back to the trap as it was pulled, then turned and fired. They moved on to more complicated tricks, one of which called for Shelby to lie down with her back on her chair, then shoot at a ball that Ben swung back and forth on a string.

Finally she attempted one of Annie Oakley's own famous mirror shots. For her variation, Shelby held a tiny mirror with her left hand, and lay her rifle on her shoulder, pointing behind her, her right hand on the trigger. Ben stood on a stool perhaps fifty feet back, holding an ace of hearts out in the air. Then, using only the mirror to guide her aim, Shelby fired backward, and nothing happened. The crowd was as silent as if the arena was a church.

Shelby took a deep breath, exhaled slowly, aimed again and squeezed the trigger gently—and the card flew out of Ben's hand.

The band began to play "In the Good Old Summertime," and Shelby laid her last smoking rifle on the table and blew a kiss to the audience, now on its feet. Then, as the wild cheers of the spectators mingled with the briskly paced song, she held onto her hat with one hand and went running across the grounds, pausing only to toss one more wink and smile over her shoulder before disappearing behind the white canvas curtains.

Shelby's heart was pounding like crazy. Johnny Baker, the celebrated marksman who had been with the show for twenty years, rushed to clasp her hand.

"Good for you, Shelby! They love you!"

The crowd had been forced to stop applauding her because another act was beginning. A wagon train, like ones that had taken so many pioneers west, was moving into the arena. The program announced that it would be "attacked by marauding Indians who are in turn repulsed by 'Buffalo Bill' and a number of scouts and cowboys." There was so much noise that Shelby was forced to yell to be heard.

"I know that my talents are meager compared to yours, Johnny, and I'm not very fast yet. That's why Colonel Cody coached me to play to the audience." Now that it was over, she felt a little embarrassed by her own showing off. "If they had Annie Oakley herself here to compare me to, I'd be booed off the show grounds!"

"Nonsense. You have star quality, and that means more than you know!" A short man, Baker was able to look right into her eyes as he spoke. "And you were smart not to try anything too hard the first time out. Go slow and give 'em those theatrics and you'll do fine!"

Vivian was waiting, too, to congratulate her friend, and Ben caught up with them after he'd stored her guns. The area offstage was crowded with hundreds of performers and horses, so it was easy to get lost. Ben had an easier time tracking down Shelby and Viv because they were among only a handful of women in the entire troupe.

"Shel!" he barked, catching her by the back of her skirt. "Don't think about goin' back to your tent; Colonel Cody says you have to stick around to meet the king and queen when the show is over!"

"What? But Uncle Ben, you'll come with me, won't you?"

"Nah, I'm not invited."

"But what will I say?" Shelby wailed. "This is terrible!"

Chief Iron Tail, waiting nearby on horseback as the Indians prepared to attack, chuckled at the sight of her stricken expression. "Shelby is not afraid to shoot a card out of her uncle's hand, but quakes at the thought of shaking hands with a mere man!"

In the midst of the laughter that followed, Vivian managed to pull Ben Avery aside for a private word: "I don't care if you weren't invited. Don't you see? You have to go with her. Shelby might sneak off and avoid the reception, or she might faint when she sees him! In any case, you must distract that awful woman Geoff's engaged to marry, so that he and Shelby are free to at least greet each other!"

"*Distract* her!" Ben hissed. "How'm I supposed to do *that*?"

"Don't be crabby, for heaven's sake. I have heard from very reliable sources that Lady Clementine loves horses. Why don't you offer to give her riding lessons in Hyde Park? Tell her to bring her friends."

"Can I charge 'em?"

Viv laughed in spite of herself. "Why not?"

The princes were clamoring to visit the Indian Village and meet the cowboys, but first they had to stand still while their grandparents received the stars of the Wild West Show.

Ever since he'd heard Cody speak Shelby's name, Geoff had been numb with a mixture of shock and joy

. . . and dread. How in the world could they meet, surrounded by not only the royal party, but also the woman he was to marry in little more than a fortnight?

He stood on the far side of King Edward, and since His Majesty cut a very large figure, Geoff could remain nearly hidden if he wished. Unfortunately, he could not make himself invisible.

William F. Cody was the first to appear, and the king and queen greeted him with reminiscences of the first performance of the Wild West Show they had attended with Queen Victoria in 1887.

"Wasn't that a grand day?" Buffalo Bill agreed. "It was a high point in the history of our show! There were four kings present, from Greece, Saxony, the Belgians, and Denmark, and I took all of them for a ride in the Deadwood stagecoach!"

King Edward nodded. "Yes, and I, as the mere Prince of Wales, sat with you as you drove. Perched up on top, swaying and jolting with each bump and turn, I believe that I was treated to a more thrilling experience than the monarchs inside!"

"Do you remember also what you said to me later?"

"Yes, I told you that you had had a magnificent poker hand that afternoon: four kings!"

The laughter that accompanied this exchange seemed to relax not only the royal party, but also the Wild West performers. They came one by one, the cowboys and scouts, the international soldiers, the Indians in all the finery that they had worn during the many dramatic scenes in the show, and all the other stars, doffing their hats, helmets, and headdresses as they met the new royal family.

King Edward was particularly delighted to see Johnny Baker, for they, too, had met in 1887. The two men shook hands vigorously, the monarch heaped compliments upon the American, and then he remarked, "I missed Annie Oakley in today's performance, but that new female certainly makes up in style what she lacks in skill. I found her excessively charming!"

"Yes, indeed," chimed in the queen.

Johnny declared that he couldn't agree more. "Where is that little sprite? For all her bravado in the arena, Shelby went white when she heard that she was to meet Your Majesties." Leaning back, Johnny craned his neck until he spotted Shelby and Ben standing uneasily at the very end of the line. "Come up here, you two! The king himself is looking for you, Shelby!"

Geoff thought his heart would jump out of his chest when he saw Shelby approaching, wearing an expression of disarming uncertainty. It was all he could do not to step forward and reach for her, but with the king on one side of him and Clementine on the other, he took a step back instead.

She was radiant; lovelier and more clever and daring than ever. Everyone stared as she passed by, including Lady Clem, and Geoff felt a surge of pride. This Wild West performance of hers was outrageous, but Shelby carried it off with great style, and there were already newspaper reporters and photographers recording her meeting with the king and queen.

Edward VII was presenting Shelby to Alexandra, while Geoff shook hands with Johnny Baker. Knowing that he and Shelby would come face-to-face within moments, Geoff glanced at Ben and found with a shock that he was staring straight at him, his eyes knowing. One might suspect that uncomplicated Ben had *planned* this sticky situation!

In sonorous tones the king was saying, "Now then, Miss Matthews, you must meet the Duke of Aylesbury," and at the same moment he turned his big body so that Geoff was fully revealed.

If Shelby was shocked, she didn't show it, but she did falter for just an instant, and there was a flash of emotion in her eyes. When their hands met, Shelby caught her full lower lip with her teeth, and Geoff heard his own sharp intake of breath. Currents of electricity seemed to pass where their hands touched and between their locked eyes.

"How do you do, Miss Matthews?" he managed to say. "I can't tell you how impressed I was by your performance."

"Indeed, Your Grace?" Shelby felt as if she were being buffeted by a storm. His effect on her was more powerful than ever, and it was all she could do to breathe, let alone speak! Why hadn't someone warned her, so she could have avoided this moment entirely? It was terrible torture to rekindle the fire in her heart when nothing could come of it. It would be better not to see him at all than to touch his hand and gaze into his eyes and crave just one more embrace, one more full-blown kiss, one more moment of shared laughter. . . .

All these thoughts and feelings were squeezed into mere seconds, but Clementine needed no more than a glance to rouse her suspicions. "Geoffrey," she said sweetly, "have you and Miss Matthews met before? In Wyoming, perhaps?"

Before either of them could summon the presence of mind to reply, Ben Avery intervened, bypassing his niece and actually bowing before Lady Clem. "I hope you'll forgive me for interrupting, my lady, but I had to speak to you." Hat in hand, Ben gave her a boyish grin that displayed seldom-used dimples. "My name is Benjamin Franklin Avery, and I'm Miss Matthews's trainer . . . and manager."

"Indeed? It's a pleasure to meet you, Mr. Avery." She flushed prettily under his bold male gaze. "You handled yourself with great dexterity during the show, sir."

"Now, I won't let you be the first one to pass out compliments, my lady! I happen to know that you're a first-rate horsewoman, and I hope to see you ride. I'm giving lessons in western-style riding in Hyde Park starting tomorrow, and one of my other students told me that you might be interested."

"Really! Who was that?"

Ben didn't miss a beat. "I have to confess that I'm not very good with names, but I do remember that she is a countess, and she said that you have the best seat in the saddle of any woman in London."

Preening, Lady Clem decided that it might be great fun to learn western-style riding, and agreed to have her first lesson with Ben Avery the next morning at nine o'clock. When she turned back to Geoff, expecting to find him still gazing at that silly American girl, Clementine discovered that everyone else was starting off for a tour of the Indian Village.

With a wave, Ben left to catch up with Shelby and Johnny Baker, both of whom were engaged in conversation with the excited young princes. Geoff was waiting for Clementine. He leaned against the grandstand, off to one side, and when she approached, he cocked an eyebrow.

"Mr. Avery seemed quite taken with you, Clemmie."

"He was very kind." Her English complexion showed a bright spot of color on each cheek. "I had nearly forgotten that a man could behave toward me as if I were an attractive female."

"Well." Geoff feigned boredom, when he longed to smile with happiness. "I don't suppose I can stop you from seeing him. Riding lessons should be harmless enough."

"I hadn't thought to ask your permission!"

"Would you mind terribly if we left now?" He yawned. "I don't believe I can bear any more of the Wild West for the moment. The reenactment of the Battle of San Juan Hill wore me out so that I want nothing more than a bath and a nap."

"Actually, I could use a quiet evening myself. I have to be in Hyde Park quite early tomorrow."

As they walked off together, Geoff was conscious of a warm sense of gladness where previously there had been a void.

Shelby happened to look back herself then, just as Geoff stole a glance over one wide shoulder. Her heart was still racing in the aftermath of their meeting. It was crazy, because everything had changed in their lives and nothing could come of this euphoria except pain, but for the moment, Shelby reveled in it.

Geoff and Lady Clementine headed off toward the street, while Shelby's group made a turn at the outer edge of the arena, which brought them nearly to the Indian Village. She hung back, letting the others move ahead, waiting until she was sure that no one was looking. Then Shelby opened her hand to reveal the tiny note Geoff had slipped to her minutes before.

Standing alone while dust swirled around her, Shelby unfolded the paper, giddy with anticipation. The barely legible printing read: *Come to Warwick Rd, 10 P.M.—G.*

It was madness to even consider doing as he bade.

And it was madness to realize that love for him was still churning inside her, as hot and substantial as ever.

A small, elegant carriage was waiting on Warwick Road when Shelby started up from the corner just before ten o'clock that night. Immediately, it came toward her and a dignified coachman inquired, "Miss Matthews? His Grace has sent me to fetch you."

When she nodded, he hurried down from his perch, let down some steps, and held the door for her. Feeling as if she were in a dream set in another age, Shelby settled into the tufted leather interior and looked around in wonder as they clattered off into the night.

Was he taking her to Geoff's home? All manner of possible scenarios for the evening had run through her mind as she dressed, but even Vivian had agreed that the late hour of this assignation seemed to preclude any plans of a respectable nature. Shelby decided to go all the same. How could she refuse? Vivian, and even Uncle Ben, had urged her on, reminding her of the real, if unspoken, reason she'd come all the way to London. She had to see Geoff and talk to him again, even if it was only to make a proper farewell.

When, early in the evening, a footman had arrived at the camp village with boxes addressed to Shelby, she asked Viv if it would be wanton to wear the clothing Geoff had sent. They opened the boxes, and the most beautiful gown, cape, and accessories either of them had ever imagined spilled across Shelby's cot. Vivian reasoned that Geoff had sent the clothes so that Shelby would fit in wherever it was he was taking her tonight, so wearing them would be sensible, not wanton.

Now, glancing down at the gown that was a froth of priceless ivory lace and fine golden silk, and the evening cape trimmed in fur that caressed her throat, Shelby wondered what lay ahead of her the rest of this night. . . .

All of London seemed to be out and about. Lights glimmered hazily in the gathering mist, and the streets were crowded with carriages and automobiles filled with animated occupants. From time to time Shelby saw the winding River Thames, blanketed by fog. They had passed into a more residential area of Mayfair, she thought. Perhaps it was the Strand? Finally, the carriage drew up before a magnificent building that Shelby recognized as the Savoy Hotel. Even from the street, she could see the sparkling chandeliers and hear the laughing, well-dressed people inside.

I feel like Cinderella, arriving at the ball, she thought with a tart smile. The coachman assisted her from the carriage, and a uniformed doorman was immediately at her side.

"Would you be so good as to follow me, milady?" he asked with a kind smile. Shelby was grateful for that, having expected to be treated as if she were a woman of loose morals who was meeting secretly with a nobleman who was about to marry another woman. *Aren't you?* a little voice taunted. *Your prince won't even be seen in your company, Cinderella!*

"Good night, miss," the coachman said as she went off toward the entrance to the Savoy.

Shelby waved to him, feeling a little giddy. Inside the Savoy's vast frescoed and marbled entrance hall, she tried not to stare at the palatial surroundings, the countless electric lights that powered the chandeliers, or the spectacular crowd entering the dining room just ahead of her. It was clear that these ultrarich men and beautiful women were very important, and Shelby wished she had dared to ask the doorman about them.

At least two male members of that smart set lifted their monocles to bestow appreciative gazes on her as she passed, skirts rustling. In spite of the punishing, fashionably exaggerated S-shaped corset that she refused to endure in her everyday wardrobe, Shelby felt beautiful tonight. She glanced at herself in a beveled mirror near the elevator and saw how her up-swirled cinnamon hair caught the light, and how soft and creamy her skin was, and how distinctive were her brows and defined cheekbones and wide, full mouth.

Her heart was racing again and her palms were damp by the time she followed the doorman out of the elevator and down an elegant hallway. Stopping before a recessed, gilt-trimmed door, he gave Shelby another encouraging smile.

"I'll leave you here, milady." He bowed, turning, and soundlessly disappeared back into the elevator.

She did one of her breathing exercises, but this time discovered that it seemed to make her heart beat all the faster. Besides, she was so very anxious to see Geoff, even for one night only—

The door swung open then, before Shelby could knock, and they were face-to-face, alone, at last. His eyes widened at the sight of her, then softened visibly. "Good God, look at you. My scamp is a princess."

When he caught her hand and drew her into the room, Shelby wanted so badly to keep going, right into his arms. "Oh, Geoff . . . it's good to see you."

It seemed a luxury to be able to drink in the sight of him without fear of attracting attention. Clad in dark blue trousers that accentuated his lithe physique, a starched white shirt that was open at the neck, and sapphire cuff links, Geoff seemed to be just as handsome as ever, if more polished. But then Shelby noticed the fine lines that were more deeply etched at the corners of his eyes, and the faint hollows under his cheekbones.

"Geoff, you're starting to have the look of a rake!" she said fondly.

"What do you know of rakes, sweet?"

"Only what I read in novels . . . until I met you!"

"Come into the light so that I can have a good look

at you." Although his tone remained deceptively light, Geoff could not hide the emotion in his eyes. He took her cape and led her into the middle of the suite's grand sitting room, where a fire danced in a carved marble fireplace. Holding her small hands in both of his, he murmured, "My God, I've missed you."

Her defenses crumbled and vanished. What use was common sense when one was in love? The love she felt for Geoff seemed altogether wholesome, as rich and powerful as it had been in the simpler environment of the Sunshine Ranch, and it felt stronger than any other aspect of reality . . . such as Geoff's lofty title, his betrothal, or even the existence of Lady Clementine Beech.

"I have missed you, too." There were tears in her eyes, and in her voice. She had to bite her lip to stem the tide, and that made her look, unknowingly, all the more appealing. The little voice—sounding like Gran Annie—cautioned, *Do you want to be a loose woman? Will you let him dress you up like a doll and use you at his leisure, in secret?*

His gaze burned her creamy throat and shoulders. "You look magnificent, Shelby, but I'll confess that I am partial to the figure you cut in trousers and boots."

"These silly corsets deform the natural shape of a woman's body," she replied. "Don't you think? I look like a pouter pigeon."

"Hardly," he murmured with a dry smile. "However, I don't think that your body should be altered in any way. It's perfect just as God created it."

She knew that he was thinking about the little ribbed top she'd worn during their night of abandon at the ranch. Blushing, she countered, "Do you talk to your gently bred fiancée like this?"

Geoff drew back a bit, warily. "No, I do not. Nor do I admire her face and form . . . or even her manner."

"Then you shouldn't marry her!"

He glanced away. "I wish it were that easy."

Shelby wanted to tell him that, in spite of everything she'd once said about detesting the lifestyle of the British aristocracy, that didn't mean she wouldn't have adapted if he'd asked her to. Had she simply lost her chance back in Wyoming by clinging to the notion that Geoff might be persuaded to stay there, or had it all been pulled completely from her hands when that telegram arrived about his father's illness?

"What is tonight all about?" Shelby was surprised to hear herself speak in a heated tone. "Why did you send me these extravagant clothes and bring me to this . . . *den of iniquity*?" She made a sweeping gesture around the elegant sitting room with a view of the moonlit Thames and its thick carpets and pale yellow walls with carved plasterwork picked out in white. When her eyes lit on double doors across the room, Shelby stormed to throw them open, her skirts whisking behind.

"Aha!" She pointed to a magnificent rosewood bed with a wraparound footboard and headboard, carved with flowing vines and fruit. Drifts of embroidered pillows crowned the top of the ivory counterpane, and the lamps on each bedside table were turned invitingly low. "Could you possibly be more obvious—or insulting, Your Grace? I do not know what you take me for, but I know what *you* are—a cad!"

"And a rake?" he wondered mildly, coming up beside her. "I like the sound of that better than 'cad.' "

"I am not joking!" She closed the doors with a flourish and returned to the sitting room.

"Clearly not."

Her color was high as she raised a finger in the air.

"How do you think it feels, to be summoned in secret to this trysting place like a woman of easy virtue? Just because I—lost my head once with you, that doesn't mean you can take me whenever you have the whim!"

"Shelby, this has nothing to do with a bloody trysting *whim*, and you know it."

"Do you think I am ignorant of the ways of titled Englishmen just because I've come from America? I know all about your king, and the many love affairs he's carried on with actresses and singers, right under the nose of his lovely, gracious wife!"

Geoff wanted to interject that this had no bearing on tonight, but clearly Shelby needed to finish her tirade, so he poured himself a glass of champagne and perched on the sofa arm to hear her out. Meanwhile she reached around to lift her skirts in one hand so that she could pace without swishing.

"Today," Shelby declared, "I had half a mind to do as Annie Oakley did in 1887 and shake hands first with the queen, rather than the king! She caused a huge scandal, but she said women *should* come first, and her heart went out to Alexandra, who has to suffer flirtations and the degradation of—"

"Shelby, this is fascinating, but hardly the topic I would have chosen for tonight. Do you really mean to compare me to King Edward? We couldn't be less alike." Geoff's elegant hand reached for her and drew her against him. "Are you thirsty? Have a sip of champagne."

His male fragrance, which she'd dreamed of for months, wafted around her, and she stood between his open thighs and breathed him in. When Geoff held the fluted goblet to her lips, Shelby drank, and felt a faltering barrier collapse within her. She looked at him under her lashes, longing to sink her fingers into his burnished hair, to taste his mouth with the tip of her tongue. . . .

"I can't bear the thought that I'm some sort of cast-off," she whispered brokenly. "That you might think I could wait at your beck and call, and be placated with presents and champagne." Swallowing, she lifted her chin and said firmly, "It isn't right, Geoff. You're taking a bride you don't love, when I am every bit as fine a woman as she."

"Finer." He made a low sound and took her fully into his arms. "Oh, Shelby. My love." His mouth closed over hers; he was starving for her, aching with every aspect of his being.

Joyously, she melted into his body and found that they still fit together as two pieces of one whole. She was smiling as she opened her mouth to him, then their tongues were reunited and her tingling breasts were crushed against his hard male chest.

When Geoff tasted her tears, he felt his own eyes sting. How could he have ever been stupid enough to think that he could live without her?

"Turn around," he muttered thickly, and she obeyed. His fingers made quick work of the fastenings on her gown, and then met the challenge of the boned corset. Before he let her clothing fall to the floor, Geoff drew her back against him and kissed the side of her neck. "You know, scamp, if you came to England intending to marry me, you could have made it easier by assuming a lower profile. Do you have any idea how London will react to the notion of the Duke of Aylesbury jilting Lady Clementine Beech on the eve of their wedding to marry the new sharpshooter with the Wild West Show?" His tone was ironic.

"It's not my fault you were dull-witted enough to allow that match with Lady Clementine!" Shelby protested. Then, as his words sank in, she froze, thinking. "Geoff?"

"Yes?" He traced the line of her shoulders with feather-light kisses.

"Did you mean that? About marrying me?"

"Absolutely. I would have saved myself a gigantic lot of suffering, not to mention hours of crashing boredom, if I'd proposed to you in Wyoming and insisted that you come home with me no matter what you'd said against life here, or what I heard Ben saying to you about marrying me to get the ranch back."

"What I said to Uncle Ben . . . ?" She pieced together memories to make sense of his words. "Geoff, I was just impatient with him, and upset! I said whatever would quiet him. I didn't mean it! As for my criticisms of English society, by August I would have come with you in an instant. I would live with you anywhere! I'd wear a corset and curtsy and attend a ball every night if I could wake up in the morning with you."

"We shan't subject you to quite that much torture, my darling." He slowly drew the pins from her hair and let it down in a luxuriant spill. "I hate balls, too. We'll live most of the time at Sandhurst Manor, in the country, and that's quite tolerable. If we do just enough in London to satisfy my mother—" Geoff broke off and groaned with laughter. "Christ, my mother is going to keel over when I tell her."

"I imagine she won't be the only one."

"Oh well." Geoff let her clothes slide into a pool on the carpet. "Never mind."

Noticing the play of the firelight over her naked body, Shelby smiled dreamily. She turned to face Geoff and began unbuttoning his shirt, while he bracketed her thighs with his hands and slid them upward, in and out over her womanly curves, soaking up the satiny texture of her warm skin. When he reached Shelby's breasts, he caressed them slowly, staring at her nipples as they gradually tautened. He could hear the shift in the cadence of her breathing. She pushed his shirt back and he freed each arm in turn, then held her close and fastened his mouth on the rosy crest of her breast. His perch on the arm of the sofa positioned him perfectly so that he could suckle, sliding one arm around her waist, and find his way between her thighs with his other hand.

"This is . . . decadent," Shelby murmured, her head thrown back so that her hair swirled past her waist.

"We're engaged." His mouth was hot on her nipple. He nipped gently, then moved to the other one. "It's quite proper in this case."

That made her giggle. "When are you going to take off the rest of *your* clothes? I think I'm at a disadvantage."

She was wet when he touched her there, wet and swollen. Geoff thought for a moment that he might climax right then, like a young pup with his first lover. It made him realize how long he'd simply buried his sexuality. He hadn't been without a woman this long since he was sixteen. "I'm the one at a disadvantage, sweet," he muttered ruefully, cupping her buttocks with both hands, moving from her nipples to press kisses over ever inch of her full breasts. "You mustn't touch me—"

"Nonsense." Wearing an incandescent smile, Shelby took his hands and drew him to his feet. Her fingers worked the buckle of belt, then unfastened his trousers. "We have all night. Remember?"

Geoff clenched his teeth and found a measure of control. They kissed, feasting on each other's mouths, and he allowed Shelby to urgently caress his chest, arms, back, hips, for he understood her need.

"You've lost weight," she fretted, kissing, touching, tasting, relearning each well-loved inch of him.

"Feed me."

He spread her cape on the carpet in front of the fireplace, with the satin lining turned up, and they lay down together. In the light of the prancing flames, Geoff covered her body with his in a timeless pose of love. They shared the same wild need to mate; there would be time later for more delicate forms of pleasure. Shelby was panting as she spread her thighs for him, grunting as he pushed inside her, hard and hot as a saber, and they rocked together with the rhythm of each pounding thrust.

"Oh—love—" Beads of sweat stood out on Geoff's brow; the fire was getting hotter. When he climaxed, his teeth in the curve of her neck, Shelby wrapped her arms around his wide back and wished they never had to move.

Time passed, and she whispered, "It feels like home. . . ."

PART THREE

How many loved your moments of glad grace,
And loved your beauty with love false or true,
But one man loved the pilgrim soul in you,
And loved the sorrows of your changing face.
—W. B. Yeats

Chapter Eighteen

"If this weren't going to make such a devil of a mess in my life, I'd laugh," Geoff said as he opened the morning edition of the *Times* in front of them on the bed. "Look, the writer can't stop babbling about 'Shelby Matthews, the audacious, captivating *cowgirl* who lights up Earl's Court with her sharpshooting antics. . . .' "

"Goodness, does it really say that?" Shelby nuzzled his chest and peeked at the newspaper under long lashes.

"Yes, and every newspaper is the same. Buffalo Bill and the Wild West Show are old hat, but *you're* not, and all of London is in love with you, scamp." His hand slid under the fine linen sheet to caress her intimately then settle on the curve of her bottom. Shelby, meanwhile, pulled the pages closer and read every word, wondering what it was in Geoff's voice that suggested he really wasn't happy about her newfound fame.

She didn't want anything to spoil their perfect morning. Or was it afternoon by now? The fog had burned away and sunlight streamed through the windows facing the Thames. There were silver carts full of dishes on both sides of the bed, and Shelby had balanced a little plate of sliced peaches, buttered scones, and bacon on one of the pillows. The countless moments of bliss that made up the past dozen hours were riches for her soul. Even now she caught herself lazing in Geoff's arms and remembering their exquisite lovemaking at dawn, when the entire bedroom had been drenched in a warm, blushing glow. It was all too wonderful, and Shelby didn't want the mood to be altered by the newspaper stories. Yet . . . why should Geoff begrudge her a bit of acclaim?

"Well, you have to admit that it's very nice. I mean, in my wildest dreams, I wouldn't have imagined—"

"My love, don't you see that this is disastrous for *us*? It will be tricky enough, getting free of the wedding to Clemmie, particularly since the invitations have already gone out. But when I trot out my new choice for a bride—"

It was Shelby's turn to interrupt. "You don't need to spell it out." She fell back in the pillows, the corners of her mouth turned down. "Perhaps it would be better to wait a few months, until London Society has forgotten about the terribly undignified spectacle I made of myself as a common *performer*. Then, if we're careful to give me a new name, people might not realize that you're marrying Shelby Matthews. I mean, it's bad enough that I'm an American! Consuelo Vanderbilt might have married the Duke of Marlborough, but she brought a two-million-dollar dowry to soften the blow to the nobility."

Geoff's dark face loomed above her, his hair tousled, tendons standing out in his neck. He looked just wild enough so that Shelby was deliciously frightened. "That's enough!" he commanded.

Her heart jumped; she let him take her, kissing her until she was weak. It seemed that they couldn't get enough of each other. The mere imprint of her breast against his back in the middle of the night had set off a frenzy of half-dreaming lust: kisses that burned tender flesh too long neglected, rough caresses, daring liberties, nipping teeth and biting nails, love sounds given voice, and fulfillment beyond memory.

Now, they clung together, arms and legs twisting in the bed linens, kissing with fresh ardor, endlessly hungry for the sustenance they could only find together. Geoff sank his fingers into her hair, which gleamed like brandy spilled over the pillows. Boldly, she returned his stare, her eyes slanting a bit at the corners, and it came to him again that part of the reason he loved her so ravenously was that she would not be tamed, not even for him.

"I crave you," he whispered harshly.

When his lips trailed down Shelby's throat, his hands roaming over her breasts and belly, she reflexively grew congested, aroused, in spite of the soreness between her legs. It was crazy, the lust that burned between them . . . and yet, wasn't the fire this hot because of all the other elements strengthening their bond?

"Tell me it doesn't matter," she gasped. Her fingers closed around his warm, hard manhood and she ached to have him inside her.

Unfortunately, Geoff knew exactly what Shelby was talking about. "I *wish* it didn't matter." He was there, the sensitized tip of his shaft nudging the slick, welcoming entrance to her hideaway.

Employing her easy athleticism, Shelby scrambled out from under Geoff's strong body as if she were a butterfly escaping a collector's pin. "Perhaps you'd like to take back your marriage proposal, Your Grace! In the light of day, isn't it all just a bit too outrageous? *Impossible?*" Her voice trembled, half out of fear of his warning gaze. "Face it, Geoff, nothing you can ever say will convince *them* that I'm good enough to be the Duchess of Aylesbury." Yanking the sheet from the bed, Shelby wrapped it around herself like a toga. "You were right all along and I shouldn't have tried to change your mind. I'm proud of who I am! And now, if you'll be so kind as to call for transportation, I must return to Earl's Court." She swept toward the bathroom door, the end of the sheet making a train in her wake.

Geoff flipped over on his back, hands balled into fists that he pressed against his brow. "Shelby . . . for God's sake, don't go."

"But I have to. I have a performance to give at two o'clock!"

Geoff leaned close to Manypenny, eyes narrowed, and muttered, "I wanted to wrap my hands around her pretty throat and *strangle* her!"

The elderly manservant wore a look of unaccustomed shock. "I say, Your Grace, I don't think you ought to express such sentiments, even in jest."

"You know I don't really mean it. Aren't I allowed to make wild threats even to you?"

"Not when they concern Miss Matthews. I suspect you would call out any other man who spoke of her in such a manner."

"Never mind then, old scold." Scowling, he stood over his desk and sorted through his mail. Then, abruptly, Geoff brought his fist down on the satinwood surface and stormed, "How, I'd like to know, did I get into this coil, and how am I going to get out without either being disgraced or cut off from Shelby? Why couldn't I have siblings? It would be so much easier if I could just give this unwieldy title to an unsuspecting younger brother!"

"Sir, if I may be so bold . . ."

Geoff gave him a narrow glance. "When I rant on

and pose irrational questions, I don't necessarily mean for you to answer me."

Ignoring him, Manypenny persevered. "I would simply remind you that nothing at all will be accomplished if you stay here and shout at me."

"You're right. I need to act, hmm?"

"Exactly so, Your Grace." Relieved that the matter was back on track for the moment, the manservant followed Geoff to his dressing room and watched as he began rifling through his suits. "Sir, I've been meaning to mention that I had a rather unnerving experience yesterday. I was stepping out of the carriage at your tailor's in Clifford Street when I saw a man dart into a hansom cab . . . and if I didn't know better, I would swear that the fellow was Bart Croll."

"That is so very odd a vision for one to have that I am surprised you would even remark upon it!" Geoff replied with a trace of impatience. "Bart Croll is in Wyoming, and there isn't a reason in the world why he would be lurking about in Clifford Street!"

Manypenny pursed his lips. "Did Miss Matthews neglect to tell you that *Mrs.* Croll is in London, sharing her tent at the camp village?"

"What? How do you know this?"

"Perhaps I should confess that Mrs. Croll visited me here. It was she whom you saw getting into a carriage a short time ago." He watched the duke's astonishment reflected in his eyes. "We agreed that you and Miss Matthews should see each other again before you married someone else and it was too late."

"You knew!" he cried. "That's why you talked me into going to the Wild West Show yesterday!"

"Quite true, Your Gr—that is—"

"Never mind. I'm getting used to it." Geoff selected clothing, then allowed Manypenny to assist him in changing. "Now then, about Vivian—why is she in London? Don't say that Croll let her come alone?"

"I do not know all the details, Your Grace, but I did deduce that the marriage is ended. She looked rather like a frightened rabbit at the mention of his name, and allowed me to believe that Miss Matthews had, in effect, rescued her from a wretched situation by bringing her to London."

"So, if Bart were actually here, that would mean he'd come to find her."

"Yes, but I don't suppose it's possible, do you? It must be someone who only looks like Mr. Croll."

"I'm sure you're right, but I'll make a point to ask Shelby about it." He slipped into an amber-brown coat and let the shoulders settle into place. "That is, if we ever speak again."

Manypenny handed him the engraved, silver-spined comb and they both moved to the cheval mirror. For a moment, Geoff had a sense of déjà vu, and the year-ago night he'd decided to go to Wyoming floated back in his memory. "I was just thinking, old fellow, how much you have changed of late."

"I fear so." His great brow furrowed, considering. "Do you mind, Your Grace?"

"Only occasionally." Geoff laughed then, and Manypenny let out his breath, relieved.

"If I may be so bold, I should like to take this opportunity to point out that you also have changed, Your Grace . . . most especially since you found Miss Matthews again yesterday. It is as if you are alive again, as you were in America."

"Ah. I see your point, and I'll take it this time." He grabbed a hothouse pear from a Canton dish on his dressing table and started toward the door. "You're in danger of meddling a bit too regularly, though, Manypenny. I wouldn't mind a return to the old mute corpse demeanor—at least part of the time! Has it gotten away from you? Perhaps you ought to practice in front of the mirror . . . hmm?"

Shelby was furious by the time she returned to her tent at the end of the afternoon performance. She jumped off her bicycle and set it off to one side, then looked around for Vivian.

"There you are! Good grief, of all the days for you to stay in here—"

"What happened?" Viv's eyes were big, and she stepped in front of a huge engraved silver pot with a yellow rosebush planted in it. There was no point in Shelby seeing it until she was calm enough to appreciate it.

"Uncle Ben didn't show up!" She tossed her hat on her cot and paced outside the tent on the little wooden walkway. "Colonel Cody had to do his part, which meant that I had to cue him—and I'm used to Uncle Ben cuing *me*! Oh, Viv, it was a nightmare! I can only guess that the people were cheering because they'd read the papers and they didn't know any better."

"Did you try the bicycle trick?"

"Yes," she replied through gritted teeth. "Yes. I rode around the arena and shot at various targets from my bicycle, but the pieces from the clay pigeons I'd shot earlier were on the ground, and every time I rode over something like that, I'd veer just a bit—and I missed." Shelby gave her friend a glum look. "Twice."

"People understand that you're new. They love you because of your charm!"

"I did all I could to make up for it, miming and holding my head and riding the bicycle in a silly way—as if I were a clown in the circus!"

"No one in their right mind would take you for a clown, Miss Matthews," a male voice said from behind her. "You're much too beautiful."

Shelby whirled around to find herself face-to-face with one of the monocle-wearing gentlemen she'd seen in the Savoy Hotel the night before. "Oh! Well, it's kind of you to say so, sir. . . ."

"I am Bernard Castle," he murmured, bowing low, catching her fingers in his gloved hand and kissing them. "Your humble servant."

"Nonsense, Mr. Castle!" Shelby felt herself turning pink as she managed to retrieve her hand from his possession.

"No doubt you are wondering who I am and why I have turned up this way. . . ."

"Well, actually, yes." She tried to size him up without being too obvious about it. Castle appeared to be about forty, with reddish hair and old-fashioned side-whiskers flecked with white, a sallow complexion, and lively eyes the color of bay leaves. Slight of build, he was almost too well-dressed in a black frock coat, a double-breasted pearl-gray silk vest, light gray striped trousers, and highly polished shoes. His monocle was in place, and he carried a homburg hat and an ivory-handled blackthorn walking stick.

"I happened to see you last night as the Savoy Hotel," Castle murmured in confidential tones. "I had no idea of your identity, but one of my companions happened to have seen you perform yesterday for Their Majesties. Then, I read the glowing article about you in the newspaper and I knew that it was meant to be." He leaned closer, his face nearly even with Shelby's, and a note of passion crept into his voice. "I had to come. Did you like my present?"

"Present?"

Inside the tent, Vivian blanched as Shelby's eyes came her way. His present! She'd been certain that Geoff had sent the beautiful rosebush with its silver pot! "Um, I didn't have a chance to show you," she called, and bore the yellow flowers out into the light.

Shelby oohed and aahed over the gift, which indeed would go far toward brightening the doorway of her tent. "I like to sit here and read, though I don't have very much time now that I'm performing. . . ."

Castle was eyeing Vivian with displeasure. "I have all my servants trained to inform me of deliveries such as this the very moment I arrive at home."

"Do you? How efficient. I, on the other hand, am hopelessly relaxed. And Viv is not my servant. She is my friend, and is kind enough to help me organize my life so that we don't have to bother with a maid."

"Colonel Cody is not paying her to act as your servant?"

Shelby blinked. "I am sure you did not mean to be inquisitive, Mr. Castle, nor can I imagine that such a matter would interest you for any reason."

"You must call me Bernard, Miss Matthews." His features melted again with adoration. "If I overstepped my bounds, it is only because I feel that everyone within your circle should act as your servant. It would be my privilege to do so as well."

"That's very kind of you, but quite nonsensical! I have no servants."Shelby found herself running short of patience. What was she to do with this puffed-up, worshipful gentleman? Looking hopefully toward Vivian, she said, "Speaking of my lack of servants, where on earth is Uncle Ben? He's probably afraid to show his face for fear I'll use him for target practice!"

"Would you like me to send detectives to search for your uncle?" Castle begged.

"Certainly not!" Laughing, Shelby turned to him, on the verge of sending the fellow away with a firm set-down, when she caught a glimpse of Geoff approaching her tent. He, too, was carrying a pot with flowers in it, only his was more to her taste. He'd chosen a blue and white Chinese cachepot filled with yellow and peach narcissus, paper whites, and little snowdrops. It was an exquisite miniature spring garden, created with her in mind.

Her heart caught as she took in Geoff's appearance: rebelliously graceful and dashing, light hair combed back from his aristocratic face, a camel's hair muffler round his neck as if he'd absently donned it before remembering that the weather had turned springlike. Although she longed to simply wave Bernard Castle away and go straight into Geoff's arms, for once Shelby was able to stop long enough to consider the situation she found herself in.

Casually, she shielded her eyes against the sunlight and smiled at him. "Good afternoon, Your Grace."

Bernard Castle gripped his monocle and spoke with furrowed brow. "What, might I ask, is the Duke of Aylesbury doing here with flowers on the eve of his wedding?"

"But, those couldn't be for me!" Shelby put on an amazed expression. "I couldn't be lucky enough to get flowers twice in one day, especially ones that will keep blooming if they're watered. I'll bet you're taking that treasure to dear Lady Clementine—isn't that right, Your Grace?"

A muscle flickered in Geoff's jawline. The last thing he needed was interference in the form of overbearing, over-rich, over-nosy Bernard Castle. "Were you addressing me a moment ago, Castle? It's difficult to tell when you look over my shoulder." Then he reached for

Shelby's hand and held it a moment too long. "As for my gift, I confess that it is for you, Miss Matthews. I—We—were so taken with your performance yesterday that it seemed a small token—"

"How kind of you and Lady Clementine to think of me! You must thank her for me!"

Castle was watching this exchange warily. "It would be far too easy for one to misinterpret this scene."

"Miss Matthews knows *exactly* what my intentions are," Geoff said with a wintry smile.

It took every ounce of control Shelby could muster to keep herself from turning crimson. Inside the tent, Viv was fanning herself, swooning at the romance of it all. "Well, I must say that it's lovely to have so many friends here in London. I thank you both. Your Grace, did you see the magnificent rosebush that Mr. Castle has brought?"

"Magnificent indeed. Almost *excessively* friendly . . ."

"Not at all," Castle protested. "I aspire to higher goals. In fact, although I had hoped to ask you in private, Miss Matthews, I shall take this moment to request that you join me this evening for theater, followed by supper at the Palm Court at the Carlton Hotel. It is my habit, with my friends, to dine either there or at the Savoy, every night." He was watching her face anxiously, oblivious to the duke's darkening visage. "If you would join me, I can promise you an evening of rare pleasure. Do, please, say yes, Miss Matthews!"

Silence charged the air, then Shelby smiled suddenly and replied, "Yes . . . I would be honored to accept your invitation, Mr. Castle!"

Vivian pressed a hand to her mouth, smothering a gasp, but Geoff did not react. Victorious, Bernard Castle announced that he had another appointment and could not linger. He promised to send an automobile to fetch

Shelby that night, adding that the driver would escort her from her tent to the waiting Daimler. Then, bowing again, he hurried off, disappearing among the tents and the colorful performers who were milling about.

Geoff immediately imagined Shelby wearing the gown and cape he'd given her on her outing with the odious Castle. He very nearly demanded that she return them, but good breeding won out. Instead, glaring at Shelby, he ground out, "If you are doing this to make me jealous, I can assure you that you will suffer much more than I tonight."

"How could I have misjudged you so completely? You're a conceited jackass!" she whispered loudly, hands on hips. Vivian flinched in the shadows behind them. "Thank God you showed your true colors before I got myself in any deeper than I have already."

"Fortunately, I know that you don't mean one word of that nonsense, so I'll forgive you in advance."

"If I were a man, I'd punch you!"

Geoff laughed at this, which made Shelby even more furious. "How charmingly transparent you are, scamp. I think that we both know that you would have sent Bernard Castle on his way if you hadn't seen a way to strike out at me. How long will it be before you send word to him that you aren't feeling well and won't be able to join him this evening?" He flashed a wicked grin.

Since this was exactly what Shelby had intended to do, it made her furious that he should have guessed. "How amusing it is that you make yourself so important! Ha ha! Why should I go to such trouble on your account?"

"What other motives might you have?" Geoff tapped a finger to his mouth, pretending to consider a range of possibilities. "Are you longing to be owned? If so, Castle can pay the price. He's one of the wealthiest of the diamond millionaires and financiers whom King Edward has befriended. The circle of friends he spoke of includes the Rothschilds, Cecil Rhodes, Barney Barnato, and Ludwig Neumann. They could buy *me* ten times over."

"I will not even dignify your ugly insinuations with a response." She presented her back to him. "You and I have nothing to say to each other. You made your position quite clear this morning, and your visit this afternoon has only served to convince me that I am doing the right thing. Please go."

Looking over Shelby's head, he met Viv's eyes. Had he made his problems worse? "I know that you are tired. I'll see you later." When she made no reply, Geoff turned to leave. Just then one of the stable boys came toward Shelby's tent, leading a magnificent buckskin gelding by the reins.

Geoff felt as if he'd been struck squarely in the chest. "Good God. It—can't be—"

Charlie came toward him whinnying, pulling the reins right out of the startled boy's hand. The reunion between Geoff and his horse was so touching that Vivian began to weep. The buckskin nosed at his master's face, seeming to smile, leaning into each glad caress of Geoff's hands.

"Miss?" the stable boy murmured to Shelby, fearful lest he'd be scolded for letting Charlie go. "Did you still want to exercise him this afternoon?"

Geoff gave the lad a cutting glance. "This horse belongs to me. You may go."

Shelby nodded as well, but as soon as the boy had dashed away, she accosted Geoff with flashing blue eyes. "How dare you? You left Charlie in Wyoming, just the way you left everyone else who cared about you, and none of us thought we'd ever see you again! You have no right to barge back into our lives with this proprietary air—"

"How dare *you* not tell me that my horse was in London?" His tone was just as angry as hers.

"It seems that we both forgot to say a lot of things—until it was too late." Shelby went back into the tent, her voice thickening as she added, "Go ahead and take him, then. You're never satisfied until you have your own way."

The Carlton Hotel's restaurant was liberally decorated with elaborate potted palms. One of them brushed Shelby's nape each time the doors opened and the air moved, but otherwise she had no complaints. This was the first restaurant she had ever been in where music played softly in the background, and the snowy table linens, crystal, and silver dazzled the eye. Bernard Castle had ordered a bottle of Dom Pérignon stuck in a bucket of ice, and Shelby feared she had drunk her first glass a bit too quickly.

"How did you like the play?" Bernard inquired over the top of his menu.

"It was quite . . . interesting," she replied. They had been to see something called *The Cigarette Maker's Romance*, which Shelby had found deadly dull. Of course, she wasn't able to concentrate on much of anything, let alone the plot of a play.

"I thought it would be a special treat for you, my dear, since you come from a part of the world where entertainment is wholly lacking."

"I beg your pardon?"

"Now, now, there's no call for testiness. I do not wish to call into question the honor of your homeland, but it is a simple *fact* that the American West is a cultural wasteland, *n'est-ce pas*?"

"Non, ce n'est pas vrai!" Shelby shot back.

"I like you immensely! In many ways you remind me of my dear mother. Wait until you meet her! She's an absolute *brick*."

The manager, César Ritz, appeared at that moment to chat with his dear friend Castle and suggest choices for their meal. It was eventually agreed that they would start with escargots, and the chef would choose the other eight or ten courses.

"My friend Rothschild contends that a particularly fine dish can be confected by first taking the roe of nine hen lobsters," Bernard said when Ritz had left them.

"That sounds horrid," she decided, eyeing the champagne.

"My own particular favorite is a course wherein birds of varying sizes are cooked inside one another, like those Oriental nesting boxes." He lit a cigarette. "I do hope you don't smoke. My mother despises women who smoke. Did you know that the very first Society woman who ever smoked a cigarette in public did so in this restaurant? It was three or four years ago, I b'lieve. Lady Essex . . ." Castle paused to drain his own glass, then added, "She was an American, of course."

Shelby was speechless. How was one to make conversation with this person? Mr. Ritz approached the table again, this time wearing a cautious expression. After pouring more champagne for both Bernard and Shelby, he turned to her and bowed.

"Miss Matthews, an important call has come through for you on the telephone. If you would be so good as to follow me, I will escort your personally."

"Oh." This was even more confusing than the play.

Who in the world would be calling her on the telephone? Who even knew she was here?

"Perhaps it's your missing uncle . . . ?" Castle suggested. "Do hurry, my dear. It's vital that one consume one's escargots as soon as possible, and they should be arriving any second."

Shelby was wearing the yellow silk and lace gown that she'd bought in Cody for the party at the Irma Hotel. It was very pretty, and the emerald-green sash still set her tiny waist off to fine effect, but she knew it wasn't much by the standards of London Society. Bernard's eyes had told her so earlier, and now the patrons of the Carlton gave her more critical glances as she passed. Up came the monocles and nose glasses. Why did I ever come here? Shelby wondered, feeling as out of place as Alice at the Mad Hatter's tea party.

César Ritz led her into the velvet-tassel and palm-filled foyer of the restaurant, then peered back and forth, suddenly furtive. Shelby spied the telephone on a little desk with his reservation book, but the manager motioned to her to follow him again, this time into a tiny anteroom that appeared to be his private office.

"Miss," he whispered earnestly, "I must explain that I compromise my friendship with Mr. Castle tonight, and I beg you to keep this a secret from him. It is only because the Duke of Aylesbury is a personage of such noble, exalted grandeur that I am forced to put his wishes ahead of—"

"What does the Duke of Aylesbury have to do with this?" Shelby interrupted. "Where is my urgent telephone call?"

"Here," intoned a familiar voice, and Geoff stepped out from behind a coat rack. A aura of power surrounded him, more potent than Shelby had ever felt before. His eyes roamed over her, branding her as he took in every detail of her appearance, and she was thankful that she hadn't worn the finery he had purchased for their reunion night.

Of course, Shelby had no intention of conveying any of her fluttery emotions to *him*.

"I cannot believe you could be so rude as to interrupt my supper with a *ruse* such as this!" She heard César Ritz gasp in the doorway and knew she was on the right track. "Self-centered is too small a word for someone as vainglorious as you are, Your Grace!"

"She does this all the time," Geoff told the goggling Ritz. "It means nothing. This is the language of love for her." Before Shelby could protest, he gripped her arm in a way he knew she would find secretly thrilling. "Now then, before Mr. Castle comes in search of his goddess, I would like you to deliver a message to him, César."

"Yes, Your Grace," he agreed, wincing in anticipation.

"Tell him that Miss Matthews has been called away and regrets that she could not bid him good evening personally."

"No! He'll think I am the rudest of wretches!" Shelby cried. "Mr. Ritz, don't listen to him! Call the police and tell them the Duke of Aylesbury is trying to kidnap one of your female patrons!"

This last wild demand sent César Ritz scurrying out of the little office. Suddenly, the prospect of delivering Aylesbury's dreadful message to Bernard Castle sounded like a reprieve. He could only hope that, by the time he returned to his station, the duke would have carried that ill-bred little hoyden off into the night.

Chapter Nineteen

The Carlton Hotel was located at the junction of Haymarket and Pall Mall, in a terribly proper quarter of London known as St. James. There was an assortment of palaces nearby, as well as the National Gallery, and the Café Royal and Verry's Restaurant in Regent Street. It wasn't at all the sort of place one would expect outrageous behavior to go unnoticed, especially if one were a duke.

Geoff had long since thrown caution to the wind. When he demanded to know whether Shelby would walk or be tossed over his shoulder, she agreed to cooperate.

"I feel like a hostage in a bank robbery. You might as well be holding a gun to my back," she muttered under her breath as they exited the hotel. "I can only pray that Mr. Ritz will do as I bade and use the telephone to summon the police to rescue me!"

Geoff threw her a sardonic glance. "You are confused. *I* am rescuing you at this moment, scamp. I know you too well to believe that you actually wanted to suffer through that ten-course meal with Castle!" His voice was laced with laughter.

"This is hardly a rescue! It is an . . . *abduction*!"

A richly dressed white-haired couple were stepping out of their automobile at that moment and paused to stare at Geoff. "Your Grace?" inquired the gentleman. "Is everything all right?"

"Quite, Sir Harry. A misunderstanding, you know." He winked over the top of Shelby's head.

"Do convey our regards to your dear mother," the woman chirped as she and her husband tottered toward the Carlton.

"Certainly, Lady Maude."

When they were gone, Geoff glanced down to find Shelby glaring at him so fiercely that he had to laugh. "Why not relax and enjoy yourself? I am."

"I demand that you take me home. Where is your carriage?"

"Actually, I didn't come by carriage." He signaled to one of the doormen, who went into an alleyway and emerged leading Charlie. Geoff slipped the man a pound note, then swung into the saddle.

Shelby was nearly overcome by the sheer lovestruck madness of the moment. Finally, starry-eyed, she allowed herself to look Geoff over, and discovered that he was wearing riding boots with a familiar pair of chinos, a chambray shirt, and a tweed jacket. He still had his clothing from Wyoming! And Charlie was wearing his western saddle!

"Come on, scamp." Geoff leaned down and swept her up in front of him, sidesaddle, his arm like steel around her midriff, while he held Charlie's reins in his other hand. The hotel's doormen gawked as if they were witnessing a vision from another age, of a knight or a highwayman carrying off a fair damsel.

"Did y'see the look on 'er face?" said one as the buckskin gelding walked out among the vehicles on Pall Mall.

"Right-o," replied his partner. "For all 'er protests, she fancies His Grace!"

It was a beautiful March evening, redolent of spring.

With only the streetlights to mark their way, they cantered down side streets to the Mall, a wide, triumphal way from Buckingham Palace to Trafalgar Square. Geoff waved in a cavalier fashion to startled motorists and coachmen. Charlie, meanwhile, was completely at ease, as if he were used to London, with all its people and automobiles, trucks and omnibuses.

"Gad, but I've missed my faithful steed," Geoff said happily against Shelby's hair.

Her mind was atumble with memories of the last time they'd ridden together on Charlie's back, halfway across the world. They'd been returning home from rustling their own cattle on Bart Croll's ranch. What an incredible night that had been! Shelby leaned back against him now, and his arm tightened around her. More than ever, she realized how perfectly suited they were, for only Geoff could have guessed that this impetuous escapade was the surest way of all to win her heart, forever.

Charlie left the pavement and trotted into St. James Park. In the distance, Buckingham Palace was ablaze with light; Their Majesties were in residence. Clouds broke away from the moon, and its silvery iridescence filtered through the branches, giving a magical luster to the scene. Charlie meandered between the newly budding trees, heading toward the slender lake. Along the glimmery water's edge, Shelby discerned the first narcissus opening their star-shaped petals, bobbing gently in the moonlight, and there were thousands more rising above the grass. Soon the park would be carpeted with drifts of yellow blooms.

"I'll bring you back in daytime, a fortnight from now," Geoff promised in hushed tones. "The daffodils are spectacular, and the lake has every breed of water bird imaginable, many of which you'll be able to hand-feed." He paused, musing for a moment, then added,

"Odd . . . I often think of coming for an afternoon, but never do. For years, my only view of St. James Park in spring has been from a passing vehicle. . . ."

She didn't need to say it; life's simple pleasures were abruptly sweetened when shared with a loved one. Shelby and Geoff had never had a bad time together—or at least, they'd never been bored!

"I think Charlie's thirsty," she said.

"Do you promise not to push me in the lake if we dismount for a bit?"

"That's a very naughty notion, Your Grace, and tempting! However, since you have removed the element of surprise, I will promise." Shelby watched as Geoff lightly swung down, then reached up to catch her. She went to him gladly, wrapping her arms around his neck, suddenly yearning to fit her body to his.

Ever discreet, Charlie ambled down to the lake's edge for a drink. Meanwhile, Geoff enfolded Shelby in his embrace, and they held on as a tide of sheer need swept over them both.

"I thought I was going mad today," he said hoarsely. "The thought of that bloody Castle hovering around you—plying you with champagne and teaching you to eat cursed escargots—all the while plotting evil ways to take advantage—"

"As *you* are wont to do, Your Grace?"

"If you call me that again, I really *will* take advantage of you!" It was hard to sound angry when laughter was so close at hand, so Geoff bent her backward and covered her mouth with his. Firmly, burningly, deeply, he kissed Shelby and she kissed him right back, her tongue invading his mouth, her heart racing.

"Shelby." At last, when they were both panting, Geoff drew back, his hands framing her face. In the moonlight her face was arrestingly beautiful. "My darling."

She was shivering. Tears threatened. "I can't go on this way, Geoff."

"I love you."

"I believe you—but that's not enough. You cannot lay claim to me, to my time, and even my choice of friends, unless you—"

"I am. I've already made the appointments."

"You make it sound as if you're meeting with Prime Minister Balfour!" She couldn't suppress shaky laughter.

"I can assure you that the Dowager Duchess of Aylesbury is infinitely more intimidating."

"What about Lady Clementine?"

He stole the chance to caress her satiny cheek and throat, and then to press his lips to the leaping pulse at the base of her throat. "She hasn't been in all day. I'm not certain she ever came home from her riding lesson with your randy uncle!"

Shelby was thunderstruck, then began to giggle. "Before we imagine too much, I ought to mention that Viv persuaded Uncle Ben to help us by keeping Lady Clementine busy. Gosh, do you suppose he's actually enjoying himself?"

He paused, considering. "Anything's possible. I've always maintained that there's more to Ben than meets the eye, particularly when it comes to loving his dear niece. Perhaps he's found a way to help that suits his temperament. Deeds not words, and all that."

"It may not be anything more complicated than his love of *horses*." Shelby laughed as euphoria enveloped her. It was difficult not to throw off her slippers and begin cavorting through the daffodils. "Let's talk about something important, like the moonlight. . . ."

"Mmm." His cheek grazed the silken shell of her bodice. Gently, Geoff moved the edge of the fabric down just enough so that he could kiss the high curve of Shelby's breast. Ambrosia. But then the remnants of his day-long fit of jealousy pricked at him. "I hope Castle didn't give you this gown."

"Of course not!" Shocked by such an insinuation, even if in jest, she was also reminded of the disparity in their stations. "Do you imagine that I am so provincial that I own no proper clothing?"

"Forget it," Geoff soothed. "It was a poor joke."

"Indeed!"

"Let's not argue over nonsense. I was jealous; completely to blame." He kissed her. "Forgive me."

"I suppose we have both been rather edgy. . . ." Her voice trailed off as Geoff's feather-soft lips aroused her beyond reason. Shelby trembled with yearning to feel his hand cupping all of her breast, his mouth hot on her nipple, his body crushing hers, his knee parting her thighs. The straining hardness in his trousers was ample proof that Geoff shared her desires, and yet Shelby suddenly felt overwhelmed, as if he held the reins and she had no control whatever.

"Wait!" Weakly, she attempted to break free. "This isn't right—not yet."

Ever the gentleman, Geoff released her, but his smoldering eyes taunted her with the knowledge that he could have easily persuaded her to yield. "You have chosen an odd moment to begin guarding your virtue."

"You use sarcasm like a knife!" Tears threatened as she marched away to the waiting Charlie. When he reached her side, Shelby murmured, "I'm just confused. I know you're going to do the right thing, but it still hurts to be pushed into the shadows, while all of London believes you're devoted to Lady Clementine."

"Never mind." His groin ached. "You're right. We are both ruled by impatience of one sort or another."

"Perhaps it seems *common* for a woman to betray

such feelings, but I am still the finest woman you'll ever have the honor to know. Now, take me home." Shelby hitched up her silken skirts and petticoat, put her foot in the stirrup and easily mounted the buckskin.

Geoff was behind her in an instant, taking the reins in hard, aristocratic hands. "I love you, Shelby. You needn't worry about the future—or about being common." He chuckled. "If anything, you are *uncommon*."

Surrendering, she sighed and leaned back against his chest. "Every day brings so much new uncertainty. . . ."

"Trust me. All right?"

Blinking back tears, Shelby nodded, her heart full once again.

"I can't stay this morning," Lady Clementine Beech lamented as she slowed her magnificent gray to a walk. She was looking especially fine herself, clad in a sapphire velvet riding habit with a high white collar, her dark hair hidden under a neat, plumed hat. It was late enough that most of the fashionable set had finished their turns in Hyde Park, and Clementine and Ben had a measure of privacy. "I have an appointment."

He rode closer to read her expression. "Well, I'll admit that I shouldn't be here at all. My niece was madder than a hornet when she came into my tent late last night. I guess the performance didn't go so well without me."

"I still find it deplorable that you could have 'forgotten' to tell me you were Shelby Matthews's uncle until yesterday afternoon!" Her scolding was playful. "Did you tell her that you and I rode to Windsor and had supper in a romantic pub?"

He blushed a little under his tan. "No, not exactly. I said I was giving you a riding lesson and we decided to go a bit farther afield."

"That's quite *true*, after all." Lady Clem gave the

American a smile that was unquestionably coquettish. "In any event, she can't expect you to spend all your time attending to her needs with that horrid circus, Benjamin."

"It's not a circus—"

"Whatever." She waved a hand, smiling at him all the while, thinking that it would be heavenly if Geoff were more like Benjamin: brawny, obsessed with horses, uncomplicated, and easily manipulated. She'd always known noblewomen who had amused themselves with affairs of this sort, but her own underlying insecurity had held her back. Now that Clemmie felt attractive and desirable in the company of Benjamin Avery, it occurred to her that marriage to the enigmatic Geoffrey might not be so bad after all. There were all sorts of lovers she could take. . . . "I do wish I could stay longer this morning, but unfortunately I have an appointment at Aylesbury House in half an hour."

"Are you really getting married?" He watched her closely, wondering what else he could do to help free Geoff. Recklessly, Ben pressed, "You don't love him, do you?"

"Oh, my dear, you can't possibly understand such arrangements! In the class to which Geoffrey and I belong, marriages are *rarely* made for love. Mummy always told me that love is for children and duty is for adults." Clementine gave Ben an arch smile. "It's more a business decision that Geoffrey and I have made—or one that was made for us as children. We'll rub along tolerably well, probably not seeing each other very often, and each of us will be free to take . . . our pleasures elsewhere."

"That's crazy!" He stared, clearly shocked. "Why bother getting married at all?"

"It sounds crass," Clemmie continued in a whisper, "but I'm afraid it all comes down to money, and social standing."

"That's the most cold-blooded thing I ever heard!"

"Have I horrified you, darling Benjamin? I assure you, I am not cold-blooded in the least. How would you like to meet me later this afternoon?" Reaching for his big hand, she came close enough for their horses to touch as well. "I've taken Room 517 at the Savoy Hotel. Would you care to visit . . . ?"

He thought about her long, athletic legs, and the heat he'd already felt in her kiss. Besides, it'd probably help Geoff and Shelby if he slept with Clementine. Blushing slightly, he gave her a crooked grin. "Sure. I'll meet you there—but I gotta work with Shel first."

"Shall we say nine o'clock?" Her breasts tingled, and she daringly offered her mouth to him. There was no one else near this secluded portion of pathway, and Lady Clem threw caution to the wind. "Kiss me, my darling!"

Ben obeyed, and almost immediately they heard the crunch of wheels on the gravel. Looking up, they saw Consuelo, Duchess of Marlborough, driving a curricle that also contained the imposing, elderly Louise, Duchess of Devonshire.

Clementine froze, terrified. "I—I'll see you later," she hissed. "Go now!"

When Ben had ridden away, she walked her elegant gray to the curricle, her heart pounding. "I do hope you two won't scold me!"

The Duchess of Devonshire peered at the girl through her nose glasses. "*Scold* you?" she repeated in icy tones. "I would rather counsel you to consider your decision to marry Aylesbury before it is too late. I can assure you that one is married for a very long time."

Consuelo, the Vanderbilt heiress from America, watched with beautiful, sad eyes, but said nothing. She would always be haunted by the memory of her own tearful wedding, into which she'd been literally forced—some said sold—by her mother. If she'd dared speak her mind openly, she might have told Clementine that no amount of money or position or lofty titles could fill the needs of a woman's heart.

"I fear I must go," Lady Clem said. "I have a pressing appointment."

As she started off toward Curzon Gate, the young Duchess of Marlborough called, "Have a care, Clementine. . . ."

Those words echoed in her mind as she reached the gate and handed the gray over to her waiting groom. A Renault was chugging nearby, driven by her father's erstwhile coachman, and Lady Clem hopped into the back. Within minutes the motorcar drew up in front of Aylesbury House, one of the great eighteenth century mansions facing St. James Square.

As it happened, Geoff was arriving at that same moment, emerging from his Mercedes. He walked to greet Lady Clem and escort her into the home of the Dowager Duchess of Aylesbury.

"I have been trying to reach you this past day, so that you and I could speak privately," he said. "However, I surmise that your time has been taken up with riding lessons?"

"News travels fast." She took a chance and alluded to the relationship she suspected existed between Geoff and Shelby. " 'Twould seem that you must have been carrying on an adventure of your own, to be apprised of Mr. Avery's activities." Lady Clem glanced over to see him arch a brow, by way of ceding the point.

The new Duke of Aylesbury had dressed with care in a dark suit and starched shirt chosen to set the proper mood with his mother. When the two callers came into the mansion's entrance hall, he murmured, "I can't bear the grandeur of this place. I hope to God I never have to live here."

"People already expect it."

"Do you know," he whispered cheerfully, "I don't give a damn what *people* expect of me."

She nodded, beginning to sense what he'd wanted to talk to her about. Ingrained pride and outrage warred with a bittersweet sense of relief. Was Ben right about the aristocracy's confused priorities? Were there other avenues to greater happiness? Geoffrey seemed to believe so.

The dowager duchess received them in her favorite drawing room, which was decidedly formal, with Palladian windows dressed in plum silk, blue-gray walls, and a ceiling elaborately decorated with plaster "icing" in shades of pale yellow, blue, and pink. The gray marble fireplace was flanked by a pair of doors crowned with yellow open pediments. Geoff disliked the room so much that he wondered if his mother had chosen it on purpose.

"There you are, children," Edith Weston said in greeting. Still determinedly mourning, she wore a walking dress of black crepe, trimmed with dull jet.

The butler, a man named Whistler, whom Geoff judged to be at least one hundred years old, led the young people to chairs facing Her Grace near the fire. A cart laden with tea, scones, and other breakfast food appeared. After the conventions were performed, the servants disappeared, closing all the doors.

The dowager duchess regarded her son through nose glasses that she wore around her neck on a black cord. "Geoffrey, as this meeting was your doing, I shan't presume to lead off with wedding conversation. I do appreciate your display of breeding—visiting me at home rather than forcing me to come to you. Shall I brace myself for a shock?" She gave Clementine a bereft look. "He never brings me any good news."

"Isn't it bloody hot in here?" He got up and went to the window before his mother could tell him not to curse. "All right; there's no getting around it, no undoing it, so I may as well lay the situation out on the table."

"Indeed," Lady Clem said.

"If I believed this news might break your heart, Clementine, I would have insisted upon speaking to you alone . . . but I know you aren't in love with me." He took a breath. "You see, I have taken a stark look at this betrothal our parents arranged, and have decided that it's wrong for both of us."

"*Just* as I feared!" his mother cried. "Lady Tweedstratten wonders if Geoffrey may have been damaged somehow, to make him so relentlessly contrary. Perhaps it was that tumble he took off the nursery step when Nanny went back for her tatting. If only she were still alive so that I might inquire further into possible mishaps!"

His temper flared. "That is absurd, Mother!" He returned to stand behind his chair, and stared into her distraught eyes. "If you and Father had allowed me to grow up to make my own decisions, rather than arranging my life for me while I was still in the nursery, I would not be forced to challenge you now." Geoff's chiseled features were proud and unyielding. "Lady Clem and I are old friends, but I want more, and so should she. There is no reason for either of us to agree to this marriage, beyond the more ridiculous issues of face-saving and—"

"Money?" Clementine suggested gently.

Edith cleared her throat for many seconds and lifted an eyebrow in a gesture unnervingly reminiscent of her son. "Well said, my dear Clementine. How frequently we must remind Geoffrey that marriages among the nobility generally have less to do with love than with matters crucial to the continuity of one's title and way of life. . . ."

"I don't particularly care about building a bigger and better fortune by acquiring the Beech estates. I have other priorities for my life, and Clementine should as well."

"I knew that your father should never have agreed to let you go to that ghastly place—"

"Wyoming, Mother. And, I mean no disrespect to Father, but I am more than thirty years of age. I go where I please."

"Ooohhh!" She closed her eyes and moaned. "You haven't been the same since you returned to London. Even your father expressed concern, wondering if you'd taken to chewing one of those exotic roots one hears about—"

Geoff laughed at that, relaxing, and sat on the edge of his chair, leaning toward her. "Nothing of the sort. Again, I have done nothing more shocking than think for myself. In the past, I simply didn't care enough about my own future to fight for my beliefs."

"If it's any help at all, Your Grace, I am willing to release Geoffrey from our engagement." Clementine patted Edith's trembling hand. She wasn't one to make unselfish choices, but she couldn't forget Consuelo's eyes, or the Duchess of Devonshire's warning. Her own behavior had hardly been above reproach, and maybe it was better this way. Looking at Geoff, Lady Clem said, "I hope you'll be able to make a go of it, in spite of the gossips and the newspapers."

"What are you talking about?" Edith's voice grew querulous. "Geoffrey, what's she talking about?"

He sat back in his chair and laced his fingers together, bracing himself for a storm. "I believe she is referring to the existence of another lady. Is that right, Lady Clem?"

"I would have had to be blind not to see, Geoffrey. You were never yourself after America." Wistfully, she added, "People there seem to have a different outlook on life, don't they?"

"Definitely." He explained as best he could then, relating a whitewashed tale of his arrival in Wyoming and his "purchase" of a portion of the Sunshine Ranch. "When I began to have feelings for Shelby, I wasn't even certain what it meant. I'd never felt alive like that before. And then, there was a lot of guilt and confusion, as much for her well-being as my own—and for yours, Clementine, and my parents'. I tried very hard to lock up my heart again. Also, I couldn't believe that Shelby could love me enough to give up her idyllic life in Wyoming to put up with all the nonsense of a noble existence."

"But she followed you to England, didn't she?" wondered Clementine. "And now she is the toast of London!"

"What in heaven's name does *that* mean?" Geoff's mother gasped.

"Surely you have read about Shelby Matthews in the newspapers? She has taken over Annie Oakley's part as the sharpshooter with the Wild West Show. Geoffrey and I went with the royal party to watch her perform."

"But I had no idea that Shelby would be there," he hastened to amend, "or that she had left Wyoming at all."

Edith Weston sat with one hand splayed over her heart, her lips pressed so tightly together that they were colorless. "This is the most appalling scandal I have ever known."

"Oh, for God's sake."

Clementine, meanwhile, felt oddly weightless, and was aware of a new sympathy toward Geoff. "Perhaps," she suggested, "I ought to give the two of you an opportunity to converse in private."

Geoff walked her out. They stopped at the top of the stairs and he bent to lightly kiss her cheek. "You're a brick, Clem. I can't tell you how much I appreciate it."

"Tell me that we'll both be happier in the long run."

"It's true . . . and I think you suspect as much, hmm?"

"I don't know what will come of all this—but I do believe in possibilities now."

"Times have changed, Clem. The world of our ancestors, in which people married for every reason except love, and then had affairs to satisfy their hearts, is over—for me, at least. It's a new century." A wry smile curved his mouth. "I'd rather work for a living than marry for money."

"I'd give anything to see Her Grace's expression when you say *that*!"

"What will you do now? Is there anything you need from me?" He paused. "You aren't going to elope with Ben Avery, are you?"

She gave him a big toothy smile. "No, but it has been an instructive flirtation. Benjamin has said some things that made me wonder about loveless marriages, and his attraction toward me made me realize that another man could give me more than you would." Hope and regret mingled in her eyes.

"You are quite right! You deserve much better than *me*!"

"I'm thinking of traveling to Italy for a few months, until the scandal dies down and your marriage is more accepted. I hope to have at least one marvelous romance while abroad, and then return home in triumph, a new woman—confident, worldly, and radiant!"

Geoff laughed. "Bravo! Do you know, that riding habit is particularly flattering. You're looking more jaunty already."

"I must go now. I have an assignation with your would-be brother-in-law this evening!"

They parted then on friendly terms, but Geoff's smile

had faded by the time he returned to the drawing room. It was a devil of a role to be forced to play: the loving only son to a newly widowed mother. No one had ever taught him how to be a son at all, beyond Nanny's gentle instructions that he go in to his seldom-seen parents and deliver a little speech of some sort. Then Geoff had gone away to school, and most of his memories of parental communication were of windy lectures from his father during the occasional holiday, during which his mother would relentlessly critique his table manners, grooming, and vocabulary. Was it any wonder he'd withdrawn almost completely once he was on his own? And his father and mother had hardly seemed to mind, for they were either in separate houses, or journeying to the Continent, or doing anything other than making a family.

Shelby had been a revelation Geoff still found astonishing. Life with her was like a room full of warm light, and he had no intention of going back into the shadows.

"I shall have to meet this circus performer," the dowager duchess announced when her son sat down again. In his absence she had gotten hold of a small goblet of sherry, which was now nearly empty.

He studied her austere, beautiful face, looking in vain for clues to her feelings. "I haven't asked her to marry me yet, Mother. She may not accept."

"Surely you don't doubt for one instant that this common cowgirl will leap at the chance to *ruin* our impeccable title by assuming the status of—" Edith closed her eyes dramatically and sobbed, "*Duchess of Aylesbury!* Oh, my dearest only son, it really is too, too dreadful to bear!"

"Don't you think you're pouring it on a bit thick?"

Her fine nostrils flared. "That would be impossible, given the dark depths of this subject. Not only must we bear the humiliation and scandal of your broken betrothal to dear Clementine, but you couldn't have chosen a more inappropriate woman to replace her."

"Shelby is a treasure. She is the product of a fine family."

"Where do they live?"

"Deadwood, South Dakota."

"Really, Geoffrey, what do you take me for? *South Dakota?* Hardly a bastion of good breeding!"

"You don't know the first thing about South Dakota, Mother. And Shelby graduated from Smith College in Massachusetts. That's one of the best colleges in the *world*, and she has a first-rate mind. I can assure you that she'll be able to hold her own with anyone she meets here in London."

"I'm afraid there is nothing you or she can do to erase the stigma of her current *occupation*. It almost seems a cruel hoax, a means to test the fortitude of this poor, broken woman who has lost her lifelong mate. . . ." Edith drained the glass of sherry. "There is only one line of work that might possibly be more humiliating."

"See here, I have other appointments." Geoff stood up, his face stormy. "I have tried to pay you proper respect and include you in this discussion and decision. However, if you cannot be civil—"

"Wait!" She caught his sleeve, and now her eyes were raw, her face unmasked. "Without the Beech fortune, how are you going to pay the death duties . . . and the taxes? It was becoming a terrible worry for your father; sometimes I think that was what killed him. Servants are demanding higher wages and everything's become so expensive! The cost of installing electricity and modern plumbing was such a shock. We even spoke of selling this house in order to hang on to Aylesbury Castle—and it was the mounting pressure from creditors that prompted your father to insist you do your part now and marry Clementine. Don't you see, Geoffrey, our entire way of life is at stake!"

"Thank God for a bit of honesty at long last!" He drew his chair nearer to hers and let her clutch his hand. "Mother, I refuse to sell my soul for Lady Clem's fortune. We'll manage without it, even if taxes continue to rise and we're forced to sell one of the London homes to meet expenses. Our challenge is to adjust to the changing times. If we cannot, we'll die out completely."

"But you are the Duke of Aylesbury! You have centuries-old traditions of honor to uphold!"

"Perhaps, but I am a man first, and I will not muddle through life insisting that my honor prevents me from doing an honest day's work. I've given this a great deal of thought already. As I told you last month, I intend to manage Sandhurst Manor on my own, and I'm afraid that I shall also have to find other ways to trim our staffs . . . slowly, with due notice to each employee, of course. In the end, the improvements you and Father have been so burdened to pay for will cut expenses in the future, because we'll need fewer servants." Her hand was shaking in his, and Geoff clasped it firmly. "I won't let anything happen to us, Mother. We shall face reality head-on, rather than going on with our heads in the clouds."

"But Geoffrey . . . a circus performer? A *cowgirl*?"

"Shelby will bring much-needed vitality and courage to this family." He glanced down at his signet ring and added, "That is, if she'll have us."

Chapter Twenty

"I'VE DECIDED THAT THE DAYS I FEEL NERVOUS about performing the bicycle trick, I'll ride Gadabout around the ring instead," Shelby told Colonel Cody. They were standing together in the arena while she stroked the pinto pony's sleek coat. "She's knows me well enough to compensate."

He gave her a reassuring nod, even though shooting at glass balls from horseback was part of Cody's own act. "Good idea, little girl. You just need a little time to get used to riding the bicycle and aiming and shooting at the same time. Didn't you tell me that you only learned to ride a bicycle this past summer?"

"That's right, but it came easily to me—"

"That's not the same thing as firing a rifle at a target when you're pedaling! Maybe you should see if Carter has any tips for you." Cody was referring to the cowboy cyclist who was famous for a "bicycle leap through space, across of chasm of fifty-six feet!"

"I'll ask him, sir," Shelby promised.

Buffalo Bill started to walk away, then turned back, stroking his white goatee. "I have been meaning to remind you of a certain fact that I wish you would stress if you should speak to a newspaper reporter. We must teach them to use the term 'exhibition grounds' rather than 'show grounds.' It's difficult enough to gain the respect we deserve without those sorts of erroneous inferences."

"Of course," she agreed, having no desire to draw him out further.

"You ready to practice, or what?" Ben called. Now that he had resumed his role as her trainer, he was back to picking on her work habits again. Today they hoped to perfect a new trick that called for Shelby to pull the trap herself, then straighten and shoot the clay pigeon that she'd launched. Then, to further dazzle the audience, she would actually lay her rifle down on the ground, then pull the trap herself, pick up the rifle, and fire at the clay pigeon. So far, this last stunt required a good deal more speed than Shelby could muster.

A handsome Indian chief, named Has-No-Horse, stood with White Bonnet, Albert Thunder Hawk, a couple of Russian Cossacks, and an Arab called Hadji Cheriff, otherwise known as the Whirling Dervish. They were there to watch Shelby practice and offer praise and encouragement. She was a great favorite among all in the Wild West Show who knew her, and she was grateful for their friendship. This new family, of all colors and nationalities, told her with their warm, smiling expressions that they had enjoyed even watching her practice. She needn't be afraid to face the audience that day.

"I'll never be as fast as Annie Oakley," Shelby complained to her uncle as they readied the traps.

"Unless you're plannin' to make a career out of this, you won't need to be as good as she is." He kept his voice low so Cody wouldn't overhear. The old showman was heading off to the other end of the arena to work with the buffalo herd and their trainer. "For now, eighty percent of your act is your looks and charm and that saucy little show you put on, Shel. I've never seen an audience take to anyone the way they do to you. Faces light up. Men fall in love and women want you for their sister." He scratched his head. "It's amazing."

Shelby had been practicing for two hours in the spring sunshine when she happened to notice that Gadabout was trotting toward a little audience of her friends. It was the first time the pinto had left her side, and Shelby immediately sensed the reason. Shading her eyes, she picked out Geoff, standing between White Bonnet and Hadji Cheriff. Gadabout went straight to him, nuzzling his face and golden hair, and then she turned her attention to Charlie, who was waiting off to one side.

"Look, Ben, isn't that sweet? The horses are having a reunion. Just like old times." Tenderness welled up in her. Two days had passed since her strong words to Geoff, and she'd begun to fear that he might have given up, caught for good in the web of his noble circumstances.

"For Pete's sake, go on," Ben said gruffly. "Take a break. If you tried to keep working with him over there, you'd probably blast my ear off—or worse!"

Shelby was wearing a modified cycling costume: a white blouse with a little glen-plaid jacket and a knee-length divided skirt, worn with gray leggings and a white boater with a blue band. Her braid danced behind her as she ran toward Geoff.

He would have gladly embraced her, but Has-No-Horse and the others were eyeing the stranger suspiciously. Shelby took his arm and performed introductions, partially in comical pantomime for the benefit of those who did not speak English. They all nodded politely, but remained rooted to the spot, determined to guard Shelby.

"What do you say we go for a little bicycle ride

around Earl's Court?" Geoff whispered. "Will they allow it?"

"Don't be silly." She tried not to giggle. "I'm a grown woman." To Has-No-Horse she added, "The duke is a very special friend!"

Nonetheless, the self-appointed chaperones didn't look happy when Shelby and Geoff tied Gadabout and Charlie to a post, then got onto the bicycle together.

As they found their balance, Geoff pedaling and Shelby perched on the bar, he marveled, "It seems impossible but—this is the same bicycle, isn't it?"

"The Napoleon from Jakie Schwoob's store? Yes."

Nostalgia pinched his heart. "How is my friend Jakie?"

"Fine. He's thinking of running for the Wyoming state senate in a year or two." She reached for the handlebars as they rounded a corner. "I saw Jakie at the party for the opening of the Irma Hotel, and he misses you, Geoff. He helped convince me to try again, and soon after that party, he drove out with the piano you had ordered during the summer."

"Perhaps you'll be able to use it yet. . . ."

Shelby wondered what that meant. His tone was absent, as if he were thinking about something else. Was he implying that she would be returning to Wyoming without him? Had he come today to break the news to her?

"I've been wanting to set up a croquet course on my lawn fronting the Thames," he remarked. "Does that sound like fun to you?"

She nodded, her boater brushing the front of his jacket. Now she was completely lost as to his mood and intentions. They came into a grove of young maple trees planted a good distance from the exhibition grounds. The draft horses were stabled nearby, but the only person in sight was the Japanese magician, practicing illusions under the sheltering branches of a willow.

Geoff let the bicycle down so that Shelby could step off, then leaned it against a tree trunk. He stood for a moment, gazing into the distance, pensive.

"Well, I can't bear another moment of this!" she burst out. "If you are going to bid me farewell forever, you may as well get it over with rather than avoiding my eyes and drawing out the agony!"

He looked at her and blinked. "Has anyone ever told you that you jump to conclusions?"

"Constantly. But you know that."

Clad in a fawn coat and trousers, Geoff was looking especially dashing. His light hair was brushed back from his face in a way that made his features all the more arresting. His warm brown eyes fixed on Shelby, she began to tingle inside. "My darling, if I have seemed distracted, it's only because I was trying to think of the right words."

"Words?" she peeped.

Abruptly, he dropped to one knee before her and slipped off her glove. Then, clasping her fingers in his strong hands, Geoff gazed into her eyes and said, "Shelby, I have settled the other matters in my life honorably and now I am free to tell you how ardently I love you. You are my sun, and each moment that we spend apart I am in shadow."

"Oh!" she gasped tearfully. "Geoff, that's beautiful!"

"Hush. You mustn't interrupt when you're being proposed to." He flashed a grin at her and continued, "I can only hope that you might love me enough to do me the great honor of agreeing to become my wife."

"Well . . . I'd be a horrid person to refuse, knowing that without me you would be cast into darkness for the rest of your life!"

"Heartless vixen," he pretended to scold. "How can you tease me at such a moment?"

"I am very bad, aren't I?" Impetuously, Shelby sank down to her knees so that she might be closer to him. Her eyes were wet and her face was suffused with joy. "Oh, Geoff . . . of course I will marry you. I want nothing more for the rest of my life than to spend every moment with you."

He gathered her into a tender, secure embrace and kissed the tears that spilled onto her pink cheeks. Then, "Shelby, what are you doing down here with me? You're the woman, and I'm supposed to kneel before you in worship."

"Oh." She scrambled up, dusted off her bicycle skirt, and put her hand back into his. "How's this?"

"Much better." Geoff fished in his breast pocket with his free hand, then gently slipped a spectacular ring onto her waiting finger. It featured a pear-shaped diamond flanked by a pair of small sapphires, and Shelby immediately loved it.

"Oh, Geoff—it's gorgeous!"

He got to his feet, wincing as his knees complained. "I very nearly left the diamond alone, but when I saw the color of those sapphires, I knew they were perfect. Can you see that there's a hint of green in them, just like your eyes? They're very rare."

Shelby continued to stare at the ring, awestruck. "I've never seen anything more beautiful in my life."

"You are," he murmured. Leaning toward her, Geoff nibbled at her throat, then her parted lips, and their tongues caressed in tantalizing greeting. "*You* are more beautiful than anything." His hand strayed around Shelby's waist, then up to cup her breast. "Oh, God."

"I don't think God wants to be included just now."

Across the way, the Japanese magician had stopped

practicing and seemed to be trying to discern what was happening in the grove of maple trees. "Is that one of your bodyguards? I could be in danger."

"Uncle Ben will be looking for me," she said, plucking her boater from a pile of dead leaves.

"Never let it be said that I was the sort of bounder who tried to take advantage of a lady just because I'd put a ring on her finger." Geoff gazed longingly at her petal-soft ear. "Will you come for supper tonight? Manypenny is most anxious to see you."

"Dearest *Percy*! Can I bring Viv? She's been having bad dreams and is fretful when I leave her alone."

"By all means. Why not? Next you'll remind me that we'll have our entire lives to be alone and indulge in pleasures of the flesh."

"Believe me, Your Grace, I am as interested in those pleasures as you!" Her teal-blue eyes were playful. "But aren't there conventions that must be observed? I have a reputation to consider if I am going to be the Duchess of Aylesbury!"

Geoff drove over to get Shelby himself, and she was euphoric as they motored through the streets of London in the cream-colored Mercedes.

"This is the happiest day of my life," she announced.

"And mine, darling scamp."

"I can hardly wait to learn to drive myself! When will you teach me?"

He looked at Shelby askance, but knew better than to refuse her. "Soon. I hope that Vivian didn't mind my suggestion that she come a bit later. I asked my old friend Charles Lipton-Lyons to come by and pick her up at seven o'clock."

"She didn't mind a bit—but what are we going to do until then?"

"Visit my mother." He cringed slightly as he made this confession, but was relieved to discover that Shelby was smiling.

"Good. I've been wanting to meet her, so that I won't be nervous worrying about it day after day. How do I look?"

"Smashing." It was true. She was wearing a lovely, fairly simple yet tasteful gown of pale yellow crepe embellished with ivory silk and imported lace. The colors made an ideal backdrop for her dark red hair, most of which was currently swept up under a fashionable hat with a wide brim and frothy plums. The only jewelry Shelby wore was her new engagement ring, which she either looked at or touched most of the time.

"Uncle Ben told me that Lady Clementine is traveling to Italy. Considering the flirtation *he* had with her, it doesn't sound as if she's particularly faithful and devoted." Shelby's eyes snapped with consternation. "How lucky that I saved you from that marriage!"

"Clemmie's a good sort. She could have pitched a huge fit, but since her own conduct was hardly impeccable, she swallowed her pride and consoled herself with Ben. I think she'll be more apt to look for love when she decides again whether to marry."

"Well, I wish her luck, then," Shelby murmured. "Is there anything I should know before I meet Her Grace? I am determined to reshape myself into the ideal bride for the Duke of Aylesbury."

"Hmm." Geoff considered this question while maneuvering through the traffic near Buckingham Palace. "I should mention that my mother and I have just had the first frank conversation of our lives—about finances. Seems that the fortune isn't what it used to be, and I'm determined to manage the estates a bit differently. Your Americanism should serve us well in that area. You are hardly one to demand the most lavish of lifestyles."

"That's putting it mildly."

"Just be yourself—as always." He touched her cheek. "And try to remember that Mother takes her title and our social status rather more seriously than you might."

They arrived shortly, and Geoff took Shelby's arm as they approached Aylesbury House. Her eyes were so big that he whispered reassuringly, "It's awful, isn't it? I wouldn't mind a bit if we sold every last stone."

Inside, Geoff asked Whistler to announce them to his mother, but the ancient butler looked puzzled. "Does Her Grace expect you, Your Grace?"

"Of course."

"Odd." He wrinkled his parchment-fine brow in concentration. "Perhaps she's simply forgotten, then."

"My mother never forgets," Geoff countered. "Isn't she at home?"

"Well—yes, Your Grace, but she is about to leave. The carriage has just been brought 'round and her maid is helping her with her overgarments."

"Then we'll just pop upstairs and surprise her." Eyes narrowed suspiciously, Geoff took Shelby's hand and went straight past Whistler, who was rendered momentarily speechless by the duke's effrontery.

"Please . . . Your Grace . . . I really cannot allow . . ." The butler drew himself up, but advancing age had shrunken him so that his full height amounted to scarcely five feet.

"Don't worry, Whistler, I'll tell Mother that you threatened me with the ancestral broadsword." Geoff tossed this last over the upstairs banister, then disappeared, Shelby in tow.

"Well . . . then . . . thank you, Your Grace . . . I suppose."

Just then the dowager duchess emerged from her suite of rooms at the far end of the long, gloomy passageway. She was all in black, from her great hat swathed in net, to her fur-trimmed dinner costume, to her modest black shoes. Her face turned pale at the sight of her son and his companion bearing down on her. Clearly she was wondering if there was time to dart back into her sitting room and bolt the door.

"Mother, stand still!"

"What is the meaning of this, Geoffrey?"

Shelby had begun to wonder if they weren't making matters worse, but there was no reasoning with Geoff when he was like this.

"Will you tell me that you had forgotten our appointment?" he demanded of his mother, now standing over her wearing his most forbidding expression.

"Poor Whistler. Shall I find him run through on the staircase?" Her composure restored, she matched his chilly stare. "To answer your question, I would rather not elaborate at this time. I will say that another matter arose and I felt I should go out."

"Very cryptic," he parried. "I won't press you further in Shelby's presence, except to say that this is not a very auspicious beginning to your relationship with your future daughter."

Shelby stepped forward, extending her hand. "Your Grace, I am Shelby Matthews, and it is an honor to meet you. Also, I wish to apologize for the scene we have just caused in your home."

The dowager duchess watched Geoff first, to see how he would react, and when he actually smiled, however faintly, she was completely taken aback. "Well then . . . how do you do, Miss Matthews? I am sorry that I cannot stay and chat. . . ."

"Another time. Perhaps we could meet without your

son present." She gave the older woman her most winning smile.

Without preamble, Edith said, "Some of my oldest friends saw you at the Carlton Hotel recently, Miss Matthews. These friends are nobles of the highest order." Her voice became icier by the moment as she continued, "I understand that you were the *guest* of Mr. Bernard Castle, one of those jumped-up plutocrats who think they can *buy* position and prestige rather than earn it over centuries and by dint of the quality of one's blood." Her nostrils flared. "Mr. Castle is known for his female guests, I understand, and since you have already made such an indelible reputation for yourself in that *carnival*, it seems that everyone present at the Palm Court was aware that you were the latest of Mr. Castle's *companions*. . . ."

Geoff wished he could clasp his hand over her mouth. "Mother, that's enough," he said in deadly tones. "I won't allow you to speak another word against the woman I love, especially since your information is rife with prejudice and falsehoods."

"Were you not drinking champagne at the Palm Court with Bernard Castle?" the dowager duchess demanded of Shelby.

"I only went because Geoff forbade it," she replied softly. "And I had only met Mr. Castle a few hours earlier, Your Grace. And Geoff took me away from the Palm Court before I'd eaten one bite of food." Shelby paused, considering her next words. "However, I'm afraid that I prefer *not* to judge people in advance, or listen to gossip. So, I might have gone for supper with Bernard Castle even if I had known the rumors about him. You see, Geoff was still betrothed to Lady Clementine Beech at that time. I had no idea that I would ever be in this position."

"Did you not? 'Twould seem to me that you planned your strategy quite shrewdly, my girl; so shrewdly that my son believed you were completely guileless."

Geoff shook his head, enraged beyond memory. "What are you doing? Do you wish to separate yourself from me for the rest of your life?"

"Not at all." Edith stared back at him with beautiful eyes much like his own. "But we shall have to work diligently to alter perceptions of Miss Matthews if she truly is to become the Duchess of Aylesbury. Of course, she will have to move into this house immediately, and cease performing with that troupe of players."

Shelby managed a faltering smile. "I have no wish to argue with you on the occasion of our first meeting, Your Grace, but I have given Colonel Cody my word that I will continue with the Wild West Show through the spring. They need me."

"Have we all gone raving mad?" cried Geoff. "We're discussing long-range personal plans while standing in the corridor! Mother, you will have to give Shelby and me a chance to sort some of these matters out ourselves. We've only just gotten engaged this afternoon, for God's sake!"

"I must ask you once again not to curse in my presence, Geoffrey," she interjected coolly.

The muscle jumped in his jaw. "I'll be in touch with you soon to let you know what Shelby and I have decided."

"But—certainly you don't plan to have a wedding of any size, given Miss Matthews's background? I thought a family ceremony at the chapel in Sandhurst Manor might be nice, don't you agree? The village vicar is a lovely man."

Sensing that Geoff was longing to strangle his mother, Shelby extended her hand again and tried to speak with genuine warmth. "Meeting you has been one of the memorable experiences of my life, Your Grace. Good-bye."

The dowager duchess turned away then and started toward the rear stairway without a word of farewell.

After arriving at his own house and drinking two whiskeys, Geoff's spirits began to lighten. Shelby sipped wine, still looking stunned, while he regaled Charles and Vivian with the story of his mother's "ghastly" performance.

"Sometimes I wish she would just go to Yorkshire and live at Aylesbury Castle, since that's what she insists she would *rather* do," he said in conclusion, pacing in front of his audience of three in the library filled with Chippendale furniture, glowing wood paneling, and thousands of books. "I know that must sound cruel, but what is *she* when she behaves that way?"

Charles cleared his throat. "I don't think that Her Grace meant to be cruel, really I don't." His eyes shifted to Vivian, who was perched nervously on the edge of a hunter-green wing chair. "She's much more complicated than that; I've always sensed it."

"Indeed?" Geoff slanted a sardonic glance his way. "I can see you'd like to enlighten us, but I've had enough of my mother for one day." He dropped down on the sofa next to Shelby, gently took her hand, then looked from Vivian to Charles. "I hope you two have been dealing together tolerably well, since I threw you together without even an introduction."

"Why, Viv," Shelby remarked, "you're so pink. Are you warm?"

"No, no, just pleased—for you! Pleased to be here with you and Geoff and—Charles." Her cheeks burned hotter as she said his name. Thanks to Shelby's ministrations, Viv looked almost pretty, her hair pinned up and puffed out over carefully placed pads, her plain features enhanced with skillfully applied cosmetics, and her thin figure reshaped by a new corset and a frothy powder-blue gown. Most effective of all, however, was the soft glow of budding happiness that replaced Viv's previous frightened-fawn demeanor.

"Actually," Charles volunteered, "Vivian and I find that we get along very nicely. We have a great many shared interests."

Both Geoff and Shelby were taken aback by this last comment, but neither could think of an even remotely polite way to inquire what in the world the Honorable Charles Lipton-Lyons could possibly have in common with painfully shy Vivian Croll.

Just then supper was announced, and the foursome went into the great dining room. Shelby was staring everywhere she went in Geoff's house, fascinated by the notion that soon they would live here together as husband and wife.

"Do you like it?" Geoff asked. He'd redone the room, as well as a few others, on the advice of a high-born lover a half-dozen years ago. The walls were covered with pale yellow silk, the windows were dressed in tasteful yellow and dark blue stripes, and the furnishings were classical Sheraton antiques.

"It's lovely," Shelby replied honestly. She sensed the hand of a ghost from his past, but didn't mind. It was Shelby whom he meant to marry, against all odds and opposition. "But Geoff, there are only four places. Where will Mr. Manypenny sit?"

"Miss Matthews," Charles said with a nervous laugh, "are you having us on?"

Geoff bent next to Shelby and said softly, "Darling, we are not in Wyoming any longer. The servants have their own quarters, below us, and their own kitchen. Manypenny would be horrified by the thought of joining us."

"But you promised that I should see him tonight! I was looking forward to sitting beside him and chatting about everything that has happened to both of us since we last spoke in August!" She set her chin. "Percy is my friend."

"I'd enjoy a visit with Mr. Manypenny, too," Vivian volunteered loyally.

"All right, then. I'll go and ask him."

When Geoff had left the room, Shelby turned to Charles with a smile designed to melt his resistance. "Geoff has told me so much about you, and all your shared adventures over the years. I hope that we'll become friends, Charles . . . and that you will call me Shelby."

His eyes widened. "I say, you Americans don't mince words, do you? All right then, let's be friends. Geoff has been moping about like a lost pup since he left you behind, so I suppose there must be something to it." Charles extended his hand. "Welcome, Shelby."

She shocked him further by coming closer on tiptoe and kissing his cheek. "Thank you, Charles. You must be a wonderful friend, for Geoff to have named his horse after you!"

"Did he really? Not sure I care for that." Lipton-Lyons blushed. "Well, while we're chatting, I ought to give myself credit for bringing the pair of you together. It was I who convinced old Geoff to go to Wyoming at all!"

Before Shelby could reply, Geoff reappeared in the doorway. "Look who's come to dine with us." Standing aside, he revealed the towering frame of Manypenny, who crossed the threshold wearing a tentative expression.

"Percy! How I've missed you!" Shelby dashed straight to the elderly manservant and wrapped her arms around his torso. A big tear trickled down her cheek. "Oh, look, I'm making another scene. Do you mind?"

He was nonplussed for a moment, then a smile spread over his long face and he patted her back. "Not at all. It's simply splendid to have you back among us, Miss Matthews. Words fail me."

"Are you going to join us for dinner, then?"

"Just this once, only because it is an occasion without peer." Manypenny stepped back and attempted to regain his composure. "His Grace is correct, however, to remind you that circumstances in England cannot be as they were in America. Life is much simpler if we all keep to our prescribed roles."

"It's all a lot of pretentious nonsense, if you ask me—but of course, nobody *has* asked me, so I'll try to behave."

As they gathered around the table, with Geoff at one end and Charles at the other, Manypenny took the opportunity to lean down and tell Shelby, "I must congratulate you and His Grace on your betrothal. I couldn't be more pleased if I had made the plans myself."

Vivian glanced up from across the table and smiled at the old gentleman. When everyone was seated, she spoke up suddenly. "May I say something? Now that everything has worked out for our friends, Shelby and—uh, His Gra—"

"For God's sake, call me Geoff," he insisted.

"Thank you, Geoff. What I want to divulge is the fact that most of us were acquainted before tonight, and not just in Wyoming. I came to visit Mr. Manypenny some days ago, to let him know that Shelby and I were in

London and enlist his help in reuniting them. That same day, Charles and I introduced ourselves outside this house, but he was sworn to secrecy because I couldn't let Geoff know. So you see . . . Charles and I were already . . . friendly before this evening."

Shelby and Geoff made exclamations of pleasure over this news, while Lipton-Lyons's pale skin grew flushed again. "I was drawn to Vivian from the moment I saw her. She is demure and ladylike, yet refreshingly honest, and possesses inner strength that is rare among members of the weaker sex."

"I beg your pardon," Shelby countered. "Inner strength is hardly rare—"

"Darling, do try to relax," Geoff interrupted, covering her hand with his. "You don't need to take issue with every spoken word with which you differ . . . particularly after you become duchess. It might be wise to begin practicing now to simply smile and remind yourself that most people don't mean to be idiots; I fear that *faux pas* come all too easily to us Brits."

"I don't think I am very well suited to all these duchess rules," she replied sulkily.

The first course, consisting of julienne soup and baked mullets in paper cases, was served. While the others began to eat and Shelby eyed her food dubiously, Geoff leaned over to whisper to her, "Have I not been careful to warn you that becoming Duchess of Aylesbury is not a position to which anyone of sound mind would aspire?"

"Yes. But I love *you*, Geoff."

"I'm glad to hear it. We'll sort out the rest later."

Still whispering, she asked, "What is this horrid-smelling thing in the paper?"

"Mullet." Laughter welled up in him. "It's a fish."

She started to wrinkle her nose, then put on a very

serene expression instead. "There. Did I look like a duchess then?"

"It's a start." Waves of affection and desire broke over him, and he badly wanted to have Shelby herself for dinner.

As the meal progressed, with chicken cutlets, and then boiled leg of pork with pease pudding, and roast fowls garnished with watercress, Shelby excitedly told Manypenny about the grand opening of the Irma Hotel and how she had come to join the Wild West Show. Geoff had only heard the story in bits and pieces, so he, too, listened with interest.

"I confess that I am fascinated by this drama," Charles said, "and I was terribly impressed by your talent when I saw you perform recently. Will you be very sorry to cut short your career as a sharpshooter?"

"I don't understand," Shelby said sweetly.

"I'm referring to the fact that your engagement to the Duke of Aylesbury must necessitate your withdrawal from the Wild West Show. I thought that perhaps you would be a bit sad to leave so soon after your debut."

"But I don't intend to leave. Colonel Cody was kind enough to make a verbal agreement with me, rather than a contract, and I intend to honor it." She took a long sip of wine, adding, "He seems to feel that people may be coming to see me, though I don't quite understand it, and so I shall continue to perform through the spring, until the show leaves London."

"Shelby is used to making decisions on her own, without consulting a partner," Geoff interjected in a carefully patient voice. "We have yet to discuss this matter *together*." Then, casting about for a way to change the subject before they had another argument in public, he turned to Vivian. "I hope I'm not putting a foot wrong here, but I have been meaning to ask you

. . . how did you ever persuade my old nemesis, Bart Croll, to let you go?"

Viv went white as the table linens, gazing at Shelby with stricken blue eyes. Geoff's innocent question had served to instantly plunge her back into the horror and degradation of life in the smoky, dirty sod prison she'd shared with Croll.

Shelby rushed to her aid. "Geoff, are you vying with me for the evening's indiscretion honors?" Everyone fell silent as the footman served gooseberry tarts, trifle, and Swiss cream. Shelby took a moment to think, waiting until the guests were alone again before continuing, "Perhaps it's best to bring this sore subject into the open, then bury it forever. Since we are among friends, we can be frank, but I know that dear Viv does not wish to speak of this after tonight."

"Fr-Frank?" the girl gasped.

"Yes. There's no shame in it, after all! The truth is that Viv worked up the courage to break free from that horrid man, to leave her marriage and come with Ben and me to London—"

"Here here!" put in Manypenny. "Well done."

"Indeed," Shelby affirmed. "He was worse than a beast, and she never should have married him, in spite of feeling that he'd rescued her." She glanced at Charles. "I know Viv will explain about the tragic fire that took her family, if she hasn't already. Bart offered her shelter at the most vulnerable moment in her life, but then he mistreated her—much more than any of us ever guessed, isn't that so, Viv?"

Her head bowed, she could only nod.

"Well, she ran away from him, and since then we have heard that he *died* in some sort of accident, so it's all in the past, where it belongs."

"Died?" Geoff echoed rather doubtfully. "Good show."

Charles reached for Vivian's hand, and she raised her eyes, relieved to hear the way her friend had ended the story. "Yes. It's over. Bart can't hurt me anymore. . . ."

Manypenny's great brow relaxed. "I say, how relieved I am to hear that the villain Croll is dead! Because, you see, I had a chilling experience the other day, and I've been feeling quite haunted since then. I was in Clifford Street, visiting His Grace's tailor, and I saw a man in a passing carriage who looked exactly like that dreadful Croll! Quite an eerie moment, but now I know that it simply could not have been—"

The old manservant broke off, mid-sentence, at the sight of Vivian sliding out of her chair and onto the Turkish rug in a dead faint.

Chapter Twenty-one

"I STILL SAY THERE'S SOMETHING YOU HAVEN'T told me about Vivian and Bart Croll," Geoff said to Shelby as she perused the bookshelves in the firelit library. Manypenny, after one spoonful of Swiss cream, had retreated to the comforts of his own room downstairs, and their other guests hadn't lingered long beyond Viv's recovery from her swoon. Charles had assured Shelby that he would take care of her friend for as long as he was needed.

"I'm happy to know that you can read me so well, Geoff, but I cannot comment about Viv."

"If Bart is safely dead and no longer a threat, why did she keel over upon hearing Manypenny's little story?"

"Well," she wet her lips and examined a gold-stamped volume of Dickens, "I suppose there is always the fear that the story of his death was some sort of ghoulish mistake. Yes, that's it! Really, wouldn't *that* be a nightmare come to life? To have him turn up here?"

"But Shelby, even if that were the case, Vivian hasn't any reason to fear Bart—certainly not so that she'd faint at the chance he might be in London! He *did* let her go after all." Geoff came up behind her and leaned around to scan her face. "Right?"

"Mmm-hmm." She was dying to tell him the same horrific tale that had so shocked her: that Viv had put rat poison in Bart's potatoes and left him writhing on the dirt floor, near death. However, Shelby had been entrusted with secrets too dark to betray without permission. Instead, she held up *Oliver Twist* and remarked, "This is an awfully handsome edition. I can't tell you how impressed I am with your library."

"Can I give you a more thorough tour?" Geoff slid the book back into its niche and took Shelby in his arms. "Upstairs, perhaps?"

"Not until our wedding night, my naughty duke." Her face was lit by one of her wide, sparkling smiles.

"Let's get married, then, hmm? I hate to give Mother undue credit, but her idea about the chapel at Sandhurst Manor wasn't half bad. I'm quite attached to it, and a wedding there would be so much simpler."

Shelby didn't answer, but her smile lost its luster and there was a hint of something in her eyes that Geoff struggled to analyze. He tried a different tack. "I hope you don't imagine that I agree with her—that we should marry in the country because we have something to hide, or that you are in any way unsuitable—"

"Of course not!"

"I only mean—one would assume you wouldn't want all the fuss and pomp of a huge wedding here in London—that you'd prefer something small and simple."

"It seems that you know me very well, Geoff."

She was fiddling with another book, and for an instant he thought he saw the glint of tears in her eyes. *Damn! Why is she so incorrigibly blunt about everything else but this?* "Have I got it all wrong?"

"You must do what you think best." Shelby climbed a few steps up the library ladder and her skirts whisked toward his face. "I know that you've taken on a lot of trouble with this wedding to me, and I promised myself long ago in Cody that, if I were lucky enough to find myself in this position, I should make whatever concessions were necessary."

Was she bothered because everyone else was making decisions for her? But what about her own stubborn insistence upon continuing to perform with the Wild West Show? His head hurt. "Shelby, come down from there, would you? I'd like to talk to you."

Geoff's arms were outstretched, and she let him catch her, let him see the utterly vulnerable look in her eyes. The pins were loosening a bit in her hair, and a few tendils brushed her temples and brow.

"You are so damned beautiful." Geoff kissed her gently, tasting each curve and corner of her mouth.

Shelby released a big sigh, blinking back tears, and struggled to be set on her feet. "I don't know what's wrong with me. Perhaps you should take me home."

"Home. How can you think of a tent as home?"

"If you would pay me a proper visit there and show a little respect for my world, you would understand. We're all a family, rather like an Indian village! When the front of a tent is open, that welcomes guests, and it's great fun to wander around and visit, and to have other performers visit Viv and me. We like to serve tea and biscuits. It's lovely! We have all the comforts of home . . . including flowers planted in front. Your spring bulbs are blooming next to Bernard Castle's rosebush."

"Is that your idea of poetic justice?" Before Shelby could reply, Geoff led her out of the library and picked up an oil lamp from the Adam hall table. "I want you to see the newest addition to the house. Come on."

She peeked into darkened rooms along the way, then gasped softly when Geoff turned into a splendid conservatory that fronted the Thames. By the wavering light of the oil lamp and the moonbeams that slanted through the glass walls, Shelby could make out groupings of wicker furniture, all with plump cushions. There were plants of all sizes everywhere she looked, some in china pots on the floor, others arcing out of dishes set up on columns. Great palms, ferns, miniature lemon and orange trees, and other flowering plants gave the conservatory the look of a jungle, and the air was heady with exotic, humid fragrances.

"I love it," Shelby whispered at last, feeling his eyes on her. She breathed deeply of the rich air and walked to the window to gaze out at the light-spangled Thames. "It's the same view we had from the Savoy."

"Yes." He came up behind her and slipped his arms around her waist. The sensation of their bodies fitting together, lightly, was keenly arousing. "Shelby . . . I wonder if I haven't botched this day. I wanted it to be perfect for you; magical memories that would last for a lifetime. Instead I made rather a bad job of the proposal, and the setting was hardly romantic—and then there was that scene with my mother . . . and it seems that we've been at each other ever since."

"But you have no control over outside forces—like your mother." Her tone was still careful, as if she were gingerly ice-skating through the conversation. "How could I blame you? And, it's been a lovely day. I am overjoyed and relieved to know that we'll be married after all."

"But?" Geoff's mouth grazed the baby curls along her hairline. When she didn't reply, he said, "Perhaps you feel that you are being left out of decisions concerning our wedding and your life . . . ?"

"It's very difficult for me to be subservient, even when I'm aware of my own ignorance." Shelby tipped her head back to look up at him, her face animated at last. "I long to be so perfect as Duchess of Aylesbury that everyone who doubted will recant—but I want to be *myself*, too! Our wedding day should be for us, not for your mother, or—"

"I don't care about the other nonsense. We'll rise above it. I only want to make your dreams come true on the day we marry."

"Would you laugh if I said that I always dreamed of a fairy-tale wedding? A grand church and a sumptuous gown . . . ?"

"Of course not." Geoff was amused by the thought of his little cowgirl from the ranch wanting to wear pounds of satin and pearls, but he bit back the smile that threatened. "I'll see to it that you have your storybook wedding at Westminster Abbey. In return, will you do something to make my life a bit easier?"

"Of course! Name it!" Shelby turned to face him, wrapped her arms around his neck and nibbled at his mouth.

"Will you leave the Wild West Show? I'll never hear the end of it if my bride-to-be is performing daily at Earl's Court."

Shelby blinked. It felt as if he'd hit her square in the center of her breastbone. "No. No! I can't do that! Geoff, you know how I feel about this! It isn't just my own feelings and reputation that are at stake; my real concern is for Colonel Cody. He is in trouble financially! I cannot go back on my word."

She was trying to wriggle away from him, but Geoff held on tight. "Stop it. Look, we have to learn the art of compromise, and you have to accept some of the reality of my position as a duke. London nobility will make the wedding you want a nightmare if you try to have your cake and eat it: meaning shooting glass balls and clowning for the audience, yet expecting Society to take you seriously the next day at Westminster Abbey when you become a Duchess of Aylesbury. It's too outrageous, even for you."

"I'll do anything as long as you let me stay at the camp village and perform with the troupe until we're married."

"Let's marry away from London, at Sandhurst Manor. I actually think it would be a happier atmosphere. You can have all the trimmings and flowers and food and guests you'd like, yet we'll start off our marriage in surroundings we love and trust. Also, it will look better, given my father's death just months ago. Too many people would condemn us for having a grand, splashy wedding."

"Yes! I agree! In fact, when you put it that way, it's the best idea of all."

His lips traced the line of her throat. "Compromise can be enjoyable." He sat down on the wicker sofa, taking her with him.

Shelby nestled into his lap and traced the sculpted lines of his face with her fingers. "Oh, Geoff, I've missed you so much. It's heaven just to have time together like this, away from the world. We're going to make a terrific marriage, won't we!"

"I haven't a doubt in the world, scamp."

"Because—" She pulled at his starched collar. "—we're learning the art of compromise!"

"But practice is essential."

"Yes." When his hands firmly cupped her breasts, sensations seemed to explode inside Shelby and she arched her back. "Ohh . . . yes! Lots of practice."

Like adolescents, they fell over on the sofa, panting, and the wicker creaked in protest. The pins slipped from Shelby's hair, and Geoff plunged his fingers into the long, silky waves, kissing her ear, the pulse under her jawline, her open, hungry mouth.

"I despise all these cursed female garments!" he muttered, his tone spiced with self-deprecating amusement. "Why can't we just go upstairs?"

"Because that would be behavior unbefitting a duchess-to-be." Shelby tried to muffle her giggles. Meanwhile, that feverish ache was blossoming between her legs. "Geoff, this is crazy. Someone could come in—or see us from the river!"

"Shh."

Suddenly Shelby was gripped by a wild, joyous madness. Everything rolled away into the distance except Geoff and the reality of their love and their shared, burning desire.

When Shelby scrambled out from under him, Geoff feared that she was about to dash cold water on the fire. He felt sixteen again, alive and hard and burning in a way he hadn't known until Shelby. Christ, what a marriage it will be! he thought wryly.

"Darling—" he protested, sitting up, but then Shelby was straddling his legs, her swishing skirts billowing around them. Her breasts, alluring but well-covered, touched his face. Geoff seized the moment and molded one hand to a breast while his other hand found its way under the layers of taffeta petticoats and silk and lace gown. "God's foot!"

"Not quite," she corrected happily.

He'd encountered her beautiful leg, extravagantly clad in a silk stocking and a frilly garter. Geoff's own pants felt two sizes too small. When his fingers explored higher on Shelby's thigh, he discovered that she wasn't wearing drawers with her corset. "Oh, God . . . what are you doing to me?" he moaned, dropping his head back on the cushion. "This is cruel, you know."

"Let's compromise." She reached between then and unfastened the front of his trousers. Since he was conveniently wearing braces, she didn't have to bother with a belt. "Poor darling."

"Yes," he managed to agree, dying at the touch of her hands caressing each throbbing inch of him. "You're killing me."

"Is that good?"

"Smashing."

His fingers roved into the cleft between her legs and she instinctively thrust against the heel of his hand, again and again. She was slick and so warm that his own shaft pulsed in reaction. Leaning down, Shelby put her tongue into his mouth and they kissed voraciously. Geoff's long, deft middle finger explored inside her, her muscles tightened around him, teasing, tempting.

"Someone could come," she repeated.

"Yes. No time to waste." His grin flashed in the moonlight.

Audaciously, Shelby moved her skirts over him. They were both panting and giddy and the heat of their arousal mingled with the other pungent scents in the air. Closing her hand around him, Shelby bent him back just enough and sat over him, poised, until Geoff pressed for entry.

"I'm in charge," she asserted.

"I surrender."

Inch by inch, with excrutiating slowness, she took him in to the hilt. They were both holding their breaths, their eyes locked, and then Geoff clasped her bare bottom with both hands and she braced her own palms on his hard shoulders. When Shelby was filled with him, she rose back up on her knees, then the pace increased, thanks to Geoff's thrusting hips and his hands on both her cheeks.

"I love you," he and she said together.

The wicker sofa crackled and groaned, Shelby's skirts rustled, the lovers huffed and puffed and moaned, and the gaggle of servants standing next to the downstairs chimney shook their heads and muttered about sin and depravity and American commoners.

March turned to April just as Shelby and Geoff's romance burst into full flower. Quiet announcements were made regarding the broken engagement between the Duke of Aylesbury and Lady Clementine Beech. Lady Clem told friends that Geoffrey had changed in America, and it wasn't fair to hold him to an old bargain. By April she had left for Italy, insisting that she was eager for new adventures. Rumors had already circulated about Lady Clem's riding instructor, so news of the broken engagement came as less of a shock. An oft-heard comment was, "Everyone knew Geoff never cared to marry Clemmie, so who can blame either of them for having the good sense to call it off?"

Besides, London had other concerns. The aristocracy was looking forward to the spring and summer of 1903 with a new sense of anticipation. Queen Victoria's court had been shrouded, and even stodgy, especially during the forty years of her widowhood. When the queen herself had died, her subjects had needed time to adjust to the loss of their symbolic mother, and then King Edward's coronation had been postponed over the summer of 1902 due to his appendicitis. Only now did it seem that Society might be going to enjoy a Season replete with gaiety and grandeur.

The new monarchs had set the tone from the start. Queen Alexandra was unfailingly beautiful, tasteful, and kind. When she and King Edward decided to make Buckingham Palace their principal royal residence, he had looked at it and proclaimed, "Get this tomb cleaned up!" That might have been the credo for all of Britain. The people were feeling lighthearted. It was a new century, and even the dark old Victorian styles were being replaced by the fresh, younger influence of the Edwardians.

As Shelby adapted to her new world, she learned that on Sundays, London rested. Chimneys weren't swept, street vendors were absent from their usual corners, and the morning parade in Hyde Park was abandoned in favor of a visit to church . . . or, for many, extra sleep after a night of revelry.

The first Sunday in April, Geoff surprised Shelby by taking her to Sandhurst Manor in his automobile. They paused in Oxford for luncheon, and she had a glimpse of the mellow, golden towers of his Magdalen College. "We'll come back another day and I'll show you everything," he promised, then drove on into the pastoral Cotswolds hills, a region nearly too lovely for words.

They motored through the sunshine in the open Mercedes, Shelby's driving scarf spiraling behind her in the soft, fragrant breeze. There were masses of daffodils and violets and wild thyme, splashed over impossibly green meadows. The hills rolled gently, and the valleys were threaded with glistening streams and pollard willows.

"It's nearly as beautiful as the Loire Valley," Shelby decided, "or even the Black Hills."

"I gather that's strong praise," he replied, a smile playing over his mouth.

"Do you know, you get handsomer every day. When you smile like that, I could just gobble you up."

"Would you like to try a bit later this afternoon? I'm not quite certain what it would entail, but it sounds quite promising."

Sharp, clear joy rushed over Shelby and she almost had to close her eyes to contain it. "Oh, Geoff, I am so happy."

"Just as you should be, scamp." He gave her an intense look that made her tingle inside. "I pray for nothing else. When you are happy, the entire world is aglow."

It was a splendid day, a preview of the life that awaited her as not only Geoff's wife, but as Duchess of Aylesbury. No matter how spellbound Shelby might have been by her first sight of the salmon brick towers of Sandhurst Manor, she reacted with a measure of dignity. She tried to view it from the first as the home she would share with Geoff.

The staff had been informed in advance of the duke's visit, and they were immediately taken with Shelby. Sometimes servants could be more rigidly class-conscious than the nobles themselves, but Meg Floss and rotund old Parmenter both recognized the quality of Shelby's character, just as Manypenny had, and their warm greeting cued the rest of the staff.

Already the afternoon was waning, and after the briefest of tours, and tea and biscuits, Geoff and Shelby had to start back to London. Meg seemed particularly reluctant to see them go, for she sensed that the next duchess would also become her friend. When the servants lined up again to say good-bye, Meg Floss dared to tell the duke, "You've done the right thing, Your Grace. None of us fancied that other one a bit."

The corners of his eyes crinkled when he grinned. "Has anyone told you that you're a brilliant woman, Meg?"

"Just you, Your Grace. That's plenty."

Laughing, Geoff took Shelby's arm and they went down the stone steps to the waiting Mercedes. In the distance, twilight gathered over the ancient yew trees and the lily pond, and Shelby sensed that she was already becoming part of history.

On Tuesday morning Vivian rode over to the arena on her Josephine bicycle to show Shelby the latest edition of the *Daily News*.

"You almost had it that time, Shel!" Ben shouted. His

niece was working on the trick in which she pulled the trap herself, then grabbed for her rifle and shot at the clay pigeon she'd released. It seemed that Shelby had only missed the last one by a split second. "Don't go talk to Viv; it'll wreck your concentration!"

"You can't yell at me that way," she teased. "I'm going to be a duchess!"

The irony of this sally was not lost on Viv as she watched her friend walk over to join her. "I thought you ought to see this before someone else mentions it," she said, then opened the newspaper.

Shelby looked. There was a large engraving of her in full Wild West Show regalia, from fringed skirt to Stetson. Propped beside her was her favorite rifle, which she was regarding with a jaunty grin, one hand on her hip. Under the illustration was a bold, italicized caution that read: ***THE NEXT DUCHESS OF AYLESBURY?***

"Oh, no," she whispered miserably. "Just when everything was going so well. . . ."

Just then Colonel Cody rounded the corner, carrying the very same newspaper and beaming happily. "There you are, little girl! Congratulations on your engagement! I have to admit that I'm pleased for selfish reasons, too, because this news is guaranteed to double our business between now and June!" He wrapped an arm around her, eyes twinkling. "Why, I bet that folks who have already come once will come back just to see you shoot with your engagement ring on!"

"I'm not sure that I want to exploit Geoff's title that way, sir."

"Well, I'm afraid the damage has been done. This write-up goes on and on about the show and your tricks and talents, and tells how you're from Cody, and how you 'n' the duke met while he was out there last year."

"You know that I'm terribly proud of my part with the

Wild West Show, Colonel Cody, but there is something about the tone of this article that is demeaning to me and to Geoff, as well as the show. There is a great deal more to our history together, and to me as a person, than this."

Viv put a hand on her shoulder. "Yes, and everyone who knows or meets you is aware of that."

Shelby tried to calm herself, but it was difficult not to overreact. "I wanted people to meet me in a more proper setting before the engagement was announced this way, so that if they saw an article like this one, they'd understand that this is only a part of who I am." She sighed and shook her head. "It's just that there are so many Americans in London right now, trying to force or buy their way into Society, and they give all of us a bad name."

Cody shrugged. "Everybody wants to be a duchess like Consuelo Vanderbilt."

"Or you, Shel," Ben interjected.

"Why don't you go back to your tent and have a glass of water and calm down," Colonel Cody suggested. "In fact, take the rest of the morning off, little girl." He wrapped an arm around her. "The newspapers are fickle. Tomorrow they'll be after somebody else."

Riding her bicycle back to the camp village alongside Viv, Shelby fretted. "If only Geoff's mother weren't such a snob! She told me that I would ruin their good name if I didn't drop out of the show immediately and come to live with her so that she could work to improve my reputation. And now, when she sees the newspapers, she'll be unbearable!"

"It doesn't matter, Shelby. Geoff won't care."

"I know, but I want him to be proud of me. I want him to be able to show me off, not feel embarrassed if his friends see us together!"

"Well, we'll think of something. You're brilliant when it comes to problems like these!"

Shelby nodded, but there was a little crease between her eyebrows that would not go away, even after she'd had a cup of tea with lemon.

Geoff's reaction to all the fuss was to take Shelby riding with him in Rotten Row the next morning, insisting that he was relieved to have the entire matter out in the open. She looked lovely in a stylish green and black habit, but rode Gadabout in spite of Ben's suggestion that she take a more elegant horse.

"I seem to be of two minds," Shelby admitted to Geoff as they trotted among other riders and carriages. "I want everyone to admit that I am every bit elegant enough to marry you, but on the other hand, I want to be myself. When Ben told me that Gadabout wasn't fine enough because she's a pinto pony, I felt horribly stubborn."

"I wish you would stop worrying about all this nonsense. It's not as if anyone's opinion is going to harm us." Geoff reached for her gloved hand.

Just then the members of the Four-in-Hand Club rumbled by in their horse-drawn coaches, holding fast to the old ways against the encroachment of the automobile. Geoff greeted some of the men; others stared openly at Shelby. Her cheeks were burning when she said, "Geoff? I wanted to tell you that I've decided to leave the Wild West Show."

"What? Not on my account, I hope."

"They're going to move the show to Manchester in the middle of April, and that gives me a perfect excuse to disengage. I . . . hate to admit it, but I think your mother may have been right." She sighed, her eyes shining. "A little bit, at least. If I'm going to be your duchess, I must begin to adapt. Visiting Sandhurst Manor, I began to realize that you and I have a legacy to carry on. I want to be a credit to your family."

"That's very sweet, darling, but—"

They were interrupted as a graceful curricle drew up beside them. Holding the reins was Consuelo, Duchess of Marlborough, accompanied by a maid and a groom. Slim and dark-eyed, she was the most famous of the now-titled American heiresses, the most beautiful, and the most haunting.

Geoff gallantly doffed his top hat and gave her a winning smile. "Good morning, Your Grace. May I present to you Miss Shelby Matthews? Shelby, this is Consuelo, Duchess of Marlborough."

"Let's dispense with these cumbersome titles, shall we?" Consuelo asked. She extended her hand to Shelby and smiled. "I had to meet you. Everyone's abuzz about the great love match."

"I'm surprised to hear it described so kindly," Shelby replied. She knew that it was a grand gesture on the duchess's part to have not only greeted them, but stopped to chat, and she expressed her appreciation.

"I will be honest with you." Consuelo gazed at her fellow American with great, liquid eyes. "I adore Geoffrey, so I'm a bit jealous, as are most of those women who are talking about you. But we have a common bond. When I saw your picture in the newspaper, I felt such sympathy for you." She turned to Geoff then. "It's not my place to intervene . . . but did you know that there is to be a reception at Devonshire House on the fourteenth of April? Louisa Devonshire told me that she intended to invite you both, but someone asked her to exclude you from the list."

"Who would do such a thing?" exclaimed Shelby.

Geoff exchanged glances with the young Duchess of Marlborough. "Let me guess. Could it be—my own dear mother?"

Chapter Twenty-two

"EVERYTHING IS HAPPENING SO QUICKLY," SHELBY murmured as she and Vivian shared their afternoon tea, sitting together on her cot. She'd just finished her performance for that day and still wore her dusty glen-plaid bicycle costume. "Whenever I think about saying good-bye to everyone and not coming back to this wonderful—awful!—tent ever again, I feel like crying."

Just those words made them both grow misty-eyed, then a little giggly. Viv handed her friend a lace-edged hankie, saying, "This tent may be awful, but it *has* been a happy home. We've entertained some colorful guests here! Remember the day the entire cowboy band came for tea?"

"At least two dozen of them—with their instruments!" Shelby exclaimed. "And then we made the mistake of inviting the Hawaiians and the Filipinos at the same time, and it turned out that they didn't get along!" Laughing, she fell over against Viv and said with feeling, "I'm so glad that you've agreed to come with me when I move to the Savoy. I should be lost without you."

Of course, it was Viv who would actually be lost if Shelby went off without her, but that went unsaid. Viv, in fact, kept a great deal to herself these days, not the least of which were her incessant nightmares about

Bart. Sometimes she worried that she was going mad, dreaming of him all night long, sometimes screaming aloud and alarming Shelby. Just as terrifying were the visions that plagued her waking hours. Croll seemed to be lurking in every corner, peeking out at her from behind each light post or from passing hansom cabs.

Just when she'd talk herself out of it all, the memory of Manypenny's experience would return to bedevil her. He, too, had seen Bart staring from a hansom cab!

"Are you thinking about *him* again?" Shelby's tone was a crisp whisper. "You must stop, Viv! He is *dead*! Manypenny merely saw someone who resembled Bart, which could happen very easily in a city this size, with so many extraordinarily ugly people!"

"Yes, yes, of course you're right." Viv had begun breathing rapidly, like a child. "You always say just the right thing."

"Well, I know that you're punishing yourself with these fears because you feel guilty. At night, I share the terror of your dreams and only wish I could help you to *know* that you are good, honest, and blameless!"

"I *hate* him for forcing me to do such a horrible thing! It's not fair that he drove me to it, and now I will carry this burden for the rest of my life!" Her sweet, pale face crumpled. "I worry that this secret will always come between Charles and me. . . ."

"Oh, Viv!" She gathered her near, searching for words of comfort. "I've been so glad for you, knowing that Charles has come into your life. He appears to be just the right sort of man—kind and caring and protective—"

"Yes! He's so gentle with me. He thinks I'm an angel!"

"Perhaps you should confide—"

"No! Never! No one must know! If he knew what I

had done, he would turn from me in revulsion and never touch me again!" Tears streamed down her face. She pulled away from Shelby and stood up, wringing her hands. "Don't you see, I'm a *murderess*!"

"That's nonsense!"

"It's a fact!" Two of the Rough Riders were passing by, and they glanced into the tent at the sound of Vivian's raised voice. That was enough to cause her to sit down close to Shelby again, speaking softly. "You don't know . . . just how bad the things were that Bart did to me. And now, if Charles even attempts to embrace me in the most chaste fashion, I am overcome with panic. I am so afraid that he will lose patience with me."

"Oh, Viv, you mustn't fret so about this. You will always have a home with Geoff and me, so you needn't feel pressured to marry Charles."

She colored slightly. "That's not what I meant—"

"I know, but I also know that such thoughts must occur to you. As for your problem of getting close to him . . . I would try, no matter how difficult it may be, to explain at least a little about the reasons for your panic. Ask him to give you time to recover from your past. If you don't do this, Viv, Charles may worry that there is something wrong with *him*!"

Her blue eyes widened in horror. "Goodness, I never thought of that!"

"Why not talk to him the night of the ball? Wouldn't that be the perfect setting? And then, once you've shared a little of your secret with him, you may feel closer and safer than ever." Shelby's mouth widened into a playful smile that drew an answering blush from her friend. "That's what I like to see!"

"I still can't believe I'm going to the Duke and Duchess of Devonshire's ball," Viv said in wonder.

"Charles invited you to accompany him, so it's completely aboveboard and proper."

"Thanks to you and Geoff getting a gown for me."

"We two American commoners must uphold the dignity of our homeland!" She smoothed back Viv's limp, flaxen hair, then rose to pace across the tent. On her dressing table were sketches for not only the dress Shelby would wear to Devonshire House in two nights, but also the pearl-encrusted white silk gown that was being readied for her wedding day in May. Her mind was cluttered with those myriad details, but in the forefront was tomorrow's final performance with the Wild West Show. The costume she'd chosen was hanging on her brass coatrack, seeming to stare at her in constant reminder that her old life was ending.

Slowly, Shelby reached for her favorite Stetson and fingered the brim. "As long as I've been with the Wild West Show, I've been able to hang on to a piece of Cody," she confessed now to Viv. "Colonel Cody and every person and aspect of the show reminds me of home . . . of the Bighorn Basin and the Sunshine Ranch. I was so happy there—and Geoff was, too. We used to shoot bottles off the fences together, and I'd joke about learning Annie Oakley's tricks! Never in the world could I have imagined what lay ahead for us. . . ." Her eyes swam with tears again. "There is so much to look forward to . . . but I can't help feeling sad realizing that we can't go back, either."

Suddenly, a voice from outside the tent exclaimed, "Hey kid, you don't think you've seen the last of the West, do you? Believe me, your family's not about to let you forget where you come from!"

Viv looked worried and uncertain. Shelby stood stock-still for a long moment, then gave a loud whoop of pure joy. "Quit playing tricks on me and get in here, you big brute!"

Around the flap of the tent strode a tall young man with dark curly hair and black-lashed green eyes. He wore a wide, irresistible smile that looked amazingly like Shelby's own, and she ran to meet him. When they embraced, he lifted her off the ground, twirling her around so that a chair and two cushions went flying when her booted feet spun through the air.

"*Mon Dieu*, how beautiful you've grown!" he yelled, laughing.

Shelby was crying again. "Oh, oh, I've missed you! I didn't know how much until this very moment!"

Just then Geoff appeared. He stopped on the little wooden deck built out from the front of the tent, staring in shock, his face darkening. They didn't see him. Shelby was too busy weeping with happiness, her arms wrapped around this stranger's neck in a manner Geoff had believed she reserved only for him. The man, too handsome for his own good, was beaming down at her, his face just inches away. If something wasn't done, the scoundrel would be kissing her next!

"I beg your pardon!" Geoff said coldly, and tapped the interloper on the shoulder.

"Oh!" Shelby cried. Her color was hectic. She came toward him and started to say, "Geoff, this is—"

"I don't give a damn who he is!" the Duke of Aylesbury shouted in a deep voice, and with that he drove his fist into the man's jaw with such force that he sent him hurtling backward into a tapestry-upholstered settee.

"Beast! That was the stupidest thing you've ever done!" she raged, scrambling over the wreckage. "This is Byron Matthews, my *brother*!"

* * *

"I don't know what came over me," Geoff apologized for the dozenth time. "It was a primal urge beyond anything I've ever known before."

"Couldn't you have removed your signet ring first?" Byron asked in muffled tones. Lying on the sofa in the sitting room of Shelby's new suite at the Savoy, he was forced to keep an ice pack on his jaw and only speak through clenched teeth.

"I thought you were a bloody Frenchman, trying to woo her away from me with a lot of foreign phrases." He bit his lip and glanced hopefully toward Shelby. "I was rendered temporarily insane. By love."

"Stupid," she declared. "Idiotic. Infantile." Without looking at Geoff, she went to Byron's side and caressed his brow. "I have to go back to Earl's Court for my farewell performance this afternoon, but afterward I'll be coming back here for good. Will you be all right?"

"Mmm." His eyebrows went up. "I guess so."

"I'll go with you, darling," Geoff said to her.

"No. I can't stand the sight of you at the moment! Just send someone over after four o'clock with a wagon or something to collect my things."

He nodded, trying to look responsible. "All right. I'll mind your brother, then."

Byron's eyes widened with mock terror. "No! Don't leave me alone with this madman!"

In spite of herself, Shelby's lip quivered, but she bit back a giggle and said sternly, "Perhaps you've forgiven him, but I mean to think long and hard about the implications of this—this *savage outburst*! What might he do after we're married and it's too late for me to change my mind?"

Geoff had done penance enough at this point. "I say, pouring it on a bit thick, aren't you?"

"Be glad I'm even allowing you in the same room

with my brother and me!" With that parting shot, Shelby exited with a flourish.

"She hasn't changed a bit," Byron said through his teeth. "You're a hell of a brave man to take her on." He considered for a minute, then asked, "You don't have any plans to *change* her, do you? We've all tried since the day she was born, and I can promise you it doesn't work."

Geoff laughed. "Absolutely no plans of that sort."

"No?" He blinked. "Amazing."

Shelby's farewell performance with the Wild West Show was as dramatic and vivacious as the Little Trick Shooter herself. Throwing caution and impending duchessdom to the wind, she hammed for the capacity crowds and they roared their approval.

Buffalo Bill Cody took over part of the time for Ben, throwing the glass balls as Shelby cycled around the arena, and even holding the target for her during the mirror shot. At last, when she nodded to him, the old showman announced to the audience:

"Today, for her farewell performance, our wonderful Shelby will try one of the few tricks that has eluded her until now. Ladies and gentlemen, I ask that you give her your undivided attention as she now lays her shotgun on the ground, then attempts to pull the trap herself and pick up the gun and fire it *after the trap is sprung*! Never before has Shelby accomplished this trick, even in practice!" Cody glanced at George Foehlinger, in the cowboy band. "George, a drumroll, if you please!"

Shelby's heart was hammering as she took her place in the middle of the arena. It seemed that every member of the audience was leaning forward, wide-eyed. Realizing that they cared much more for her than for the silly trick, Shelby smiled warmly, swept off her boater, and made little curtsies to all sections of the grandstand. The people rose spontaneously.

"Bravo, Shelby!" they cried. "We love you!"

That meant a great deal coming from the characteristically reserved Britons, so she pressed her hand to her heart and threw them a kiss in return. Cody was standing a few yards away, and when Shelby glanced back at him, he chuckled.

"Too bad you can't quit now, while you're ahead, little girl!"

She hadn't felt much enthusiasm for the show in days, but now the old charge of adrenaline returned. *This is my last trick!* Listening to the drumroll, she let the rhythm come inside her and willed herself to be fast enough this time.

The audience continued to stand, silent now.

Shelby's eyes went over the steps to the trick. The gun was her new favorite: a 12-gauge, double-barreled shotgun with a short stock and a light trigger pull. It was just like one of Annie Oakley's own, and Cody had suggested it for Shelby, saying that it was perfect for a petite woman.

But had she set it on the ground an inch too far away? No. No, this time she could do it, because she wanted it enough.

When Shelby raised a finger, the drumming stopped. She then pulled the trap, got the gun into her hands, fired at the clay pigeon that was flying through the air—and hit her mark. It was nothing compared to the complicated and difficult tricks that had made Annie Oakley famous, but the audience adored Shelby and they cheered as if she had accomplished the most astonishing feat ever.

The band struck up "In the Gold Old Summertime" as she scampered around the arena, throwing kisses, then lightly ran back to her bicycle and pedaled away behind the curtain. Buffalo Bill could be heard trying to quiet the crowd, then he gave up and boomed, "Let's say good-bye one more time to our own Shelby Matthews. As you all know, this is her last performance. We'll miss her terribly, but we couldn't be happier that she is leaving us to become the bride of the Duke of Aylesbury!"

She took off her boater before going back into the arena, and the spring sunlight burnished her long, braided hair. It seemed that Shelby had a radiance that made people feel close to her even though they were far up in the grandstand. The affection that poured down on her from these countless strangers brought tears to her eyes. Cody came to meet her, embracing her in front of the audience.

"You've been a joy—and a help to the show, little girl." His white goatee tickled her cheek as he added, "We'll miss you."

Johnny Baker, the other legendary sharpshooter, was emerging from behind the curtain to embrace her, and then Iron Tail and a parade of Indians, and the Whirling Dervish, and the Cossacks, the Hawaiians, and all the cowboys who had hidden their infatuations from Shelby. She began to cry openly, smiling at the same time.

"We'll have to move this farewell party backstage so we can get on with the show, folks," Cody announced at last to the beaming spectators, "but I know you all wish Shelby as much luck in her new life as we all do—"

Just then, a tall, devastatingly handsome man with gilded hair came down from the grandstand. His arms were filled with a magnificent bouquet of peach, pink, and white long-stemmed roses; perhaps a hundred or more. The crowd buzzed as he strode out into the arena and headed straight for Shelby Matthews. He walked with the graceful, aristocratic strength of a lion, and waves of whispering rippled through the audience as they identified the man.

Shelby saw Geoff advancing toward her with a decidedly predatory gleam in his eyes. Her friends from the Wild West Show backed away as if it had all been planned, and she found herself all alone in the arena, blushing and uncertain as Geoff drew near. How magnificent he was! Wide-shouldered and lean-hipped in a dark blue frock coat with a crisp white shirt, he seemed to become more intensely appealing each day.

It came to Shelby that this was the greatest gesture Geoff could have made: to stand beside her in the middle of the Wild West Show, before thousands of Londoners and dozens of newspaper reporters. Tears slid down her cheeks as Geoff put the roses into her arms.

"Am I forgiven?" he murmured, smiling at her under his lashes.

"Don't be silly." She buried her face in the fragrant blooms to hide her tears. "I love you."

Then, to Shelby's shock, Geoff dropped to one knee in the dirt and bent his head before her. The crowd cheered louder than ever, and women could be heard sobbing over the din. Someone began to shout, "Long live the Duke and Duchess of Aylesbury!" and the audience took up the chant.

"You are the most amazing man," she said, and ran a hand over his golden hair. "Do, please, get up."

He kissed her hand instead, then rose in one lithe movement and smiled down at her. Shelby proudly took his arm. Colonel Cody came forward to escort the couple from the arena, the cheers and good wishes of the audience echoing after them as they disappeared behind the curtain.

Backstage, all the other performers crowded around to congratulate them and bid Shelby good-bye, but they had to let go because the show was still in progress. Finally, the duke and his bride-to-be walked together back to the camp village.

"'Twould seem that you no longer worry that the Wild West Show will tarnish your title," Shelby mused, a note of mischief in her voice. "I hardly would have expected you to advertise our attachment in this manner. Can you imagine what your mother would've done if she could have viewed the scene in the arena today?"

"Devil take my mother. As for the other matter, let us agree on some rules for our marriage, hmm?"

"Let me hear them first."

"I'll own up to my occasional words and acts of male folly, if you'll agree to *forgive* me more cheerfully. How's that?"

"Brilliant. However, I couldn't possibly make any promises."

"Your brother informs me that it's impossible to change you."

"That's true. I'm very impetuous . . . yet irresistible, don't you think?" Shelby threw her arms around his neck and kissed him passionately.

"Quite," Geoff agreed when he was able to speak. He swept her up into his arms then and carried her into the tent. Wooden crates were piled everywhere, so he set Shelby down on top of the biggest one, about four feet off the ground. "I suppose it wouldn't be too awful if we do quarrel excessively, as long as you put just as much vigor into making up with me."

Shelby was churning with emotions: euphoria over her performance and the execution of the trap-pulling trick, bittersweet regret and gladness that her time with the Wild West Show was ended, and anxious excitement about the future. Finally, ever-present, coating every other feeling, was her love for Geoff.

Their faces were inches apart, eyes locked. He fit his hands around her waist. Shelby linked her pretty calves, encased in pearl-buttoned leggings, behind his back. "Yes. I may not be able to make promises for my temper, but I can promise to make up with you in style." She kissed Geoff lingeringly, melting into his arms when he began to deftly invade her mouth with his tongue. One of his hands splayed over the middle of her back while the other cupped her breast, rough and tender all at once.

Hot desire pulsed between Shelby's legs. "I wish I could just take off my clothes right here," she confessed.

Geoff's eyes raked over her body and his jaw clenched. He wanted her so badly it hurt. Often he woke in the night, aching for Shelby, not just in lust, but longing to feel her sleeping in his arms. "I wish we were married right now," he said raggedly. "I miss you all the time." He pulled her flush against him. "I want to be inside of you—"

Voices outside the tent announced the arrival of the footmen and grooms Geoff had assigned to move Shelby's possessions. Vivian had come along to direct them. As Shelby disengaged and straightened her clothing, she gave Geoff a helpless look. "Tonight I'll be settled at the Savoy," she whispered.

"Right." His left eyebrow shot up. "With your brother and your best friend and God knows who else!"

She caressed Geoff's cheek. "I love you. Thank you for today."

He bent close, his breath warm on her ear. "Why is it that, so much of the time, love feels like torture?"

Caught in a long line of carriages arriving at Devonshire House, which sprawled behind brick walls along Piccadilly, Geoff looked at his three companions in the landau and yawned. "We haven't even set foot in the place, and already I'm dead bored."

Shelby laughed. "Why are you complaining so much these days?"

Charles Lipton-Lyons squeezed Vivian's hand and offered, "It's actually his habit. As long as I've known Geoff, he's found every aspect of life in London numbingly tedious."

"Yes, but now *I'm* here!" she rejoined.

"My point precisely," Geoff agreed. "There are so many *better* things to do with our time, yet we are constantly ensnarled in these social duties. . . ."

Viv blushed to the roots of her hair, and Shelby cuffed the duke's hand. Their landau had reached the portico of Devonshire House, and servants swarmed to assist His Grace's party. Light poured from every window, and the sounds of music and raised voices danced out on the night air.

"It's like . . . a fairy tale," Vivian murmured.

"Just try to look as if you are perfectly at home," Charles suggested gently.

She wore a beautiful gown of sea-foam crepe, with a froth of ivory lace at her bosom to add volume where nature had skimped. Shelby had given her pearls to wear, and had seen to it that Viv's fine hair was styled to best effect. It was doubtful that anyone would mistake Vivian Croll for a noblewoman, but she possessed integrity and intelligence, valuable commodities that could not be purchased or taught.

"Don't leave me, Charles. As long as you are holding my arm, I'll be fine."

It was hard not to stare as they went first into the gigantic hall, which was supported by pairs of pillars. Beyond was the famous crystal staircase, a marvel of wide white marble steps curving upward to the huge ballroom, where most of the guests were gathered for the reception.

"Look," Viv breathed. "The handrail is *glass*!" It sparkled in the light of a magnificent gas-lit chandelier. Everything in the house was gilded, it seemed, adding to the impression that they had stepped into a fairyland.

Upstairs, Charles took Vivian into the ballroom first, to get a sense of the crowd. Out on the stair landing, Shelby leaned over the crystal balustrade and gazed down over the marble and mirrors and the lavish arrangements of flowers.

"It's all too beautiful for words."

"I was just thinking the same thing about you, love." Geoff regarded her warmly. This ordeal was almost worth it, to see Shelby looking so ravishing. Her exquisite gown was fashioned of light *ciel*-blue satin with a décolleté bodice edged in pearls and crystals. The pointed, tiny waist and draped skirt were embellished by more glistening stones, embroidered in a pattern of leaves. The gown's sleeves were short and puffed; dotted mousseline de soie under a ruffle of beaded satin. To finish the effect, Shelby wore eighteen-button gloves and carried a fan, all created to match the gown. Because Geoff had argued that Shelby's hair was jewelry in itself, she had pleased him by wearing only a six-strand pearl-and-sapphire dog collar, her engagement ring, and simple pearl combs in her Gibson Girl–styled hair.

"These occasions are much easier for you men, since you only have to get out the same winged white collar, black tie, and tailcoat," she said, straightening his tie. "But no matter what, you are always the handsomest man in every room."

A wry smile touched Geoff's mouth as he thought that he'd never appreciated his looks until the moment he'd realized they gave Shelby pleasure.

Charles and Vivian reappeared, frowning. "I b'lieve they may have heard you were coming. Your mother and her friends are guarding the doorway, and they cut me dead when we walked in."

"Let them," Geoff ground out.

"It gets worse. Three different people, including the Earl of Clyde, already asked me if I'd heard about your little performance with the Wild West Show today. Lord Clyde said that you had 'made an exhibition of yourself and dragged your rarefied title through the dirt.' "

"He can go to the devil."

At that, the furrow in Charles's brow only deepened. Viv put a gloved hand on Shelby's arm. "These people have been giving me terribly cold stares, but at least they don't know, or care, who I am. Shelby, I'm worried that if you go in there, they'll do something horrid and cruel."

Geoff stubbornly shook his head. "They can't hurt us, and I want them to know that," he said. "Puffed-up bloody peers need to understand that we don't give a damn about them if they're going to be rude to us."

Shelby met his eyes, her own flashing with determination. "I'm ready if you are, Your Grace. Lead on!"

Watching them enter the gigantic Italianate ballroom, Charles grimaced and muttered to Vivian, "I say, it's rather like sending the Christians off to greet the lions. . . ."

Chapter Twenty-three

TWO ROOMS HAD BEEN COMBINED TO FORM DEVonshire House's ballroom, and the effect was dazzling. The coved ceiling was gilded and decorated in the palazzo manner, while the silk walls were covered with great, gilt-framed mirrors alternating with tall windows and priceless paintings by such artists as Jordaens and Rubens.

Even the unflappable Shelby gasped.

"Steady on," Geoff muttered. His eyes roved over the dense crush of gayly chattering guests, searching out key faces and noting those who were already staring and whispering about the newcomers. Sure enough, there was the Dowager Duchess of Aylesbury, together with a phalanx of her most loyal friends. They were all peering at Geoff and Shelby through their nose glasses.

Finally, Louise, Duchess of Devonshire, stepped out of the group and walked forward to greet her guests. She had been the wife of two dukes, known for decades as a beauty, but now, at seventy, the first thing Shelby noticed about her was her overuse of cosmetics.

"Geoffrey, my dear, it is lovely to see you back from your . . . excursion to . . . ?"

"Wyoming, Your Grace." Geoff took that opening to introduce her to Selby, who behaved with impeccable decorum, using beautiful phrasing and all the right forms of address.

The duchess's makeup cracked when she smiled. "I must confess that I did not expect to find the 'Little Trick Shooter' to be so elegant a woman. Perhaps some people have misjudged this match."

Bowing gallantly, Geoff lifted her gloved hand to his lips. "Once again, I am impressed by your keen powers of perception, Your Grace."

"Foolish boy. You've always been too handsome for your own good." She tapped him with her fan, then lowered her voice to add, "I am sorry about the muddled guest list. I've been awfully torn about the entire business, but Edith is one of my oldest friends. . . ."

"Never mind," Geoff said. "Is His Grace here tonight?"

"When I last saw Cav, he was sitting in a chair along the far wall, pretending to listen to the orchestra, but actually asleep." Louise turned to Shelby. "I fear that my husband prefers sleeping to any other pastime."

Geoff laughed. "I remember being with my father once in the House of Lords. The Duke of Devonshire was sitting nearby, actually snoring, so Father gave him a polite nudge. He roused himself long enough to consult his watch and exclaim, 'What a bore! I shan't be in bed for another seven hours!' "

Amidst the laughter that followed, Shelby's eyes strayed back to Geoff's mother. "Would you think me terribly rude if I were to leave you for a moment, Your Grace? I believe that I ought to greet my future mother-in-law."

"Dear child, your courage is commendable, but I really can't see that it's wise."

"I won't make myself into a different person . . . but

I can turn the other cheek." Anticipating Geoff, she added, "And I must meet this challenge alone."

A hush seemed to sweep over the ballroom as Shelby left Geoff's side and walked toward the dowager duchess and her allies. Watching the young American draw near, they all wore wary expressions, as if they expected her to somehow demonstrate her poor breeding.

"Good evening, Your Grace," Shelby said in tones of genuine warmth. "I wanted to greet you myself, hoping to begin to build a happier relationship with you. Has Geoff told you that I will no longer be appearing with—"

"Yes, I know," Edith interjected, appalled to think that Shelby might speak the name of the Wild West Show in these surroundings. She looked away then and began to converse with one of her friends.

Shelby swallowed. She glanced hopefully toward the other women, but they resolutely ignored her, executing what was known as the "cut direct." Her eyes stung. How could they be so cruel to a stranger? She wished she could look back at Geoff so that he'd come to her rescue, but that would signal defeat.

So she gathered her courage and said, "Have none of you any manners? Or, more importantly, *kindness*? I have done nothing to hurt you. My only crime is loving Geoff and having a mind of my own."

The peeresses looked pinched and shocked, but before any of them could react, Consuelo, Duchess of Marlborough, emerged from the larger crowd of guests. She crossed the parquet floor, smiling, embraced Shelby, then led her away from Edith and her friends.

"You have earned the respect of everyone in this room," Consuelo whispered. "There are nobles who are *nice*, most particularly Her Majesty, the queen. I mean to encourage my own friends to override the power of Geoff's mother."

"I already feel so much better!"

"I'd love to help with your wedding preparations in any way I can. Would that suit you?"

"Yes, please." Shelby's face shone with sincerity.

"Let's go to meet Her Majesty, then. She asked specifically to speak to you. She is only here for a little while, having ventured out without His Majesty this evening."

"I hope she doesn't mean to scold me!"

"Not at all. It was she who bade me fetch you from those hideous women."

They arrived before Queen Alexandra, who was chatting happily with her daughter, Princess 'Toria, and with the pretty, golden-haired Daisy, Princess of Pless. However, upon glimpsing Shelby, the gracious queen broke off and held out both hands to her.

"How brave you are, my dear Miss Matthews!"

Shelby curtsied, pink-cheeked, then put her fingertips into the queen's hands. "Very frightened, actually, but determined. I mean to be a very good wife to Geoff, Your Majesty, and I don't think I deserve to be snubbed."

"Charming. We shall see to it that you are included at court, won't we, ladies?"

Consuelo slipped an arm around Shelby's waist and smiled at her. "There, you see, everything is going to be just fine. I was terrified as well, when I came to England. They told me that I must learn every word of *Debrett's Peerage* so that I didn't make any mistakes!" She laughed at the memory. "You've already learned the most important lesson of all: you are true to yourself."

"Yes." Shelby looked around at her new friends with

a beguiling smile. "I'm glad to know that's good, because I don't seem to be able to help it!"

"I do hope that the weather improves for His Grace's wedding," Meg Floss said to Parmenter as they both indulged in a second cup of tea in the servants' kitchen. It was a gray, drizzly day and no one felt much like working. "Of course, it will be May, so we should expect sunshine."

"Just so." The old butler's jowls waggled slightly when he nodded. "So much to do in less than a fortnight!"

Gathered round the big table were Lilith the cook, the groom of the chambers, a pair of footmen, and several kitchen maids and housemaids, all eager for more news about the wedding. "Now, tell us again, Meg, what His Grace wrote in the letter," Lilith asked once again.

"Actually, Miss Matthews wrote most of it, and she was as frank and charming in the letter as she is in person." A smile lit Meg's thin face as she glanced down at the creamy vellum writing paper decorated with Shelby's script. "She explained that she and His Grace have decided to have the wedding that suits their characters best, rather than doing only what London Society expects."

A wave of murmuring went around the table. "Seems to be a very sensible girl," Parmenter observed.

"What else did she write?"

"Miss Matthews confided that she had always dreamed of a storybook wedding, but that the usual affair at St. Paul's or Westminster Abbey would be too formal and stiff."

Parmenter nodded. "Just so."

"How sweet!" Lilith cried.

"She and His Grace agree that they'll have just the

sort of wedding that would suit them best right here at Sandhurst-in-the-Hole, with their friends around them! Miss Matthews wants all the trimmings, though, and plenty of guests coming in for the day, so we'll be working awful hard to prepare all the food and do up all the silk ribbons and such. She wants the chapel like a garden, she says." Meg consulted the letter before adding, "Miss Matthews is counting on all of us to make her dream come true."

"Did she really write that last bit?" asked Jamie, the groom of the chambers.

"Indeed she did. And she has a warm way about her, even on paper." Meg sipped her tea, considering. "I believe they may live here most of the year. After all, Miss Matthews is used to a *ranch*! She'll prefer country life, I'll wager."

"Just so we have instructions and time enough to prepare properly for this wedding," Parmenter said, as he resumed worrying.

"Do you suppose that Consuelo, Duchess of Marlborough, will come?" Lilith wondered. "I read in *Tit-Bits* that she has become a great chum of Miss Matthews."

Before anyone could comment on this, there was a knock at the back door of the servants' hall. "Perhaps it's the coal man," Meg said. "I'll go and see."

When Meg pulled open the heavy door, she discovered an unpleasantly grizzled old man standing outside. His frayed collar was turned up against the damp, and he had several days of white stubble covering his hollow cheeks. The fellow had been rolling a cigarette with stained, cracked fingers as Meg opened the door, but now he looked up and his sunken eyes sent a chill down her back.

"How may I help you, sir?"

"I'm lookin' for work, ma'am," he replied in a raspy voice.

"You're an American!" she exclaimed in surprise.

"Somethin' wrong with that?" He took a step toward her.

"Certainly not. In fact, our master, the Duke of Aylesbury, is about to be married to a lovely American woman. It's simply that we don't encounter many of you out here."

The light in his eyes grew brighter. "I need work."

"I am Meg Floss, the housekeeper here at Sandhurst Manor. What is your name, sir?"

Momentarily flummoxed by her question, he stammered, "Uh—it's Ted. Ted, uh—Bart. That is, Bartell. Ted Bartell."

All of her suspicions piqued, Meg replied, "Well, Mr. Bartell, I'm afraid that we don't have room for any more employees. In fact, His Grace is searching for ways to trim the staff here, and already some of us are looking for work in the village."

"Would you turn away a hungry man who's willin' to work?"

His words struck right to her kind heart. They could find something for him—outside. "Come in, then, and we'll give you a hot meal . . . and some soap and hot water. Perhaps we can find something for you to do for a few days, then; long enough for you to earn enough to carry you along into May." Reluctantly, Meg stood back so that the horrid man could enter. "The grounds keeper may need you. We're having the wedding here in the chapel, in less than a fortnight, and there's a great deal to prepare."

Ted Bartell smiled suddenly, like a ghoul. "Good. That's just the kind of news I was hopin' for. . ."

* * *

Byron Matthews poured champagne for his friend, Adam Raveneau, Viscount Thorncliff, and stuck another bottle into the ice to chill.

"Better not uncork that one until your relatives arrive," Adam cautioned.

"Hadn't planned on it. Actually, I think that Geoff meant all three of these bottles to be for them, but they don't drink very much." He grinned. "One should be enough."

"It's good to see you again, Byron. I'll never forget those days in Honfleur—"

"Mmm. That brunette. What was her name?"

"Chloe. *I'll* never forget! And that inn where you were trying to get an audience with Monet—"

"La Ferme Saint-Simeon. What food!"

"I can still taste the wine." He sipped his champagne again and ran a hand through glossy black hair. "It's an amazing coincidence that your sister is marrying Geoff. I've known him forever, and I thought he was incapable of love."

Byron cocked his head slightly, listening. "I think I hear my sister. She's packing, you know, for the trip down to Sandhurst Manor tonight."

"Hard to believe the wedding's tomorrow, when your family's only just arriving this afternoon—"

"Shh!" His voice dropped to a whisper. "Try to remember that she doesn't know they're all coming. She thinks Uncle Ben is going to give her away tomorrow—so keep your big mouth shut!"

The door to the main bedroom swung open then and Shelby emerged, fresh and lovely in her traveling gown of old rose *peau de soie* brocaded in delicate blue flowers. "Oh, hello, Adam! You boys have been chatting out here for hours!" Her eyes flicked over the empty champagne bottles. "Will you two be up to helping with my trunks? I wouldn't want you to hurt yourselves!"

"We were having a serious conversation about my *art*," Byron intoned.

"Oh, have you sold a painting?" she teased.

Adam Raveneau had risen and was observing Shelby with hooded gray eyes. "I hope that Geoff knows how fortunate he is to be marrying a woman as beautiful, witty, and—"

"Headstrong," supplied her brother.

"—as you, Shelby. Do you happen to know any other American heiresses who would be interested in marrying a handsome, titled Englishman?" He gave her a piratical grin. "I'm trying to raise the funds to restore our family estate in Barbados."

Shelby gasped in mock horror. "I am shocked! How can you speak of the sacrament of marriage in such cold-blooded terms? Besides, I am not an heiress. Geoff was attracted to something other than my money."

They all laughed, and Byron tried again to get her to describe her first encounter with Geoff. When she refused, again, he said, "I'll get Ben or Titus to tell me. One of them must know."

"I'm just glad that revealing the circumstances of our first meeting was not a requirement for marriage." Her eyes were alight with mischief. "I could never have become a *peeress*!"

"Give us a hint."

"All right, but this is all I will reveal: I was wearing a horsehair mustache." Shelby's eyes took on a faraway look as Byron and Adam laughingly tried to make sense of her silly clue. How long ago it seemed! Her eyes grew wet with longing for all the people and places she missed in Cody. She saw Manypenny again, bowler-clad, perched stoically on the sunlit pile of trunks in the middle of Sheridan Avenue, a tumbleweed whirling past. She could smell the spring air and conjure up the rich hue of the afternoon's twilight during that initial ride together in the buckboard, back to the Sunshine Ranch. *I hated Geoff then.* Closing her eyes, Shelby took in the shape of his shoulders as she had that day, when he saw the house for the first time and sat forward in the seat. His eyes had been intent with feelings and a sense of promise that even he hadn't understood.

How hard she'd tried to drive him away. . . .

Byron came up beside her. When they were together, it always felt as if they were still kids. His instincts were either to tease her or protect her, so sometimes he felt lost trying to relate to his sister as an adult. "You aren't having second thoughts, I hope?"

She shook her head, smiling, but her chin quivered. "I was just thinking about Cody, and how happy we all were at the ranch. I wrote Titus a long letter, but it's sad that he can't be here for the wedding. If only Cody and London weren't so far apart!" Accepting his handkerchief, she wiped her eyes, laughing at the same time. "It seems that I can't stop crying lately. Tears of joy, mostly. I'm fine as long as I don't think about how far away home really is. I mean—it's going to be a wonderful wedding—"

"*C'est vrai*—don't forget your big brother is here!"

Shelby lay her head against his shoulder and sighed. "I know. But I miss Mama and Daddy . . . and all the people I dreamed would be with me on my wedding day."

"Well, I know they all wish they could be here, too. I guess that's the price you pay for getting married in England." He patted her back gently. "Let's talk about something more cheerful. Where's Geoff? What about the rest of the plans? Is this going to be enough time—

all of us showing up in Sandhurst the night before the wedding?"

"The staff there has taken care of everything, and this is the only night we'll all stay at the estate. After that, you'll have to go to the village inn or come back to London. But you understand that we're giving up this suite today, don't you?"

Byron blinked once. "You mean I'm out on the street, then?"

"Did you imagine that you were going to have a room in my house indefinitely?" She watched his face. "Byron, are you broke?"

"What? Hell, no!" But his face was paler.

"Come and stay with me, old fellow," Adam rejoined. "I haven't much, but you're always welcome."

"I'm on the verge of selling two excellent paintings. When those deals go through, I'll be able to take a suite of my *own* at the Savoy!"

Shelby bit her tongue to refrain from suggesting that he put his earnings in the bank for a change. Her brother was beginning to remind her more and more of Stephen Avery, their wandering grandfather. "Anyway, the other plans are certainly less elaborate since we're having the wedding at Sandhurst Manor. I'm only having two attendants, and we've been able to trim a lot of the obligatory names from the guest list. The day is designed to fit our tastes, rather than ducal etiquette." Shelby wore a wistful smile. "My life is going to change tremendously when I become Duchess of Aylesbury, and not even Geoff can help that. I want one last day to be, unabashedly, myself. . . ."

"Sounds absolutely fitting," Byron assured her, then asked innocently, "When are you going back to Wyoming?"

"I—I don't know yet. I've made up my mind not to

look beyond our honeymoon. We're going to motor through France during the rest of May. In June, Geoff wants to take me to Royal Ascot and the Windsor house party—"

"The Season's only two months long, and you'll be in France for half of it," Adam put in. "I know it sounds ominous, but Geoff's title is weighty. Now that his father is dead and it's on his shoulders, there are obligations that he will have to fulfill." He pinched her cheek. "You, too, my beauty."

"I know. Perhaps I'll enjoy it all," she said hopefully. "Meanwhile, let's get my trunks out of the bedroom and ring for the bellman. Geoff will be here any moment with some relatives of his who have just arrived by ship—from the Continent, I believe. We are all going down to Sandhurst together."

"Relatives, eh?" Byron loved surprises. No sooner had he and Adam dragged the trunks out into the sitting room than a knock sounded at the door. "Perhaps that's the bellman," he said gaily.

"Let him in, then."

Byron went into the little entryway, out of her sight, and opened the door. When Shelby heard low voices, she called out, "I hope that the trunks aren't too heavy—"

Her brother peeked around the corner at her. "Brace yourself for a surprise!"

Like a vision, Madeleine Matthews appeared, elegant and radiant in a suit of white silk with black dots and a ruffle at her neck. Setting down her dotted parasol, she opened her arms to Shelby. "We've come for your wedding!"

"I think I'm dreaming. I didn't think this was possible!" Shelby replied in disbelief. Then, she hurried into her mother's embrace as waves of emotion surged through her. "Oh, Mama! I've missed you terribly."

"It sounds to me as if you've done very well without my meddling!" Maddie said fondly.

"Geoff really loves me."

"So he assured us all the way from Albert Docks!" Holding her daughter close, she whispered, "Darling, he's every bit as wonderful as you said. I can see now that you were absolutely right to come to London. The duke will provide the sort of stability you need in your life."

"Yes, Mama, but he's a lot of fun, too!"

Just then, Fox appeared with Geoff, both of them smoking cigars. "Doesn't my hell-raising daughter have a kiss for her daddy? Did you really think we wouldn't come, just because you were half a continent and an ocean away? You must have mixed your family up with some of these sissy Brits!"

Overjoyed, she lifted her skirts and ran to him, her eyes blurry with tears. "This is the best wedding gift anyone could have given me. I realize that Gran Annie and Aunt Sun Smile and so many others couldn't come all this way, but I do wish Titus could be with us, since he helped bring Geoff and me together." Shelby clung to Fox's big shoulders and sighed. "Titus is our link with the Sunshine Ranch. . . . Oh, well. I guess I can't have everything."

"Why not?" Geoff rejoined from the entryway, where he was leaning against the wall and smoking his cigar. "You've never settled for less before."

And there was Titus Pym, peeking around the corner at her, doffing his new bowler. "I had to come, lass. Have you a kiss left for me?"

She let out a whoop of joy, tears flowing freely now.

Hugging the little Cornishman, Shelby commented on his new checked suit and shiny pocket watch.

"I had to look the part for our crossing on the SS *Celtic*. It was a luxury ship, you know, and filled to the brim with rich folk." He touched his nose. "I don't know if I took too much sun or too much ale while we were at sea."

The last bottle of champagne was uncorked, and Adam ran out for more. Everyone stood together and Fox made a toast—"To the enduring love and long marriage of the Duke and Duchess of Aylesbury!"—and then they all sat down and began catching up on all the news. Maddie put Byron between her and Fox on the sofa, for it had been three long years since they'd last seen their son.

Fox delivered letters of congratulations from Gran Annie and Sun Smile and several other old friends from Deadwood. Titus also had been entrusted with messages for the happy couple. Jakie Schwoob had written them a touching note, expressing his regret that he, too, could not attend the wedding of his dear friends.

Then, already misty-eyed, Shelby opened a large lacy envelope. She took out an elaborate greeting card, covered with doves and roses and cherubs carrying hearts. The flowery message read:

Let this lovely heartsease
Our best love convey,
Long may joy surround thee,
Care keep far away!

Then, plainly printed at the bottom, were the words, "Best wishes to valued friends from Cal, Lucius, Jimmy, and Marsh."

Shelby looked at Geoff and saw that there were tears

in his eyes. She bit her lip. "Goodness, how I miss them!"

"Those were exceptionally happy times." His voice caught. "Remember the day the boys first tried to teach me to rope?"

"Reminiscing's well and good, but you don't imagine your days at the ranch are over, do you?" Titus demanded. "I'm takin' Benjamin home with me, and I expect to see the pair o' you riding up the South Fork Road before the summer's out. Fair enough?"

They both looked wistful, and Geoff replied, "I wish I could give you my word. . . ."

Shelby summoned a bright smile. "It's just that we can't possibly get away before Royal Ascot and the Windsor house party. There are so many exciting activities that one enjoys when one is a duchess!"

"Oh, really? You're startin' to sound like that big bag of hot air, Manypenny!" Pouting, Titus added, "Just don't forget who used to change your nappies, Your Grace! I happen to know that your arse is no fancier than next girl's!"

Geoff's eyebrows flew up as he protested dryly: "Age has weakened your memory, my good fellow, particularly in this case." He lifted his glass. "I would like to propose a toast to my bride's superior derriere."

Laughing, they all cried, "Here, here!" and drank.

Later that night the Dowager Duchess of Aylesbury arrived at Sandhurst Manor with Charles Lipton-Lyons and Vivian Croll. Vivian looked exhausted from the drive in the company of Geoff's mother, and no sooner had they entered the house, followed by Edith's own servants, than Viv received a lecture on the impropriety of her own status.

"My dear child, it is quite shocking for you to be

seen traveling with Charles without your maid. People will talk."

"But I haven't a maid," Viv replied with an effort. "To be brutally frank, I am Shelby's maid!"

The older woman gasped, turning to Charles. "Great heavens. Dear boy, were you aware of this?"

"Quite." Protectively, he took Vivian's slim arm.

"What is becoming of Britain's youth? Have these ill-bred Americans put a spell on you?" Just then Edith was diverted by her son, who came to escort her into the dining room. It seemed that the other guests had been urged to begin eating rather than wait for the other tardy arrivals. Hearing this, Edith said, "But Geoffrey, it is scarcely eight o'clock! Only barbarians dine before eight-thirty!"

Having been warned in advance about the dowager duchess, the Matthews family and friends managed to refrain from quarreling with her during the remainder of the meal. However, their tempers were sorely tried.

While Edith was waiting for her first course and the others were eating strawberry tarts, she struck up a conversation with Maddie. Even though Shelby's mother had traveled to England from the American West, Edith gravitated to her because of her air of quality.

"Were you raised in South Dakota, Mrs. Matthews?"

"No, actually, I was born in Philadelphia and lived there until I was twenty years old. And, even then, Deadwood was just a few months old and quite . . . rustic. The Black Hills still belonged to the Sioux Indians, and life there was dangerous and difficult." As she spoke, Maddie enjoyed watching Edith's eyes widen and her mouth drop open. "I had been gently bred, and was quite unprepared for such an existence."

"How could your mother have permitted you to go?"

"She had died not long before, and my brother Benjamin and I went to Deadwood to join my adventuring father." With a twinkle in her eye, Maddie added, "I must tell you, Your Grace, that you remind me of my mother. She was very like you." A bit of a snob, she thought, smiling.

"Why, that's a lovely compliment, my dear." The dowager duchess finished her sherry and smiled extravagantly. "Aren't you charming! What a pity you've been forced to stay in such a horrid place as—what is it? West Dakota?"

"Actually, the Black Hills of South Dakota are very beautiful, and Deadwood has grown into a fine town. I couldn't have wished for a better place to live and raise my children."

Her Grace waved a hand dismissively. "But what do you *do* out there in the wilderness? How *hideous* it must be to be forced to be polite to a town filled with backwoods commoners!"

Unable to restrain herself a moment longer, Shelby interjected, "My mother is a marvel. Not only has she adapted to life in Deadwood with grace and good humor, she and my father also lived among the Sioux Indians for several weeks. That was in 1876, just before the Sioux lost the Black Hills and were forced onto the reservation." It was fun, Shelby thought, to watch Edith's eyes grow bigger and bigger, but it did seem prudent to postpone information about Sun Smile until after the wedding. "The Indians gave Mama a beautiful name: Fireblossom!"

The dowager duchess pursed her lips. "How very . . . uncivilized!"

"On the contrary," argued Geoff. "Given Mrs. Matthew's beautiful bright hair, Fireblossom seems a fitting and eloquent name."

"Yes," agreed Maddie. "I am proud of it." She gave

him a nearly indiscernible wink. "Has Shelby told you *her* Indian name, bestowed when she was still in diapers?"

"No!" He leaned forward in pleased expectation.

"Wildblossom!"

"Perfect! I wonder why she never mentioned it?"

Shelby spoke up, joining in the laughter. "You've been bad enough, calling me *scamp*, Geoff! I didn't want to give you any more ammunition."

The dowager duchess looked on with a pinched expression. "How very quaint. Shall she be known as *Duchess Wildblossom*?"

"Mother!" Geoff stopped there, not wanting to spoil everyone's meal, and gave the Matthew's family an apologetic smile. Maddie finished eating and excused herself. Stepping into the library, she waited for Fox. Only a minute passed before he appeared in the doorway, followed by Titus, Byron, and Ben.

"I don't want to stay here tonight with that woman," Maddie said firmly. "I'd rather go to the inn."

"There are plenty of other wedding guests staying there," Fox agreed. "We'd probably have a fine time in the common room."

"Do you think Shelby's feelings will be hurt?" her mother worried.

Ben shook his head. "Not a bit. She'd run from the duchess herself if she could—and so would Geoff! Later, at the inn, I'll tell you the story of the Duchess of Devonshire's ball. Shelby told her future mother-in-law off in front of half the names in *Debrett's Peerage*."

"Good for her," Fox said, then he turned to his son. "Byron, why don't you go and explain to Geoff and Shelby. Tell them that we've decided it will be too much trouble to unpack here tonight, then move to the inn tomorrow. Easier to make it all one step."

"Brilliant," Maddie said approvingly. "Now we can relax for the rest of the evening, and I'll get a good night's sleep rather than fuming over that woman's insufferable manners!"

"I have a notion it'll be less complicated for Shelby as well," Byron said.

A half hour later Geoff's Mercedes was brought around for the Matthews party to borrow. As Maddie, Fox, Byron, and Titus all squeezed into the automobile, Ben stood on the front steps making arrangements with a footman to bring their luggage along in the manor's Sunbeam Mabley.

"I'll drive," Byron announced to Ben when he approached the Mercedes. "I think I remember the way."

He wore a distracted expression. "Sure." Then, as they started down the dark drive, Ben stole a look back at the hunched-over old servant who was carrying their bags to the other automobile.

"What's wrong?" Byron asked.

"Nothing." He continued to frown, though, and finally twisted around to search Titus's gnomelike figure scrunched into the rear seat. "This is going to sound crazy, but you know who that man looked like—the one wearing the cap, who was skulking around getting our things into the other vehicle?"

"Who?" Titus barely had room to breathe.

"Bart Croll . . ."

"It's true," Titus replied crossly. "You do sound crazy!"

Chapter Twenty-four

"LET'S HAVE A GAME OF BRIDGE," THE DOWAGER duchess commanded as she finished her meal. Each course had been trotted out to her, she picked one or two bites at the most, then waited to be served again. Now, finally, she had nibbled one berry from her tart and set down her fork with a note of finality.

"I don't play bridge," Shelby lied, thrilled to think that she and Geoff were able to escape at last from the table.

"Of course you don't. How foolish of me to have hoped that you might. And your little maid, of course, would not play, either. It takes an exceedingly keen intellect to grasp the game of bridge, you know. I consider it more an art than a game." Edith regarded her son through her nose glasses. "Where is Charles? If we can locate Charles, we only need a fourth. Do you suppose that Parmenter plays bridge?"

Geoff very nearly let his eyes cross in response to her question. Instead he replied, "Mother, this is the eve of our wedding; hardly a time for bridge. In fact, I thought I might show Shelby around the manor. Would you care to join us?"

"Not in the least." She rose from the table, the corners of her mouth turned down sulkily. "I will go to my room and read poetry. Ask that good-looking red-headed footman to bring me some sherry."

"Good night, Your Grace," Shelby offered. "Sleep well."

Geoff watched her black-clad figure rustle toward the hall and could not resist calling, "Mother, I don't suppose you might have brought something other than black to wear tomorrow . . . ?"

She threw a sharp look over one shoulder. "How selfish you are, Geoffrey! I am in *mourning*!"

When she was quite sure the dowager duchess was out of earshot, Shelby whispered in Geoff's ear, "So *that's* what it's called!" and they both fell back in their chairs, overcome with laughter.

It took Shelby to draw Geoff out about Sandhurst Manor. He'd forgotten some of the history himself, so they brought Parmenter along on their tour. The old butler trundled along the passageways ahead of them, pointing out the fifteenth century tapestries in the gallery, the bedchamber where Queen Victoria had slept in 1864, the billiard room and smoking room that had once served as the children's wing and had included a nursery, a schoolroom, and a playroom.

"It's been too many years since there've been little ones in this house," he ventured. "Meg was just saying that a house this size needs children to give it light."

"That's a lovely turn of phrase," Shelby said warmly.

Geoff cleared his throat. "I can take a hint."

They came into the great hall. Its Tudor style had been obscured in recent years by a grand piano, potted palms, and a bust of the Duke of Wellington. Parmenter said, "I like to think of the way this manor house looked during the Tudor times. Have you ever seen the sheaf of engravings made by the third earl, Your Grace?"

"No. Wait—perhaps, once, when I was a boy. Before they packed me off to school."

"There were flowers strewn on the floors then. Hyacinths and roses and clover and such. And Andrew, the third earl, liked to paint in here because of the great windows." Parmenter let his eyes rest on Geoff's face. "His lordship was an artist."

"I know where you're going with this, Parmenter." Geoff turned to Shelby. "People believe that I resemble this particular ancestor, who lived during the sixteenth century."

"We've all noticed that Miss Matthews bears a likeness to his lordship's French countess, Micheline. Would you like to see the paintings, miss?"

"I'd adore it!" she exclaimed. "I want to know all about every one of your ancestors, Geoff. We should make certain that all the records are written down so that the facts aren't lost." As Parmenter led them up the stairs to the eighteenth-century balcony that ran the length of the hall, Shelby slipped her hand through Geoff's arm. "It's time that someone paid attention to your heritage."

"Perhaps people may expect you to live at Aylesbury Castle now that you are duke, Your Grace," Parmenter wondered.

"This is my home." He looked at the paintings, illumined by gaslights built into the balcony walls. "I remember now, Parmenter. You may leave us."

It was eerie for both Shelby and Geoff to stand on the balcony, overlooking the arched hall with its priceless linen-fold paneling, and realize that on the morrow their lives and families would be joined. Together they examined the paintings made nearly five centuries ago by the third Earl of Sandhurst.

"This is Andrew Weston." He pointed at a man who could have passed for Geoff himself but for the jeweled doublet with its slashed, puffed sleeves. "And this is Micheline, his wife."

A strange chill coursed down Shelby's spine. Indeed, this woman bore a strong resemblance to her, though her hair was more the lighter shade of Maddie's. Their eyes were the same, though: lively and determined.

There were children. Two, then four. Paintings of Micheline with her children. A whimsical portrait of a spotted spaniel. Horses.

"They bred horses," Geoff murmured.

"Why don't you have dogs?"

"I do. They're in the kennels, next to the stables."

"Geoff, it's time to make this house a home again!" Shelby's voice rose, impassioned. "The gardens need to be tended so that they have character again. The rooms here must be furnished with regard to history, not passing fashions like those potted palms! And the dogs should be in the house where we can enjoy them!"

"We could fill the stables again," he said, catching the spark of her enthusiasm. "Sandhurst Manor could be a stud farm. Horse racing is all the rage in England now; it could ensure our financial security."

Shivering with excitement, Shelby wrapped her arms around Geoff's chest and they held on tight to one another.

"I never thought to have this feeling for my heritage," he said in soft wonderment. "It's taken you to awaken bits of me I never knew could live."

"I'm delighted to hear it." She turned her face up to his kiss as the tall-case clock in the hall below struck midnight. "Goodness! I had better had get my beauty sleep if I'm going to be a proper bride."

"Maybe you'd sleep better in my bed. . . ."

"What in the world put that notion in your head?"

"Wishful thinking, I perceive." Geoff smiled ruefully. "I suppose I can wait one more night."

"Pleasure postponed is pleasure enhanced, Your Grace!"

As Shelby and Geoff were kissing good night in the doorway to her suite of rooms, Charles was next door, sitting on the edge of Vivian's bed with his arm carefully placed around her shoulders.

"Shh! They'll hear us!" Viv cautioned.

"Darling, there's no cause for alarm. I'm quite certain our friends would be delighted to know that our romance is progressing so nicely."

"But it's only been a few months!" Her face was pale and anxious. "That is, of course I care for you, but that does not mean I can allow you to take liberties—"

"Why not? I love you, Vivian. I know you were hurt by that man you had to marry. I think of you as a bird with a broken wing, and I hope that with my gentleness and caring, you'll learn to fly again. I respect you, and I would *never* do anything to hurt you!" They had spent nearly this entire evening alone, and Charles had had such high hopes that, at last, his beloved would allow more than a chaste kiss. Every ounce of his being longed to shower her with tenderness and kindness, to enfold her body in his arms, to attain a level of intimacy in keeping with the feelings he knew they shared. To be rejected, again and again, was humiliating to him as a man. "Vivian . . . I am not asking for . . . favors. I only hope for some sign that you care for me—"

"Oh, I do!" Tears sprang to her eyes, and suddenly

her hands went out to him, clutching at his sleeves. "I love you, Charles!" Then, horrified by her own audacity, she drew back. "I'm just not ready yet."

"Vivian, darling, I love you, too!" Long-suppressed passions boiled up inside him. "Please . . . please . . ."

His dark eyes were feverish with need, and she thought, Just one kiss . . . I've done that before. . . . Squeezing her eyes tightly shut, she puckered her lips, and his mouth touched hers, carefully.

When she didn't protest, Charles drew her into his arms. He made a tremendous effort to hold back, to remember that Viv was nothing like the women he'd made love to before, and he must not let his body overpower his mind. Was she softening? Another kiss, and Viv seemed to relax. Her hand touched his back.

"My darling," Charles muttered, "I have never cared for anyone this way. I ache, night and day, to prove my love to you."

Forget about Bart! This is different! And for a moment Viv believed it, even felt it. Charles was tender and dear. She tentatively returned his embrace, and then his arms tightened, his lips parted, his breath grew ragged, and a silent scream rose from the depths of her soul.

Although Vivian made no sound, her torment somehow reached Charles through the haze of his own physical need. When he looked at her, he saw such raw terror in her blue eyes that it dawned on him that her problems were deeper than anything he could simply persuade her to forget.

"Please, *don't make me—*" Vivian choked when she found her voice.

"Of course not!" he replied, aghast. "Never! I love you and I will wait for you to trust me." And yet, a stain of sadness spread within him as he wondered if that day could ever come. "Viv, dear, I believe I'll pop on over to the inn and stay there with the others. Would that be all right?"

Her relief was evident. "Yes." She was breathing hard in the aftermath of her panic. "I'll be better tomorrow, Charles."

"I know, love."

She was lying across the bed, weeping for them both, when she heard the Sunbeam Mabley chug to life out in front. It was a curious-looking, noisy motorcar, and Charles had to travel a fair distance down the road before the sound died away completely.

Drained and dry-eyed at last, Viv rose off the grand four-poster bed and went into her bathroom to wash her face. When she closed the door, she saw Bart Croll sitting on the edge of the claw-footed bathtub.

It's another vision—like all the other times. . . .

Certain she'd only imagined him again, she stifled her screams because she didn't want to disturb the house. By the time it came to her that he was *real*, Bart had grabbed her in a punishing grip and forced a gag into her mouth.

"You'd of been better off with that pretty limey, bitch." He took another of the silk ties he'd stolen from Geoff's closet and bound her hands. Then he leaned right up to her face, staring with his black, burning eyes, and he smiled. "Didn't you believe me when I said you could never get away from me? You didn't really think you could *kill* me, didja? Now you're gonna have to pay for tryin'."

Vivian wished she could die at that instant. He pulled her along with him back into the bedroom, and the sight of the bed filled her with horror. But Bart had other things on his mind, and at first Viv was grateful for the reprieve.

"I got a cast-iron belly," he said, then pointed to the pistol stuck in the waistband of his trousers and laughed at the pun. "I was sick for a couple days, but then it passed—and the only thing I cared about was makin' you hurt like you did me."

Don't you know you already had? she thought, but she couldn't speak, and the pitiful look in her eyes was familiar to him.

"Let's see." He pretended to think, scratching his stubbled cheek. "What are you scared of, woman?" His eyes scraped her soul again. "How 'bout a little fire? You still have bad dreams about that fire that kilt yer family?"

While she stood there, trembling, Bart rolled a cigarette, then lit it with a delicate oil lamp Charles had placed on the bedside table for atmosphere.

"Trouble is," he growled, exhaling the strong smoke, "I don't want to just pay *you* back, I want yer fancy friends to suffer, too! The minute they showed up next door to my ranch, things started goin' wrong. You think I don't know they made you try to *kill* me?" He was snarling now, puffing madly on the cigarette. "I *hate* them folks! Luckily, I been learnin' my way around this place, and I know just what to do t'pay alla you back. We're gonna make a nice big fire, Viv, just you 'n' me. Won't that be *fun*? You 'n' me used to have lotsa fun!" He cackled, coughed, crushed the cigarette on the rosewood table, then picked up the oil lamp. Grasping her thin waist, he yanked her along behind him. "C'mon, bitch."

Viv had made herself go numb, just as she had back in the sod house in Wyoming. She followed him obediently, glassy-eyed, through long corridors. *It's only death,* she thought. *It'll be over soon.* Perhaps the others would be able to escape. It was fortunate that

Geoff's suite of rooms was on the ground floor and everyone else had gone to the inn. The servants were far away in their own wing. Geoff would rescue Shelby—

Throwing open a door, Bart pushed Viv onto a staircase landing. Below them sprawled the manor's magnificent great hall; above was the railed balcony that bisected the two-story walls. Bart's oil lamp sent wavering orange shadows over the hand-carved paneling and heirlooms that marked the progress of six centuries of the Sandhurst earldom.

"Looks like this place'll go up like tinder-dry sagebrush in August." Bart smiled at the oil lamp and drew off the glass chimney. "Ain't this fun, Viv?"

After Geoff had left Shelby at her door, she postponed sleep in favor of looking over everything she'd need tomorrow. Her gown was exquisite; fashioned of four different kinds of delicate lace. Her veil would be secured by an understated tiara that had belonged to the seventh Countess of Sandhurst. Finally, Consuelo's gift had been extravagant Parisian lingerie for Shelby to wear under her wedding gown.

Her inventory of the bridal accessories was interrupted by the sound of an automobile starting up out in the drive. *Who can that be?* she thought. Crossing to her windows, Shelby drew back the curtains and dimly made out the figure of a man who appeared to be Charles Lipton-Lyons, chugging off in the Sunbeam Mabley down the long, moonlit drive.

Immediately she worried about Viv. Had something gone wrong between them? Perhaps she should go and say good night and they could have a last bedtime chat, just as they had each night when they lived together in the camp village.

Shelby had just opened her door when she was assailed by second thoughts. Viv might already be asleep. After all, it was nearly one o'clock and they all were tired. Or she and Charles might have actually had a romantic experience together and she was enjoying the afterglow.

Don't be so nosy! Shelby scolded herself. But what was that smell? The unmistakable odor of strong cigarette smoke made her nose twitch. Then, in the next instant, she knew that it was Bart Croll. It didn't make any sense, but Shelby knew. She turned out her lights and waited, listening. Voices came to her. Viv's door opened and Shelby caught a faint, sour, unwashed whiff that was unmistakably Bart.

Oh, dearest Viv! Her eyes stung in empathy, but she couldn't allow herself tears. She remained completely still, listening, watching as Croll emerged into the passageway, an oil lamp in one hand while he pulled Viv along with the other.

Shelby waited until they turned a corner at the end of the corridor, then she bent next to her bed in the darkness. Underneath she had stowed her guns from the Wild West Show. Most of them were either shotguns or rifles converted to use shot, because Colonel Cody considered long-distance bullets too dangerous around such a big audience. However, she still had the Winchester repeating rifle she'd practiced with on the ranch. It would serve her needs well enough tonight.

Grimly, she loaded the rifle and slipped extra shells into her pocket, then crept out into the corridor.

Sandhurst Manor was a virtual rabbit warren of passageways, but luckily Bart had left his stench for her to follow. She was just passing the last suite of guest rooms when a door suddenly flew open and frightened Shelby so much that she thought her heart might burst.

"What in heaven's name are you doing? What's happening?" It was Edith, decked out in a lavish, beribboned, lace-trimmed combing gown. He white hair was lying across her bosom in two long braids. "Something's wrong, isn't it? Why are you carrying that hideous gun?"

Shelby had immediately pushed her back inside her rooms, closing the door behind them. "For God's sake, hush up! I'll brook no argument from you on this matter, Your Grace. There is a man here in the manor at this moment who means us all harm. You must stay in here and not make a sound until I have—disposed of him."

"But—this is unthinkable! You cannot do this! Geoffrey must be summoned—"

"Geoff's rooms are downstairs. This villain came into Vivian's bedchamber, which adjoins mine, and he has taken her hostage. Geoff can't hear us or help us now; you'll have to trust me." Shelby started to open the door again, then glanced back at her goggling future mother-in-law. "You may wish to admit that it's not so terrible that I'm a sharpshooter. I'm the best person to have on hand at this moment; better in fact than Geoff!"

She couldn't spare another moment to argue with Edith, so she simply went out and shut the door, wishing she could lock the dowager duchess inside. Determination and fury coursed through Shelby's veins as she followed Croll's cigarette smoke to a small door she recognized as the one she and Geoff had used to leave the great hall balcony.

Her heart was pounding now. Through the heavy door she could hear Bart's gravelly voice, no doubt heaping words of degradation on her dear sweet Viv. Turning, Shelby found the nearest staircase and followed it to the first floor. The massive doors to the great hall were open; through them she glimpsed the play of the lamp's flame over the paneled walls.

"Where shall we start, huh, Viv?" Bart was saying in a coarse tone. "Up here, on the balcony?" He jerked the tie that bound her wrists, bringing her along with him up the steps. Vivian's eyes were closed and she was crying through the gag.

On the top step, to Shelby's stunned disbelief, he held the flame of the lamp to the stair rail that ran the length of the balcony. Slowly the fire began to catch and spread, illuminating the portraits of Andrew and Micheline and their family.

"You like that fire?" he asked Viv. "Remember the night your family died—how they *screamed*—"

"That's it, you bastard," Shelby muttered to herself. Leaning around the doorway, she raised the rifle to rest in the hollow of her shoulder. However, the moment she cocked the hammer, Bart's head jerked up. He went for his own pistol, all the while searching the fire-illumined shadows for his enemy.

Shelby's heart thudded. Why doesn't he stand still? she thought wildly. His own gun went off then, narrowly missing her.

Bart reached for Vivian and pressed the pistol to her head. "Put down yer gun and come out, or I'll kill her!" he snarled.

The sight of her weeping friend, gagged and tied and trembling with terror, swept Shelby's own fear aside. Croll gave her no choice! Employing the speed she'd worked so hard to perfect at Earl's Court, Shelby aimed through the fire for his heart, preparing to shoot even though a near miss would mean shooting, perhaps killing, her dearest friend.

Crack! Her bullet found its mark and he staggered

backward, pulling Viv with him into the flames that licked the balcony floor.

"Burn, you bitches!" Croll yelled. "I won't die!"

It was Vivian who recovered her senses long enough to wrench free of his death grip. She reached out then with her bound hands and gave her husband a shove that sent him crashing through the burning rail of the balcony.

"Hurry, Viv! Come down the stairs!" Shelby cried. To her relief, her friend obeyed, and they met moments later. Their tears mingled with soot as Shelby untied Viv and held her close. "He's gone. Dead! You and I did it together, and he'll never hurt anyone again."

The echoing gunshot had roused the entire household, and footsteps already sounded in the corridors. Soon they'd all be there to help put out the fire before it spread farther, but one person had silently witnessed most of the drama.

"I say," Edith, Dowager Duchess of Aylesbury, exclaimed from the doorway. Her hands were pressed to her ears in reaction to the deafening rifle shot. "Good show!"

The wedding was postponed a couple of days to allow for notification of the proper authorities, the disposal of Bart Croll's body, cleanup of the fire damage, and an airing out of the sixteenth century chapel, which adjoined the great hall. Most guests were notified of the delay by telephone, and the others simply arrived early and waited patiently.

It seemed, however, that the mood at Sandhurst Manor was one of celebration rather than tragedy. Bart Croll, who had been haunting their lives, was unequivocably dead, and Viv no longer had to carry the burden of believing that she was a murderess.

It was as if a cloud had lifted. Better still, Shelby was not only the bride-to-be, but a bona fide heroine. To her own astonishment, Edith could not stop telling anyone who would listen that Shelby had saved their lives as well as one of the family's ancestral homes and all its irreplaceable, historically significant contents.

The morning of the wedding found Manypenny helping Geoff to dress.

"Have I told you, Your Grace, how pleased I am for both you and your bride?"

"Yes, you have." Geoff pointed to a speck of dust on the shoulder of his morning coat.

"Now that you are settled and you no longer need me to steer you clear of ruin, I have been thinking of retiring."

Geoff had been checking his reflection in the mirror while pinning a white rosebud to his lapel, but Manypenny's bombshell brought him up short. "But what would you do?"

"Might I remind you that I am eighty-two years of age? Do I not deserve a few years—or months—of leisure?"

"It's just that I can't imagine you sitting in the servants' quarters with your feet up, Manypenny."

"Actually . . . I intend to return to Cody, Your Grace. I would like to end my days on the veranda at the Sunshine Ranch."

Geoff's expression of outrage was tinged with jealousy. "Do you truly intend to just go away and live apart from me?"

"You are free to join me, Your Grace. And I should assure you that I have received permission from the future duchess. We've discussed this matter at length and she approves completely."

"Hmm." Geoff frowned. "Well then, good luck."

The manservant turned away, smiling to himself. "I appreciate your generous good wishes, Your Grace. I know that we will both be very happy in our new lives."

It killed Geoff to think of Ben, Titus, Manypenny, and the boys all enjoying the pleasures of the Sunshine Ranch while he endured Royal Ascot. "Do you know, old fellow, I wonder if I ought not reconsider our plans to honeymoon in France."

"I thought you might, Your Grace. As I recall, Wyoming is simply spectacular by the end of May."

The duke gave him a grudging smile. "Just so, cunning old fellow."

Upstairs, Shelby's rooms were filled with women. Maddie, Consuelo, Vivian, and even Edith were all chattering happily together while Meg Floss helped Shelby dress. It could not have been a finer spring day, and the air was redolent with romance and joy and the scents of the garden wafting through the open windows.

When the bride was ready, Viv put a bouquet of trailing white roses, lilies of the valley, and lilacs into her hands, and the other women stood around to compliment her beauty.

"How excited you must be to become the Duchess of Aylesbury!" Meg cried, awestruck.

Shelby's smile seemed wider and more radiant than ever, and her teal-blue eyes sparkled with joy. "Actually, my only thought is to be Geoff's wife. The duchess part is—" Edith was listening intently, so Shelby censored herself. "—just a wonderful added bonus!" Turning to Consuelo, Duchess of Marlborough, she put out a hand. "I mustn't forget to thank Her Grace for her generous assistance . . . and friendship, freely offered. I am so honored that you've agreed to be an attendant today."

Consuelo's dark eyes were soft with affection. "It is I who am honored to be a part of this wonderful celebration."

Maddie went to give her daughter a last hug. "You are so beautiful I want to cry," she murmured. "We must all go down to the chapel now. It's time."

Consuelo went ahead to see if her husband had arrived, but Vivian lingered behind with Shelby, grateful for these last minutes alone with her friend.

"You look lovely," Shelby told her, then fussed with one of Viv's curls that wanted to droop a bit. "How are you feeling? Better?"

"I keep remembering your advice—to remind myself, over and over, that Bart was an evil man and nothing that happened was my fault—"

"And that Charles is *not* Bart. Just give yourself time with him and I am convinced that you'll begin to open up like one of these roses."

"I already am. I feel . . . lighter now. The thought that I'd poisoned and killed him was a terrible weight on my conscience—and then, those dreams, and the times I saw him in London . . ." She shivered at the memories. "I actually thought I was going mad!"

"But you were not. And all of that is in the past. Look how well everything is turning out, Viv! Even Geoff's mother has changed her tune!"

"We are very lucky, aren't we?"

"Incredibly so."

"Charles has been wonderful to me these past two days. He felt terrible that he wasn't here to save me himself, but the realization that our lives can only get better is becoming clearer all the time. My demons have gone." Vivian actually smiled dreamily, a gleam of true romance in her eyes. "I think everything is going to be all right."

"Dear friend, I'm so happy!"

Laughing, they shared a handkerchief to dab their eyes, then checked Shelby's veil and Viv's champagne and rose gown and bouquet, and then they went out into the corridor where Fox was waiting.

"Look at my little hellion." He shook his head in wonder. "I never would have believed that you could go from being a cowgirl in curly angora chaps to a duchess in Belgian lace."

Beaming, Shelby took his arm. "The secret is, I always believed I could be *anything*—and nothing has ever seemed out of reach to me. Why not try to reach *all* the stars?"

"Why not indeed." Fox kissed her cheek. "Are you ready to go to your bridegroom?"

"Oh, Daddy, I'd run to the chapel if I could!"

From the floor below, Shelby heard Bach being played on the organ. Holding tightly to her father's arm, she waited for Viv to lift her train, and then she stepped out with anticipation toward her new life.

EPILOGUE

Rowing in Eden!
Ah, the sea!
Might I but moor
To-night in thee!
Might I but moor
To-night in thee!
—Emily Dickinson

"I, SHELBY, TAKE THEE, GEOFFREY . . ."

Her voice quivered with emotion. Each word of Shelby's vows held special meaning for her, as if the time-honored speech had been created just for these two lovers.

The chapel was bathed in a golden light that seemed to soften the guests' faces and dim the sound of the vicar's voice, until all that remained were Shelby and Geoff and their rich bond of love.

"With this ring, I thee wed," Geoff declared as he stared into her eyes in a way that made her shiver. "This gold and silver I thee give. With my body I thee worship . . ."

Every inch of the chapel seemed to be filled with flowers, more spectacular than all the treasures in Westminster Abbey. There were pink-frosted blue delphiniums, together with fairy spires of columbine and coral bells, while ruffled tulips mingled with sun-drenched daffodils. The altar was banked with bouquets in glorious disarray: lilacs, old roses, sweet peas, daisies, cornflowers, foxglove, stephanotis, and regal lilies. A trailing ivory moiré ribbon adorned each pew, the bows crowned by jewel-toned primroses. The effect was opulent and unpretentious at the same time.

Shelby couldn't believe how handsome Geoff looked

in his cutaway coat and gray-striped four-in-hand tie, and he thought she was utterly exquisite; glowing and womanly. All his ancestors seemed to be smiling down on Shelby, who wore her heirloom tiara and fragile lace with grace. Even the most regal guests looked pleased now that they had seen Geoff's American bride for themselves.

"I now pronounce you husband and wife," the vicar intoned, and Shelby went into Geoff's strong arms, dazed and delighted.

"Can we leave now?" he whispered. "Alone?"

Her heart raced. "Meg's promised candied violets on our wedding cake. I have to see it before you—"

"Better not say it in church."

They were both wearing broad smiles as they turned to face the waiting the guests. The strains of Bach's "Wedding Cantata" filled the chapel, and Shelby trailed Belgian lace and sunbeams in her wake.

"How many other women have you lured into this pool?" Shelby called teasingly to Geoff, who was getting undressed in the next room. She was reclining in the deep-tiled Moorish pool-bath that was sunken into the floor of his decidedly decadent bathroom. Geoff had lit countless candles, in brass holders, and they flickered exotically on every inch of dry tile.

He paused in the doorway, his eyes darkening at the sight of her luscious form, barely discernible under the water. Shelby's cinnamon curls, so carefully coiffed for the wedding, were now pinned up loosely. The scented water lapped just above her nipples.

"You do me an injustice," Geoff protested. "I have only enjoyed this room in solitude, until tonight . . . although I may have *dreamed* that you were here with me."

"I've been wondering all day if we're not dreaming together. Can real life be so . . . so—"

"Never mind. There isn't a word for this. I know, because I've been puzzling over it myself, without success." Geoff had already removed every piece of his clothing except for his white shirt. It pleased him to see Shelby admiring his sculpted legs, and watching as he took off the stiff wing collar and cuffs, then opened the buttons, one by one.

"I suppose it's very bad form for a duchess to stare at naked men," she remarked with mock solemnity.

Geoff bit back a grin. "If none of the duchesses who instructed you mentioned that *particular* rule, then I wouldn't give it another thought."

"It's all right, then?"

"Yes, but only if the naked man in question is the duke," he corrected. "Your *own* duke. Not Devonshire or Marlborough or Cumberland, you see."

"That's fine." Shelby's face was illuminated by a winsome smile. The clock on the bedroom mantel struck midnight, but she wasn't a bit tired. It seemed that the euphoria of her wedding could carry her through endless days without sleep. "I think I'm delirious."

"Think nothing of it." With his white shirt open, so that she had glimpses of his muscled chest, Geoff brought in an icy bottle of champagne from the bedroom. He eased the cork out and let it fly in the direction of the pool. Giggling, Shelby splashed to safety.

"Is there room enough for me in there?"

Her blush was visible even in the rosy glow of dozens of candles. "I'm all mixed up," she admitted, accepting the glass of champagne Geoff had poured. "I feel very . . . passionate, yet shy, as if we've never been . . . alone together before."

"Well, it has been a long time. Forever, it seems!" With that, he doffed his shirt, and met her wavering gaze. "Will I do? No second thoughts?"

For a moment Shelby couldn't speak. He was magnificent—still the lithe, powerful golden lion she'd imagined one night long ago at the Sunshine Ranch when, after their rustling adventure, Geoff had lifted her into his arms in the kitchen and carried her off to teach her the wonders of physical love. . . .

Her expression ended the banter. Geoff joined his bride in the pool-bath, the long muscles in his thighs flexing as he immersed himself in the warm water. "I think a sip of champagne is in order for your case of wedding night nerves, scamp." When they both were holding the crystal flutes of shimmering gold liquid, Geoff murmured, "Here's to the best day of my life, and to a future that promises only improvements. I love you, Shelby, and I'll do whatever it takes to make you happy."

His unspoken meaning was not lost on her. They touched glasses and drank, and instantly the bubbles seemed to race through her veins. "Uh-oh. This must be very special champagne. It's working already!"

"Then perhaps I shouldn't give you any more. I don't want you keeling over."

She held fast to the stem and sipped again. "I have to make a toast of my own. Here's to the best day of *my* life, which must make it *our* life! I am going to be a very good duchess, so that you won't have to make any more sacrifices for my happiness."

They both considered their toasts, sipped again, and then Geoff's fingers grazed her breast under the water. Immediately his body reacted. "Before we move along to the, uh, grand finale, I ought to tell you that I've decided we both deserve a temporary reprieve from all this ducal nonsense."

"Our honeymoon in France, you mean?"

"Honeymoon, yes, France, no." He slipped his hands around her slim waist and drew her close so that they bobbed against one another. It was delicious torture. "Manypenny has persuaded me, nay *begged* me, to bring you to Wyoming for the summer."

"Manypenny?" she echoed in confusion. "But Percy wants to retire from your service! He is looking forward to the peace and quiet. I hardly think that he would attempt to persuade you, certainly not *beg*—"

"Never mind that. Additionally, I don't think we should feel obligated to spend this Season in London. People will understand that you miss Wyoming and cannot make this adjustment so suddenly."

"First you blame Manypenny, and now *me*?" She tried not to smile. "I'll go with you to the ranch for our honeymoon, Your Grace, but only if you are man enough to admit to your wife and your peers that it's you who desperately miss Wyoming."

"I've been away longer than you have."

"Have I your promise?"

"You drive a hard bargain, Your Grace." Geoff was laughing now, holding her on his lap in the water, and the pressure of her breasts against his chest nearly drove him mad. "Yes, I'll promise, but only because I know you'll make plenty of promises of your own before *this* night is out! Ha-*ha*!" His voice rose dramatically, rather like a mad pirate shouting from his quarterdeck.

"I do hope the servants can't hear you, darling," Shelby chided. "They'll be whispering for days."

Chuckling, he found a cake of almond-scented soap and began to wash her back, and then her arms. It was keenly sensuous work.

"This is sweet," she remarked. "We must do this *often.*"

They took turns, lathering one another bit by bit, touching gently, expertly, tantalizingly, and sharing plans for the future. The anticipation built, and Geoff turned on the taps to let more hot water into the bath.

Finally, when they were both slippery clean, rinsed, and feverishly aroused, Geoff's eyes turned predatory. "Come here, my little Wildblossom."

Thrilled, Shelby straddled his hips, and his hands clasped her hips in welcome. No longer timid, she slid her arms around Geoff's neck and kissed his eyes, nose, cheekbones, and then the mouth she so adored. Geoff made a low sound somewhere between a growl and a purr as he deepened the kiss, turning her in his arms and parting her lips so that his tongue might explore completely.

"God, how I'm missed you."

"You've mentioned that in the past," she gasped, "but perhaps now that we're married, you won't have to miss me anymore."

His kisses seemed to burn away the water on her neck, throat, and breasts, inspiring her to come up on her knees and bring more of herself out of the water. They kissed hungrily for long minutes, savoring each long-awaited taste and sensation. Finally, as she dropped her head back, he nipped at her throat, shoulders, and took a nipple into his mouth.

Sensing magically just what it would take to bring her to the brink, he suckled and kneaded each breast in turn. They swelled in reaction, and Shelby felt the blood surging into her nether regions as well. "Oh—Geoff! What—how—"

Her own hands moved convulsively over his chest, soaking up the texture of the wet hair and the lean strength she'd dreamed of, night and day. Was it possible that nothing could part them again? Tears trickled down her cheeks. Shelby pressed forward against the steely shaft of his manhood, begging wordlessly for fulfillment.

Geoff came into her an inch at a time. "Oh!" Shelby exclaimed, momentary panic replaced by a powerful surge of passion. The buoyancy of the water lent a new dimension to their lovemaking, and Shelby was able to return his thrusts with ease.

The candles threw dancing golden light over the tiled walls and over the newlywed Duke and Duchess of Aylesbury as they clung together in joyous torment. They kissed, tasting, savoring, then shared a gaze of miraculous understanding. Closer and closer they came to the precipice, to that little death that so intensely affirmed life. When at last they reached the edge, gasping, Geoff and Shelby fell . . . not down, but upward, toward the stars.

Strolling along the vast, spotless deck of a newly christened passenger ship, Shelby closed her parasol and turned her face up to the June sun. The ocean stretched out to the horizon, reminding her of the endless prairies of her childhood. *Soon*, she thought, *I'll see Cody again . . . and the mountains, and the ranch, and all our friends. . . .*

No matter how many times Shelby envisioned their homecoming, her sense of euphoric anticipation could not be diminished. What a wonderful summer she and Geoff would have!

"Your Grace," a steward murmured at her side, "would you care for refreshment?"

"No, thank you, Mr. Collins." She gave him her complete attention. From her elegantly coiffed hair to the hem of her new Parisian demi-saison gown, Shelby exuded the grace, beauty, and kindness of a genuine aristocrat. "Is it true that we may reach land by tomorrow evening?"

"Oh, I should think so." He dipped his head. "We expect to make this first crossing in record time."

The great steamships that were being built in the new century seemed to become faster with each Atlantic crossing. It was no longer uncommon for one to be able to sail from Europe to North America in less than a week. Shelby thought that they were very lucky to be living in so advanced an age. Why should she and Geoff not travel from London to Wyoming as often as they desired? English Society would scarcely miss them!

"Can I assist you in any other way, Your Grace?" the steward inquired before backing away.

"Yes." She gave him a radiant smile. "Have you seen my husband by chance? I left him in the smoking room."

Collins looked rather uneasy. "I . . . I think I may have seen His Grace on the upper sundeck, having a nap."

Shelby smiled to herself as she went in search of Geoff. For now, they were playing the roles of duke and duchess, but soon enough they would be at the ranch, wearing old familiar clothes as they raced on horseback to the base of the mountains. It was amazing, but it seemed that, with care and compromise, she and Geoff could make all their dreams come true.

It's more than luck, Shelby thought as she moved along a row of deck chairs filled with passengers basking in the sunshine. Everything comes together when the time is right. Her willfulness was giving way to trust: trust in God, in herself, in Geoff, and in the wonder and goodness of their love.

Nearing the last few deck chairs, Shelby wondered if Collins had been mistaken. There was no sign of Geoff. She was about to turn back when she noticed the man in the next chair. His face was covered by a large white Stetson hat, but there was something familiar about the rest of him.

He wore a white shirt with cufflinks, tailored tan trousers, and handmade shoes. His hands were folded over his chest; a signet ring glinted on one lean finger.

Shelby's joy was so profound that her heart ached. Blinking back tears, she perched on the edge of the next deck chair, set down her fluffy parasol, and watched him for a few moments.

When he stirred, Shelby leaned forward and lifted the Stetson hat just enough so that he could see her. Her eyes twinkled. "The Duke of Aylesbury, I presume?"

Chuckling, Geoff reached up to caress her cheek. "Have you, by chance, heard of a disreputable cardsharp called Coyote Matt?"

"Your Grace would not lower yourself to consort with such a person, would you?"

He drew her down, hid their faces with the Stetson, and murmured, "Lower myself? Nothing I'd like more."

They both were laughing as they kissed.

Author's Note

So many of you have written to tell me that you loved *Fireblossom*, the story of Shelby's parents, and I want you to know how much I appreciated every letter. I'm sorry to say that some of them were lost before I was able to respond. A lot happened in the Wright-Hunt household in 1993: we suffered the loss of my father in April, my husband graduated from USD in May (Jim's a history teacher!), and we moved to Sioux City, near my mother, in September. I just wasn't as efficient as usual, and some of my mail was misplaced. If your letter was one of those lost, I sincerely apologize and appreciate your understanding.

Since you enjoyed the historical notes at the end of *Fireblossom*, I thought I'd add some here. Thanks to a wonderful trip west that yielded some obscure research materials about Cody, Wyoming, I was able to provide a lot of detail about the town's gradual progress. I should add that Cody continues to thrive and now numbers more than eight thousand residents. Jim and I spent many hours at the incredible Buffalo Bill Historical Center, which encompasses four unique western museums, and we stayed in Colonel Cody's own suite at the still-operating Irma Hotel!

Many of the characters actually lived: Jacob Schwoob, Etta Feeley, and all the Wild West Show performers named and described. The events surrounding the opening of the Irma Hotel were recorded carefully, and I adhered closely to those details.

I should mention that Shelby's family home in Deadwood was inspired by the real Adams house, which was restored a few years ago and transformed into an inn. It's a fascinating showplace.

As for the portion of the book set in England, the Wild

West Show did tour there during the weeks I placed them at Earl's Court. Also, the train crash that killed Cody's horse and injured Annie Oakley really happened—so the situation I created for Shelby was, theoretically, possible! The new king and queen did attend the Wild West Show, as described, on March 14, 1903.

Buffalo Bill grew older, his debts mounted, and he tried to keep various incarnations of Wild West Shows in business. Annie Oakley never rejoined the show. In 1912, when Cody was sixty-six, everything had to be auctioned to pay his creditors. Later, he organized a movie recreating the Indian Wars and toured with other circuses to generate an income. His health grew increasingly worse, and he died in January, 1917, in Denver. Although Colonel Cody's wish was to be buried in Cody, Wyoming, he was laid to rest on Lookout Mountain in Colorado.

Consuelo (Vanderbilt), Duchess of Marlborough, was an intriguing historical figure, and the Duke and Duchess of Devonshire were real as well. Consuelo may reappear in the book after next, along with Adam Raveneau, Viscount Thorncliff.

One more note for the truly faithful: Yes, Geoff's look-alike ancestor was Andrew Weston, Earl of Sandhurst, and hero of *A Battle for Love*, which was set in 1532.

Have I forgotten anything? I'm working madly in 1994. I've finished *Scapegrace*, the rollicking story of Nathan Raveneau and Adrienne Beauvisage (offspring of past heroes and heroines). It's set in 1818 England and the exotic-yet-British island of Barbados, and I know you'll love it as much as I do. I've now returned to Edwardian times, writing the mate to *Scapegrace*—Adam Raveneau's story, *Tempest*. It was fun to meet him in advance in *Wildblossom*.

I cherish each of your letters, and all the good wishes and encouragement you send, even through thoughts that don't make it to the mailbox. Keep reading, and I'll keep writing.

Cynthia Wright Hunt
Sioux City, Iowa